T0304861

Justin Myers is an author and journalist from Shipley, West Yorkshire. Perhaps best known for his work as The Guyliner and his *Impeccable Table Manners* blog, Justin's writing has featured in many leading publications, and his popular newsletter *The Truth About Everything** has been running since 2017. Justin now lives in London with his partner, and is desperate to get a dog. *Leading Man* is his fourth novel.

theguyliner.com
@theguyliner

Also by Justin Myers

The Last Romeo
The Magnificent Sons
The Fake-Up

LEADING MAN

Justin Myers

SPHERE

SPHERE

First published in Great Britain in 2024 by Sphere

1 3 5 7 9 10 8 6 4 2

A CIP catalogue record for this book
is available from the British Library.

Hardback ISBN 978-0-7515-8351-9
Trade paperback ISBN 978-0-7515-8352-6

Typeset in Perpetua by M Rules
Printed and bound in Great Britain by
Clays Ltd, Elcograf S.p.A.

Epigraph quotation by Stephen Sondheim is taken
from the 23 April 1973 edition of *Newsweek*.

Papers used by Sphere are from well-managed forests
and other responsible sources.

Sphere
An imprint of
Little, Brown Book Group
Carmelite House
50 Victoria Embankment
London EC4Y 0DZ

An Hachette UK Company

www.hachette.co.uk
www.littlebrown.co.uk

For Sophy and Sam

*'I prefer neurotic people. I like to
hear rumblings beneath the surface.'*

— STEPHEN SONDHEIM

One

I wish I looked good wet. You know what I mean. Some people wade out of the sea in full photoshoot mode: a vision, sparkling rivulets of water clinging to their tight torso. Stepping out of the shower is their peak aesthetic; hair wet, smooth and glossy, slicked down their back like paint, or tumbling into perfect, glistening curls. Water gathering at the tip of their nose, yes, but adorable somehow, diamond droplets swelling then falling, gracefully, delicately.

Me? Soaked, I look like I've just heaved myself out of the Union Canal, after fighting a dog. My eyes disappear, my face bloats, and my hair spikes into a soft-rock guitarist's wig. Droplets don't nestle on my face, water sluices down it, cascading off my too-spiky features. Nosferatu auditioning for a shampoo commercial, basically. And that's how I looked, trying not to appear flustered, strangely drenched from the short walk from cab to pub. I'd not bothered arguing with the cabbie, who was adamant the safest place to stop was halfway down the street and not right outside. So much for June. Foiled again by Edinburgh's microclimate – never satisfied until it's found somebody's chips to piss on. Wherever you live, whatever you think you know about June, it does not apply in my hometown.

This wasn't one of our usual places, we were at least half a generation too young to be here, and the staff uniform of Hawaiian shirts felt sad rather than ironic. There they were. Daisy and Tam. My team. The crew. My rock and my hard place. I stood and took them in for a few seconds, perched on high stools peering down with amiable imperiousness – two swans realising they'd followed the breadcrumbs into a pigeon coop by mistake – both trying to talk over each other. Daisy gesticulating in chaotic semaphore, Tam shredding his paper napkin in frustration as he failed, again, to interject. Then, the punchline, and the eruption of their bawdy laughter that turned heads three tables away. Followed by the primal urge, mine, not to miss a second more of it, to be right there in the middle of the two people I loved the most. Wet or not, time to make my entrance.

As she always did, Daisy waved exaggeratedly like she was welcoming me back from the Somme. I returned my usual greeting, a coquettish wave and a clutch of my imaginary pearls. We revelled in our clichés. As I approached, her smile briefly dropped in recognition of my sodden frame, realising this was perhaps her fault. Rain couldn't dampen the swell of joy I always got from seeing her, though, so we kissed hello, exaggerating our 'mwah' like fashion designers.

'Leo! You're never late! Hang on. Oh God. I'm sensing this drowned rat look is down to me.'

'Please never get a job as a satnav. You said to meet in the bar where Tam got the two investment bankers to pay our bill. In the West End.'

We never called bars or restaurants by their actual names, only labelling them according to whatever scrapes we'd got into last time we were there. The Bar Where Daisy Threw Up Into a Martini Glass. The Pub Where Tam Lost a Shoe.

'Are you mad at me? Please don't be. Sorry. I forgot that happened twice. You know how bankers love a bit of Tam. I meant East End, obviously. I was sweating over a seat plan for a work barbecue and texting at the same time. Big beer company thing. My head was up my hole.'

Tam finally glanced up from his phone. 'Literally organising a piss-up in a brewery.'

'It's a private garden, actually. For four hundred people.' Daisy didn't usually get things wrong. She was hyper-organised; it was her entire living. Her kitchen had fancy cupboards that unfolded into all kinds of impressive origami formations. We'd spent many afternoons at university eating instant noodles and watching extreme organising programmes featuring people who couldn't throw away receipts from 1977, and Daisy had been categorising her socks ever since. She could locate any item in her flat within forty-five seconds. 'Four hundred! And three hundred and ninety-five of them are men. They all call me sweetheart, and instead of choking them to death, I have to giggle. Giggle!'

'Our Daisy does not giggle, not even for us.' Tam leaned in for a kiss but recoiled slightly from the wet fabric of my coat. 'Poor Lion, you're soaking. Don't get my shirt wet or it'll be nipples o'clock.'

'Oh no,' I said, disrobing and trying to wring out my fringe at the same time. 'Then everyone will be looking at you, your worst nightmare.' I blew him a kiss to neutralise the dig, and he blew one back in mock consternation.

Daisy slid a glass to me, dripping with condensation and the ghost of an ice cube inside. They'd been waiting ages. 'I asked the barman if they had anything . . . y'know, booze-free, and he laughed and told me to suck the juice out of his bar cloth.'

'Maybe he's practising jokes from his Fringe show,' I said. 'You should've marked him out of ten.'

Tam beamed the watery smile of a man two drinks ahead and not listening. 'You know, there's an alternative timeline out there where Leo drinks lager. I wonder which one is having a better Friday.'

Bloated by gas and gluten? Not in this cardigan. Tam was always invoking the multiverse theory to cajole us into spoiling ourselves. Having an extra pudding (Daisy), blowing half the mortgage on denim (him), and getting reacquainted with tequila (me), even though I hadn't drunk in years.

Daisy giggled. 'Maybe I should've sucked his cloth. Can kitchen spray make you high? Lion, remember we tried to sniff aerosol when we were thirteen but did it wrong and I sprayed Lynx in your eye?' I'd known Daisy a long time. Half the scars on my body came from bumps and dares she made me do.

After a quick dash to the loo to blast my soaking bones with the hand dryer, I properly took in their crooked smiles and glassy stares. The eternally naughty schoolchildren. And hammered ones at that. It was 7 p.m.

'Are you two day-drunk?'

'Oh my, Miss Falconer,' squealed Tam. 'I love that "why haven't you done your homework" voice! Only thing I miss about teaching. We're not day-drunk. Are we, Daiz?'

'No! More . . . um, afternoon tipsy. I knew you'd be snowed

under with last-day-of-term shit. I had a half day and Tam's consultation fell through.'

'Memorial Japanese garden, big job.' Tam shrugged. 'Customer's inheritance was smaller than they thought, so they didn't fancy remembering the dear departed after all. So we met for coffee.'

'Which you . . . poured into a martini?' I was joking, these sly digs were our main energy source, but even after all these years, I sometimes felt tiny prickles of jealousy when I arrived to the fun a wee bit later than everyone else. The more I looked at them, the more elastic their movements became. This was the trouble with not drinking: watching the world turn to jelly before your eyes. 'End of term is next week, by the way. I've been loitering with zero intent in the staffroom since about half-two.'

Daisy blinked rapidly, realising she had, again, dropped a clanger. 'God, I don't know what's wrong with me. Of course it's next week. Lion, I'm worse than one of those mums who gets on the news for sodding off to Zakynthos and leaving her kids with only a loaf and squirty cream to last them two weeks. I'm so sorry!'

I was graciously accepting her apology – knowing it wouldn't be the last of the evening – when we were interrupted by one of the bar staff, looking horrified to be carrying a silver tray, upon which wobbled three glasses of prosecco.

'Have we walked into a wedding dress shop by mistake?'

The waiter looked at me with murderous eyes. 'Aye, very good. Guy over there sent these. With his compliments. For you in particular, apparently.'

I didn't know what to say. Not that it mattered, he wasn't looking in my direction – the target was Tam. Obviously. A few tables away, an attractive man – a good decade older than us, out of my league but nudging the underbelly of Tam's – raised his own glass of prosecco and smiled. Daisy already had a flute halfway to her lips when Tam gently grabbed her wrist.

'Nope, don't drink that. Sorry. Send it back. Thank the, uh, gentleman but I can't accept.'

Tam had never turned down a free drink in the decade-plus I'd known him. He was a sucker for a compliment, especially from a stranger. Tam could easily have acted in a soap or worked the changing rooms at the big H&M if he hadn't gone into teaching. He had peacock tendencies, but I suppose if I looked like him I'd have fanned out my feathers too.

'I'm a new man.' He looked very serious. 'No more drinks from randoms.'

I laughed. 'You'll be dead of dehydration by August.'

Tam's eyelash fluttering and ability to tune out dull conversation had kept us in gin and tonics throughout our twenties. Nobody could resist telling Tam 'this one's on me, gorgeous'.

Daisy made a desperate grab for the tray but the barman was already backing away with a shrug. 'Whoa! Let me drink mine.'

Tam peered over his shoulder to see if the man was still looking. 'No! Because he'll come over. It should just be us. Tonight is about Leo! Here's to the end of term!'

I tried to calculate how many martinis were swimming inside them, and how long I had until they were talking backwards. 'Again, you're a week early.'

'Besides, if he'd really wanted to impress me, he'd have sent champagne.'

This would sound arrogant to casual eavesdroppers, but Tam attracted ice buckets like picnics drew wasps.

'I don't think it's the kind of place where they have champagne on ice, Tam; they just run the prosecco under the cold tap for ten minutes.'

'Actually, champagne would be very fitting, because I have some news.' Tam took a deep breath, held out his left hand and tapped his ring finger. Upon it . . . nothing.

'Had a French manicure? Engaged to the invisible man?'

'Not the invisible one, no. Fabrizio proposed. I didn't want a ring.'

I ricocheted between shock and euphoria. Happy for Tam, and what would be a licence to spend a fortune, his favourite pastime, but how long had those two been together? Was it even two years? I wasn't sure I'd actually heard them have a conversation any deeper than agreeing to order a pizza and a pasta dish and split them. They called each other 'babe' a lot; Daisy and I would always share a quick grimace whenever they said it. Extra points if Tam saw us doing it.

But it was bound to happen. They were both achingly photogenic, and Tam had dropped enough hints; every time he saw a canapé he'd exclaim how perfect (or unsuitable) it would be for a wedding. Daisy was smiling. Kind of. More of an embarrassed smirk, maybe. She already knew!

'I got this instead.' Now I knew why usual tight-hugger Tam didn't want my wet, mangy coat sullying his beautiful shirt, as blue as the summer sky I hadn't seen for far too long. He thumbed the collar. 'Prada. More practical. It'll give me much more pleasure than a ring.'

'What about the wedding? You gonna tie a Gucci sock round your finger?'

I'd been ribbing Tam about his materialistic side for years, but he took it in good fun, reminding me that collecting sec-ondhand knitwear wasn't a personality. 'I'll insist on a ring for the big day, obviously.'

I was hyper aware Daisy wasn't joining in. She was staring at her phone, scrolling, brows knitting together and springing apart in reaction. Any light prodding went ignored so Tam seized the opportunity to reveal his wedding plans. It would be in Italy, in August the next year. Italy. Glamorous. August in Italy. Hot. I mentally scrolled through my wardrobe – it took all of five seconds – checking for suitable outfits. We only got seven minutes of summer in Scotland, I'd never bothered building up a seasonal 'look'. I had two pairs of shorts, one which grazed my knees and a considerably more teeny-weeny pair that grazed . . . actually, never mind.

'Won't your mum and dad want something more . . . um, Hindu? And more local?'

'I don't think they're expecting anything traditional from me. My brother's got that covered. And my mum's always wanted to go to Italy.' Tam winked at me. 'I'm paying for the flights, we'll be travelling together. All of us. You, Daisy, sig-nificant others. Patels and pals on tour.'

If I had as much credit card debt as Tam and Fabrizio I'd sleep for precisely one hour a night, sixty minutes of unfiltered nightmares. But Tam could never leave anyone out, and he and Fabrizio, chief critic for a listings mag and thus fond of swishing about grandly, both liked their gestures big and bold.

'Jesus, Tam, how many flowerbeds will you have to dig over to pay for that?'

'It'll be fine, I'll start smuggling vodka into pubs in sun cream bottles, like we used to at Pride.' He swatted away my concerns as he might a bluebottle from his picpoul. 'I like the idea of arriving in a flock. It's chic. Don't get the abacus out, Lion. You can congratulate me now, if you like.'

I raised my lukewarm glass of lime and soda. 'Sorry, Tammy, that's so generous and lovely. Congratulations. You're made for each other.'

Tam beamed, easily placated. 'I'm really sorry about the end-of-term thing, I've been out the game too long. I work to a different timetable now. This time next week, we'll have another go. Somewhere nicer.'

Ah. There it came, that little extra effort to swallow, the invisible grit in my eye. 'Can't. It's Dad's anniversary.'

'Oh, baby.' I couldn't bear seeing Tam's face crumple into sadness; such a waste of his looks. I was an ugly crier, but it was no big deal; not much of a shift from my regular resting face.

I guided us back to the upcoming nuptials, conspiring over how we could make his father's inevitably heartwarming speech less embarrassing, settling on engineering a volcanic eruption timed with his favourite joke, that Tam was the first of his kind in the family – by which he'd mean gardener, not gay. There'd been a great uncle in Bhavnagar with a large hat collection who never married.

When Tam slipped off to the bathroom, I gave Daisy's wrist an affectionate squeeze. 'Oi, this is the doomscroll police. Come back to us.'

I had a distant relationship with my phone. I wasn't on socials, so lacked an emotional crutch when conversation lulled or I found myself alone and conspicuous, waiting for someone – or rather two certain someones. I didn't think for a minute any of my students would remotely care what their drama teacher got up to in his spare time, but since Mr Foreman from maths had been found wearing cycling shorts on a dating website – 'Passions: French cuisine, nature, spelunking' – he'd been known as Spunky Frogs' Legs. Better to stay offline.

'You knew, didn't you? The proposal.' I saw a light flicker on inside her, like a fridge door opening, then a traitor's grimace. 'You were there!'

'Not intentionally. I didn't know he was gonna do it. It was a couples' thing. Me and Seb, Tam and Fabrizio. Cocktails. You don't drink those. And you don't have anyone . . .' She tried to pull back from the edge of that particular cliff. 'I promised not to say. He wanted to tell you himself.'

Not drinking, not being on social media and not having a partner was, to my friends, like I'd checked out of the twenty-first century. It had been three and a half years since I let Peter go. I say that like he didn't want to go, but he did, very much; I'll never forget the vim in his eyes when he'd unplugged the kettle and packed it in a box, reminding me, 'I bought it with the John Lewis gift card my granny gave me, remember?' I had as much luck finding someone suitable enough for one of their 'couples' things' as I did winning the giant teddy at the arcades with that big metal claw. Not even a near miss. I didn't want to win anyway – once you snag the prize, you stop playing, and there were plenty more games to come.

I decided not to give her a hard time. 'How was it, then? The big yes?'

Daisy brightened, relieved to expel the gossip at last, like trapped wind. 'It was really sweet, but Fabrizio's not a natural at the old public speaking. To say he writes for a job, I mean. He read something off his phone. A poem.'

I'd always imagined myself sharing that moment, a tear forming in my eye, sweeping violins as I turned to my other half or – for better dramatic effect, actually – an empty chair. Lost in the beauty of the moment. Never mind. Daisy assured me her boyfriend Seb had filmed it – although it was hard to hear everything because Seb kept whooping and hollering positive affirmations. He had a life coach.

'It killed me keeping the secret, Dandelion. In twenty years it's only the second thing I've not told you.'

Daisy kept confidences like colanders hold water so I found this very hard to believe. 'What was the first?'

'I've forgotten, washed away on a tide of prosecco. But it must've been juicy. Get me drunker and I'll remember.'

A challenge nobody could win. Her phone started going full angry vibrator in her hand.

'Just take it, I don't mind.'

'Thanks, Lion, I'm so sorry. God, another sorry. I'm spitting them out like a machine gun.'

She stalked off to the toilet to 'focus' as Tam returned sporting the grin of a CEO who'd won a billion on insider trading.

'That's Seb driving her mad, I assume. What they arguing about this time?'

Tam squeezed the lime from his gin and tonic right into his mouth. 'Daisy alphabetised her paperbacks but Seb reorganised them by colour and then . . . he turned them round so only the edges were showing. He saw it on a makeover show at 3 a.m., pissed.'

Any minute now, Daisy would return and say she was leaving, to make up a bed for Seb on the sofa.

'It's so she never knows what time he gets in, you know. Doesn't have to face the truth.'

'I know, she'll be calling you in tears later, hope you've no plans.' Tam was slurring now. By my calculations, he was five minutes away from peeling himself off that stool and slithering into a cab.

'This isn't about the paperbacks, is it?'

Tam sighed with disappointment. 'No. They lowkey messed up the proposal, to be honest. Don't say anything though. She caught Seb chatting up some yah girl from the uni. Same old. Poor Daiz.' Tam shivered at the memory. I'd witnessed enough of Seb and Daisy's showdowns to know they never happened in quiet corners; it would've been a popcorn moment. 'Look, what're you doing tomorrow, assuming you're not reassembling Daisy's heart in front of *A Chorus Line* or whatever? Fancy coming shopping? Early wedding prep?'

Daisy reappeared, her frown lines set in concrete, slamming her handbag on the table. 'Of course he doesn't. He can't go into town on a Saturday afternoon and trail round after you. He'll see all his students, shoplifting. Too horrifying.' I actually had zero plans, and being Tam's bag carrier didn't seem too bad – even if we did spend most of our time together running his many errands, he always chose good lunch venues.

I didn't have a chance to answer anyway; Daisy was thrusting her phone into my face. I caught two words of the text she was showing me – 'hysterical' was one.

'Literally every woman I was just chatting to in the toilets thinks Seb should be clawing his way out of a shallow grave somewhere outside Linlithgow.'

'I'm not sure you should listen to wasted girls trying to have a piss in peace, Daisy.'

'Oh, I dunno, Tamish, why shouldn't she? I trust their authority.' If I kept them talking, maybe I could hang on to them a while longer. My lime and soda hadn't even activated my acid reflux yet. 'Westminster has the House of Lords, Holyrood has ten Lauras in the Silk Rooms toilets. Send him down!'

'Exactly, Lion! Toilet gurus taught me everything I know about men. Anyway . . . ' I knew what was coming. Exit Daisy Forbes. 'I'm heading. Please don't be mad at me, Lion. Why don't we have lunch Sunday? I've got some time between my HIIT class and an argument with my mum about something my dad did in 1997.'

Almost every lunch Daisy and I had eaten in the last year or two had been sandwiched (ha!) between two other appointments. Sometimes in cars. She must have had permanent indigestion. 'Sure, sounds good.'

'Barry. I can't wait to have a proper catch-up.' She leaned in and lowered her voice to a whisper. 'I'll play you the video of the proposal and you have to pretend it's gorgeous, okay?' Laser focused on the argument she'd be having in about thirty minutes' time, Daisy swept out into the wet evening, the open door sending us an unseasonal gust of wind to fill the space where she once was.

'That's that, then.' Tam looked at me thoughtfully. 'How are you?'

'I'm brand new, cheers.'

Tam chuckled. 'Good.'

From over my left shoulder came a scream somewhere between blood-curdling and excited. 'Oh my God! Mr Patel!'

I turned to see a skelf of a lad, no more than eighteen, skip over, then fling his arms round Tam who tried his best not to recoil. 'You were my fave teacher. Remember me? Archie? Archie Lockhart?'

Tam showed every one of those glorious teeth in a smile wider than the Forth Bridge. 'Of course I do!' He didn't. Not a bit.

'Oh my god, it seems like such a long time ago, primary seven. Can't believe it! My sister said you gave up teaching! Why? You were brilliant.'

This was the teacher's curse, but didn't happen often, if you were lucky; I usually tried to make sure I socialised in dives no underage drinker would be seen dead in, but once your students came of age, the chances of an unwelcome reunion rocketed. Tam answered young Archie's questions with the guarded discretion of a diplomat caught in a brothel and made polite enquiries about Archie's life since they parted company eight years earlier. Archie turned to me briefly and smiled, perhaps recognising me as the teacher who'd booked him for smoking in the girls' toilets once he'd made it to high school, but more than likely not.

'Anyway, lovely to catch up, I'm here with my pals.' Tam and I spotted a group of embryos in tight sportswear choking down alcoholic ginger beer. 'See you around?'

Once the lad departed, Tam groaned as if looking into a mirror and seeing Yoda look back at him. I rubbed his arm. 'First time, huh?'

'I forget they grow up, become real people, get reeking in bars.'

He hopped off his stool, made a show of rearranging himself, running his finger round the inside of his waistband to make sure his shirt wasn't untucked, sliding his watch round to be face up. 'You wanna head somewhere else?'

I could tell his early start on the martinis was catching up with him. 'Let's call it a night. Catch up tomorrow?'

'You don't mind?' He looked grateful.

'Nope. One of us will be getting a call from Daisy soon anyway.'

'You mean you will. Hopefully she won't leave it too late. You might be back home and tucked up in your own bed by sunrise. I'm sorry I'm bailing, I'm useless. Let me know about tomorrow. It's ages since we did a gays-go-shopping day. We can get the train through to Glasgow if you want. Ooh, how about a drag brunch?'

'Sounds great.' I leaned in for the kiss, steadying Tam as he wobbled.

'Goodnight, gorgeous Leo.'

And he was gone. My hair was still damp.

Daisy's tearful phone call came at 2.30 a.m. Tam's hungover apology and cancellation landed eight hours later. I wasn't surprised, or even disappointed. It was comforting, in a way, to know they never changed. That's what I loved about them. And I suppose the fact I knew them so well, yet loved them all the same, was exactly what they loved about me.

Two

There are two types of people in the world: those who think they're the centre of the universe, and those who know, beyond all doubt, that they're not even close. Life has hierarchies. All social circles have their main players and supporting roles. It's not always a bad thing. Supports are important, they keep the roof from falling in. There's even an Oscar for them. *Chicago* – for example. Nobody's going to deny Catherine Zeta Jones steals the whole damn thing. Well, maybe not nobody. I put this to my mother one Sunday afternoon, who responded that Renée Zellweger had been 'a revelation' and that my preference for Catherine Zeta Jones was British bias. She did concede, however, that at least Jones was Welsh and not English, which would've been the final insult. Regardless, not everyone can be centre stage; some of us aren't built for it. These hierarchies are flexible, though, depending on who we're with. Sliding scales. In some rooms we're kings, but a few steps in another direction makes us serfs again. I always had a knack for not only knowing my place, but accepting it, shrugging off being picked last for football, coming third in writing competitions or being a regular victim of queue jumping. I was the type of man you'd have to search for in a group photo.

Daisy was epicentre to her core; she drank wine like a camera was on her. She was now the lone woman in our tiny circle and, like all friends you can't live without, started out as an enemy. Well, not really, I was only eight, but I used to be so jealous. No, hang on, envious. She wasn't overly popular, but even from a young age had the air of someone unwilling to be fucked with. Her parents' separation turned her into the most nihilistic eight-year-old imaginable. At school, I feared Daisy until she made it impossible for me to do anything but adore her. We finally bonded over our mutual love for pop music; mine unabashed, hers a secret because worshipping Steps clashed with her ambition to headline Glastonbury someday. At eleven, she offered to be my first girlfriend. Well, girlfriend might be overstating it — we tried scissoring, fully clothed, in her summer house but felt nothing through our tarpaulin-weight kids' jeans out of Next.

'I think you're gay,' she'd said after fifteen minutes of urgent frotting. 'I can tell. My granny does the tarot. I won't tell anyone.'

Our sexual awakenings began in earnest. Daisy, with non-regulation 'Dad said I could do it' dyed hair and huge DM boots, was a curiosity. This made her desirable. Back then, I couldn't think of anything hotter than being drooled over by boys with bad skin in unironed school shirts yellowing under the pits from twenty squirts of Lynx. Nobody drooled over me; I gave St Bernards cotton-mouth. The limelight and Daisy were never far apart, but her main competition these days was Tam, especially now he was in the throes of planning a wedding.

I'd resented Tam at first when Daisy turned our twosome into a triangle. She'd stumbled into him in the uni bar, dragged him over and did her usual 'Look, Leo, another gay! He's funny!' introduction. For a moment I was struck with anxiety. Now she'd found a good-looking one, it occurred to me Daisy may no longer need me to fetch her a latte and two Hedex every Sunday morning, but Tam had immediately disarmed me with a slightly mean joke about a mutual enemy. I didn't need to tell him I hated this person – a pig's carcass of a man who studied sports science and flapped his wrist whenever I walked by – Tam just knew. So he stayed. You can't let the good ones go.

I was happy with my spot on the sidelines, grateful to take in drama rather than create it, the clean-up operative who put everything back together again, steering the ship away from icebergs. My last flirtation with centre stage was when Peter left, but this was quickly usurped by a pregnancy scare for Daisy – not hers, but a woman Seb was dating just before he met her, he said – and Tam's then-boyfriend returning to his ex, which left Tam homeless and needing my spare room. Just like that, I was back in my supporting role.

I knew my place at work too, took comfort from it. Experiencing school as a teacher was a world away from my awkward teenage years, remarkable only for being tall. Dare I say I was cooler now? Being a drama teacher suggested more interesting depths than the top layer of the onion portrayed. I told myself that students enjoyed my classes more than double chemistry – and I was the only classroom to offer geometric-print beanbags and a thinking corner.

My assigned role here at Bucklemaker, Edinburgh's most

arty and liberal high school, was sassy creative with theatrical tendencies. Why fight the stereotype? It had its advantages. If I rolled my eyes, it was on-brand, but any sociology teacher who pulled the same act would be labelled difficult. My (vanishingly rare) strops were a genius's outbursts; in anyone else they would denote a breakdown. Perched next to me on this particular ledge of the pecking order was Mica.

'Morning, peasants.'

In she strode, that last day of summer term, clutching her school-branded thermal cup which, judging by her wired expression, must've contained her second triple shot of the day. The end of summer term wasn't as much fun as you'd think: too much exuberance. Somebody always got cocky and ordered a Chinese takeaway to afternoon registration, or shagged in a cupboard, or broke a leg. Nobody wanted to be the teacher dashing to A&E and missing end-of-term drinks.

'Hello, handsome.' Mica flicked my ear as I muttered my hellos. I liked Mica because, aside from lying that I was handsome, she was very direct – for instance, she'd correctly identified the wee patch of vitiligo at the corner of my mouth within seconds of meeting me. I knew where I was with her. We were quite different – I'd only been inside a nightclub after 5 a.m. twice, while she'd spent most of her twenties experimenting with ecstasy before having her daughter fifteen years ago. A decision she regretted, she joked, once she realised it would mean never again having possessions she could truly call her own. Mica, however, considered us similar – we both had one eye bigger than the other, and neither of us ever agreed with the public when picking *Strictly* winners. We were also, as she loved to point out, two sassy best friends who were much more interesting than any of the lead personalities jostling for attention in that staffroom.

'Six sweet weeks of nothing. You excited? You still haven't told me what you're doing.'

The only thing in my diary was helping Tam with wedding travel plans, and pretending to enjoy the plays, gigs, and Fringe comedies that his future husband could give me free tickets for, to say thank you. 'No major plans. Just gonna enjoy summer in the city.'

'Said nobody ever.' Mica's laugh cut through the air like wire through an Orkney cheddar. The entire social sciences department, lined up against one wall like the front row of a circus, flinched. 'What, two sunny days on the Meadows, forty days of rain, getting crushed by tourists in every pub? Stop it. They're not plans.'

Mica did the same every summer. Two weeks seeing family in London 'with actual summer weather', two weeks some-where blisteringly hot abroad, and the remaining two weeks arguing with her daughter in their Morningside flat and texting me to join her for drinks at a festival pop-up. Sometimes I'd go.

'You live like an extra in your own life sometimes. Up your main character vibes, I keep telling you.'

She did indeed. Constantly. I didn't really do plans. I waited for things to happen, preferred to be asked than to arrange. Made life a bit of a mystery tour; I quite liked seeing where I might end up. Plus, if you don't ask, nobody can say no. I didn't mind my diary being blanker than a mannequin's stare anyway; made a nice change from term time.

'Look at this lot,' said Mica at a volume that would be mildly disrespectful at a funeral and gesturing in the general direction of our colleagues. 'Waiting for an audition that's never gonna come; centre stage is where the fun's at, babycakes.'

'Drama analogies, Meesh? On the last day of term? Come on.'

'So long as you're hearing me. Fag?'

'Please don't call me that.'

'Every time. Don't you get bored of that joke?'

'No.' I followed Mica to the fire escape and we shuffled round the corner of the building until we overlooked the car park, the only place on campus you couldn't be spotted from a classroom. She lit up and I breathed in deeply, enjoying that warm, toasty scent when someone first lights a cigarette – precious seconds before the smell becomes an acrid blend of formaldehyde and crematoriums. Crematoria? Whichever.

I didn't smoke. Mica didn't smoke. Officially. But we had the Emergency Cigarette Protocol. We co-owned a packet of cigarettes, kept in my locker. Occasionally, if we'd had a bad day, the protocol was invoked. Only one of us was allowed to smoke, the other would have to watch. We weren't allowed to smoke at any other time, and if both of us needed a cigarette, it would cancel out the craving and we'd agree not to bother. Our reasoning was, if we smoked like this, only together, but never actually at the same time, we'd never get addicted (again). It was hardly worth it anyway, really. If the students smelled smoke on you they'd give you hell all day. We tried smoking wearing a surgical glove for a while, before admitting it made us look unhinged. Instead, Mica had a bottle of awful supermarket perfume in her desk – another deterrent as it masked the scent of her regular Black Orchid – and I had a can of talc-scented Mitchum so, post-protocol cigarettes, I had the whiff of a newborn fresh from a nappy change.

'Why are we hitting Miss Nicotine today, Meesh?'

'April's last day before mat leave, isn't it? New face next term. I hope we don't get one of those strategy types who wishes they'd applied for *The Apprentice*.'

'Shit, yeah. Results driven. A disruptor. Asking what we think of the syllabus.'

As one of the deputy heads, April looked after the arts subjects, but she was fairly hands off. Fairly everything off, really. We did as we liked, got through the year well enough not to make the front of the *Evening News*. Our only taxing duties were, for Mica, to arrange an art show, music teacher Joe – known as Joe Music for obvious reasons – would throw together a recital, and I'd have to stage an end-of-year performance for parents to dutifully film on their phones. So long as nobody died, April was happy. Maternity covers made us nervous. Her understudy might want to keep things ticking over, fine, but there was always one teacher who'd overdosed on *Everybody's Talking About Jamie* or *Dead Poets' Society* and was desperate to inspire a West End musical, or who thrived on extra paperwork because it made them look busy.

April's office looked like three filing cabinets had been fucking in it. She was sitting catatonic, staring into the chaos, a stapler and folder of coursework resting on her bump.

'I've been looking for this for five years,' she said. 'It had to go to mitigating circumstances in the end. I hope he got into St Andrews.' She sniffed up. 'You could've invited me outside and blown smoke in my face.'

'How you doing?' I said. 'Emotional? Ecstatic to get out of here?'

'All of it. I know this sounds old-fashioned, but I can't wait to sit at home and stare at my baby. Even if they're a crier. It's gotta be better than this.'

April had no idea who'd be replacing her, and didn't seem to care, as long as they didn't burn the place down. 'Or maybe I hope they do.' All she asked was that we didn't throw her under the bus. 'If they ask about my . . . processes, say you'll check and get back to them. Then avoid them until the end of the academic year. Okay?'

Like everyone going on extended leave, April was worried she'd be exposed as an impostor and banished to the corner of the staffroom where the blinds were stuck shut or worse, given a registration group of her own – calling out attendance gave her hives, she said.

'Be nice to them, but not too nice to them,' said April shooing us out of the door to start the day, 'remember, every time you betray me, a puppy gets stung by a wasp. Love you.'

Six long, chaotic hours later, Mica heaved her bag onto her shoulder like it contained all the world's problems. 'You coming to the pub?' She saw my face. 'Oh fuck, why not? Don't leave me with Emerald.' The head of art, prone to melodrama – Emerald refused to eat in the staffroom because the defibrillator next to the coffee cupboard reminded her of the fragility of the human heart. 'She's dying to fill me in on how her husband always stays late at work since his supervisor got implants.'

'I can't. Mum wants me round. I didn't realise Emerald was the suspicious type.'

'You kidding? She phones the husband's office putting on funny voices to check he's still there. This is the level of chill I'm dealing with. None. What's going on with your mum that's keeping you from buying me sixteen Bacardis?'

'Dad's anniversary.' One more brief spell as a leading man, a year after Peter left. My dad died. Cancer. I missed the last few days of term that year, spent them holding my father's hand for the first time in my life, watching petals drop off the flowers someone had brought. Someone. Peter, I mean, clawing his way back in. Arm round my mum's shoulder. 'Anything you need, Dawn.' Ever the suck-up.

Mica saw the game was lost. 'Okay. But I wanna see you during these six weeks, you hear?'

'I hear you.'

Three

My dad and I were very different. He liked watching the boys boot them in at Easter Road and I preferred the high kicks of the 'Mein Herr' backing dancers in *Cabaret*. But there were sweet overlaps. When I'd beg to play my Steps CDs in his dusty Mondeo, he'd jig along. He'd claim he liked the brown-haired lassie best, just like me, although even then he knew we'd spend very different evenings with her, given the opportunity. He wasn't too bothered I was gay so long as I didn't end up on drugs or living in London, especially working in fashion. He'd been to London twice and both times claimed to have seen someone doing cocaine in the café of a now defunct clothing store on Oxford Street.

For most of my teenage years, my mum's time was taken up with my brother Duncan, whose hobbies included getting into fights at bus stops, stealing pints from men big enough to slice him in two, and talking his way into the knickers of girls he'd blank once he got what he wanted. A mother's worry can only spread so thinly, so it was Dad I came out to on a match day, standing outside the Cabbage & Ribs pub, aged fourteen.

I remember trying to get the words out as Coca-Cola bubbles whooshed up my nose like caustic soda round a U-bend.

My dad had looked round to make sure nobody else heard, then said, 'You're sure about that, then, son?'

'Aye.' I always said 'aye' to my dad; he only ever said 'yes' if he was wearing a tie.

'Alright, then.' That was that. He took my mum for a Chinese a few days later and must've told her; she brought back a bigger bag of prawn crackers than usual and said I needn't share with Duncan if I didn't want. Which I very much didn't.

When Dad died, my brother and I were surprised to be left a bit of money; we'd always assumed that, aside from the house, they hadn't a pot to piss in. At the wake, Mum, brandishing a polystyrene plate overloaded with vol-au-vents said, through pastry-encased teeth, 'Your brother'll pish all his up against the wall, son, and that's up to him, but do something decent with yours, put a wee deposit on a flat somewhere.' I got a bargain on Salamander Street in Leith from a rail-thin divorcé who was having trouble selling because prospective buyers were put off by the scrap yard opposite – there wasn't a brand of fridge on the planet that I hadn't seen there in its final rusting place.

Mum struggled with widowhood at first; she still warmed up two kinds of pie every evening and her idea of therapy was to sit cross-legged on the floor listening to 'At Seventeen' and smoking a Benson & Hedges right down to its balls. Gradually, she came out the other side, went back to work. She was getting there. The only problem was my brother: every few months he was chucked out by whichever woman he was lying to at that time, and would return to his childhood bedroom, demanding beige, high-saturate dinners. He couldn't do anything for himself – he'd gawp at the microwave in terror, like it was the control deck for *Apollo 11*.

On the one occasion Tam came face to face with Duncan, at Dad's funeral, he took me aside and said, 'Maybe this isn't the time, but you can't be related to him, you just can't. Do you want me to get a DNA swab test?'

I never saw flowers in our house until my dad was dying; I always think it's a shame the person being commemorated never gets to appreciate their beauty, but now I always took a bunch for my mum. I walked through the unlocked back door into the kitchen with a bouquet I knew she wouldn't have a vase big enough for, and the first thing Mum said was, 'Harvey Pearce.'

'Hello to you too. What?'

She shoved aside the laundry basket she'd been rummaging in, got two mugs out of the cupboard, and flicked on the kettle in one fluid movement. 'Rab and Lynda Pearce from the flats. Mind them? Harvey was the son. There was a girl, too, Emma. Mind?'

I did. Harvey was in my class, and we played together; our parents were pretty close. They'd moved down south when I was about eleven and they became names on Christmas cards. 'Did they come to Dad's funeral?'

'Rab and Lynda did.' I could feel Mum getting irked I didn't have instant recall of someone I'd barely thought about in two decades. 'Not Harvey.'

'Come on, Dawny, out with it. Is he dead?' There couldn't be many reasons she was bringing him up; the only texts she sent me were updates on who was ascending to the angels that week. I'd had to delete the family group chat.

'Stop calling me Dawny. It's disrespectful.' She stirred the coffees forcefully to show her disapproval. 'He's not dead, drama queen! He's moved back to Edinburgh. For work. You should give him a call.'

I conjured up memories of Harvey Pearce. They were faded, replaced by slideshows of good places to get a curry, every millisecond of the London revival of *Company*, and names of every student I'd ever taught, but the haze started to lift and a few things came into focus. He didn't like to get his hands dirty, he had a year-round penchant for shorts, and enjoyed arguing over who got to command his Lego space station. I couldn't imagine Harvey was desperate to relive these highlights. 'Yeah, maybe.'

'I said you would.'

'Who to? I mean, to who? No, to whom?'

My mother went back to folding laundry – Superdry polo shirts, my brother was back. 'Lynda! I said you'd call. No, hang on. She said Harvey would call. I gave Lynda your number. Looks better if you call him first.'

I sat at the tiny, battered foldaway kitchen table to avoid towering over her and sipped my coffee. Bloody sweeteners in it. I'd never taken sugar or anything like it, ever. 'Nobody phones anyone anymore. How does it look better?'

'More welcoming.' A long tube of ash fell off Mum's cigarette into the basket of clean shirts. 'He's on his own. I said you'd be free tonight.'

'Tonight?! What about Dad's anniversary?'

'Peter's taking me out for a Chinese.'

Hearing his name was like that 'sharp scratch' the nurse always warned you of when taking your bloods. Every time. My breakup with Peter had been decisive, clean – but Mum never acknowledged the memo. Post me, Peter had thrived, marrying 'Ben' a year to the day after we gave up the flat. A doctor, too! Mum always liked Peter – everybody did – and after Dad died I didn't want to deprive her of her few remaining connections to happier times (for her, anyway). I tried not to begrudge her visits from my ex, and his new husband's daughter, Ava, who my mum doted on. So long as our paths never crossed, I could handle it. My eye still twitched, though.

'I could've taken you for a Chinese.'

'You're not adventurous with the menu. It's embarrassing. You can eat spring rolls any time.' Head tilt. Here it came. 'Your dad wouldn't want your old friend sitting in the house by himself, would he?'

I remembered Harvey Pearce on his bike, chapping at the door, asking me out to play, a melting Calippo in his hand. I didn't like the idea of him now, as an adult, behind a door nobody was going to knock on.

Mum read my face like it was the menu at the Happy Rickshaw. 'I'll get you this number.'

Four

Having no social media presence of my own, Daisy and Tam volunteered to scour all channels for me, to make sure Harvey didn't have any racist tattoos or was a football bore — but there was nothing.

'I'm getting a plumber in Kirriemuir and someone from Essex who does slightly out-of-time formation dancing with his two brothers,' said Daisy over an emergency video call. 'They've got bright white hoodies on. Why on earth wouldn't you have social media unless you were trying to hide something?'

'I quite like the mystery of it,' said Tam. 'Look, if it gets too "straight male", text us and we'll FaceTime and camp it up and be, like, egregiously annoying, so he'll run a mile.'

'So . . . you'll both act completely normally, then?' I blew the obligatory kiss. 'Look, if he murders me, promise you won't start a true crime podcast.' Daisy laughed like a hairdryer on a cool setting, Tam hung up.

I figured Harvey would be as keen on this enforced reunion as I was, so I decided to text, make myself sound busy and offer a vague promise of a meetup one day. Eventually. Within seconds, my phone rang. I jumped. I'd forgotten it could do that; it had been on silent since 2014.

'Uh, hello? Leo?'

Harvey. Obviously.

'Harvey Pearce! I believe our mothers have been conspiring.' I used my most calming parents' evening voice, reserved for weary parents in need of some good news after ten rounds of disappointment.

A short chuckle. 'I thought I'd grown out of my ma making playdates for me, but no. Horrendously embarrassing. Sorry.'

He sounded nice enough. Weary, apologetic, the voice of someone behind the ticket window of a railway station dealing with his eighth complaint of the day about a missed connection at Dundee. But there was something else.

'You sound totally English now!'

He laughed gently. 'No! Don't worry, I still roll my Rs.'

For some reason, I blushed.

'Look, you don't have to,' he said, sounding slightly more Scottish. 'But I'm free tonight and Mum's expecting a report back.'

'As a teacher, I strongly encourage you to finish your assignment.'

We arranged to meet in the safest straight pub I could think of, in the West End, the heterosexual heartland. Just the right side of showy, monogrammed paper coasters, a mixed crowd, and decent alcohol-free beers so I wouldn't be guzzling fizzy water all night. Somewhere a straight man could feel comfortable but not in charge. I foresaw the standard evening for two old acquaintances: a round of drinks each to reminisce and realise you've nothing in common anymore, before an ill-advised third you agree to out of politeness, sipped in harrowing silence. One thing I missed about alcohol: being able to talk shite through an awkward lull.

I realised, walking in, that I had no idea what he looked like now. It didn't matter; the moment I was in the door, an elegant, toned test-tube of a man called out. I recognised the aged-up face of the ten-year-old I'd known, clear bright blue eyes crinkling as he said hello, handshake strong and sincere. His body had morphed from the hazy sack of meat we carry around in childhood into a svelte, well-maintained machine, everything in perfect proportion, heightening my own oaf complex. I could feel my sense of balance corrupting, my limbs stretching like strands of chewing gum. He was a pristine filament of flesh, muscle and 100 per cent cotton, not a hair out of place, he must've floated here. Everything fit perfectly: a long-sleeved T-shirt, in navy, no stains or lint or worn cuffs like most of my wardrobe. His jeans looked expensive. His trainers gleamed so hard I had an urge to stamp on them.

His first words: 'You're tall.' Disappointing.

'Oh? I was five-seven when I left the house.' Ten points to me.

'Sorry, that was a dumb thing to say. You know you're tall. I'm an idiot.' Redemption!

'It's fine.' I noticed a theatrical roll of the eyes. Hmm. A slight hunching of the shoulders while he called himself an idiot. Self-deprecating.

He didn't ask about my vitiligo or question that I wasn't drinking, which suggested he'd been briefed beforehand.

Hang on, was this a setup?

My mother had never taken an interest in my love life,

beyond wondering why I hadn't snared Tom Daley before he was snapped up. Was Harvey Pearce gay? I quickly scanned internal childhood footage for limp wrists, interest in the Spice Girls, or liking trains, but came up blank. I decided to look out for the usual giveaways.

We plunged into small talk, job interview politesse. He'd never adjusted to living in England, he said, and ditched his Scottish accent quickly, to survive. Adolescent pain! Not unique to little gay boys, though. The usual issues with his parents – no mention why. Finally, he'd moved to London to sort his life out. A bell chimed in my head. What else would a wee gay prototype do but high tail it at the first opportunity to the safety of the brightest lights and the tallest skyscrapers? Body language-wise, he was indecipherable as hieroglyphics. So still, controlled. He spoke calmly, without emotion. He worked in construction. Oh. Masculine! But the management side, more logistical. Yes, he wore a hard hat onsite but would be more likely found in a suit and hi-vis than dusty overalls. Sounded hot. Ding ding. We covered nicknames. He'd been 'Sauce' at high school.

'HP, you see. It died off, thankfully. Why Dandelion?'

'Oh, man, it's bastardisation upon bastardisation. Leo the lion, right? And I'm tall, as you helpfully pointed out . . . so it was lanky lion for long enough, then Dandelion because it sounds like "lanky lion" when you do it in a funny voice.' One of Daisy's many drunk 'characters' was a sadistic six-year-old who pulled wings off butterflies. 'I don't mind it.' It meant I belonged.

'Didn't we always say at school that touching dandelions made you pish the bed?'

Next topic of our corporate icebreaker evening: hobbies.

He did mindfulness every day, loved yoga, and was really into breathing. I managed to choke back a giggle. Wasn't everyone 'into' breathing? You didn't have much choice. I was in the middle of telling him how much I loved musicals and staying up late on YouTube watching videos of soldiers surprising their children for Christmas, when he interrupted me.

'Look, personal question, but . . . are you gay?'

'I'm sorry, what?'

'Did I offend you? It's just, I wondered. You seemed quite . . . you know, when we were kids. Not that there's anything wrong with that.'

I've always been quite . . . *you know*. Effeminate, camp. I used to try hide those flourishes that gave me away, but it was like plugging a leak in a pipe with your finger – soon enough, another would gush out somewhere else and we'd be drowning in rainbow water. When I started teaching, I realised it was better to own it. I couldn't do my job trying to rein in my exaggerated sighs and my arms' tendency to reach for the farthest corners of the room when I spoke, so I let my students take me as they found me, and it seemed to work. Whatever they said behind my back was none of my business.

'What gave it away? My love of musicals? God, yes, gay as hell. My most treasured possession is a reply from Stephen Sondheim when I was fifteen.' I took a chance. 'You?'

He nodded. Knew it. I tightened my mouth to stop a smile leaking out.

'Maybe not gay as hell,' he said. 'I mean . . . is hell gay? 'Cos, like, it sounds like a giant barbecue, and straight men love those.'

'Course it is! All that red leather. Satan has literal horns, and a big fork for poking people up the ass.'

Harvey laughed, and, I swear, his shoulders dropped a few inches closer to sea level. That sweet release. Our radios had finally tuned to the right frequency. The rough outline of the first half hour began to fill with colour.

He'd never forgiven his dad for making them move so often. 'I had no control over my own life, you know?'

'Totally. Kids are so powerless. You can't make any decisions, good or bad, until you leave school. Sometimes I sit and eat a tin of cold beans for my dinner, just because I can.'

Harvey grimaced as the barman handed us our drinks and spilled some of my faux mojito. He dabbed it with a napkin. 'I've been a clean freak since I was a kid.'

'I remember. Always running inside to wash your hands.'

'Do you?' He looked touched. 'I'm way worse now. I learned about the micro biome cloud and it ruined me for two years.'

'What's the micro biome cloud?'

He pulled a face like he was watching someone lick the filling out of an apple turnover. 'It's basically a cloud of filth that hangs around everyone. All things. Every person. Fart gas, dead skin, bacteria. It's always there. Like an ex, maybe.'

I blushed. I never talked about Peter. But when you bring up an ex with a stranger – a gay stranger at that – you're working out whether they're an ally, I suppose, and also whether they want to be a successor.

Harvey spotted my change in expression. I never play card games. 'Tell me about yours.'

I had a standard routine on the rare occasions I was forced to address the breakup. 'Not much to tell. He was an English teacher. We argued about whether I should use semicolons in my Christmas cards. Weekends ruined by debates over "imply" versus "infer". And then . . . ' I liked to call it The Unpleasantness in my head but I wasn't ready for questions. 'Then he left.'

'Why?'

'He found someone else.' I reached for a one-liner. 'That last six months, the only place he wouldn't put his cock was back in his Calvins. Sorry to be coarse. I don't miss him. That's it really.'

'That's funny.'

'It's also the truth.' Ish. 'What about you?'

The faraway look in his eyes told me he'd been the one receiving the Dear John. The usual platitudes laced with excuses. Matt. Worked in property. A lot in common at first – a love of knocking down walls to make spectacular garden extensions, especially – but began drifting. He was a good person. No hard feelings.

I tried to tap into the undercurrents. Drifting? What kind of idiot would let this man float away? I decided he must've been a real piece of work, this Matt, and Harvey was too nice to say. I created a crude caricature in my head, imagined Matt criticising Harvey, constantly yucking his yum. Sour, unsupportive, no fun, always begging to leave parties early or complaining of a headache but refusing to take paracetamol. Things I'd never do. Not now, anyway, not now I'd learned my lesson. Little twitches of envy surprised me, so I snapped back into the present, watched Harvey's mouth as he spoke. His teeth were perfect, like they'd come pre-assembled and slotted into place by archangels. I ran my tongue over my own crooked pebbles, as if saliva would magic them into perfect straight pearls like his. He'd had them 'done', in Chelsea, he confessed later.

Before we knew it, the sloppy barman was whipping away our glasses and wishing us goodnight. Our voices echoed off empty walls; we were the last in the place. We spent a couple of strangely uncomfortable minutes gathering ourselves up and making our way outside. He asked if I'd like to do it again. I tried to decode his intentions. Do it again as friends? Or do it again, but do a bit more? Seeing Harvey again would feel significant. It would be rude to let things dribble away, participate in mutual ghosting, like I had every other man since Peter. My mum would ask questions.

My mind raced. Would we end up doing it? Me and Harvey Pearce? Naked? Could I have sex with someone I'd known as a child? Wouldn't it be icky to leap from *Junior Monopoly* twenty-five years ago, to adults coming inside each other? I remembered his pasty little body in play-fights in paddling pools or braving the salty chills on Porty beach. What memories did he have of my body? Would he even be curious to see how little was going on under my shirt? He'd left Scotland before I'd even heard of hormones, but now he was a man, who did cardio four times a week, with a whole new body beneath that tasteful navy outfit, waiting for a reply and a handshake.

I held out my hand like I was placing Scrabble tiles back into the bag and said, 'Cool, yeah, sure.'

Five

My single life progressed along two trajectories – the real one, the one I lived in, which involved quietly getting on with things, and the one outsiders saw, which had several stages, similar to the grieving process, or a project to build an orangery on the back of a townhouse. The first few months after Peter left was the 'Too Soon' period. If I happened to mention meeting a man, any man, I'd get the dreaded Head Tilt of Concern in response. Daisy and Tam took breakups badly, so they'd say I was rushing things, as if I were choosing wedding venues rather than hooking up. Eventually, to avoid scrutiny, I clammed up about these encounters.

It was a flawed strategy that propelled me into the 'Back Out There' era. That's where they thought I should be after six months: back out there, finding Peter 2.0. I was already very much 'Out There', just not in a way they understood.

Dragging myself to the Cameo one night to watch a three-hour superhero dirge, I came across a flyer with three disastrous typos, for a social group called Menergize (I know, I know). Its members were gay or bi men, many as dull as me, who'd go on theatre trips, park runs, or do drawing classes. Activities. Trips away. Like a very twee stag night twice a month. More, in summer. It was perfect, until I made it complicated. I may be no looker, but you should never underestimate the novelty factor as an aphrodisiac; I slept with one or two of the members. Well, three. Okay, four. And a half, if we're counting handjobs. Each was looking for commitment I was unwilling to give, and they transformed from rivals to allies, teaming up against me, looking for blood. No boy had fought over me since the two football captains had argued over who didn't get me in their team; the spotlight was exhilarating but unwelcome. One day, Glen, the chief menergizer (he chose his own title) took me aside, put his Papermate behind his ear and said if I were his son he'd give me a good thrashing. Holding in my laughter, I agreed it might be best to exit Menergize with what remained of my dignity.

Next stop on the singledom sympathy trajectory was 'Just Want You To Meet Someone', blurted out one Hogmanay by frustrated Daisy and Tam, who were sick of staring at empty chairs at birthday meals.

'All you ever say is that everything's "brand new". How can it be? You live alone.' Tam couldn't be alone longer than five minutes, which explained his serial monogamy.

'And you don't drink!' boomed Daisy. 'How can you pull without the one thing that makes people hotter?'

I shut that down quickly. The fact Daisy fell off her stool seconds later helped.

Sick of my lack of cooperation, we progressed to 'How's It All Going', vague enquiries whether I'd met someone asked with the detached sincerity you might expect from a shopping mall Santa once you're on his knee. I loved my friends, they meant well, but some people don't feel useful unless they have someone to worry about. The real answer – that I really was absolutely fine, as far as I could tell – wasn't enough of a story. Once it was clear I wasn't interested in a relationship, the comments dried up.

But now? Might I have found someone? An actual attractive man? Harvey was obscenely good-looking. Honestly, shockingly so. My previous personal best 'I can't believe how hot this guy is' was a one-nighter with a model who was high on something he licked off a key and said he loved 'Slavic faces'. Harvey made him look like a half-eaten pie, and being a semi-forgotten character from my past made him more intriguing. Every so often I felt faint traces of familiarity, a lingering conspiratorial bond from shared childhood secrets.

'I was a late bloomer too,' he said, kindly, the next time we met, even though we both knew the 'too' wasn't necessary. I'd grown into my face a little and my height and length of bone were less bizarre now I wasn't wedged into a uniform, but I was still as hot as I'd been at school. Not very. There'd been no Valentines, no midnight phone calls pulsing with adolescent longing, or being consensually groped at prom. Instead of beauty, I had humour, so I had pals, but not admirers.

My first sexual experience happened where nobody knew me. At seventeen, Mum and Dad dragged me to a caravan park in Blackpool for my final family holiday so they could get drunk in unfamiliar surroundings. I attracted the attention of a plain-faced children's entertainer. He was only four years older, but the gap between us felt generations wide. His furtiveness and detailed instructions where to put my hands led me to believe I wasn't the first young holidaymaker to find themselves pressed against the fire escape behind the onsite snacketeria. He timed my sexual awakening with expert precision between compèring knobbly knees contests, while my parents drank pear and lychee cider and watched a comedian tell vaguely homophobic jokes only tens of feet away. He messaged me a while after, sent poorly composed nudes, said he'd come to Edinburgh, but eventually the communication dried up; no doubt he found some other sucker. Literally. But my loss of innocence beamed signals into the sky: in my last term an equally unappealing boy from a different school became my boyfriend by default, because we allowed each other to do things we'd only read about online.

Once I started telling Harvey about my clumsy sexual exploits, over messy tacos in a chain restaurant, three days after our first meeting, I couldn't stop. His face was so open and trusting, he followed my cues to laugh, but held back if the memory hinted at being a painful one. The Menergize story slipped out. I enjoyed the look on his face as he tried to work out where the hell this was going.

'You were intimate with four of them?' Intimate! There was something so gracious in the way he tried to romanticise my sleazy past. 'I'd never have guessed you had it in you.'

'That was the trouble,' I said. 'I did, often.' Vulgarity is a defence mechanism. He reddened. 'I couldn't believe they were attracted to me, so I went for it. The sun shone, I made hay.'

'Why couldn't you believe it? You're not exactly ugly.'

'Thanks for the "exactly". I know. I'm okay, I won't scare children.' A lie. 'But I wanted to be striking, you know? I used to lie in bed and imagine the things I'd do if I woke up drop dead gorgeous. Then I decided to do them anyway.'

'That sounds pretty empowering.'

Not really. All that time I wasted wishing I were hot, with

no discernible way to make it happen, went on longer than it should've, right up to my late twenties. What if the little patch of porcelain by my mouth, or its cousins at various points of my body, disappeared overnight? What if my dark thatch of stiff hair suddenly lightened and loosened into luxuriant waves that fell around my face? What if my eyes changed from dark, expressionless, peering currants into bright, blinking jewels that gazed or sent sensual glances across crowded restaurants to slick-haired men in tuxedos? What if my stature withdrew slightly to a respectable six feet, and my protruding rib cage retreated behind sculpted pecs atop granite abs? I imagined my arms and legs solidifying, toned, and moving in fluid slo-mo. Whatever. Every morning I looked exactly the same.

Harvey was looking at me as you'd stare into a fire in a schmaltzy drama to show tension. 'Who says you're not already gorgeous?'

'Mirrors! Shop windows! My Auntie Jenny after three snowballs on Boxing Day!'

He laid his hand over mine, his tanned skin on my bluish paw. Lovely nails. We'd touched before, polite handshakes, but now I felt electricity. 'Can I say . . . I get it's a way of keeping your guard up, but you don't have to play comedian, you don't have to try to be funny. Not with me.'

'I wasn't trying. I am funny!'

'You can be yourself.'

'I am.'

'Are you? I see something else. Maybe something others don't see.'

Was this real, or a mindfulness podcast? 'Would you like to see something in me that others have never seen?'

He laughed, but had the weight of the world on his eyebrows. 'There you go. Deflecting. Be serious.'

I felt a flicker of irritation. We didn't know each other well enough for psychoanalysis; it even annoyed me when Daisy and Tam tried this kind of thing. Life isn't serious, why shouldn't I joke my way through it? 'Light and breezy keeps things easy.'

'I know your waters run deep. Don't be afraid.'

I felt seen, and mildly infuriated, so I said, 'Oh' and stirred my cranberry juice with my rapidly disintegrating paper straw.

Our third meeting – I hesitate to call it a date, he kept his hands above the table – he took me to a stand-up night, a pre-pre-pre-Fringe warmup in a basement venue that smelled like divorce and mildew. I'd swerved dinner at Daisy's and given only vague excuses, but I'd either have to tell her how things were going with Harvey soon, or never see him again. The comedian was terrible, regurgitating outdated memes, dreary anti-English jokes and referendum patter, even though he was from Penge. Halfway through, Harvey tapped me on the knee – all this fraternal touching was bringing out my inner Jane Austen; I was desperate for him to throw a glove at me.

'Can we go?'

We made our way to the exit as quietly as possible, but the comic spotted us and pointed at Harvey. 'Looks like this guy and his portable hat-stand can't hack it. You going back to Europe to buy a nice chapeau?'

What did that even mean? I was embarrassed for him, then realised I was the hat-stand. Harvey turned toward him with the slow agility of a tai chi instructor. I steeled myself. There was no surer antidote to the first flutter of attraction than seeing a man flex his temper in public. Was Harvey violent? Withering? Nasty? I had no idea.

He put his hands up to his chest and said, 'Nothing personal. Have a nice evening.' We left. That was it.

I was stunned. Euphoric. Such a classy move. Debonair. He smiled as we hit the pavement. 'Never mind, eh?' My mindful God.

Fourth time, our first dinner. A restaurant Fabrizio had reviewed and raved about. The waiters were starchy gays and nervous young women in obligatory tourist-ready tartan. We were whisked to one of the nicest tables, with a view over the New Town. The Harvey effect, I assumed; waiters usually parked me as close to the toilet as they could without laying a tablecloth over a urinal. Harvey ordered for us, the one thing that didn't come with a jus, or encased in mist under a cloche. Fish and chips, with a 'smear' of peas. As Harvey picked up the salt grinder, the waiter tapped his index finger on the dense tablecloth.

'Just to let you know, sir, the potatoes are already salted, so you may want to taste before adding more.' I now noticed the snowy crystals on the golden chips, glowering at me. And, yeah, salt can glower, okay? My heart quickened. Peter would've exaggeratedly ground a volcano of salt over his plate to prove a point.

Harvey smiled thinly, popped a chip in his mouth. 'Hmmm, good shout. I'll still need a tad more, but thank you.' One swift turn of the mill. The waiter receded into the shadows. I watched every flake of salt tumble onto that plate, then gazed into Harvey's eyes.

Shit, I thought, I have to hang onto this zen master.

Six

As we careened toward our thirties, Daisy decided what we really needed in our social circle were even more gay men. It took me a while to work out exactly why. She'd met Ross at a party in a hotel room while playing hooky from an event she'd organised three floors below, and he'd been a floating member of the gang ever since. Daisy wasn't a collector of people or anything so calculating, but there was always method in her madness. Ross's USP was his house in Edinburgh's most affluent neighbourhood, The Grange, a towering monstrosity he was forever extending up or out. Every facade had an expensive glass ulcer welded to it – and was brilliant for entertaining. Ross loved having parties. What was infinite wealth if you couldn't smoosh it in the faces of your nearest and dearest unfortunates?

I try to see the good in most people, but a dark, obscuring fog always descended with Ross. He was the kind of acidic gay man you'd think was long extinct if your only knowledge of gay men came from soap operas. I was never quite sure how old he was, but he said he'd been fired from his job as cabin crew for posting mean things about Cilla Black on a messageboard so he was definitely a full-grown adult at the birth of the internet.

I sound bitchy, I know, a bit of a gay cliché myself, and I'll own that, but the first time he met me, he said: 'You look a bit like Bernard Butler. No, Brett. Actually, I reckon more Neil Codling. You basically look like all the members of Suede mashed together.' He'd called me Mashed Suede ever since.

Ross was much nicer to Tam, always reminding him how handsome he was, praise Tam was only too happy to guzzle up. I used to wonder if maybe he was trying to get into his knickers, but even if Ross hadn't resembled a Disneyfied Habsburg, he'd have got nowhere with Tam. Despite tongues constantly unrolling like red carpets in front of him, Tam wasn't promiscuous. He hated the idea of hookups gossiping about him in nightclub toilet queues, and with good reason: if you fucked Tam, you'd want people to know about it, and Edinburgh is small. Daisy too would fawn over Tam and paw his chest, calling him a heartbreaker, though Tam was always the one getting roundly dumped every two years or so.

Men who left Tam behind fell into a few different camps: unable to believe their luck, but intimidated by his good looks; horrified by the percentage of his wage he spent on brunch; sick of how much marking he did in an evening; or, once he gave up teaching for gardening, how early he got up to shovel horse manure over someone's rhododendrons. Imagine being so beautiful, men were too frightened to stay with you. Couldn't relate. I once made the mistake of asking Daisy why she constantly complimented Tam.

'He's insecure. It's like crumbling flower food into a vase of drooping tulips. Have you never noticed sometimes? His red knuckle? He bites it when he's upset.' I'd never considered hot people lacking confidence before. If I looked like Tam, I'd dance like everybody was watching and I'd love it, I'd break hearts, I'd stage coups. 'You don't need me to do that to you, do you?'

'No, of course not, I'd hate it.'

'Well then!'

'It's just that it never occurs to you.' Unwelcome as it would be, I'd at least have liked the opportunity to bat away objectification.

'I do think you're lovely,' she'd said, with crushing maternal kindness, and I swear my two front teeth twisted over each all the more in sympathy.

Ross's over-designed glass-and-concrete maze was being put to good use. In an effort to upstage Daisy and me, Ross had offered to host Tam and Fabrizio's engagement party. I'd promised my mum I'd be on trolley pushing duties while she blitzed IKEA, so I arrived late to what I'd been assured was an 'informal' bash, damp with (yet more) summer rain. Naturally everybody else was togged up like it was a regular Saturday night at Jay Gatsby's. There were young people serving – university students, I assumed – and a man with a Monaco tan making cocktails at the kitchen island. I fastened the buttons on my denim shirt all the way up to the top and found Seb and Daisy, already steaming, fondling Tam as you might feel up a stripper at the social club. As always, I felt that happy jolt in my stomach seeing them, the fun yet to unravel, the opportunity to bask in their glow.

'Dandelion!' Daisy folded herself round me. Red wine. Tam pecked me on the forehead – vodka and Coke, doubles, at least – and Seb held out his fist to bump – Peroni – but I missed. He stuck his tongue out. Really long. Daisy said it was exhausting being on the end of it. That wasn't the only thing keeping them together, he'd put up the lion's share of the deposit on their flat and . . . beneath it all they did love each other, probably. He was hot, at least, and wasn't one of those boyfriends who hardly joined in (like Fabrizio, although I'd never say this out loud) – Seb always had something to say. He'd talk to anybody – literally, he had to be torn away from philosophical conversations with buskers outside Waverley station – and although he was, to be honest, kind of dim, it was endearing and attractive, in a way. He was addicted to self-help podcasts and most of his patter was quoting them back to us, Confucius in an Oliver Spencer polo shirt.

'Hi, bitches,' I quipped, turning myself up to eleven as I sometimes did if ice needed breaking, 'what we bumping our gums about this evening?'

Seb and Tam's eyes bulged with the guilt of two public schoolboys caught straddling a soggy cracker. 'We're just doing "Beast or Boring"!'

They loved a drinking game. This one was fairly simplistic: you went round listing people – anyone, friends, celebrities – and debated whether they were a beast in bed, or . . . you get the picture.

'I thought we'd covered this,' I said. 'You're beasts and I'm allegedly boring.'

Seb wrapped his arms around me from behind, brave of him given his hangup about his height. 'For the record, Dandelion, I want you to know that I always say you're a beast.'

I'd been planning a subtle mention of Harvey, test the water, but I didn't want to rate him 'beast or boring' in front of people who'd never met him. Nothing to tell anyway. We'd shared a brief kiss on the lips at the end of date number five — no tongues — but he sped away before I had a chance to ask him in for a Nespresso. For the rest of the evening, I almost didn't want to drink anything, or brush my teeth, in case I washed away the feeling of his lips on mine. I don't know what you'd call it. A glow, maybe, a weird energy that excited me, because even with that short peck, we'd crossed a line, moved to the next stage, and it hadn't felt weird, or uncomfortable. It felt like permission to be happy.

'Stupid game, anyway,' moaned Daisy. 'I've got one. Tell me what disaster or terrible event you were obsessed with as a kid. Every kid has one. Mine was *Titanic*, obviously. I even had a poster of that old newspaper front page on my wall. "All drowned but 868." That film was a god to me. I was basically a horse girl but with a huge hulking ocean liner instead of a pony. I know yours, Lion.'

'You do?'

'Hindenburg!' She clapped her hands in joy, strange considering she was talking about a calamitous, fatal fireball. But it was true, I was briefly fixated on the tragic glamour of an airship disaster. That and ancient train crashes.

'Don't forget the Tay Bridge collapsing. I did a ten-page project on that. Tam, what was yours?'

Tam chewed his nail. I noticed a light bite mark on his index finger, above the knuckle. 'Not sure. Let me think.'

'Let me!' shouted Seb. 'The Gulf War!'

'Bit tasteless,' said Daisy, as if judging a fancy dress contest.

'It changed the world!'

'Yes, I know.' She was slurring now. 'But it's not gothic enough. Too modern. Too real. Tammy, what's yours?'

Fabrizio appeared, leaning in for a millisecond-long hug. He was smoking again. And on the Pernod cocktails. He snaked his arm round Tam's waist, drawing him in tight and taking his hand, stroking the finger where, come next August, there'd be a tasteful and expensive golden proof of ownership. Tam shifted his body to accommodate him, enjoying the attention. The pieces of a jigsaw clicking into place. I found myself wondering if Harvey and I would do that one day, coil round each other, not caring that everyone could see.

'I know. Bonnie and Clyde.' Tam hugged Fabrizio tighter. 'I thought it was so devastating, but so . . . beautiful.'

'Not strictly a disaster or major catastrophe, Tam.'

'Pretty catastrophic for them, Lion, they're dead. I know they were bad people or whatever, but it was very poetic and that is a banging film. The one with Faye Dunaway. Who I adore, obviously. They did it for love.'

'And money!'

Fabrizio seemed agitated so we had to explain our game to make him feel included. He looked almost disgusted. 'I didn't get the horn over thousands of people dying. I read nice books and played with my toys, you sound like mental delinquents. I was a wee shy boy in Anstruther, barely had any pals except Al and Lee.'

'My poor shy babe,' cooed Tam. 'In another timeline, we'd have been friends. I was just the same.'

Nonsense. Why do hot people always claim they were crippled by shyness as kids? Are we supposed to believe that? Same when A-listers love to insist they were ugly dorks at school.

Tam was not shy. He was wearing mermaid leggings the night we met him; his favourite toys as a child were a feather boa and a megaphone.

Ross appeared, assessing me with the hawkish eyes of a man who argued with fishmongers about the weight of their pollock. 'Leo! So good to see you, though you're looking tired, honey. Still decompressing from last term? I've got a Sephora discount code for anti-wrinkle serums; let me know if you want it.'

'I wouldn't want to deprive you, Ross.' I turned my attention completely away from him, back toward my friends. 'I tried that place you raved about the other day, Fabrizio.'

Daisy's sonar was activated. 'You went to a new restaurant without me? What the hell?' Daisy assumed that when she couldn't see us, we stayed in suspended animation like the *Toy Story* ensemble whenever a child is in the room.

'Didn't trust you not to spill soup down yourself.' I blew the obligatory kiss.

'Maybe I could've used one of your hundred cardigans as a bib.' A kiss came back my way.

'Anyway, as I was saying . . . we didn't really rate it, the restaurant. We . . . I was quite disappointed.' The 'we' would have them chattering in their cabs home. Tam and Fabrizio exchanged a look.

'Oh,' said Tam with a hint of fluster. 'Everyone has an off night, I guess.'

'Who, the restaurant, or Fabrizio?' I winked. Always a bad idea. Instead of looking cheeky or scampish, I gave the impression a bee had just flown into my eyeball.

'Sorry you didn't have a good night, Leo,' said Fabrizio, icily. 'Why don't you leave an online review? Have your say.'

'Oh . . . no, I mean . . . I'll leave it to the professionals.' I noticed a drawbridge going up. I resolved to wait until Tam was fuzzed up by further Stolichnaya and ask why Fabrizio was so touchy. 'Have you two done speeches yet? Shouldn't you be climbing on a table and declaring undying love?'

'Nobody's climbing on any fucking tables,' hissed Ross. 'I must go tell the servers to mingle more with the canapés; I've not seen so much as a stuffed olive for an hour.'

Tam breathed out deeply. 'We should have had this in a bar. He's wiped the bottom of my glass about six times.'

'Better to save our money for the main event, babes. I fancy an Aperol Spritz.' Fabrizio chucked Tam under the chin, as you might a toddling godchild. 'You want anything, babes?'

Tam's eyes went Bambi-wide. Daisy and I exchanged a quick look of cringe that Tam definitely spotted. 'No, thanks, honey, I'm good.'

Fabrizio squeezed my arm not entirely gently as he glided away.

Tam hugged me, I felt his drink slosh onto my shirt. 'You missed the speeches, Lion, but I said lovely things about you and Daisy. Oh, do you want me to get a cloth for that? I'll be getting banned for making a mess. That reminds me . . . how many Hail Muscle Marys did you have to chant before Ross let you back over the threshold?'

Ah yes, small detail: I'd been blackballed from Ross's last party because of a canapé incident at the one before. I'd rather not go into it right now but I still get triggered whenever I see a white carpet or baba ghanoush.

Seven

The next Sunday afternoon, Harvey invited me to his flat, a relocation package rental through his company, down one of Stockbridge's smartest streets. His neighbours were investment managers, or little old ladies still refusing to sell up and move somewhere more suitable for a Stannah stairlift. It was beautiful, if decorated in the minimal style of transient accommodation – wooden floors or cream carpet, stark shelves with the odd generic ornament, more mirrors than one person would ever need. Although it wasn't homely, there was something reassuring about its icy clinical grandeur. Harvey claimed not to have many possessions, but I could tell by his eyes that somewhere out there an attic groaned with memorabilia.

We stood in the gleaming kitchen, metres apart. The tiles had glittery champagne-coloured flecks in impenetrable onyx. He was still unused to the layout, the cupboards having been arranged by someone determined to make life one long sudoku, he said, hissing in frustration as he searched for the right glasses, and dainty dishes for the coalsack-sized bags of snacks I'd brought. The non-alcoholic wine he bought me had the insipid taste of water from a grape-crusher's foot spa, but I said it was delicious and smiled until my cheeks hurt.

His top two buttons were undone and I noticed a light matting of hair underneath. Very exciting. I was nervous. I think he was too; he fussed with cushions and couldn't seem to get his words out. We moved into the living room. Spotify's finest vaguely sexy playlists burbled from his Bluetooth speakers as he kissed me, deeply, on the sofa, like he wanted me to know exactly where this was going. This change of speed felt like when you dream it's Christmas Day and really hope it's true when you wake up. Before the end of the first song, he'd relieved me of my chinos, swiftly, like he was peeling a banana. I loved the feeling of the back of his head in my hand, the bumps at the base of his skull, the taut nape of someone who spent too long staring at a badly positioned computer screen. Good kisser, attentive, forceful. Just the right amount of appreciative moaning. This was not amateur hour. His scent was enticing: citrus, wood, immaculate bathrooms. There was a crispness and order to him, his touches tender but methodical, yet something mysterious lurked.

When his fingers snaked round the fly-front of my M&S trunks, I had a flash of doubt. Was this right? We'd been kids together, our mothers spoke on the phone three times a year, his parents had eaten tuna and cress sandwiches at my father's funeral. Most of my sexual encounters were 'one and done'; I didn't want to add Harvey to that list, make it embarrassing, or sordid, or have to send a 'there was no spark' text then block his number. Harvey was different. Harvey was special. Harvey gave me that light, airy feeling I thought was never coming back. By making me wait for this, he'd entangled me in feelings I'd struggle to escape. I didn't want to, that was the thing.

I was happy to be led. However: now was my last chance to stop – you cross a line when you see each other's cocks, even if you never lay eyes on them again, or stay friends and never talk about it. It's always there; what you saw, how they taste, what they look like when they come – even if you don't get that far, it's easier to imagine it.

I was suddenly aware my mind was drifting and Harvey had stopped, his fingers still inside my fly.

'You're thinking this might not be a good idea.'

Where his hand was right now, it felt like a very good idea.

'No, not at all,' I lied, 'it's just . . . '

'Been a while since Menergize?'

My laugh broke the tension. 'I'm a bit nervous. It's . . . you.'

Harvey sat up straight, removed his hand. 'Did I do something wrong?'

'Hell no, the opposite, I think I'm gonna pass out. But . . . I'd hate to spoil this. I do a lot of one-night, er, things. They don't always end well. But they do end.'

He dipped back down in his seat and hooked his hand under the hem of my trunks. 'Maybe it shouldn't be a one-night, er, thing?'

There it was again, permission to be happy. To let myself fall into it. This wouldn't be like the others, because Harvey wasn't like the others. I knew what was making me nervous. It wasn't my body, or things going weird and ruining our friendship; I knew if I let Harvey in, I'd end up falling hard, I'd be his, and the idea was thrilling, scary, and absolutely brilliant.

He held my chin between his thumb and forefinger, I could taste his hot breath, his eyes didn't break their hold on mine for a second. 'Should I carry on?'

Doing it for the first time on a Sunday? Scandalous. One in the eye for my lapsed Catholicism. My mouth too sandpapery to speak, I nodded. His other hand went back up my shirt and the next thing I said was his name. Shouted it, actually.

Eight

'Have you ever tried yoga?'

Now there's a question. I had not. Harvey ran his hands up my bare legs and pressed lightly at the base of my spine, where he claimed he could feel tension. He said yoga would be fun, might help with any stiffness. I swallowed the joke to spare us the embarrassment.

'Won't it be difficult? I'm quite long.'

'It's for every shape and size,' he said, 'you'll be a graceful willow.' They droop, don't they, willows? He kissed the tip of my nose, like leading men did in films. I murmured excuses about not having the right kit; he had spares of everything. 'This is pretty loose on me, should fit you,' he said as I eased on a T-shirt the width of an ankle sock.

Harvey's yoga studio was an intimidating, glass-fronted carbuncle – an aesthetic some people love, believing it aspirational to be sassed by a bored receptionist or told they're worthless by a personal trainer. We changed in silence in a lunar-bright locker room that smelled of dashed hope, trying not to look at anyone's dick, before waiting outside a room with one glass wall. The queue was all women but for one gay guy I recognised as a barman from one of the places at the top of Leith Walk. He nodded an 'alright' and I nodded back. Harvey raised his eyebrows.

'Menergize?'

'No!'

The women were about my age or older, some could've been mums of my students. I knew experts when I saw them, lithe and focused in mind, body and ponytail, as they held tightly rolled yoga mats and chugged water from bottles resembling miniature milk churns, patterned with jolly looking fruits.

The doors opened and the women scurried to what must've been their usual spots. Back row, every corner, filled. Nowhere to hide. I thought it best to copy Harvey exactly. We unrolled our mats in sync. He removed his trainers and socks and placed them at an angle to his mat. I did the same, before quickly putting my socks back on — I didn't believe in baring my toenails to strangers unless five feet of water was available to dive into.

The instructor — 'Cate with a C,' Harvey said — had the kind of voice that asked for Manuka honey at expensive brunches, and gave gently scolding feedback about long waits for a salted caramel affogato. Her aura was patience, a safe pair of hands; the entire class relaxed in her presence. Almost. My shoulders seemed welded to my ear lobes; I felt about as relaxed as a cat counting through their lives while looking up at a plummeting anvil.

A light tap on my arm. Harvey beamed. 'You'll love it.'

In that second, I believed him. But once we began it quickly became clear I was out of my depth. I got some of it right; I'd done stretching with my students so it wasn't quite like getting a wardrobe to bend. Manuka lady's voice was calm and breezy, so zen she almost came out the other side and began to sound threatening. Perspiration slicked my forehead and shoulders as I switched between my approximation of the cat and cow poses. Was I sticking my bottom out too much? What did 'tuck your tailbone' mean, anyway? I looked over at Harvey but he was lost in the moment, his movements swift, graceful and balletic. My limbs clunked into unfamiliar contortions. A woman caught my eye and gave a sympathetic smile, confirming that I was basically a tangle of shoelaces in a bamboo T-shirt.

'Now spine balancing,' said Manuka lady, on her hands and knees. 'We're gently extending our left leg back, and acknowledging that shift in our centre.' Everyone else seemed a step or two ahead, crouched like Superman. The granular instructions were for my benefit, I realised. 'Now out with the right arm, in front, extending as far as we can, push into that bright future, shake hands with the luck and love and light that's waiting.'

My left arm, unused to being asked to do anything other than lift a coffee mug if my right hand was busy changing the channel, swayed and rocked like a Dubai skyscraper in a tornado. My entire body juddered and finally succumbed to physics at exactly the moment I caught Harvey's eye. His encouraging smile switched to concern as my chin thundered onto the mat, my teeth clattering in my head. People behind winced in sympathy. Cate with a C approached and, with the calm efficiency of a mortuary attendant, folded me back into position. Sweet relief for all of three seconds, before she manhandled my knee back to the mat and wrenched my arm up toward the sky like she was grabbing the last drumstick out of a family bucket.

'And into a twist. Deep breath.'

It was too much for me. Boom! Chin met mat once more.

'Okay, everyone let's thread that arm through.' The rest of the room twisted in perfect unison. Manuka lady's eyes bored into mine as she kneeled next to me.

'Listen, doll,' she said, in a non-Manuka voice that gargled gravel and consonants for breakfast. 'How about you sack this move off and we'll bring you back in for the old downward dog? Okay?'

Once it was over, everyone filed out of the class, sending me commiserating smiles, even a pat on the back from the barman guy. I mopped at myself halfheartedly with a lurid pink microfibre towel, while Harvey punched instructions into an app that would have spirulina smoothies waiting at the juice bar a mere four metres down the hall.

Manuka lady got her zen voice back. 'How do you feel after the practice?'

'Like practice is never gonna make perfect!' I waited for Harvey and Manuka lady to laugh but they didn't. 'That was the most taxing hour I've spent since my mum did the full version of "I'd Do Anything For Love" at karaoke twice in a row.' She wouldn't leave the stage, even amid the boos. Someone had to throw a stool in the end.

'First time's always a challenge.'

'Last time for me, I think. I know my chin is made of strong stuff but I'll need a titanium implant if I carry on.' You hear yourself differently when there's no laugh waiting at the end of everything you say. Tam and Daisy would've howled, but this tough crowd defeated me.

'You don't think you'll try again?' An echo of disappointment in Harvey's voice.

I was about to say it wasn't really my thing, but . . . how did I know? Why couldn't it be? How did you work out whether something was 'for you'? How long should you give it, how many chances? Yes, I'd fallen over six times – the barman from CC's was counting, I heard him. Yes, something twanged in my back after what Cate with a C had called 'a bridge'. And yes, the room smelled faintly of mushroom pâté and everyone in the class would definitely report you to the council for mixing up your recycling, but . . . I could do it for Harvey.

So: 'Perhaps. I'll wear a crash helmet next time.' His smile reached right to the sides of his face. I wanted to do everything I could to keep it there.

We perched on the kind of uncomfortable stools specially created to stop anyone accidentally enjoying the concept of sitting, and sipped smoothies the colour of Cookie Monster's balls. Harvey was making a good fist of lying that I'd actually done very well, and that his first time was even worse, when I heard the unmistakable 'Dandelion!' that could only be Daisy Forbes.

I shouldn't have been surprised to see her; she'd been searching for self-improvement in the bottom of a wheatgrass shot since we graduated. She was drenched from forty-five minutes of noughties techno spin class.

Her innocent face was fooling nobody as she nudged me and introduced herself.

'Hello, Daisy. Great to meet you. I'm Harvey.'

'Oh Harvey, what a lovely name.'

Sensing, correctly, that Daisy was the kind of friend who knew how to behave in front of strangers, but would need as many details about him as possible right that second, Harvey excused himself to do ten minutes in the steam room.

'Maybe see you in there?'

There was absolutely no way I was letting Harvey see me slouched and sweating in lighting I couldn't control, but I said 'Absolutely,' and waved him off, anxiously waiting for Daisy's onslaught.

'Oh my God, you dirty dog. Is that . . . the old friend? I thought it was just an awks kind of thing where you meet for one drink and immediately block all calls. But you're doing it! The way he looked at you!' Daisy whipped my smoothie out of my hand, sniffed it, wrinkled her nose, then handed it back. 'More importantly, what the hell are you doing at Pique Yoga? Are you lost?'

'He's just a friend.'

'Bollocks! Did you do yoga to impress a boy? That is wild. Tam will be frothing at the—'

'Can we keep it between us?' I wasn't ready to put a name to whatever was happening with Harvey. I was enjoying the ride too much. It felt new, yes, but solid. This wasn't a filthy secret. I gave Daisy a quick précis of my entanglement so far. I could see her brain repurposing the story, adding adjectives, and excising punctuation, for retelling in my absence.

'You dark horse! Tell me about the body. It looks unreal. Are you afraid of it? And the sex! Was it hot, and depraved? Did you scream? I bet you did.'

These were the words of a woman either not getting any or not liking what she was getting. 'Why do you care? Seb has the best body on earth!'

'I know but I see it all the time. It's like my Le Creuset pans. I was so excited to get them but now I use them every day I'm bored. And they're so heavy. And a pain in the hole to clean.

So please . . . everything. Let me live vicariously through your cookware.'

An unusual pivot to prurience from Daisy. She didn't tend to see me as a sexual being, or ask things like this, not since she'd outed me to myself aged eleven. Whether I'd found love, or had a crush on anyone, yes, but seldom curious about my sexual activity. Hot people, like Daisy, always assume anyone who looks like me, or worse, doesn't have sex. We're allowed to be in relationships with similarly afflicted munters, but casual sex, they think, belongs to them. I was glad, really; it kept their noses out of my trough.

Sometimes Daisy mentioned men she thought I might like but didn't expect me to fancy; I was supposed to settle. Little did she know there's a market for literally everyone out there. You really get to know how others see you by the people they fix you up with. They don't know that, occasionally, hot people fancy us too, or that average Joes with wonky teeth and noses splatted across our face like custard are perfectly capable of finding each other ourselves. But now I'd found somebody smoking hot and, I could see, it had changed the prescription of Daisy's Leo-tinted spectacles considerably.

I employed my favourite weapon: deflection. 'I'm still working out what goes where. Not ready to whack my thoughts up on TripAdvisor yet. How are things with Seb?'

She was pretty sure he was about to propose, but worried he'd do it too soon. 'I feel . . . we need to wait until Tam and Fabrizio have done it, like after their wedding.'

'It's next summer. Ages away.'

'Isn't it vulgar to be engaged at the same time as your friends? Like you're on one of those reality shows where they have a mass wedding. A bit attention-y. God, what if Seb proposes at the wedding? He might. Anyway,' she said, 'I've got a matcha tea date with my old therapist and you, lanky *liar*, have an appointment with Harry in the steam room.'

'Harvey!'

'Ooh, I love the way you say his name. Have you made him scream out "Leo" yet? I bet he yodels it.'

Nine

I'd forgotten what it was like to have regular sex. Like, with the same person. More than once. Layers of fear stripped away, new ones added. Nice to know what to expect but still shocked by the novelty. At first, I insisted we turn the dimmer switch down to 'creepy attic in a horror movie', and always got dressed straight after my shower, in the bathroom, so he wouldn't be subjected to my fleshy xylophone skeleton slinking to the bedroom draped in a towel. Well, I say draped. Fabric didn't drape around me, it hung off me; in a towel, I looked like a flag at half mast.

He never said those annoying things people say when they dismiss your insecurities, but his eyes were reassuring.

'This is a load-bearing hang-up, I'm afraid,' I said one day as I attempted to put my underwear on under a towel. 'Take it away and a whole lot of other shit comes crashing down.' He laughed, my favourite form of feedback.

Harvey wanted us to shower together. Our bodies, upright, with the lights on. Harvey looked at me thoughtfully, carefully – just long enough to let me know he appreciated my imperfections. Trust formed, I gave it a go. His bathroom had a sloping roof and I didn't like being hunched against the glass, buttocks squeaking. In the end, I awkwardly dropped to my knees, still sore from my violent assault by yoga, licked Harvey's flat belly and finished off the morning the best way I knew how.

After, he gently wiped my face with a towel and traced his finger round the vitiligo patch, acknowledging it for the first time.

'I saw some of these on your body as well.'

His eyes flicked to my shoulder, down to my hip; he gently stroked my thigh next to my balls. He wasn't the first man to do a stocktake of my pigment malfunctions. Sometimes I'd even interrupt to point out one they'd missed.

'Will you get more? Will it go away?'

'Nobody really knows. It waxes and wanes. I might not get more, or I might end up with it all over my face. Not a lot I can do.' Multiple people, including many doctors, told me it could be worse. As if I didn't know. 'You forgot the white blob of hair at the nape of my neck, by the way.'

'Is that one too? It's cute.' He kissed the patch. 'Is Daisy a good friend?'

'My oldest friend. Apart from you, I guess. She's a rock. Mostly. I expect you have a team of gal pals in London yourself.'

I detected a glimmer of . . . what? Regret? A frown? 'Good to have someone like that in your life, someone who'll do anything for you.'

I wasn't sure about that – for my last birthday she'd bought me a car air freshener and under-eye concealer. I'd sold my car five years earlier, and my dark circles gobbled up every millilitre of that concealer as a hot crumpet would devour butter. 'You have that too, don't you?'

He brightened. 'Course.'

Maybe the best part of being with Harvey was the excitement of new discoveries becoming familiar. Nothing was mundane. His final suck on the toothbrush after cleaning his teeth — four minutes exactly, which put my brisk ninety seconds and an awkward floss to shame. Drying his hair on full heat, because he had shiny hair that moved, and not my lank helmet that would frizz up at the merest hint of a clement breeze. Whistling cheerily while he prepared bone broth for his packed lunch. Reciting his daily affirmation as he shook granola into our bowls.

I had to relearn couple behaviour. Not using the last of the milk, holding in flatulence during tense scenes on TV, pausing for his response to my jokes rather than filling the gap with my own canned laughter.

We hadn't said the boyfriend word yet. Maybe we wouldn't, ever. I had no idea where it was going, but I was happy tagging along. I had to face facts, though. We'd had a lovely summer break getting to know each other, but seeing, or dating, or boyfriending, or regularly bumming, a teacher in term time was vastly different from the holidays. There was my midweek running club, staying late for drama club, or overseeing detention, marking, and catching up with Daisy and Tam and their better-ish halves, too. I didn't want to be one of those friends who got a man and disappeared, like . . . well, like Tam was prone to doing early on. Harvey suggested we set aside one night during the week, Thursday, to see each other and spend some of the weekend together.

I always loved seeing Mica again after a summer apart, although she wasn't in a terrific mood when term started up again. Her daughter Sasha had spent most of the holidays waiting for a boy to message her back. 'Bleeding scrolling nonstop, that finger of hers is gonna fall off.' As a result, Mica had convinced herself a major teenage pregnancy storyline was imminent. 'That's all I need, a little one on the rampage when I've just gone back to fitted carpets. I want my baby to have fun, be free, just . . . '

'Just not that kind of free?'

'Exactly. Speaking of little ones, April had a girl, did you see? She's calling her Linnet. It's a type of bird.'

'Better than Thrush or Swallow, I guess.'

Everyone was on best first-day behaviour, wearing light colours to show off their tans, or patterned shirts to stretch out summer's last dregs. The Fringe still had two weeks to go so the city was full of holidaymakers, the bars were still open late, there were cool things to go see after work. It made the first week or so back at school a little more bearable and the students didn't start back for two days, so we could breathe easier. Aside from Mica, who called Emergency Cigarette Protocol. She smoked two in quick succession on the fire escape, going through every possible horrible thing that could happen to her daughter in the next ten years, half of which Mica herself had done in her youth, before berating me for not meeting up even once.

'What's been keeping you so busy? Or who?'

I was about to tell her, I really was; I knew she'd be positive, listen without judgement, maybe chuck a few sage words my way like 'hang onto the good ones' and 'never let a man apply roll-on deodorant in front of you, total passion arsenic', but something stopped me. I don't know what.

'I tried yoga.'

'Fucking hell, you must've been bored. Come weightlifting with me. I see you're giving stubble a go, I like it.'

Inspired by Harvey, whose jawline always had an immaculate outline of bristles. Yes, I was that basic boy who copied his heroes. 'Oh cheers. Wasn't sure because of the—'

'Oi, you two.' Neil the physics teacher, who according to Mica ate only one cheese sandwich for his evening meal at 4 p.m., stuck his head out the window to tell us April's stand-in was doing one-to-ones with the 'arts and farts' teachers. Mica was next.

She was back ten minutes later. 'Whew.'

'What? Are they horrible?'

'Well, he spent the first half blowing smoke up my arse and the second . . . pumping me for data. There isn't one thing about my department he doesn't want to know. He's direct. Prepare to be . . . pumped. Oh, and I reckon he's one of your lot.'

'Catholic? Tall?'

'Silly. No, you know.' There was a hand gesture; I won't repeat it here.

A name plate was already in place. Impressive. *Mr A. Campbell.* I spent a couple of seconds working out what the students would call him behind his back. Something to do with soup, maybe? Do teenagers eat soup?

He sat behind his desk, the composed authority of Mussolini waiting for his daily report on how the trains were running. He was cute, though, no denying it, in an obviously new jumper – I could see the creases from where it had been folded on the shelf. His wavy hair was kind of a dark red, and a bit of a mess, but on purpose, I think. It worked, anyway. Blue eyes behind a very nice pair of glasses that sat on what my mum would call a 'good strong bridge', and when he stood to shake my hand, I was delighted to see he was tall. Not as gangly as me, but nearly. Six-two, maybe.

Working for men always made me nervous — even gay ones like Campbell clearly was. On his desk was an empty iced coffee cup. If you know, you know. There were a couple of unpacked boxes on one chair and, like any transient being trying to create permanence in their current resting spot, he'd brought a plant with him. I noticed a still rolled-up poster leaning against a cupboard too, waiting to be tacked to the wall. I wondered what it might be. Educational inspirational quote? *The Catcher in the Rye* first edition cover? He looked the type. It was a risk — just how much of your personality did you want to reveal to students sent in for a bollocking?

'Mr Falconer.' Voice ever so slightly weedy, not like Harvey's. I realised I was staring.

'Leo, please. Nice to meet you, Mr Campbell.'

'Alex, please.' He peered at me as he released my hand. 'Leo, you've got a wee bit of . . . '

Oh shit. I knew what was coming. I tried not to double-up from the tsunami of ensuing cringe. Did I let him finish, or jump in? It was the longest split second of my life.

'Something on your mouth, the corner.' His finger went to his own mouth to point where, as if I didn't already know. Fuller lips than Harvey's, actually.

'Um, no. I . . . it's vitiligo. A skin condition.' I recited my script. 'I've had it about five years. There's no pigment, you see, so any hair that grows there is white. I haven't been sucking off a snowman or anything.' And right there, I lost Alex Campbell, I

could tell. So crude. With a stranger! My new boss! He sat down slowly, mortified. The meeting never recovered. He asked the usual questions someone asks a drama teacher when they meet them for the first time – did I used to be an actor, did I want to be an actor, did I know any famous actors, and did I think any of my students had potential to be a successful actor? (No, no, no, and yes.) The only one he skipped was 'Do you find it rewarding?' which no teacher would ever ask another in all seriousness.

He wanted to observe one of my classes. Uh oh. My teaching style was unconventional but effective. I basically channelled every bored GP's receptionist I'd ever met. Amiable detachment, it helped build a rapport. I pretended we were all there at gun point, forced to work for a lovely qualification that wouldn't matter once they were working the fryer at the Foghorn Creamhorn chicken shop and bakery on the next street over – but we could try to have fun while we were there. I'd never had any complaints, but to a casual observer it might appear like an existential crisis. Beginners, that would do it. New intake wouldn't give away my bad habits.

'Sounds great, looking forward to working with you,' he said. 'Also, before you shoot . . . Chris said you're the man I need to ask . . . end-of-term shows. Can I see a list of ones you've already staged?'

Chris, head of drama, excellent at delegation and disappearing midway through a question. We had a stock rota of adaptations, and reused the scenery every time. *Little Shop of Horrors*, the ancient stage version of *Grease* with only half the good songs, and an original one written by the previous head of drama, who'd left in 2010, a vague *Chicago* ripoff. Campbell's glasses slipped down his nose in disappointment.

'Leo, I'm a star-chaser. I believe in aiming high.' Oh good, a year of being micro-managed by Buzz Lightyear. But I liked to be liked, and always aim to leave a room with everyone thinking I'm a sweetheart, so I smiled and nodded enthusiastically. 'We can do better than the same old shows. Have a good day.' Our first encounter was over.

'Well?' Mica was breaking protocol, pulling desperately on a cigarette, solo, on the fire escape.

'Your lungs won't make it to October at this rate. I made a joke about snowman spunk.'

'Why?'

'To relieve the tension.'

'Did it?'

'No. I get the impression he thinks I'm an idiot, and you know what that means, don't you?'

Mica took such a long drag of her cigarette I thought it was going to turn inside out. 'Yep. You'll end up proving him right.'

Ten

I've never had hobbies. Not real ones, anyway. Hobbies needed equipment, planning, dedication. My twice-weekly runs and gossipy dinners in chain restaurants aren't exactly the kind of pastimes you'd be invited on a podcast to talk about. My only true hobby was not being at work, leaving Mr Falconer hanging on a peg in the drama department office, a windowless box room with a kettle and a wall planner dotted with red exclamation marks for deadlines we ignored.

My ex Peter had only ever read books or drunk red wine, but Harvey was a one-man personal statement for an application to Harvard. Yoga, pilates, wine tasting, flower-arranging – 'I used to go to a wreath-making workshop every Christmas' – CrossFit, you name it.

'I like a target,' he said. 'A goal in the distance. Gives me a sense of achievement. Running feels aimless.'

I preferred not to know where I was heading; I never timed myself or set specific aims. I just ran, until I couldn't anymore.

'How about we do something you enjoy today?' Harvey said

one Saturday morning, as I was licking doughnut jam off my elbow to stop it dripping onto his pristine floor.

I thought it might be too early in the . . . let's say relationship, to sit in jogging bottoms miming to the original cast recording of *Sunday in the Park with George*, so suggested a long walk instead. 'Would you like that?'

'I would if you would.'

We caught a cab to the Botanics and ambled round. Summer was gasping its last breath, crushed petals everywhere. Trees were still luxuriant and green, but I spied hints of orange, plants gratefully beginning to wilt after a summer of standing to attention. I cooed at flowers, making bad jokes in funny voices about their Latin names sounding like Roman centurions, jokes I hadn't made since I'd last dragged Peter there. Harvey's laughs were more muted. Maybe he was bored. That terrified me. I didn't want Harvey to find me dull. I made my escape plan, a spectacle that could never be boring.

'When was the last time you climbed Arthur's Seat?'

'Don't think I ever have.'

'An Edinburgh boy never seen it from the top of the world? Scandalous! We must rectify that at once.'

It blows visitors' minds that Edinburgh has a huge dormant volcano practically in the middle of it, but I barely notice Arthur's Seat; it's always been there. Listening to folk not from Edinburgh talk about my hometown always feels like they are describing somewhere else. 'You're so lucky, it's so beautiful,' they say. Well, yes, it is; but, to me, growing up there, its beauty wasn't significant. It was the city where I'd grazed my knees, worried about homework, had my heart broken for the first time, and made a start on the emotional baggage I'd be

carrying for years to come. Volcano or no volcano, castle or no castle, that would all still have happened.

I'd kind of forgotten my way, not having clambered up there in at least a decade. Silence can be interpreted as an unstable lid on simmering panic, so I chattered away about previous climbs. Young and drunk, with Daisy and whichever boyfriend was around at the time, smoking badly rolled cigarettes, gawping at sunsets, almost breaking our ankles as we stumbled down the gentlest slope, back to where we'd had the foresight to park her car.

'Would you ever run up it?' Harvey's trainers were for stepping out of Jaguars in, not climbing slumbering volcanoes, and he was struggling a little, his ears turning puce.

'No, God. The marathon kind of goes round it. I'd do that, one day.'

'How can someone who's not into sport go running as much as you do? Join a club even?'

'Well, it's easy to get started. I didn't want to go to the gym or buy special equipment, Lycra, protein shakes, make it a thing. With running, you don't need to prepare, or buy anything special. It's just trainers on and go!'

'You don't stretch before you run?!'

'I'm stretchy enough!'

'So . . . you like running because you don't need to commit?'

'Yeah, I mean no, it's . . . no, not just that . . . I . . . oh, it sounds silly.'

Harvey stumbled on a rock and quickly suppressed a 'Shit'. 'It doesn't. Go on.'

I'd never been one for emptying the contents of my head over other men, or anyone, but Harvey could draw water from dust. 'I'd see men running, looking . . . kind of aerodynamic and polished . . . '

'Not beetroot red and sweaty? They can't have been running that fast.'

'Ha, no, if they were I couldn't see it. I used to look at their bodies and want one just like theirs.'

I thought he might laugh, but he didn't. 'What's wrong with your own body?'

You can't often say you how you really feel about your appearance; people don't know how to react, they try to shut you down with weak compliments. Maybe Harvey would be different; we'd skirted round this often enough.

'I didn't like my body. Still don't, actually.' Looking at other men, I couldn't work out where these bodies came from. Was it genetics? Diet, exercise, sport? Just dumb luck? They seemed out of reach. I couldn't ever see my body transforming like that, it looked like too much hard work. So I accepted my fate, I wasn't meant to look that way. 'I'm envious of a lot of men. Their bodies. Of yours, if I'm brutally honest.'

He ignored that indirect compliment, but didn't tell me I was being stupid either. 'So you go running to perv over other men? I respect that.'

The sun was in my eyes so I couldn't see his face, but the warmth in his voice reached out like a hug. 'No, not that.'

I did look at men a lot, though. It was in my DNA, after all, depending on which scientific journal you believed. I liked my prize hunks as much as the next gay man, but I knew being a man with 'something about them' could be an even bigger prize. Working out what that something was – it wasn't always a physical feature – and plotting how to make it yours, was the goal. Even I had that 'something' to a degree; that's how I'd reeled Peter in, he'd told me as much.

'So . . . ?' Harvey was waiting for elaboration.

'Oh, right, sorry. Well, when I look at other men, with bodies like that, I'm not . . . I don't lust after them. I wonder what it's like to be them. To move like that.' And also to have strangers watch you as you race by, and want you, or imagine you naked beneath the shorts, but I kept that fantasy to myself. 'Does that make sense?'

Harvey stopped, he was panting now, and wiped sweat off his brow, looking faintly disgusted to get his sleeve wet. 'How much further?'

'Nearly there.'

'Okay. This is . . . can I ask a personal question, but . . . do you think your low self-esteem is down to your ex? The cheating?'

I shrugged off the chill shooting down my spine. 'For someone who looks like celeriac, I have pretty decent self-esteem.' Didn't everybody look in the mirror and think *not you again* from time to time?

'You say these things a lot. Jokes, but . . . icebergs. Like there's way more beneath. There's self-deprecating and there's self-flagellating.'

'Quite long words for a builder.'

'Do you mind?' He laughed. 'Answer a question without a joke, I dare you.'

This didn't feel like something to discuss while busting for the toilet and trying to climb a volcano rather too close to sundown. Luckily, Harvey pressed on.

'It's just . . . you speak like someone who's experienced great trauma and maybe hasn't quite dealt with it yet.' He patted my arm as if to reassure me I was safe. 'This isn't a dig, by the way. Is this why you've been single for a while? Your last boyfriend cheating is not on you.'

'I'm good for self-esteem. Honest. I'm not lonely or heart-broken. I haven't held back. I've had plenty of sex.'

'I know that. What about relationships before . . . him? University?'

'I had a boyfriend my first year. From home.' Ricky Johnson. His cat used to watch me blow him in his terracotta-walled dining room, telly on full pelt.

'You stayed together? Unusual.'

It certainly was. Daisy had spent the entire journey to Glasgow on her phone promising Blair or Will or Frazer, or whoever it was, that their love would never die. As soon as she registered the calibre of the pheromone-bubbling talent testos-teroning off the walls at the Freshers Ball, she called him to say this long distance thing wasn't working. He lived twenty miles away; we'd been there three days. It made her decision to stick with Seb even weirder, now I thought about it.

'What about the drama thing, then?' Harvey wheezed. We were nearly there. I could see a few tourists, and some sullen teenagers smoking at the apex ahead. 'Is that a way of getting validation? Might you have been an actor if you, uh . . . '

Weren't so ugly, maybe? I was breathing too heavily to answer; all those fire escape cigarettes with Mica had to stop. A sudden surge of energy sent my legs charging forward. I practi-cally threw myself onto the flatter ground of the summit, then slumped against the grass. Seconds later, Harvey did the same.

'Being in a theatre, loving theatre . . . you breathe a certain kind of air that only a few people can breathe, it's like your DNA is wired up differently.' I took a couple of deep breaths, feeling my pulse start to slow again. 'It's a feeling like nothing else. You don't have to deliver big monologues or belt out the finale to feel it. It's being backstage, stitching a costume, painting scenery, even nipping out to the sex shop for your leading man's poppers.' I turned to Harvey to check he was smiling but he was staring ahead so hard at distant Fife I bet they could feel the heat in Burntisland. 'It's not a desire to be in the show, or even run the show. You want to be part of the energy that makes it happen. Every lead, every non-speaking part, every wee cog, line, light, note of music, every part of the building . . . it's just as important as everything else. Everyone fits in.'

'I thought all actors were divas, all writers pricks, that kind of thing.'

'No, not good ones, not ones who love it for what it is. When it's working, you're maybe just one brick in a wall, but the best wall, the strongest wall, a beautiful and useful wall.'

'I can relate to a good wall. So why teach? Why not get out there, in the theatre, in the thick of it?'

Money, mainly, but nobody wants to hear that from a teacher. It's a mistake many people make, assuming those who worked in teaching are frustrated, bitter also-rans who couldn't excel in the subject they now teach. And with drama, or theatre, even more so. I wasn't interested in being centre stage. In any part of my life.

'I get the best bit. I get to share my love for it over and over. I'm like a drug dealer, giving them that good feeling, but instead of fucking them up, I'm providing something that'll stay with them.'

'Captain, my captain, eh?' Harvey turned, finally, and smiled. 'I hear you. Just checking your motor's running okay.'

I was well rehearsed when it came to justifying myself; I was proud of this performance. 'It is.'

'Cool.' His face darkened. 'This, up here. Isn't my kind of thing.'

'Let me guess. Need a medal when you get to the top to make it worth it?'

He didn't smile. 'Something like that. Can we go?'

As we doddered back down, I reached for his hand and he curled his fingers round mine. He squeezed three times.

'What's that?'

'It's a little sign. Let you know I'm here.'

'I know you're here. I can smell your Aventus.'

'Leo! It's symbolic.'

Why three squeezes? One for each letter of my name? Or SOS? The three little words? A 1-2-3 count-in before he sang the chorus of 'Livin' La Vida Loca' at me? I had to know. This was my trouble. I searched for meaning through explanation, rather than expression. I liked to know where I stood.

'Why three?'

'One for you to notice. Two so you know it's me. And the third is a bonus. My dad used to do it when I was wee.'

'That's so cute.' I suddenly felt an overwhelming wave of grief for my own father. 'Okay, so have you ever smoked?' He shook his head. 'Oh, me neither.' I lied so brazenly, like I did it for a living. 'My dad told me there's a superstition about lighting someone's cigarette? How you should never light more than three fags off the one light. Or is it two? I can't remember. Comes from soldiers in the trenches Anyway. One light, the enemy sees it. Another, they aim. A third, they fire. Clever, huh?'

'Okay, so I guess my third squeeze means you're worth the risk.' Harvey smiled. 'I won't do the squeezing thing if you don't want.'

I wanted. I did. A lot.

Harvey suddenly dropped my hand. 'Ah, we should've got someone to take our picture at the top. Let's grab a quick selfie.'

I don't really do photos. There's no such thing as a quick selfie for me; I'd need retakes that I'd be too afraid to ask for. 'No, it's cool.'

'Aw, come on, everybody loves a wee selfie.'

'I don't take them.'

'Not ever? Not even when you drag your boyfriend up a volcano?'

Ahem. Excuse me.

He said it! I heard it!

This was too surreal. I needed a reset, so I wouldn't get lost in my excitement. I smiled tightly to conceal my raptures. 'Aren't they a bit vain?'

'Nothing vain about a selfie. I snap a couple a day.'

Did he? My joy deflated a touch to hear that. Where did these selfies end up? Nobody ever kept a private collection, did they, to peruse alone? Selfies craved audiences. My face gave me away again.

'Just to check in, you know,' he said. 'See how the rest of the world sees me.'

A confusing compound of excitement and fear and happiness was making my head spin. In the blurry euphoria, I spoke without thinking.

'Harvey. I need to know, before I . . . ' I was going to say before I got hurt but it sounded dramatic. 'I have to ask. What do you see? In me, I mean. I don't know your normal type, but I'll hazard a guess I'm not it. I'm not, you know . . . I don't have a proper body, even with my running, I'm a teacher. It doesn't make sense. Shouldn't you be with someone who can bench press, uh, a hundredweight?'

'Do you actually know what bench pressing is?'

'No! Don't interrupt. Please. I don't want you to waste your time. Okay? Or mine, if I'm honest. Is this a kink? You into really weedy guys who are invisible when you see them stand side-on?'

He laughed. 'Yeah, that's why I don't eat spaghetti. I get hard as a rock, right there in the restaurant. I'm also really hot for guys who won't give themselves a break.'

I risked sending him running, I knew that, but it was important to me. Everyone knowing their mark, word perfect before curtain-up. 'This isn't about self-esteem, okay? This is me knowing myself and being secure in my limitations. There's a million buffer bodies waiting on a thousand apps.'

He stopped walking. So I stopped walking. 'I'll only say this once.' There was determination in his voice. 'I waited a long time to meet someone like you. Right? You feel like home. I hope that means something. Now, stop a second. Step back.'

I stood, mute, heart racing, head pounding, trembling with the sheer, bold sentiment of it all. He reached into his pocket, took out his phone, held it up, and snapped a photo.

'There. That one's just for me. Come on.'

I followed.

Eleven

'Can I borrow you for a few minutes?' – words no sane person ever wants to hear. It usually preceded a bollocking, a firing, or a debt being called in. But I slapped on a smile when Alex Campbell stuck his head round the staffroom door, dropped that eight-word bombshell, then vamoosed. On the few other occasions I'd been summoned, that walk to Campbell's office felt like the slow shuffle toward the electric chair. If there's one thing I've learned about bosses, especially enthusiastic stand-ins keen to make their mark, it's that they expect you to be hyped and upbeat at all times. This usually wasn't a problem; I liked my job, it was a terrific excuse to wear a cardigan, expected of me almost. But something about Campbell rubbed me the wrong way, despite that rolled-up poster turning out to be *West Side Story*, my very favourite musical. Mica, who'd psychoanalyse a probiotic yoghurt if it stayed in the communal fridge long enough, decided we were too similar.

'If you mean because we're both gay, that's extremely homophobic and I'm reporting you to the council.'

She threw her head back and laughed. 'They'll tell us both

to grab a palette knife and fight it out. And don't forget I know how to use those things. Anyway, Naomi's calling.' Ah yes, the students' nickname for Campbell had nothing to do with soup in the end; they went for Naomi which, I had to admit, was genius. 'Run along! I'm telling you – peas in a pod.'

Campbell's office became more personalised every time I went in. He was what Tam called a 'plant gay'; today, I recognised a new mother-in-law's tongue. Peter once bought one for my mother and on learning its name she'd laughed like the front three rows of a Billy Connolly gig for half an hour. Campbell always stood up for my arrival which I suppose was meant as a mark of respect but felt patronising.

'Mr Falconer, do you embrace being challenged?' He'd never again called me Leo since that first day. Without waiting for an answer: 'I've a project I know you'll be great for. Grab a pew.' A pew. God. 'You're free until fourth lesson, aren't you? I'll get us coffee.'

Refreshments? A challenge?! This spelled trouble. Once back from the staffroom with two chipped mugs – one featuring the city council logo and the other inscribed I SAW THE PANDAS AT EDINBURGH ZOO – he swiped through his grand plan on an iPad that didn't have a single finger smudge on it. Looking at previous end-of-year extravaganzas I'd staged, he concluded, just summarising here, that they were shit, I was coasting, and the shake-up I needed was to somehow commission, cast, and stage a new, totally original show that would put Bucklemaker School on the map. Which map, he didn't divulge, but I doubted the 3D foldout map of Broadway theatres in my kitchen drawer would be in need of an update.

'I want to build a community around this,' he told me, in

his usual 'corporate away day' tone. 'Expressive arts, working alongside art and design towards a common goal. Imagine you're staging the Notting Hill Carnival, or Mardi Gras.' There was dreaming big and there was profound delusion.

It was bad news for Mica too – he'd noticed our 'bond' and wanted us working together. The feckless heads of department had struck again.

'Chris and Emerald both agreed you're the best person to take the lead.'

Pair of bastards. Chris was the only teacher I knew whose Vauxhall Insignia rolled out of the car park at 3 p.m. on the dot; that man would delegate going for a shite if he could.

'I know what you're thinking,' he said, not remotely knowing what I was thinking because if he did I'd have been on a disciplinary, 'but I see great potential in you and your department. I know I can tease a lion's roar out of these pussycats. The wonderful Joe from music is already on board and I'll be giving Mica our exciting news as soon as we're done.'

This didn't sound up for negotiation, but I could really do without it. 'Mr Campbell . . . I'm grateful for the opportunity, but this is a big task.'

'That's why I'm telling you now.' Campbell's laptop beeped for an incoming message; he looked at his screen and frowned before cracking his knuckles three times. 'You're more than up to it; this will be a walk in the park if you push yourself.'

Or allowed myself to be pushed. 'Do I have a choice?'

A flicker of disappointment across his face, a short stab of guilt in my gut. 'I need you on board for this. I want to make an impression, show everyone the arts are just as important as adding up and writing and frothing up corrosives in test tubes.

Creativity's taken a battering. Like it's some frippery. We know better, don't we?'

He was right, that's what killed me. I had been a little too cosy. And wasn't it nice to be seen, told you had potential, by someone who barely knew you? Chris never checked in with me, the least I could do was give this guy a break. Try new things, same as I was with Harvey.

'Absolutely. I'll start sketching some ideas. Original songs might be tricky.'

'Let's do half and half, a few covers, a few new ones. Written by the students, obviously. As for ideas: I'm way ahead. I'm imagining a kind of scripted talent show. Showcasing different pupils' abilities through songs, acting, the staging. I want every-one to pull together. Whatever we do, it's gonna be terrific. Could you ask Mica to pop in?'

Back in the corridor, away from the blinding light of Campbell's enthusiasm, the buzz from his flattery began to fade. I'd agreed to surrender almost all my free time for the next few months to something that would be over in about two hours.

'Shit.'

Silver lining: I couldn't wait to see Mica's face in exactly ten minutes' time.

Twelve

I'd never dreamed, back playing with his Lego *Star Wars* set, that one day Harvey and I would both be grown-ups, going out for dinner, let alone actually . . . doing it and falling in love. At least, that's what was happening to me. I hoped he felt the same. We had a connection, I enjoyed being with him, and the sex was wonderful. I had it all. I couldn't quite believe my luck. Sometimes, childhood memories would reach through time, mostly hazy and idyllic, but occasionally some would sharpen and remind me my insecurities weren't new.

For instance, as we entered a place, people would look at him – understandable, he was good-looking, his calm, measured demeanour commanded authority. Then they'd turn to me and, maybe it was in my head, but after years of practice I'd learned to pick up on infinitesimal muscle twitches. They'd pause a millisecond longer, trying to work out what we were to each other.

It reminded me of being younger, and socialising the only way kids know how – hanging out in town somewhere, or outside the flats –and someone from school seeing us together.

He'd never deny me, or ignore me, but I remembered, clearly, how he'd inch away. I wasn't uncool or unpopular particularly, but my sexuality was written all over my face, even before I'd worked it out. Maybe Harvey had been frightened my proximity would make people see him through a different filter, or that he'd be guilty by association. I don't know whether he remembered this, or saw anyone looking now, but sometimes he'd reach for my hand and give me three squeezes, or shoot me a quick smile, doing penance for a crime he didn't know he'd committed. It almost made the staring easier to bear. Maybe he'd had a point about my self-esteem. I didn't really confront it. Either way, I decided the best thing was to leave those feelings in the past, back with the boys playing Lego. The future was our backyard now.

Grown-up Harvey was a different animal from the kid I'd shared many a water-pistol fight with, anyway. He was disciplined but liked to reward himself too. We went for afternoon teas in ornate dining rooms, or minimalist lunches in chic restaurants. He booked the larger seats at the cinema, the ones where they bring you a drink – he'd have a maximum two glasses of wine, never just the second cheapest on the menu – and we'd spend half an hour after, critiquing the film in the dead serious faux intellectualism you try out on new partners to show them you're a cut above. I was usually the only responsible adult in the room, but Harvey relieved that burden gladly.

I'd always had this ridiculous fantasy, inspired by something I saw on social media. This gay couple, impossibly perfect to an almost scientific level, treated every piffling occasion with great ceremony and importance, so had unlimited supplies of bunting. They travelled extensively, to places with hot, milk-white sand lapped by inviting peacock-blue oceans. Swimwear companies paid them to pose conspicuously in indecent trunks next to their expensive toaster. One of them had a Parisian mother or something, so they celebrated Bastille Day, and that was the last post I ever saw on social media before I deleted my accounts, save for some light stalking over Daisy's shoulder. The two men, who only had eyes for each other, so happy and in love, in matching Breton tops, pastries elegantly laid out before them, clinking champagne flutes with one hand, fingers interlocked on the other, probably speaking French. My Bastille Day Ideal, I called it. I wasn't stupid. I knew it couldn't be all idyllic. Light only looks bright because darkness is nearby. But that didn't make me want it any less. And now it was mine. Harvey. Social media ready. Except . . . he wasn't on it either.

'Feels like a licence to envy. I'd rather focus on what I've got,' he'd say, which I loved, as it sounded clever but not dismissive. I used it a few times at work and got an appreciative nod from Campbell. It sounded much better than 'I don't want my students seeing how I live'. The small snag in my ideal was Harvey didn't like going to bookshops, one of my favourite rainy Saturday outings. He'd skulk by the biographies, flicking through the photo pages and rolling his eyes at the captions. That same face from the Botanic Gardens. He didn't have a favourite book, but he liked to take photos and he was good at it. The one of me on Arthur's Seat had kind lighting that sort of obscured my nose; he printed it out and propped it on his otherwise empty bookshelves. I was delighted. I let him take more.

One Saturday morning in October, I was sorting through potential song submissions for the end-of-the-year show and wondering whether the students should consider therapy, when Harvey said he had a surprise. Another phrase up there with 'Can I borrow you?' I'd always liked the idea of surprises but it was the execution that worried me. I was still traumatised from pretending to love an ugly painting Tam once gave me, before he realised he'd got the tags mixed up and it was meant for Daisy – his actual surprise for me had been a massage.

'Let's see if they can get your neck to actually turn, Dandelion. When you cross the road you look like Robocop.'

Surprises from Peter had been 'Surprise! I've booked that weekend away you've repeatedly said you have no time to go on, to somewhere you don't want to go but I do, so now I'm going to sulk for ever!' Or 'Surprise! I'm leaving you for a doctor!' – although I did actually quite like that surprise in the end.

Harvey's surprises, though, showed he'd been thinking of me. He led me to his car. On the passenger seat was a gift-wrapped box.

'Don't open that. Not until I tell you. Get in.'

Another childhood memory – he was fond of ordering me about. I didn't mind so much now; there was a little spark to it. Turned me on a bit.

'Harvey, is this lacy underwear or a butt plug or something because . . . you'll need to warn me if you don't want me to scream.'

He giggled, then calmly raised a middle finger to the driver who'd just cut him up at the lights. 'Nothing x-rated. Sorry to disappoint. Won't be long.'

We headed out of Leith, stopping and starting in traffic. Rays of unseasonable warm sun appeared in brief glints. Harvey pulled at his collar. Merino wool. Long sleeved polo shirt. The colour of wine. He looked great in it, but his face was almost a perfect match. Traffic got to him. Finally, the bottlenecks cleared, green lights shone for miles and his agitation lifted. We drove into Portobello. A stroll on the beach maybe in search of ice cream or, preferably, a hot chocolate? Nope, the glimpses of coastline rushed by; I watched road signs for clues.

'Are we going to Penicuik? Daisy's gran lives there. She broke her hip in the birthday card shop. I should take her some flowers.'

'We're not! I mean, it's a surprise, wait and see.'

I'm antsy on car journeys, and the box was perched on my knee like a bored tabby flexing its claws, so after half an hour, he let me open it. His nervous energy willed me to like whatever was inside; his eyes kept flicking from the road to my lap. I carefully untied the ribbon, anxious not to knot it up, gravely lifted the lid of the box like a bomb disposal expert, and looked inside. Tissue paper, secured by a little round sticker.

'You're making a meal of it. How long did it take you to open presents on Christmas morning?'

'Sorry!'

I tried, and failed, not to tear the paper as I unpeeled the sticker. I unfurled the layers to find, elegantly folded, a pair of shorts. Hmmm. Purple ones with scattered dots and dashes, like Morse code. I took them out, stroked the material – soft but weighty – and peered inside them. Netting. Swimming shorts. I hadn't braved swimwear since my last obligatory ten-metre relay in Primary 7 – black regulation swim shorts that started out baggy and dare I say trendy, but shrunk into hot pants by the end of term.

'I don't really swim.'

91

'Sure you do. We used to go swimming.'

Harvey had gone swimming. Diving from the top board, as I'd paddled nervously in the shallow end, imagining all the horrible things that could go wrong.

The car turned down a dirt track and jiggled and swerved so much it was a relief not to have to speak while Harvey concentrated on driving. We stopped and I spied, peeking through some trees, a loch. A reservoir probably, I wasn't sure where we were.

'We're going swimming now? Here?'

'Yep. You never heard of wild swimming? Haven't you picked up a newspaper in the last ten years?'

'You said you weren't outdoorsy.'

'Not for trudging up a boring old hill, no.' I imagined the Scottish Tourist Board's arterial flutters if they heard this damning review of Arthur's Seat. 'This is wellness. It takes you on a journey. I did it all the time in London. It really helped.'

A wave of discomfort. 'Helped with what?'

'It just helped. Come on.'

We stood at the water's edge and he explained what we were going to do. A little paddle out toward the middle, he said, then back. Another go if we felt up to it, which he was sure we would. The loch was beautiful in its bleakness. The trees almost naked, the hills in the distance casting ghostly reflections in still and glassy water. I imagined it was wonderful in summer, but it was not summer. I noticed a couple of swimmers already in there, and a group of laughing women wading back to shore in fluorescent swim caps and bright pink bathing suits.

'Cancer survivors. I swear you'll never feel more alive than this.'

'I can't wear those tiny swimming shorts in there. I'll freeze to death.'

'Not even a little dip?' Harvey laughed. 'Joking! The trunks were symbolic. I've got wetsuits in the car.' Wetsuits? Of course he did. Men like Harvey had wetsuits. 'Secondhand but deep cleaned.' Christ.

Of all the things I'd imagined Harvey doing to me in the back of his car, helping me change into a wetsuit wasn't one. It appeared clean enough, but something in its scent told me it had seen things no wetsuit should see. Its previous occupant seemed to haunt every nook. It was also god knows how many sizes too small. To his credit, Harvey's face didn't crack as I emerged, taking cautious baby gazelle steps on the gravel, in my waterproof bodystocking that left nothing to the imagination in the most uninviting way.

'Your calves look good,' he said.

'My toenails could do with a trim; I look like a raven.'

I watched, rapt, while he changed into his wetsuit, which clung like paint to his body's best features, before we tottered to the water's edge. I felt the crunch of nature and the soil's secrets beneath my feet. What might be in the loch? Fish, I supposed. Corpses? Harvey said this reservoir provided Edinburgh with most of its water; I didn't like the idea of my anxiety ending up in my kettle one day. I hovered, one foot above the water.

'I'm not sure.'

'I'm with you.' He took my hand. One, two, three little squeezes.

'Okay. Let's go.'

My squeals – one for every centimetre of my body I managed

to submerge – rang off those hills. It wasn't so much the cold, but the sensation of the water; it felt gelatinous, almost, through the suit. A sentient oil slick edging up my body as Harvey gently pressed down on my shoulder. As water came up to my chest, my breathing became shallower and quicker and while I certainly felt more alive, mortality was a more pressing concern. My foot tried to find the loch floor but we must've been too far out. I wiggled my toes, and kicked about, desperate to feel dirt or stones or tangles of weeds or anything, but instead located only Harvey's shins. His face slowly changed into a mosaic of worry; he took his hand off my shoulder and moved behind me, his arms round my waist. It felt like he was about to drag me under so I kicked away from him. He caught me again and I realised he was pushing me, but not under, only out toward the land again. I stumbled out of the water, and slowly sank to my knees, muscles rigid, my lungs useless paper bags flapping away in my chest, my stomach heaving.

Harvey crouched next to me and started dabbing my face with a towel. 'Please don't cry, Leo.'

We drove back toward the city in silence. Once we crossed the bypass, it felt safe to talk, back on neutral ground again. I reached out and touched his thigh. 'Sorry. I don't know what happened.'

He smiled. 'At least you tried.'

Hearing his voice took away the loch's last remaining chills from my bones. I didn't want him to feel bad that it hadn't gone to plan.

'You know what, though, in a way, I get what you mean, about it being invigorating and stuff, I do feel quite . . . yeah, invigorated. Alive. Definitely.'

'It wasn't for you, it's fine. There's loads of other stuff we can do. I thought . . . you know if we got that body of yours out there, if you saw what it was capable of . . . you'd be less hard on it.'

I'd seen exactly what it was capable of: panic. It made his effort even more heartbreaking. Maybe I could try harder. 'How about we give it another go? Like, spring, maybe?'

'It's fine. We don't have to talk about this again.'

'I want to. Seriously.'

He put his hand over mine as we pulled up outside my flat. 'You're on.'

Thirteen

Number one question people ask when they find out you've given up drinking: 'Do you feel better/different?' I'm sure the answer for some people is yes, they've acquired superpowers and can now identify who's at the front door before they open it, on smell alone. Mind you, I could actually do that if Tam had done a hiya-spritz-dash through Harvey Nichols' fragrance counter on the way to mine. Aside from waking with a clearer head, I didn't feel much different.

When I first gave up, Daisy and Tam became immediately concerned – not for my wellbeing, but that I'd acquired a photographic memory overnight and would log their drunken misdeeds to present in a dossier at our next meeting. I did my best not to judge, but, yes, there was something demeaning about watching them break down in tears defending their favourite Disney princess (Daisy – Jasmine; Tam – Belle) or stagger into the street, zips down, threatening to golden shower the gutter.

As a good friend I promised I'd never cast up their deranged or dangerous misdeeds. I didn't need to; aside from chips from Piccante on the way home, their favourite drunk pastime was loudspeakering to their social media followings, live. Thrillingly, Daisy once accidentally posted a mullered tirade on her work account about the (shamefully low) number of crisps you get in a bag. The hysteria the next day was supersonic – I believed my sporadic tinnitus stemmed from Daisy's guttural scream down the phone that her career was dead – but in true Daisy fashion, her (clueless) boss assumed it was a hilarious form of guerrilla marketing, and gave her a bonus – 240 packets of cheese and onion Discos.

Most drinkers have a sweet spot hidden somewhere between merry/chirpy/buoyant and maudlin/abusive/total collapse. Tam's and Daisy's varied depending on what they were drinking and where, but if you caught them in the middle, you'd have a ball. Unfortunately, this sweet spot lasted about twenty-five minutes.

I didn't know why I'd avoided introducing them to Harvey for so long. No, I did. A man could be turned off for ever once he met your pals, couldn't he? Your friendship dynamic might seem totally normal to you, but to an outsider: a pack of pricks. And with new lovers, your friends' eyes are searchlights, landing on things you might have missed. It'd be like watching a horde of estate agents trampling through my flat and uncovering problems I'd long tuned out. What flaws might they dig up on Harvey? Or worse, what might they miss? Again.

On nights out with them, Peter claimed he felt like spicy chicken wings being picked apart, but he could always hold his own. He and Tam would love debating bad novels – two wannabe professors battling it out for intellectual supremacy.

'He's always right, isn't he?' said Daisy once. 'So clever.' Every syllable an incision.

I'd already been found out by Mica, who wanted to know why I was coming into school on a Monday 'looking like the original good time that was had by all' and claimed I had a 'Ready Brek glow' all around me, a reference I'd had to Google.

For the big intro, I insisted on something informal, a back-street pub in Leith, near enough home to escape if it got a bit much. Daisy disregarded this completely; now she'd finished re-alphabetising her paperbacks, she wanted to organise me. Pulling a favour with her boss, she reserved us a table at some supposedly exclusive rooftop bar in the New Town where the bouncers' aggression better suited guarding the doors to the crown jewels and not patrolling a tacky watering hole packed with over-mortgaged fortysomethings dressed like pyramid scheme fraudsters. It was very not me: I felt conscious of my grubby Converse. Harvey looked an absolute ride in bottle-green cashmere and gleaming white spaceship trainers, so I basked vicariously. Daisy looked effortlessly stylish and Tam was Croisette-chic in white T-shirt and tan trousers. He looked terrific, but didn't need to hear that from me.

'You look like a cigarette,' I said, while kissing him hello.

Daisy sent 'the men' – Seb and Fabrizio – to get drinks while she and Tam dutifully went through their routine for Harvey's benefit.

'Do you like my hair?' Daisy had acquired a fringe. First thing she did when anxiety came calling was have a hairdresser shear it away. 'I was going for Stevie Nicks.'

Tam fluffed it with his fingers. 'Which era?'

'1977, but on the wagon. Why, which era did you think?'

'I dunno. Eighties rock chick? That video where she's sitting in a barn?' This vagueness was fake – Tam's ringtone was 'Edge of Seventeen' when we first met.

'No! *Rumours*-era hedonism, but keeping her head clear to record "Dreams" the next day. Is it not?'

'In an alternative timeline, I'd try running a matte clay through it for extra zhuzh, but here, it's perfect. You're her double.'

Daisy switched her attention to Harvey now. 'Where do you get your hair cut, Harvey? It's lovely. Isn't it lovely, Tam? Leo, it's lovely, isn't it?'

My warning glower went unheeded. Harvey didn't seem to mind. 'Place near my work. West End.'

'Ooooh, we were up the West End the other night, weren't we, Tam? A copper had to help me find my handbag.'

Tam and I locked eyes. 'Indeed. A handbag you had not, in fact, brought out with you.'

'Small detail, yes.'

Standard Daisy on a night out. One I wasn't invited on. Everyone was looking, waiting for me to say something. 'How come I didn't get to hear about it?'

'It was three-for-two tequila shots, so not very Leo two-point-oh.' Tam winked. 'Every other song was Little Mix, they didn't play anything from *Oklahoma*.'

'You know, I can go to clubs and not drink.'

'What, and actually enjoy them? Sticky carpets and Lambrini vomit and all?' I feared Daisy might be rapidly exiting her sweet spot, but a squeeze of her hand reassured me. 'What about dancing?'

'I've never danced sober.' Tam looked horrified at the suggestion.

'God, same.'

'You'd be able to remember everything the next day. All the gyrating. Can't think of anything worse.'

They were on sparkling form; everything was aligning. Harvey laughed out loud. I was happy. 'Well, next time, if you can bear my disgusting freakish abstinence, I'd love to have the option of telling you I can't come.'

'Point taken,' said Tam. 'Next traffic light tequila party, I'll buzz you.'

Seb and Fabrizio returned, grappling with frosted glasses, most of whose contents seemed to have been spilled down the backs of whoever they'd elbowed out of the way to get to us.

Fabrizio handed me my water. Just water. No garnish, or ice. He clocked my disappointment. 'There was a jug on the bar so I thought it was easier.' He welded himself to Tam. 'What are we talking about, babes?'

'Nothing,' said Daisy, leaning on Harvey and lightly touching his chest, as she often did with Tam; her fingertips had never once so much as grazed my sternum. 'Harv, I need you to nip to the bathroom soon so we can tell Leo how great you are, but behind your back. Is that okay?'

He laughed. Again. Those teeth! Those eyes! All mine! But in a very non-possessive way! 'I do need to, actually.'

Once he was out of sight, Tam nudged me. 'Works both ways, you know. You could have invited us . . . wild swimming.'

Daisy clapped her hands like a seal. 'Wild swimming! Lion! That's smug coupledom gone too far.'

Why couldn't I do smug coupledom for a change? Tam and Fabrizio were always tangled up in each other like charger

cables; Daisy and Seb had their tired Taylor and Burton act.
'Get to fuck.'

'What was it like?'

'Invigorating, actually!'

'So's vinegar in a paper cut! Did you enjoy it?'

'Shut up, Tam. Yes, I did.' It was easier to lie. Maybe I had
kind of enjoyed it? The sex after was hot, anyway: it was a
happier memory if I merged the two, and understood the role
of the first part in securing the second.

'He's lovely, but . . . sporty. How can you stand it? I can't
bear sporty gays. Feels so treasonous, like all those horrible PE
lessons never happened.' Tam's toned, wiry physique was, as
he was fond of pointing out, 'superior Indian genetics' and five
days a week humping wheelbarrows of soil about. He'd visited
the gym at university only to get Tooty Frooties out of the
vending machine. 'At least Fabrizio draws the line at Peloton.
Don't you, babes?' Tam turned to his fiancé, who was showing
Seb a viral video of a dog that had learned to fire a machine gun.

'Respect to you for doing that actually, Lion.' Seb didn't look
up. 'You know fortune favours the brave and you miss 100 per
cent of the shots you don't take.' Thank you, Gandhi.

Soon it was my turn to go to the bathroom. I tried to be
quick so they couldn't interrogate Harvey. I didn't want them
wheedling anything out of him that my mild probing hadn't
yet uncovered. My worries were, as ever, misplaced. When
I returned, Harvey was deep into the glass of wine brought
to him only minutes ago, and had the rosy glow of a racon-
teur enjoying an enthralled audience. Tam and Daisy were
open-mouthed.

'Dandelion,' said Tam, in the kind of voice you might use

after your husband has told you that, actually, he was responsible for those bodies the police had pulled out of the canal. 'Menergize?'

No. Oh no. My blood surged, doing handbrake turns in every kink of my arteries. I opened my mouth but nothing came except the taste of mild embarrassment.

Daisy retracted her tongue, which had been lolling out the side of her mouth. 'You fucked the lot of them? That's why you used to go to Menergize? I thought it was a boring old book club . . .'

'Or some kind of knitting circle where you talked about how oppressed you were,' said Tam, with roguish glee. 'If I'd known it was a nonstop fuck-fest I'd have come along to pick up some spares.' Fabrizio tutted. 'Before I met you, of course, my babes. I can't believe it. You sly devil.'

'Dark horse, even.'

Seb slapped me on the back. 'Lion, buddy, I never knew you were such a man-whore; always thought you were saving yourself for . . . well, after Peter.'

Sly devil. Dark horse. Man-whore. I sensed I'd lost something. Not just my dignity. A light had shone into a corner I'd kept for myself.

Harvey, for his part, looked shellshocked. 'I . . . assumed they knew.'

Now they did, I'd never hear the end of it. 'I didn't take holy orders after I . . . after my relationship ended. I only slept with four of them, over the course of . . . I dunno, two years? What did you think I was doing on nights I didn't see you? Staying at home with my prayer book?'

'Does sound a bit seedy, chap, to be fair,' said Seb. 'Getting off with the whole group. Is that a gay thing?' Seb, lecturing me about being seedy! Imagine!

Tam stepped in. 'No worse than your "straight thing" of meeting at the watering hole, then going off to rut. Like fucking hippos.'

Daisy, knowing me best, sensed my irritation. She breezed on, perhaps hoping to offload excess fuel before it ignited. 'We always thought you were too picky. I was always saying, wasn't I, Sebby, "Too picky, our Dandelion." I really did.'

I'd heard this before, the undercurrent that maybe I had no business being 'picky', that a gargoyle shouldn't have standards.

'Turns out you weren't so picky after all. Sticky, mainly.' Tam's face flashed with admiration and devilry. 'I'm seeing you in a whole different light now, Lion.' He clinked my glass with his. 'The darkest of all the horses. Dark as those delightful peepers of yours.'

Harvey didn't say much on the way home. We undressed in silence. I liked looking at his body in the glow of the lamp; I saw him looking at mine too, and I didn't mind a bit.

'I can't believe they didn't know.'

'Sorry. Hope it wasn't too embarrassing.'

'I thought they were your best friends?'

'They are.'

Harvey sat up in bed, looking perplexed. I traced my finger down from his shoulder and gently circled his nipple. I didn't want to analyse it. It didn't have to mean anything. He didn't flinch at all, but the covers stirred.

'I feel sad for you.'

'Why?'

'That you felt you couldn't tell them something so . . . well, something that happened to you.'

I leaned over to kiss his chest now, in the hope of distracting him. A tested negotiation technique with a high success rate. He licked his lips and swallowed.

'Didn't you like them?'

'I did,' he said, his voice low. 'A lot. I'm just surprised. I thought you told them everything.'

'Ah. I don't.' I traced my finger up his thigh now; he breathed in slowly, half closed his eyes. I nearly had him.

'What do you talk about, then?'

'Them mainly.' I could've listened to Daisy and Tam talk all day – in fact I often did. Tam's gap year, spent with someone who'd since become a minor celebrity, was still a rich seam to mine for scandal. 'They're born entertainers.'

Harvey slid down to lie flat next to me. 'You can tell me anything. I'll never judge, I'll never make fun.'

I ran my hand over his belly. 'If I tell you what I really want to say now, you'll blush.'

'Whisper it.'

Got him. Awkward conversation averted. We kept the light on. No dimmer switch.

Fourteen

December is probably the hardest month not to be a drinker. I don't miss nursing rapidly flattening prosecco at house parties or concocting rancid cocktails from leftover spirits and liqueurs, but coming up to Christmas, the ceremony around booze intensifies: mulled cider, your gran knocking back gloopy advocaat, pretending Bailey's is actually nice, hip flasks at Hogmanay. Yet December was the month I gave up.

Depending on how well I knew those asking – and people almost always ask – I'd say I fancied starting Dry January a wee bit early and carried on, or wanted to be fitter, or, if someone was prying too deeply, that I'd developed an intolerance. I read that could happen once, in a magazine while I was waiting to get a filling replaced, and it seemed like an acceptable excuse that would see off any questions – it was also much easier than the truth.

I'd tried avoiding Alex Campbell most of autumn term, but hiding in corners is hard when you're six-four. I'd heard he'd installed a swish Italian coffee machine in his office which seemed so uncharacteristically extra that I was briefly intrigued, but I didn't relish showing him my blank notebook containing the zero progress I'd made on the show. Mica had run out of excuses when he came looking for me.

'You're only ever in three places, Leo: staffroom; arts office; drama studio. He's gonna get you.'

Finally, on the last day of term, via the medium of a Post-it on the door of every room I walked into, he asked to see me. Mica mischievously suggested he was going to ask me out ice skating, or to deep-throat a big bratwurst at the German market.

'Admit it, he's cute. In a geeky way. Like you.'

I couldn't find him cute. It was in my DNA to hate all bosses, especially men. 'I'm not a geek!'

My plan was to arrive late to the meeting so there wouldn't be enough time to go into detail, but the bastard must've been psychic, because he surprised me two hours early, as I was ripping pages off a flipchart filled with profanities after a class brainstorming session. Things always took an obscene turn when I said, 'Yes, you can write absolutely anything.'

'Mr Falconer, thought I'd come find you while I had a spare ten.' A 'spare ten', ugh; the breezy vernacular of a rich financier trying to be hip while ordering beers in a curry house. 'Just wondered how you're getting on.'

'Generally?' Something about Campbell made me act like the surly twelve-year-old I'd never actually been.

He didn't flinch. When it came to dealing with insolence, he was a pro. 'Our show. Do we have a script? A title, even.'

'We're workshopping at the moment, but you know, even Sondheim couldn't make it happen overnight.' He could actually, sometimes, and Campbell's thin smile told me he knew that. He pushed his glasses back up his nose and I wondered, briefly, what he'd look like without them. Vulnerable, maybe. I immediately felt bad for being a bitch.

'How about I walk you through it?' I offered, somehow inventing the entire concept of our show on the spot: characters, twists, every scene. As I was rattling it out, I made a mental note to blab it into my Voice Notes as soon as Campbell was gone, and to warn Joe and Mica, who would definitely both kill me. I kept expecting him to stop me, say we couldn't do it, but instead he listened with unreadable serenity as I talked him through my concept for a talent show within a play – just like he'd suggested.

'So leading up to the finale, the evil talent show judge, who you'll remember has been in hiding so far . . . well, he gets unmasked. Big solo, sees the error of his ways, realises you don't need to be exceptional to be entertaining, you can just be yourself, you know the drill – then a big, bastarding ensemble hoedown to show there's no hard feelings, then whump! Curtain. Fucking. Down.' My expletive rang off the walls. 'We're calling it *Hidden Talents*.'

If Campbell had guessed I was winging it, he didn't show it. 'Sounds epic. When will you have a script for me? January? So I can run it past . . . well, the management team?'

Ah, that was it. Campbell's carnivorous league table-obsessed overlords needed to be slung a carcass. Mine. I could've said fine, January works, got him off my back, but, again, something about him made me want to upturn tables. I'd literally invented an entire two-hour show in minutes – although he didn't know that – could I not have five seconds to rest on my laurels?

'Mr Campbell, I don't have an elite writers' room like an American sitcom; this is made by students.'

'Surely you have some bright stars who can . . . '

I felt quite powerful – and a bit like a traffic warden – as I raised my hand to interrupt. 'All my students are great. In their own way. Yeah, I've one or two big stars who could help me churn this out first day back.' He looked pleased, which annoyed me. 'But I'm making a show with the moral "everyone has value, stardom is not the only endgame". I'm not focusing on bright stars, I'm using all talents, all levels. Everyone gets a shot on a Mr Falconer production, okay?'

He looked suitably chastened. 'I've a lot riding on this, I've taken a chance.'

I got this. I even felt for him in a way. But I was in competition with maths, English and science. Subjects that everyone, including their teachers, would tell students were more important than frivolous shit like drama or art. 'If they're not in drama club or the exam cohort, I get one academic hour a week to show them the magic.'

I'd made him look like a dick. I actually regretted it. He shifted from one foot to the other. This obviously hadn't gone how he'd expected. 'If there's anything I can do . . .'

I laughed. 'Aye, can you rustle me up a cultural shift that reminds people the arts are pretty crucial, sometime within the next two weeks? That would be great. Otherwise, some slack would do.'

He took off his glasses and rubbed his eyes. Very handsome. Bastard. My own eye twitched. 'Absolutely. Errr, Merry Christmas to you.' I felt a bit sorry for him; I didn't even laugh as he walked into three chairs on his way out. Banged his shin quite hard on the last one.

Mica slinked in as he was leaving. 'What's that smell? Could it be . . . Sexual Tension by Calvin Klein?'

'Just regular tension, I'm afraid, supermarket own-brand.'

'Come on. Give into it. Having a boyfriend and a work crush at the same time is very main character vibes. I know you've got it in you.'

'I don't want it in me. Get your scarf. Emergency Cigarette Protocol incoming.'

Fifteen

My mum was gavotting round the kitchen to Sally Oldfield, wrapping presents and tipping sherry down her neck when I walked in. She hurriedly ditched the glass in the dishwasher, looked over my cat rescue shop cashmere cardigan and rolled her eyes.

'Did Noel Coward die for nothing?' she said, before regaling me with her usual rundown of the gradual degeneration of former schoolmates stalking the aisles of the big Sainsbury's, her personal equivalent of the *Vanity Fair* post-Oscars party. 'Lorna Casey wasnae looking her best. Rail thin. Skull and rouge. Ken Ball's away to Turkey on Boxing Day for a full set of veneers. He needs to as well, that one brown fang swinging in his mouth.'

I stuck my head round the living room door to find my brother in full holiday mode, watching *Jingle All the Way* in a snowman onesie. He ignored my hello. 'Who are these presents for?'

'Regifting! It's stuff the teachers got me. Sending them to the care home.' Mum was lucky to be the most popular secretary at the school she worked at, which I'd attended, but most of her staff treated her like she was ninety – she practically drowned in bubble bath and talc gift sets every year. 'About Christmas Day, actually. There'll be some extra bodies.' It wasn't unusual for Mum to invite the odd waif and stray for dinner – Christine from two doors along had chain-smoked her way through three or four turkey dinners over the years, and Shireen from Mum's school left her horrible husband one Christmas Eve and brought along her three adorable children. Good practice for Duncan, I'd said, when the inevitable paternity suits came knocking.

'Cool, who's squeezing round the table this year?'

Mum inhaled sharply, like she was about to tackle 'O Mio Babbino Caro' on stage at the Playhouse. 'Okay, so you know Peter's husband is a doctor?' It had been mentioned a few hundred times, yes. 'He's working Christmas Day so I've invited him and Ava.'

Peter? My ex, Peter? For Christmas Day? All day? Here? No. It couldn't happen. Listening to him fawn over Mum's cooking, sharing mildly misogynistic quips with my brother, gently ribbing me using in-jokes that once felt like they bonded us but turned out to be exceptionally weak glue. And never breaking eye contact with me for a second. I didn't want to speak that language again, be that man.

I hadn't laid eyes on Peter since my dad's funeral, his arm coiling through mine, even though I tried to keep my body tight and closed. He always found a way in. How could Mum do this? If only she knew. I blamed myself. My oblique references to The Unpleasantness, the constant assurances I had 'moved on', the truth hiding in plain sight. I could only answer in a squeak.

'Peter?'

'With Ava, uh huh. Nice to have a little one here Christmas Day.'

My lip quivered, emotion rushing to the surface. I hadn't cried in front of my mother since the funeral, where she'd pierced my grief by telling me not to wipe snotters on my sleeve because the service was being broadcast over webcam to Auntie Ann in Brisbane.

'You know me and Peter broke up? I did tell you that. That's why he's married to someone else.'

She didn't hear me. My brother galumphed into the kitchen in his fleecy cartoon hazmat suit. 'Won't it, Duncan? Be nice to have a kid here Christmas Day?'

He grunted. This would almost certainly be the worst day of the year; I had to extricate myself from it, now.

'I meant to say, actually.' I willed my brain to snap out of its shocked Cornetto-freeze and find a good excuse. It was no good, I had to scorch the earth. 'I can't come Christmas Day, I'm spending it with Harvey.'

'Who's Harvey?' My brother shovelled three cheese-topped crackers into his mouth at once.

'Harvey Pearce?' I knew Mum's look of old – the face of a woman discovering £20 at the bottom of a charity shop handbag, the woman who rigged the meat raffle at the Craig's Anchor on Great Junction Street. Excitement. Delight. Curiosity.

'It's not a big deal.' Her mouth and eyes opened wider and wider in anticipation. 'But, but . . . we're . . . together.'

'Together?! What does that mean? Together like Kylie and Jason? Together in electric dreams?'

'He's my boyfriend.' I heard my brother retch. Prick. 'It's

early days. We're gonna have a quiet Christmas. Romantic. Together. Just us.' This was nonsense; Harvey was heading south for a family Christmas, so I'd now be hiding in my flat by myself. Mum had a thousand questions and many more reasons why I should bring Harvey for a cosy Christmas lunch with my ex and his child, but I played my ace. 'It's best, you know, to spare Peter's feelings. Might be awkward for him.' She wouldn't want to upset St Peter. 'We can pop up Boxing Day?'

I'd deal with getting round that lie later. Placated and a little giddy, my mum wandered off to find a present for Harvey in her cavernous regifting cupboard, while my brother stood chewing his way through an entire pack of chorizo slices, mouth open — his face looked like a caesarean in progress.

'Bit shitty, no? Not coming for your dinner? Selfish. That's you, eh?' It blew my mind we'd once called the same uterus home, but I guess you shouldn't judge a house by its previous occupant.

'I don't want to sit and pull the wishbone with my ex.'

'You're pumping some new guy. Time you got over yourself.' Ha! Said the man back living in his childhood bedroom because he gave his girlfriend gonorrhoea.

'Would you have Christmas dinner with one of your exes? Assuming they dropped the restraining orders, of course.'

'Fuck off. I dunno, man, Peter seems pretty chill about it. You're the one with the problem.' He shrugged and padded back to the living room, the world's most flammable snowman.

'Thanks for your insight.'

Harvey liked it when I laid my head in his lap, so he could stroke my ear or twist my hair round his finger while we told each other about our day. Months ago, I'd have worried I looked silly splayed out like an attention-starved chihuahua on his huge sofa, but as Harvey said, 'What's actually wrong with attention? It's nice. Come.'

I felt safe, which made me confessional: I warned him I'd made him an accessory to my desperate lie. 'Maybe I can stomach it. I'll go. Brave it. It won't be so bad.'

'Don't expose yourself to negative energy. It doesn't have to be a lie. Let's make it real, do Christmas together.'

Part of me had hoped he'd say that, but I never dreamed it would happen. Had I manipulated him into this? 'Really? I don't think it'd be right for me to come to your mum and dad's when I've dingied my own mum.'

'No, I mean, let's do it here. Just you and me. My mum and dad will understand.'

Would they? Why would they? Harvey never really spoke about them. Was he avoiding a tense Christmas too? Then, the intrusive thought: were they as hung up on Harvey's ex as my mother was on mine? 'Do they know about me?'

Harvey rapped his knuckles on the arm of the sofa. 'Not yet, I wanted to keep you to myself a while. You don't mind, do you?'

'Not at all.' I did a bit, even though I'd told my mum about us only an hour earlier. I wondered how long it had taken Harvey to introduce them to Matt.

'I will, though, tell them. Right now. That's settled. Christmas here, me and you.'

So we did it, ticking more rom-com boxes than any previous Christmas with a boyfriend. Bastille Day Ideal Plus. There was a last-minute dash to get a tree, picking up the scraggiest, least loved bunch of twigs because we felt sorry for it, draping it in tinsel and far too many lights, and hanging baubles with the reverent care you'd reserve for clipping your first baby's toenails. On Christmas morning, he woke me with booze-free champagne and strawberries, then there was sex in Santa hats – mildly disturbing how much of a turn-on the headgear was, to be honest – and we opened our gifts. For me a slightly too tight, yet beautiful, cashmere cardigan to replace my charity shop number, and for him, a secondhand Lego Space set, just like the one we'd played with as kids. At first he gawked at it like he'd walked into the wrong hotel room and caught someone eating a meringue with no shirt on.

'What's this?'

My stomach lurched. He didn't love it. I'd failed. I'd really wanted to nail this. As I started to explain, the memories slowly broke across his face like a sunrise.

'Oh yeah. How wonderful. What a blast from the past. This is so cool. And look at us now, eh? We made it to the moon.'

He really said that. Unprompted. Wasn't reading off his phone like Fabrizio. Actual romance, in real time. Elation rippled through my body. I didn't even mind when I got up for a glass of water and stood barefoot on a mini Lego satellite dish.

Harvey allowed himself a day of indulgence with no yoga or meditation, and we feasted on Marks & Spencer's very finest 'cook everything for twenty-five minutes on a preheated baking tray' festive favourites. He declined joining me for a Boxing Day run, but accompanied me to my mother's, who gazed in awe, trying to connect the elegant man she saw now with 'the dumpy wee shite who never flushed my downstairs cludgie'. He was, she conceded, gorgeous – she told me so when he went to the loo, which we heard him flush twice.

I had to ask, though I didn't want to: 'How was your day, Mum?'

'Beautiful, son, beautiful. Wee Ava's an absolute doll.'

'Did you get any nice presents?' I braced myself for whatever flash gift Peter had bought her to humiliate me further.

'Aye, Ava made me a gorgeous picture.' She pointed to the fridge door, and an artwork of primary-coloured splodge. 'Peter got me one of they special hot chocolate machines, but he wasn't sure where I was with my cholesterol. Thoughtful, isn't he, not many people would make that connection.'

I wondered if Harvey might tense up at the mention of Peter's name. He didn't. I probably would've, if Harvey's mum started banging on about the mysterious Matt. 'What's wrong with your cholesterol? You never said.'

'I didn't want to worry you, son.'

'But you didn't mind worrying Peter. Well, telling him.' Ah, there it was, the slight flex of forearm from Harvey I'd been waiting for.

'He's made of stronger stuff. You overreact. Dramatic.'

'And Duncan?'

'Duncan can't even spell cholesterol. There'd be no point.'

Harvey knocked back the glass of Bailey's my mother had put in his hand only minutes earlier. 'Well, Mrs Falconer . . . Dawn . . . it's been epic to catch up. You haven't changed a bit. Shall we?'

Back in the car, we sat watching clouds of steam curl from our mouths as we fastened our seatbelts.

'Shall I drive? You had the Bailey's.'

'No. What's your brother's take on Peter?'

'Duncan? He's thicker than a Boxing Day turd. The only thing he takes is the piss.'

'That's an uncharitable thing to say. You should channel that negativity elsewhere. I can't imagine missing Christmas at home because of my ex.'

'No, but you missed it because of me, which was because of him. Anyway, Mum and Peter always got on.'

'You didn't, though.'

'No.'

'Just so strange. I don't want to say it's disloyal of her, but . . .'

The car pulled away and I turned back to Mum's house to see if she was waving at the window like she sometimes did. She wasn't, but I didn't look away, I kept watching the twinkling lights in her window get smaller and smaller.

Sixteen

Every year, during that weird festive perineum where everyone is coming down from Christmas Day but still high on the impending New Year, Tam, Daisy and I would meet in Robbie's Bar on Leith Walk for our debrief, comparing gift hauls, and any scandals, before listing every single resolution we had no intention of making. Usually, my content would be lacking. Daisy was always embroiled in some family drama, forcing down two separate dinners to appease her parents who still scrapped over ownership of her like rats fighting over a discarded kebab. Tam's parade of showy try-hard boyfriends compensating because he 'didn't celebrate Christmas' meant he'd always outclass us on the present front – even though his parents always put up a tree, and made a stocking, despite showering him with gifts for Diwali only a few weeks earlier.

Me? Well, I'd smell a little different, drenched in whichever fragrance Mum had bought and signed 'from Duncan' on the gift tag. Tam, who'd once eaten 'the best roast dinner of my life' at my mum's, always asked in minute detail what I'd had for Christmas lunch – 'So the sprouts, roasted or steamed?

Any garlic in the mix?' — but usually my update was unlikely to have tabloid journalists salivating. This year was different. I'd lived a fairy tale.

'You know those movies on that channel that shows Christmas films twenty-four-seven,' I gushed. 'You do! There's a perfect little town about to be razed to the ground to build an incinerator or something, so the friendly and gorgeous . . . let's say artisan chocolatier, well, she's about to lose the shop she vowed to keep going as the last wish of her dying grandfather . . . '

Daisy, natural born fact-checker, raised her hand to stop me. 'Your grandad ran a chocolate shop? I thought he painted the Forth Bridge?'

'Not me! The film lady! Anyway, in these films, it always turns out the man in charge of the bulldozers is her old high school boyfriend and even though his entire career and future financial stability hinge on his driving a JCB right through her pralines, he can't ignore that irresistible attraction and warming festive glow that tells him they belong together.'

Nobody had asked Tam what Fabrizio bought him yet, so he was getting restless. 'This sounds like a shit movie.'

'Shut up! So they get married on the bulldozer, which they convert into a quaint little tea shop that he can park outside her chocolate shop and sell perfect little steaming cups of Earl Grey to go with her . . . I don't know . . . ferret and diesel-flavoured truffles. You get me? My Christmas was that good, that sickly sweet, that amazing. Yes.' Yes!

'Oh Lion, that sounds fantastic. The dream,' said Daisy, her alleged delight not reaching her eyes. She'd stretched to a third Christmas dinner this year — Seb had invited his parents up from London, and only told her two days before. 'I was straight to Sainsbury's, bought as many foil-tray warm-ups as I could, only for Papa Seb to announce he'd booked us a table in the Balmoral. Obviously didn't trust my cooking.'

'Daiz, you didn't trust your cooking either, otherwise you'd have actually cooked,' said Tam, who'd whisked Fabrizio away to a hotel in the Highlands. 'We room serviced everything. Well, until Fabrizio got an automated alert from his credit card company. I ate Christmas dinner in a robe. A waffle one.'

'Tam, if I did that, you'd think I was having a nervous breakdown.'

'Have you still got those candy-cane and Christmas cracker pyjamas, Lion?' He turned to Daisy. 'Honestly, lodging at his, I saw a whole other side to our Leo. The nightwear! Tell me you've since destroyed that moth-eaten dressing gown you've had since you were a teenager? It's like a minidress!'

'Of course I have!' I hadn't.

'Right, more drinks.' Tam only had to smile to put a rocket under every waiter in a ten-mile radius, but this wasn't that kind of place. He handed me his card. 'Can you go up, Lion? You never get ignored at the bar. I need more info on this picture-perfect Harvey Christmas. I don't get it. Are you choc-olate shop lady or tea-drinking bulldozer dude?'

Mica listened patiently to my retelling as we watched our gloomy colleagues troop into the staffroom with the enthusi-asm of someone going to the GP to have a lump checked. 'This Harvey chick sounds like he was constructed in a lab. I'm happy for you, though.'

She didn't look very happy for anyone, least of all herself, after a full-on Christmas with an antsy teenager. 'Sasha didn't care about the tree, didn't want half her dinner, didn't pretend to like the socks and knickers from her nan. She used to know her manners.'

'She's growing up.'

'She's growing into someone who's hard to be around. I don't get it. I can get twenty-five kids listening to me no problem, but one at home, who I've fed and kept in trainers for a decade and a half . . . ' Mica began to route in her humongous bag and brought out some sketchbooks. 'And this show, hanging over my head all Christmas. This is what I've got so far, concepts-wise, but I need a proper outline. I've got some ideas.'

I'd forgotten, of course, to tell her I'd kind of invented the whole show in a panic to make Campbell back off. I never told Joe, either. Shit. It kind of got away from me, caught up in my festive fantasy. Mica took it well. Quite well. Well-ish. Okay, once she stopped swearing.

'Sorry, there was that boring drama with my mum, then Harvey cancelled his plans for me and . . . '

'Yeah yeah, your chocolate bollocks Christmas. Brilliant. You've gone full main character, well done. If Campbell starts bugging me, I'm sending him your way. Head back in the game, please.'

I hated Mica being mad at me, especially when she was right. I wasn't usually so unreliable but, I suppose, it wasn't like I tested myself much. Easier not to let anyone down that way. I promised everything would be sorted by the end of the week, and tried to get round her with the promise of a drink, but she had to get home and play jailer to her daughter.

'Some boy at school was asking for pictures of her feet. Feet! We're living in a sewer.'

We saw Campbell sweep by the staffroom and instinctively ducked – despite our combined age of 80+ we were reduced to scared kittens – but he didn't seem to notice. He didn't even react when student teacher Alfie – French and Spanish, possibly gay, but more likely merely overzealous with the pomade – waved and wished him a happy new year. The door to his office definitely slammed. Shit.

I turned to Mica. 'Don't say it. This week. The show will get done. Definitely.'

I should've made a start on preparing that week's drama club, but there is nothing like a huge to-do list to send me into procrastination overdrive. Excess stardust from my magical Christmas hung all around me; the lights still twinkled everywhere, tinsel lurked in shop windows. Usually, Monday nights were for watching vintage gameshows or bad high school productions of *Hamilton* on YouTube, but I found myself on autopilot, skulking round a convenience store buying carbs I didn't want. The woman behind the counter called me 'sweetheart', so I hit the bright green smiley on the customer feedback pad to show my appreciation for the endearment. Dawdling home, I wandered into a bar I used to go to before I met Harvey, lured by its blinking, or maybe malfunctioning, fairy lights in the window, fashioned into the shape of a great big . . . well, you can guess.

Sometimes, if I'd been speaking to a guy online and couldn't gauge whether meeting at his flat would result in my name being read out on *Reporting Scotland* after the words 'the deceased', I'd arrange to meet here. There was something quaint about its refusal to embrace any post-millennium interior design trends: bouncy, cracked laminate floor sandblasted by noxious chemicals for decades; rope lighting along every cornice; the walls white, I supposed, underneath the many layers of posters promoting a roster of drag acts, karaoke sessions, bingo nights, comedy sets, fetishwear whist drives – all nights I'd haunted over the years when trying to work out what was out there for me. Nothing, usually. ('Ooh, she's different!' – Tam, constantly.) It was soothing, in an end-of-the-pier way. No pretensions, nobody looking down on anybody, everything offered and taken at face value.

Although it was Monday, and the place nearly empty, lights strobed in time to the noughties pop and R&B honking from the speakers. Dry ice dutifully belched into the room every four minutes. A barman who hadn't smiled since the last episode of *Sex and the City* nodded in acknowledgement but was shoved out of the way by a much friendlier, younger barman clearly desperate for human interaction. He seemed disappointed when I ordered only a pineapple juice, checking with me more than once that I didn't want tequila, vodka, rum or all three added to it.

'I'm just here for the ambience, doll.'

I was about to sit at a table when I imagined what a miserable tableau it would make for anyone walking in, so opted for a nonchalant lean, as if having a quick livener before dashing off somewhere else. I leafed through a few scattered flyers, enveloped by a thick plume of dry ice. As it began to clear, I glanced up and. I. Saw.

Him.

A ghost.

Leering at me through time.

The devil in Ted Baker.

Peter.

He was totally still, staring straight ahead, no doubt watching me fade up into view as I was him. My breath caught in my throat. This couldn't be happening. My feet were welded to the spot. I remembered a time when seeing him materialise through a mysterious fog would've thrilled me. He was alone. Husband at home, perhaps, or saving lives in the NHS, or watching their perfect daughter ace a school spelling bee or something.

What happened now? What did I want to happen now? I had nothing prepared; I'd genuinely hoped never to lay eyes on him ever again. There's a time when a relationship first ends, where you wonder how you'd react if you bumped into them? It comes at the strangest moments, about to turn a corner in a supermarket, or walking into a restaurant and scanning the blur of faces in case one sticks out. I'd been spared until now. Would he come over? Surely not. No ex so lousy with acrimony would, out of sheer decency. But I underestimated him, like I always did.

He stepped towards me. It's weird. How can something happen in a flash yet take place in slow motion? He told me I looked well, I think; I can't quite remember. The world didn't end, our surroundings refused to acknowledge this momentous and horrifying event. 'Don't Think I'm Not' continued to hammer away in the background. Facing Peter now was like peering between the tines of a fork for the first time; it's obvious, in a way, that the vile buildup of grime and bacteria must've always been there, but you still can't quite believe how grisly it is.

I made polite enquiries about his husband, he lied in return that he was sorry to have missed me at Christmas. On the surface, it was civil and composed, but that energy bubbled under, the power struggle of our relationship, still there in muscle memory. His eyes flicked to my patch of vitiligo then quickly swept the rest of my face for another.

When my vitiligo first appeared on my face, Peter was sympathetic in that way people are when they're relieved the bad thing happening to you isn't happening to them.

'I don't know how you're coping,' he'd said, literally wringing his hands in an impressive rendition of concern. 'I'd die if it happened to me. God, you must feel terrible. I still love you for who you are.'

People think of building resentment as simmering or fizzing inside you. A Trevi Fountain of bile, regret, and anger spunking off in all directions, lacerating your innards until you're left raw and burning. Not quite. With Peter, it was a loch, swirling, gently sloshing inside me, or sometimes perfectly still. Rising quietly, gently eroding my dignity.

'What are you drinking?' That last year together, after I gave up, he used to sniff my drinks, trying to catch me out.

'Pineapple juice.'

'Very refreshing. Still off the sauce, then?' He slugged back what I guessed was his usual double rum and Coke. So much Peter-related data still took up valuable space in my head. 'I'm glad.' Another speciality, making me sound like I used to be a drunk, forever hovering at rock bottom. 'Your mum says you've met someone. That's brilliant. Seems you've really turned things around.'

'Thanks.' I was glad the chirpy barman had put my drink in a thick tumbler; I was gripping it so hard, a more delicate glass might have shattered. I did my best to keep it steady, resisted the temptation to clamp my other hand round it. No trembling, he didn't deserve it.

'Are you okay? Do you want me to grab you some water? You seem a bit . . . anxious. Work still putting you through the mill, is it?'

I tried to keep my breathing even, but he was still very, very good at this. He'd been near me for no longer than two minutes and I already felt bilious. 'I'm brand new, thanks. Totally fine.' How many people who say they're fine actually mean it? Daisy was always pulling me up on it.

'Your mum was saying you're Tam's best man. Old Tam getting married! Never thought I'd see the day.' Proof he'd never taken much interest in my friends. This day was always coming for serially monogamous Tam; he led the charge in many a marriage equality march – admittedly, in disguise, in case his pupils saw. 'Big responsibility. You all organised?'

He was always fond of subtly suggesting I was a mess, even though he'd been the slob when we lived together. I didn't want to talk about Tam, bring Peter into my friends' world again. I liked that his knowledge of them was archaic, closed off, a mystery unsolved. But obviously my mother, who considered silence offensive, was key-carding him into it anyway.

'I'm not best man. Tam's brother is. I'm just turning up.' Information tumbled out of me. Born in a different era, in another country, Peter, a natural-born prefect, would've headed the KGB.

'Oh, right, I must've misheard. I'd have thought you were a shoo-in for the top job. Look, I just want to say . . . '

'Say what?'

He was so close I could smell the fur on his tongue. 'I understand if you find it difficult to . . . forgive me for how things ended. And maybe it's hard for you, to . . . I don't know, to see me and your mum still getting on.'

My mum was a poor judge of character; she was immovable on her opinions of disgraced entertainers from her youth. 'It's not up to me who my mum is pals with.'

'I could always confide in your mum,' he said, earnestly, knowing I'd struggled to do the same. 'Dawn's always been very understanding, you know, about us, your troubles, the drinking and everything . . . '

The drinking? I wanted to leave, so badly, but I was still rooted to the spot. It was good, in a way, to hear this out of his own mouth. An ugly mouth, I saw now. Sloppy, too pink. How had I ever allowed myself to enjoy the feel of it on me? I'd wondered how he'd managed to worm his way back into my family, who knew he'd cheated on me, if not the rest. I'd never probed, too afraid to lay The Unpleasantness bare. But now it made sense, how he'd discredited me. It can't have been that hard. The uppity son who thought he was a cut above, who played his cards close to his chest. Offered even the tiniest titbit on what was happening inside my head, my mum would've torn Peter's hand off. Crushing, really, how easily they must've believed it. It also explained why my mother now hardly drank at Christmas since Dad died, despite spending many a night down the social club standing on tables singing 'Robert De Niro's Waiting'. Even my brother would sip his tinny of Tennent's carefully in front of me rather than slosh it down his front like he used to. Mum had spent most of her childhood watching various members of her family risk, and lose, everything for one more drink. How could I ever untangle whatever mythology Peter created to tap into that familial shame, get himself off the hook and leave me on the outside looking in?

Observing my discomfort, he offered a pacifying smile. 'I'm sorry, I don't want to drag that up. In fact, all I want is a clean slate between me and you. There's something I should've told you. Something you have a right to know. I don't think I could accept your forgiveness until I have.'

I wasn't offering any forgiveness, I wanted to say, but my tongue decided to stay put.

Peter slowly licked those fluorescent nduja lips of his. I watched them part, one small thread of saliva between them refusing to break until the last second, when he placed his hand firmly on my forearm and said, with the brutal clarity of a doctor declaring time of death: 'Me and Tam. God, this is so hard to say. We had sex.'

No.

'It was just the once. Did he ever say? About a year before we broke up.'

God. No.

'You'd had a bit too much to drink, had gone to bed, and it just happened. It meant nothing, obviously.'

This couldn't be happening. It had to be a dream.

Peter smiled awkwardly. 'I really hope it doesn't spoil the wedding for you. I hope you'll forgive me. And Tam, of course.'

Right on cue, a column of dry ice billowed between us. As the pieces of my shattered heart landed in every corner of the planet, my survival instinct kicked in. I scooted sideways and out through the sweet-smelling mist to make sure that by the time it cleared, I'd be gone, vaporised like the wicked queen in a low-rent panto, so he'd never have the satisfaction of seeing the devastation on my face.

Seventeen

Like all new boyfriends, Peter started out charming and accom-modating. We met the old-fashioned way, in a terrible gay bar – long since shuttered – where I was in my usual spot on a bar stool with a wonky leg, slinging back long vodkas and guarding jackets while Daisy and Tam carved up the dance floor. Peter's friends hadn't shown up; he was ordering restorative shots, saw a lonely looking boy at the bar, and offered him one as consolation. We bonded over teaching, of being slightly out of step with the rest of our family, and, allegedly, 'tired' of the gay social scene.

What might it be like, we wondered aloud, if we didn't have to do this anymore? Nothing quite so grating as young people who act like they've done fifty years at the coalface of gay partying, but we all suffer the pretension. Knowing this handsome man was certainly only a day tripper from the friend zone, I made no effort to seduce, but must've shown him that 'something', I suppose, the strange magic invisible to me that I had no idea how to harness. He liked the idea of a nerdy boyfriend, I think, someone with quirks, just enough social awkwardness for it to be endearing, a few dents and scratches in my confidence that kept me grounded – on the understanding I would, eventually, elbow my way out of the chrysalis.

He changed. I didn't. He was more ambitious at work, used retail therapy for validation, became curious about the world around him in that way good-looking people always are, because they know it's theirs for the taking. His bedtime reading got heavier, his favourite movies more obscure, his clothing labels read dry-clean only. The higher he climbed, the less adorable my wise-cracking dweeb act became. You could say we plateaued. It felt like a nice way to live, for me: I didn't create drama, I didn't harbour unfulfilled aspirations, I knew myself and saw the best in others until they showed me otherwise. Peter never said it, but there was a sense I was holding him back, that I'd clipped his wings somehow. We moved in together, and as he placed the last box on the floor of the living room, he looked round, smiled, and said, 'This is it, then,' the grim resignation of an inmate unpacking his toothbrush in his cell.

Then, around two years before we broke up, it was like he'd been rebooted. He'd bounce through the door after 'a quick jar on the way home' and delve for ingredients in the fridge, making a show of grabbing pans out the cupboard.

'I'm gonna cook for us! One of my specials! Sit back, relax!'

I remember that warming relief. He was okay, better, out of the doldrums, less surly and frustrated. Crisis averted, I was enough, this was working. One night, though, he returned home late, face dark and inscrutable. Doors slammed, the soulless ping of a microwave ready meal. Later, I worked it out: there'd been someone else. Like Tam, Peter could never be alone. Before we met, he'd gone from one man to another; quick outfit changes like a Fringe show. I didn't kid myself Peter nursed even a tiny microbe of guilt and ended the affair; Peter was dumped. Maybe there'd been nothing at all and Peter had been lost in a crush that gave him enough hope to plan his exit from my life more kindly than he eventually did.

Once back down to earth, he drank more. I often joined him, hoping it might drown our sorrows quicker, but they floated — giant turds of sorrow bobbing on that loch of resentment. Despite doing his best the night before to create one, Peter never got hangovers, so in the mornings, over strong black coffee, while clog-wearing elephants tangoed inside my cranium, Peter would put his first-class English degree to good use, weaving tales which sounded like science fiction. He'd tell me, with the pained disappointment of a parent trying to see the best in their loser child, of my embarrassing behaviour the night before: slurring, idle threats, crying, committing violent acts against furniture. I was speechless with guilt and shame, terrified by this stranger within, but also curious: what unlocked this side of me? I'd been drunk with Daisy and Tam more times than I cared to remember — or even could, after machine-gunning tequilas — but they never mentioned anything like this. Were they embarrassed by me? Protecting me? Frightened of me? Of me?!

According to Peter, drunk me had the social graces of a werewolf mid-transformation, a violent side that negated my thirty years of saying 'please' and 'thank you' around two hundred times during any interaction with a waiter or person working a till. I started to think of myself in the third person, a helpless Dr Jekyll wading through ugly memories of my Mr Hyde exploits. What if I started showing myself up in public? What if my students' parents saw me? At my first job in Glasgow, one of the year heads went through a messy divorce and rocked up to presentation evening white-wine-drunk and took a piss in a football tournament trophy while hollering 'Flower of Scotland'; I didn't want that to be me. I didn't even know all the words to 'Flower of Scotland'.

I considered asking Daisy and Tam. Was I a bad drunk? A scary one? Or did I save this behaviour only for Peter? Didn't that make me an abusive boyfriend? I wasn't sure there was any comfort to be wrung from seeking their counsel. When it came to confiding in each other, they did the confiding and I dispensed my advice, usually ignored. Dishing my own problems was always tricky – Daisy and Tam had been through a lot. Anything could trigger a suppressed trauma, so my dilemma would remind them of some potboiler of their own, needing immediate dissection. It was quicker, in the end, not to say anything.

But something didn't sit right. Peter and I didn't actually speak much on nights out, or even when we sat and drank together, so my alleged transformation into a ranting monster seemed not impossible, but strange. The only remaining explanation was something I didn't want to face: Peter was lying. If he was lying, he was trying to make me feel bad, and if he was trying to make me feel bad, he didn't love me, and if he didn't love me . . . he would leave, and at this point, I couldn't imagine life without him or beyond him. The chokehold of the status quo. Peter was so connected to my present, thinking of him as history petrified me. I'd get over that later. Too late.

I toyed with using hidden cameras – my brother knew a wannabe Bond who filmed his cheating wife with a camera secreted in a box of After Eights. In the end, I started scribbling notes to myself before bed. What I'd done, the last thing I'd said. Often, it was drivel, and sometimes I forgot altogether and would spend the first fifteen minutes of the next day desperately searching every corner of my thundering brain. I had no way of knowing whether drunk me was a reliable narrator anyway. So I went undercover.

A party. Ross celebrating getting a new vacuum cleaner or something, who cared. I mixed Peter his traditional two 'getting ready' rum and Cokes but poured only a tonic for myself, without telling him. At the party, I realised nobody questions you so long as there's a glass in your hand – a tactic I still use with strangers. Anytime I was handed a drink, I'd pretend to sip then ditch it for a non-alcoholic version as soon as I could. Peter was yammering away to other people most of the night; whenever I walked into a room, he'd turn his back, like a kid who thinks all there is to hide-and-seek is covering their face. Being sober as everyone shedded their inhibitions was an eye-opener. Tam's mouth turned filthy, his then-boyfriend Keith mentally packing his belongings. Daisy became clingy, to me, to Tam, but most of all Seb, who she hunted down every half an hour to check . . . well, to check he wasn't doing what he was usually doing. Ross's citric barbs, which I usually dismissed as a relic of the age he came out in, back when people treated everyone like shit as a defence mechanism, became less playful and sounded more pathetic. When I refused a canapé – a greasy square of beige filled with a pesto, in the advanced stages of E. coli – Ross pinched my waist.

'Worried you'll put the weight back on?'

'What weight? There's never been any weight.'

'Spiky little wallflower. Nothing worse than a fatso who gets skinny and thinks it makes them interesting.' His beady eyes sparkled at having landed a knockout punch.

Ordinarily I'd have shrugged or played along, but the devil got hold of me and I liked it. Sober, I could say what I wanted without stammering or skipping a syllable.

'When was the last time someone smiled when you walked into the room, Ross?'

I was never short of a sassy reply but sober this felt like even more of a slam to the balls. 'Were any of us born? Who was president of the US? Or was Walter Raleigh still over there digging up potatoes?'

'You're drunk,' he spat, and stalked off. He'd have forgotten by morning, but I'd always have that moment.

In the cab home, Peter moaned about being trapped with dullards all night. 'How much have you had to drink? You can barely speak.'

'I'm fine,' I said, but faked a wobble as I searched for my door key. He poured himself a final rum while I escaped to bed. The next day, I crept to the lounge feigning the pain of a thousand prosecco-laced daggers. Peter was in black loungewear, sipping coffee, and doing toe stretches while watching something loud on television, a white woman with corn rows preparing an approximation of gnocchi. I covered my ears, and winced as I sat. I waited.

'Aren't you going to say sorry?' He didn't look at me.

'What for?' Maybe Ross had complained.

'For your behaviour.'

Behaviour. Such a teacher word. I tried not to use it, but Peter was never off duty. Still, a part of me doubted myself. The last shreds of my delusion. I retraced my steps, looking for any opportunity I could've been an ogre. At the door: Have you got your key? In the cab: Have you got your scarf? As we left:

Did you say goodbye to everyone? Before that: Shall I order a cab? I could've gone on. 'What?'

'Don't want to remember? Cool. I won't mention it. It was very upsetting, that's all, I don't understand what I did.'

I can still taste the fear. 'Tell me.'

'Fine. Don't shoot the messenger. These are direct quotes.' He flicked off the TV. I suddenly missed shouty gnocchi lady; I felt very alone. 'You wished you'd never met me, couldn't stand the sight of me, even hearing my voice . . . ' He stopped and choked back a tear and, honestly, I was impressed. 'That sometimes . . . what was it now? Oh yeah, it would be nice if I'd just disappear.'

I had him. He was lying. Unless I had an evil twin – who only Peter could see – this hadn't happened. I'd never talk that way. I wasn't spiteful, drunk or sober. These weren't my words, Peter was reading me the contents of his own head, what he wished I'd say so he could play victim. Everything had changed, yet nothing had changed. I found myself saying sorry, I'd never do it again, because the alternative was too frightening. Did I sometimes feel that way about him? Maybe, on the nights he made me feel small and alone. But he still had a hold on me. Lightning couldn't strike twice, I'd never meet someone else who'd overlook everything that was wrong with me. Wasn't it better to be half loved, or have the memory of it, than not be loved at all?

But a change was coming. If I was to get through it, I needed a clear head, to be on my guard. I didn't touch another drop of alcohol. And even though I knew Peter was lying then, it didn't mean he was lying now, about him and Tam, did it? Stopped clocks and all that.

Eighteen

I might not be ambitious, but avoidance has always made me industrious. In those last days with Peter, I joined every school committee I could – sobriety gave me heaps of time. Same when my dad died, I focused on the extracurricular, making promises I had to deliver on, firing off so many ideas that my colleagues grew sick of me, eager for my inevitable slump. Those first few days after seeing Peter in the bar, I kept telling myself over and over it couldn't possibly be true. Peter wasn't afraid to wound; no way would he have resisted telling me before now. More importantly, Tam would never do that to me. Or to Peter.

But then, in quiet moments, my personal archives would play on a loop in my mind. Their arch banter, amiably arguing about books so loudly people in the pub would look over. 'Let's agree to disagree' – what else did they agree to do? Fuck? On my lounge floor? When I could bring myself to imagine it, I saw them defiling my plush shaggy rug out of that posh furniture shop in Stockbridge. Peter's pasty body slithering on Tam's undulating, sculpted contours.

No.

No!

They wouldn't. He wouldn't. It was too much. This was Peter at his manipulative best, knowing I'd overthink and catastrophise and spiral, hoping I'd confront Tam and destroy everything. Tam, who loved me like a brother. Tam, who despite his filthy drunken patter, believed in love, honour and romance way more than me or Daisy. No. The greatest compliment a gay man can give another is friendship with no conditions attached. What Tam and I had was pure.

I couldn't burden Daisy with this; she would've made it bigger than it needed to be. She could elevate a missing lip balm to top story on the evening news. She was ailing with seasonal flu, anyway – missed her jab appointment, distracted by a sale on wardrobe organisers in John Lewis. Confiding in Harvey was out too. I couldn't let Peter infiltrate our bubble. Harvey was otherwise engaged, anyway, first by the flu he must've caught from Daisy, then a week in Frankfurt for work. He rejected my offer to play nurse.

'You can't get sick. Your protégées depend on you, Mr Sondheim.'

So I put my head down, worked on the script, performing my best rousing monologue to my drama club and S3 and S4 classes to encourage them to help deliver a masterpiece. When I wasn't working, I ran. Harvey lent me his car while he was away, so I drove to the edges of civilisation – well, out near the airport – and pounded unfamiliar ground. On and on and on, relentless, all weathers, until my knees buckled, and my chest heaved, and I couldn't see Peter's leering face anymore. Harvey's car smelled of him, of us. I'd never liked being a passenger in any car but – this sounds weird – in Harvey's driver's seat, my body absorbed his strength and composure. I felt safe. I practised driving like him, patiently, gently – except when he floored it at amber. A piece of him was with me, he'd trusted me with something precious. Just a car I know, but still.

One day, I don't know why, I pulled over, still panting from my run, and peeked in the glove compartment. I wasn't sure what I was expecting to find, a little clue to a part of Harvey I didn't know, maybe. There was a photo. A man, in a running vest. London Marathon, I guessed. Medal nestling in dark chest hair, proud beam dominating his face. Matt.

And another, the two of them this time, standing by some climbing wall or something. Matt was holding a small trophy, a boulder in glimmering gold. I'd seen it in Harvey's flat, on a high shelf; it hadn't occurred to me it wasn't his. Harvey looked on, smiling widely, eyes flaming with adoration. I was shaking as I took in Matt's face for the first time. Wholesome. Clear. Handsome. Hair swept to the side, a few strands in his eyes in that hot, casual way of romantic heroes in airport novels. My hair never fell over my eyes, unless I got caught in a downpour. I was intruding, felt dirty. I returned the photos and snapped the glove compartment shut. Cogs of uncertainty clunked back into action. Had the photos always been there, or was Harvey looking at them recently? How long had he owned this car? It didn't matter. Harvey was with me now. Harvey didn't care about Matt. Fuck his hair. Matt was history. I was the future.

When the *Hidden Talents* script was more or less done – I still had to nail that final solo – I took it to Campbell's office with a flourish. He'd seemed in dire need of lightening up since the

Christmas break, so to impress upon him the ceremony of the occasion, I printed out a copy, fished a cheap velvety cushion out of the props store, and lay the papers on it, bowing while I placed it on his desk as if handing over the Koh-i-Noor diamond. 'Your script, my liege.'

I waited patiently for my laugh but got only a smile that barely used half a calorie. 'Thanks.'

What to do? Sit? Stand? Jazz hands? 'Hope you like it.'

'I'm sure I will.' He went back to his screen. What? No 'I knew I could rely on you' or similar plaudit from his bottomless vaults of positivity? If I'd walked in ten feet tall, I was now down with the grasshoppers. He could've at least shuffled the pages.

'If you've any questions . . .'

'I'm sure I won't. If I do, I'll get a note to you.'

Was that it? Okay, so Lin-Manuel Miranda wouldn't be heading for early retirement if he read it, but I'd poured everything into eighty-five minutes' worth of comedy, drama and campery. All I got was the promise of a note? When I've made an effort I like to know I've impressed. I pride myself on being the speediest and the best behaved person airport security will meet that day. Maybe even week. I've always mopped up praise like ciabatta through spaghetti sauce. 'I'll leave it with you, then.'

'Great, thanks.'

I closed the door carefully to quash the temptation to flounce. I found Mica in the staffroom in a furious speed round of texting Sasha, denying permission for whatever rite of passage her daughter was demanding now.

'That was quick. How'd it go?'

'I don't know.' But I found out soon enough.

I was rearranging my beanbags after a boisterous class when Campbell marched in, script in hand. Obviously more than a note's worth of feedback. No glasses. Giving contacts a go, or left his specs in the office? His eyes were puffy, whites raw and pink like he'd been chopping onions. Bit early for hay fever.

'You said it was finished. Where's this solo?'

I explained I couldn't find the right cover version to redeem the villainous judge. Joe Music already warned me his students were threatening to protest on the rugby field if he tried to force them to write more songs.

'Why hand it in if it wasn't finished?'

'Hand it in? I . . . ' Wow, suddenly I was back in maths class, Mrs Larrad with purple talons outstretched for my algebra homework, which I'd jettisoned in favour of *Carousel* on some obscure movie channel at 1 a.m. 'Like I said . . . we haven't found the . . . '

Campbell tossed the script on my desk. The pages fanned out like playing cards. 'This is a waste of my time. I need to see a finished project. You're handing me a sandwich with no top layer of bread.'

I could deal with the sarcasm, but the tone stung. 'Open sandwiches are popular for those on low-carb . . . ' He wasn't smiling. 'Right. I'm sorry.'

'I thought you'd embrace this challenge. Have I misjudged? Do we need Chris or Emerald to push things along?'

He really didn't know those two well enough if he thought for even a second they wouldn't make it more of a disaster. 'We don't. Your bread is on its way. No sweat.'

He walked away without a word. I sat staring at the floor,

chastened and embarrassed. Maybe I wasn't good at my job. Maybe I'd been winging it all these years. 'Fuck. Great big balls of fuck.'

'Mr Falconer?'

I jumped and turned to see Iqra, one of my students, emerge from my 'cosy corner', an alcove off the main studio with shelves of old scripts and magazines for 'inspiration'. It wasn't unusual for a student to drag a beanbag in there at break and mess about on their phone. I didn't mind, usually.

'Shouldn't you be on your way home?'

'I forgot my key and my mum's not back until five. Look, I heard you and Naomi, uh, Campbell.'

'*Mister* Campbell.'

'Yeah. Um. I've, like, got a song.'

'A cover? For the solo? Does it actually have lyrics? Is it . . . lewd? It doesn't have a dance routine, does it?'

Iqra had the good manners to laugh at my approximation of a very old person being introduced to grime music. 'Sir! No, I wrote it.'

I immediately retreated to my inner databank for information gleaned about Iqra in the three years I'd been teaching her. Never more sassy than was necessary, which was good (always disappointing when a student didn't have at least a little bite – I was running a drama class not a finishing school); she thought acting was lame but liked creating dialogue and was interested in lighting and sound; and I'd never heard her sing a note.

'I think it's good. Someone with a decent voice could do it. It's on my phone.'

I'd taught my students there was no such thing as a bad idea. It wasn't always true, and sometimes I had to politely smile through some stinkers, but encouragement could supercharge even the most switched-off student.

'Can I hear it?'

'Yeah, but not when I'm here, okay? And don't play it to anyone else. My voice is really bad.'

'I'm sure it isn't.' She mailed me the song and heaved her bag onto her back and made to leave. 'Why didn't you submit this before?'

'I didn't know it was allowed. I don't do music; I can't play instruments that good. I sound like fireworks when I sing.'

'At this stage, Iqra, I'd consider asking the rats living by the canteen bins if they had a song for me.'

'The canteen has rats?!'

'Ehhhhh, no. Just my joke. I can't guarantee I'll use it, but . . . I'm looking forward to hearing it.'

'It's good, sir, I think.'

I pressed play, praying for Sondheim, expecting dirge-period Lloyd Webber, and getting . . . a truly beautiful song, one that could be something special with a bit of work. Iqra's voice wasn't as bad as she said – she could've easily understudied for a reality TV star in a limited West End run, but the song required more power.

I found her the next day and asked for a word – she glared at me like I'd asked to frisk her for controlled substances.

'I'd like to play the song to a few other people, like Mr Robb and Ms Harrison and Mr Campbell, so we can consider it for the show.'

'No way.'

I had a brainwave: 'If you send me the backing track and lyrics, I could record a quick demo to play for the others . . . '

'Can you sing, sir?'

It'd been a while since I'd necked five Jägerbombs and grabbed a karaoke mic, but as I proudly told Iqra, I'd played the lead in my school production of *Beauty and the Beast*.

'Which one were you, sir?'

'Just send the track, thank you, Iqra.'

I recorded it a few times, mailing the least terrible take to Mica, Joe and Campbell. Mica's phone was grafted onto her hand and she never let messages languish unread. 'Mate, if I'd had a phone when I was a teenager, I'd have been a nervous wreck. Playing it cool? Forget it,' she once said. She loved the song. Joe was grateful I wasn't asking for more solo ideas. We had it! I knew it. All I needed was the nod from my nemesis. He'd read the message. But no reply. Not that night, not Saturday and not Sunday. To make things worse, Harvey messaged Sunday night to say he was staying in Frankfurt an extra two days. I'd been looking forward to driving out to Edinburgh airport and going rom-com daft in arrivals. I'd made a banner and everything. Was I losing my head? I didn't care, I wouldn't miss it.

By Monday morning, I was ready for war. I marched to Campbell's lair and was about to barge in when I remembered the summer I'd worked in Gap as a student and had swept back the fitting room curtain to find a man massaging his prostate with a clothes hanger. I knocked, heard a weary sigh, and thrust open the door, to find Campbell looking ... well, like he'd had quite a weekend of it, scrolling through his phone with the same expression I use when checking my bank balance two days before pay day. I thought it best to launch straight into it.

'I didn't expect a ticker-tape parade, or Vegas showgirls

waiting in the car park this morning, but an acknowledgement would've been nice.'

He didn't look away from his screen. 'What?'

'The song. The script. I got it done . . . with last-minute help from Iqra Habeeb. You never replied.'

Campbell moved his head slowly to face me, like it was made of stone. Nothing so annoying as someone being really calm when you're hyped and hysterical. 'It was the weekend, Mr Falconer.'

Okay, he had me there, but he wasn't concerned about my free time when he was breathing down my neck. 'What did you think of the song?'

'It's fine.'

Fine?! 'Is that all?' Now I understood why that word got on Daisy's and Tam's tits so much.

Campbell took his glasses off and rubbed his eyes. 'Leo . . . must we do this now?'

Whoa. The 'Leo' disarmed me, reminded me I was talking to a person, not the automated bot who lived inside my mortgage helpline. I shouldn't have bowled in being aggressive; I wasn't good at playing antagonist. A single tear tracked Campbell's cheekbone. I was losing face rapidly.

'Right, well, okay. I was just asking. I . . . Right then. So . . . give me the green light when you get a minute.'

Glasses back on. His business persona immediately reclaimed possession of his body from whatever fragile ghost he'd almost let me see. 'Consider it green. Your next mission is to draw up a rehearsal schedule so I can make sure I'm available to help out.'

You know in cartoons when . . . oh I don't know, Wile E

Coyote realises the piano falling from the sky is about to squish him and his eyes bulge out in horror? Yeah, that.

'Schedule? You'll be sitting in? On my rehearsals?'

'I'm hands on. Did I tell you I directed a variety show at my last school? So, sooner the better. Shall we say Wednesday?' He made a show of shuffling papers on his desk, which I could plainly see was overflow printer debris with nothing of consequence on them. 'I must crack on.'

I left his door open to let him know how much I hated him in that moment; whoever had brought that tear to his eye had my full respect.

Nineteen

Outside school, I was never one for making plans or heading up group activities. My brain didn't work that way. Harvey, like Daisy, was one of life's great organisers. He'd always nudge me into coming up with a plan for our day together and I'd pretend to think really hard – making 'mmmm' and 'ooooh' noises to show I was concentrating – before flopping back on the sofa and giving in. 'What do *you* think we should do?'

One night Harvey cancelled our date because he had a presentation to finish. I tried not to overthink this into meaning he was sick of generating ideas and was seconds away from dumping me. Since getting back from Frankfurt he'd been more affectionate than ever – they weren't kidding about absence making the heart grow fonder. A night apart would make the next date even better, I told myself, but I was still at a loose end. Well, not entirely loose. I could've worked on stuff for *Hidden Talents* but I was at a very tricky stage getting to grips with the misogyny in the dialogue written by my resident troublemaker student, Calvin McLeish. An attitude learned, no doubt, from a father who'd told his wife to shut up in front of me at parents' evening. He drove a Tesla.

I hadn't spoken to Tam and Daisy in the last month or so, not since I'd seen Peter. They probably didn't notice; I never fired off an initial text and I often took ages to reply, or cried off meeting up because of a school problem. But it was almost becoming a thing. To me, anyway. The longer I left it, the harder it would be to act normal next time I saw them.

So I did the unthinkable, the unpredictable, the . . . perhaps unwise thing of dropping in on Tam unannounced, like we were in a nineties sitcom and not the kind of people who usually sent twenty-plus messages in advance to confirm a quick drink after work. I suppose I wanted to know how I'd feel, seeing Tam, knowing what I knew. I'd spider-diagrammed every syllable of what Peter said and had, by this point, convinced myself Peter was lying to cause trouble, for the fun of it. He was always jealous of my closeness to Tam and Daisy, and the warmth that came from years of knowing what someone would say next.

Tam opened the door with enough force to pull down a supporting wall. He stood breathless, distracted; if he'd been thirty years older and not someone who couldn't even say the word 'pastry' let alone eat it, I'd assume heart attack or perhaps a strenuous hour on Fabrizio's Peloton.

'What are you doing here? I mean . . . hi, cool, but . . . no, come in. Come in.'

Fabrizio was out, but not long departed, I could tell – a news channel foghorned from the TV. Tam preferred true crime podcasts – horrifyingly, he found them relaxing. 'Quite reassuring that my life could be so much worse.' He only watched the news if he heard a celebrity died and, as far as I knew, flags flew at full mast in Hollywood that night. Something was wrong. He poured me a Diet Coke and grabbed himself some wine. He stopped, put the wine back in the fridge, and took out a Diet Coke instead.

'Ooh. My impact.'

Tam laughed but it was forced. 'Get fucked, you Jesuit. I'm sure you've got a secret gin still in your flat.' A hurried blown kiss. 'Ooh, hang on, do you fancy a hot chocolate? I bought one of those machines. You know. You put the flakes in.'

Just like the one Peter had bought my mum for Christmas. There was no escape. 'Christ. What's wrong with a pan and a whisk? You don't even like chocolate.'

'You know I can't resist Debbie on that shopping channel. It's the way she taps everything with her acrylics. Anyway, it's for guests. Nice guests. So not you.'

'Come on, then. Have you had a row?'

Tam nodded. That angel face, no wonder his mother had spoiled him.

'You should've called. What's up?'

'Don't you usually see Harvey tonight?' I was impressed he'd been paying attention.

'What. Is. Up? Or should I guess? You've found out he refers to you as "this one" on his Instagram?'

Tam's hand zoomed to his mouth. 'Did Daisy tell you? I know. It's awful. Is it worse or better than being "The Boy"?'

Knew it. 'Seriously, Tam. Spill, or I'll be forced to try my first headlock.'

With the energy of a marathon runner seconds from

finish-line collapse, Tam reached for the remote control and muted the White House press briefing. 'Money. His lack of. My spending it. Ugh.'

'Start at the beginning.'

'Remember that night at Ross's when you said you went to that shit restaurant?'

'Well, not shit, according to Fabrizio, but not great for us. What about it?'

'It's exactly that. It was a shit restaurant.'

'But Fabrizio raved about it! Constellations of stars in that review! Patti LuPone doing "Don't Cry For Me Argentina" at the Grammys levels of praise.'

'Which year at the Grammys, because, frankly . . . Look, no, anyway. He hated it.' Tam got up from his chair and sat next to me on the sofa, close, as if hidden mics were recording our conversation. 'He's been taking . . . encouragements, to help pay for the wedding.'

'Kickbacks?'

'Shush, Lion, Christ! I may have gone a teensy bit overboard and we're having to . . . accommodate.'

'Things can't be that bad.' Tam's face alone contradicted me. See, he couldn't hide from me. Peter was definitely lying. 'If I can help in any way . . .'

Tam had the decency not to laugh at the suggestion I'd be in any position to pay for anything other than the rice to be thrown after the vows.

'It's my fault. I wanted it to be perfect. On reflection, paying for everyone's flights to the wedding was ambitious.'

'I did say. Look, people will still come without an all-expenses trip, if that's what you're worried about. We're not famous.' My smile was supposed to be reassuring but Tam looked unnerved.

'He's ordered me to scale things back.'

'Smaller weddings are lovely.' Tam's spending was nothing new, though. Even before Fabrizio, his attitude to credit had been buy now, panic later (or just move house). This row had to be about something else.

'His boss went to that new place, Thistle Locale, you know the one, all leopard print banquettes and art that looks like butt plugs?' Harvey and I had paid the GDP of a small principality for limp reheated nachos there once. 'Obviously it was shit, and will be closed by Easter, so he was pissed off that Fabrizio raved about it. I said to him, where does it stop? What if Burger King offer him a grand to give them five stars?'

'How about, "So nice to finally get my hands on a decent whopper"? He can have that for free.'

'You cow,' said Tam, digging me in the side, but laughing. 'You're right, I should've called. You always know what to say.'

Not always, I thought, remembering Campbell's wounded expression as I'd left his office. Tam asked after Harvey, and I tried not to gush too much – not after he'd just had an almighty row with his fiancé.

'I'm so happy you met someone, Lion, and that you're . . . uh, that we get to see you like this, you know?'

I didn't. Not really. See me like what? How did he normally see me? I thought of an intelligent response that would get Tam to open up immediately. Alas: 'Huh?'

'Well, me and Daisy were saying. Nothing bad. The Menergize thing. Those guys. Why did you keep that from us . . . well, from me? I can kinda get maybe not wanting

Daisy to go all . . . Daisy about it. Were you embarrassed or something?'

'No, course not. I just wanted to see if any of them were going anywhere and when they didn't, that was that. Nothing to tell.' What a liar. The truth would hurt Tam and make me look bad. Graeme, Mark, the other one, and the other other one. Jake, was it? They'd never have fit in, wouldn't have survived the scrutiny. They were perfectly nice, friendly men, with enough social awkwardness to make me feel one podium spot ahead. But pit them against Daisy and Tam, and Fabrizio, and Ross, and everyone else fluttering about our circle, and they'd crumble. They were like me, magnolia lads, resplendent in their plain-ness. There was only one slot for a gangly cardigan enthusiast in this mob. I'd have needed to play interpreter, decoding their niche hobbies, dietary requirements and talent for finding joy in small things, stuff born winners like Tam and Daisy would never even think about. I'd have to endure the terror in their eyes when they realised they didn't belong. They weren't bad friends, we weren't an impenetrable clique, but we had our own way of rubbing along, and you either got it, or you didn't. Like Peter, though, Harvey was pre-packed, specially formulated; he looked, smelled and acted the part. He was a winner. Even if he didn't quite slot into the dynamic, he could handle it.

'So . . . Harvey's going somewhere? He's the real deal?'

The door slammed and Fabrizio strode in with the brash-ness of someone not expecting to find a visitor on the sofa wolfing sea salt and balsamic flavour crisps out of a bowl Tam once made at a singles' pottery class. Immediately subdued, he hugged me without touching me. 'Hey, Leo. Great to see you.' I hoped his fictitious reviews were more convincing.

I stayed five more minutes and yakked on about my show, to reassure Fabrizio we hadn't been talking about him, then invented a small lie about my brother cooking dinner for me, which almost made Tam choke. Duncan's entire diet came in a flat box, delivered by a man in a motorcycle helmet.

'I'll see you out.'

I paused at the door. Tam shivered in the cold air, for effect more than anything.

'Please don't overdo this wedding. All anyone wants is to see two people they love tie the knot, hopefully not round each other's necks. Okay? Small is good.'

'Sure. I'll downgrade your flight to being fired out of a cannon from Calton Hill. How's that?'

'Perfect.'

Twenty

In any job, you have to care about the customer, or at least make a good fist of pretending you do. But when you're a teacher, it's never clear who your customer actually is. Your headteacher? Head of year? Course director? Your students? Their parents — who, at times, certainly treat you like their customer service rep for a faulty kettle? Maybe it's society as a whole? You can't factor them all in, that's the problem. You must focus on one.

Given I'd spend five hours or so a day under their terrorising gaze, I prioritised my students. Not every teacher did, and I won't judge those who chased league table rosettes or end-of-term cupcakes. But seriously. You can't please everyone, and you shouldn't try. I was learning this the hard way, trying to cast the role of the evil judge to sing Iqra's show-stopping solo in *Hidden Talents*. Iqra ignored my assurances this would be a star-making role for her, reminding me she couldn't sing (she could), that she was happier backstage, and warning me that having The Big Bad of the show turning out to be a Muslim girl was a terrible look — despite the song's redemptive theme. In fact, she said, that made it worse.

'Evil Muslim girl stays hidden all through the show, sees the error of her ways thanks to a load of white stage kids, then, like, jumps about singing we're all equals? Yikes, Mr Falconer.'

Only one student openly wanted it. Lewis Cunningham, the matinee idol of S5. Hyper-talented, with the naked ambition of ten starlet-era Marilyn Monroes, he'd take on anything as long as it had the highest line count. And he did count them: if he didn't run out of fingers twice when going through any script – even a quick scene to demonstrate a rehearsal technique – he'd ask for a casting change. He was a decent enough kid, as most classroom horrors were deep down, but he believed attention was a finite resource and wanted to hoard as much as possible. He had his eye on the solo, but there was one problem: he already had a meaty role as one of the plucky fame-hungry upstarts – not exactly a stretch – and refused to give it up. I was glad this technicality kept the role from him; I wanted someone else to experience the enlivening heat of the spotlight.

One afternoon, I was caught in a last-minute 'where the hell are my keys' panicked pocket-search at the school gates when an attractive blond couple who looked like siblings from a period drama blocked my path. It took a second for me to recognise the father's upturned nose.

'Mr Falconer! The part. The judge. You. Teacher. Right?' Doug Cunningham, Lewis's dad, barking at me like I was a sodding Alexa.

I gave my finest diplomatic grin, enjoying Mrs Cunningham's evident revulsion at my crooked gnashers. They were concerned Lewis was missing a terrific opportunity. I resisted the temptation to answer it would be the first of many if he didn't watch his attitude.

'Mr and Mrs Cunningham. The show's a joint effort between three drama groups. There are twenty-one students in Lewis's class alone, and not enough speaking roles to go round, least of all enough to give him two.'

'Look, I wasn't sure about this acting lark, to be honest. I was worried he might . . . well, you know.' Mr Cunningham winked. Most unsettling. Of course I knew. Lewis Cunningham was not remotely gay. He didn't have the right walk. 'But the kid's got talent in spades. He wiped the floor with them in *Grease* last year. Why shouldn't he have two?'

There it was. Lewis Cunningham was talented, confident and guaranteed to develop moviestar looks – yet it wasn't enough. They wanted him to have everything.

'This isn't how I operate, Mr Cunningham. I'm here to teach all aspects of drama, not just acting, to everyone, not only the most talented. Lewis will have ample time to shine.'

'Not if we pulled him from the show.'

I'd heard of angry parents withdrawing permission for sex education or social studies but not drama. 'Participation in the end-of-year show is compulsory for students aiming for a qualification in drama, Mrs Cunningham.'

'He can turn down the lead role. You can't make anyone act. Lewis told us.'

I wondered what curfew negotiations were like in the Cunningham household, or discussions of what to have for dinner, threats of retaliation over uneaten pomegranate salad. Could I afford to lose my star singer? I was willing to take the risk. I'd put him backstage polishing boots for wardrobe.

'That would be a shame, Mr Cunningham, but I have other students who'd be thrilled to take it on.'

He came close to my face, not in a threatening way, but more like a cat trying to work out how seriously to take your stare. 'Who's your superior?'

I could argue the toss or accept the inevitable, and give Lewis the role. Ah, fuck it, I thought, delay the agony a day or two. 'That would be Mr Campbell, our deputy head, responsible for arts education. Must dash. Have a lovely evening.'

A note was waiting the next day. I left Mica trying to find a clean mug in the dishwasher, which was clogged with Emerald's porridge as usual. 'Wow, he must really fancy you if he wants to see you before your face has woken up.'

I refused Campbell's offer of an espresso and a seat. 'I prefer to stand.' Something in me wanted to snap his laptop shut on his fingers.

'No need to be melodramatic. This isn't a firing squad.'

I sat, my cheeks sizzling. By the time the Cunninghams had got to him, my contribution to the controversy had turned from a polite refusal outside the school gates to Godzilla grabbing them by the throat and declaring I was hellbent on ruining their son's career.

'Are you gonna make me give Lewis the solo?'

'No, I'm not. But they said no other student's good enough to do it.'

And there was me thinking Mr Cunningham ran a car showroom and his wife worked in planning at the council – I'd no idea they were qualified Hollywood talent scouts!

'That isn't the point,' I said. 'He can't hoover up all the good parts. What about Iqra? And Calvin? And . . . well, most of them. When do they get to shine?'

'Not everyone has what it takes to be the lead, though.'
Didn't I know it. 'They'll pull him from the show if another
student does it. They're calling it discrimination.'

'Fucking hell.' I tried to read Campbell's expression.
Bemusement? God, wasn't he tired of our little exchanges?
Wouldn't he rather be compiling budget reports or . . . whatever it was April definitely never bothered doing when she was
here? 'Sorry to swear.'

'I have a solution. Staring me in the face, really. Or the ears.
I want you to do it.'

'Do what?'

'The solo. You can sing, you sounded incredible on that demo,
you know, the one I didn't listen to fast enough for your liking.'

What the hell? I liked my anxiety dreams to stay where they
belonged, as fantasy. I couldn't get on stage, not as a grown-
up. I imagined the gasps from parents as I aimed for, and sailed
right past, every note, students smirking as I gyrated with the
pathetic unease of an uncle at a wedding. 'I recorded that on
my phone, in half an hour.'

Campbell stood up. 'Then you'll be even better with a
proper mic, a set behind you, students doing harmonies.'

'I'm a teacher!'

'Exactly! Show parents why their child's talent is better
moulded by you. The Cunninghams agree it's the fairest solution, and it means Lewis is still our leading man.'

'The Cunninghams? Why are we pandering . . . look, you
don't understand. I'm not an actor or a singer. I don't want to
be on stage. I don't have the . . . what it takes.'

He wasn't listening, started bustling me out. The door was
open, I was already in the corridor.

'You can't do this.'

'No, but you can. Your job is to help your students reach their full potential, my job is to help you reach yours. It'll be fantastic, Leo. So glad you're on board.' He grinned widely, the use of my first name disorienting me again. He knew. 'I believe in you, truly.'

I didn't care if he believed in me. I wasn't a toddler peering over the edge of a two-metre diving board. This was revenge; he was setting me up to fail. Bastard.

Twenty-One

Those three little words — that magic curse that binds you together. Harvey hadn't said them yet. How long had it been now? I wasn't counting in case focusing too forensically might make it come undone. Okay, I was counting: eight months. A long time without the three little words — but our three little squeezes acted as a stand-in. When I'd asked Peter whether he loved me, he usually replied, 'Of course I do,' and it never quite rang true. It was another two years before he admitted he didn't, and I certainly believed him then; he was wheeling two suitcases out to a van paid for by the man he was leaving me for. Peter had never been in love with me; we'd mistaken a fleeting sexual attraction and similar likes — books, beer, boys — for strong enough foundations for our prefab relationship.

All I'd ever wanted was to know what it was like to have someone to fall in love with me. I'd grown up on declarations of love, soundtracked by Sondheim. Furtive glances, secret kisses, champagne in hotel rooms and star-crossed lovers gazing across parks or dreamy cityscapes. It's not too much to ask, is it? To feel the overwhelming rush of being adored, so forceful you need to grab onto something to avoid being swept away, even though you wonder, as you try to focus, whether drowning in it would be so bad. Harvey was the closest I'd come to that heartstopping, rapturous feeling, and I didn't want to break the spell.

So, for every day Harvey didn't say 'I love you', I thought of the times Peter did, but hadn't meant it, or used it as a bargaining tool. Harvey was more show than tell. I felt his love, the glow of it, the tingle, the excitement from being around each other – a light in his eyes, the quickening of his footsteps toward me, the graze of his hand on the back of my neck as we embraced hello – even though he had to reach up a bit. It was all there, unsaid. Love came from showing me I lived in his thoughts. A cup of tea waiting on the kitchen counter (he once brought me one in bed but I was so nervous about spillages on his pristine linen, I could barely drink it). A message every lunchtime, checking in. He not only remembered my varying complaints about my working day but referred to them much later, reciting names and their misdeeds with a stenographer's accuracy.

This desire to make him happy – and perhaps extract the sacred three words from his lips – meant I found myself saying I was open to trying out another of his hobbies. He suggested the gym, which . . . Well, I'd never fancied institutionalised fitness, membership cards felt like an obligation to fail, but I agreed to book an induction 'soon', once school quietened down.

Early workshops for the show started and it was dark when they finished. Campbell offered me a lift home in his car, which I noticed was no longer valeted and featured the genesis of a coffee cup museum in its footwells. I refused politely. Harvey liked to come collect me. He'd be waiting in the exact same space at the far end of the car park, phone lighting up his face like a beacon that made me feel slightly unusual as I walked toward it. I didn't need to hear those three words.

One evening, however, it wasn't Harvey waiting, but Daisy. My immediate thought was catastrophe. Somebody was dead. My mother. Seb. Harvey! Campbell was wittering about some trifling script issue – still miles from a final draft, he was a master swords-man wielding his red pen – but all I could focus on was Daisy's haunted face – the look of someone who's just remembered there are tiny mites that live in your eyelashes. It had been ages since I'd seen her; a kick of guilt made me swallow, hard. Daisy's gaze fell upon Campbell. She squinted, then made a face you might pull if you were trying black pudding for the first time and weren't sure what to make of it. 'Isn't it . . . aren't you? Alex, right?'

What the . . . ? Weirder still, Campbell seemed to know her. 'Hey, yes . . . uh, Maisie?'

'Daisy. I had no idea you . . . knew Leo.'

Knowing Daisy Forbes as I do, I knew for a fact she was about to say 'I had no idea you were a teacher' but quickly realised they'd discussed it at length wherever they'd met, which made me ask that exact question.

'It was at Tam's, Lion . . . ' I could feel Campbell's ears prick-ing up at my nickname. 'He's, like, Fabrizio's bestie.'

'Not quite.' He looked embarrassed, like I'd caught him lip-synching in the mirror. 'Our mums ran the ice-cream shop together.'

I looked at Campbell as if he'd just fallen out of the sky. Why the hell had Tam never mentioned this? Then . . . a brief snippet of conversation last summer, amid wedding-based stream of consciousness. When he'd said Fabrizio's friend Al was coming to work at the school, I thought he'd meant Alfie, the trainee. That would explain why, whenever I asked him about growing up in Anstruther, Alfie would look at me like I was handing him a scientology pamphlet.

I was dumbfounded. 'Are you Italian?'

'Italian mama, the Alex is from Alessandro.'

'Why didn't you say you knew my friends?'

I could feel his cringe second-hand. 'I didn't want to be unprofessional or make it awkward.'

Why wasn't I at Tam's that night? Maybe I'd been bumped off the invite list for him. 'I didn't know you could get red-headed Italians.' What a stupid thing to say.

'My dad looks like a can of Fanta head to toe.' He sounded completely different from every other time he'd spoken in front of me. Human, almost. Knowing even this level of detail was too much, like realising famous people have body odour.

Daisy cleared her throat to remind us she was there. 'Now we've got Alex's chromosomes cleared up, why don't you join us for a drink?'

The last thing I needed was Daisy adding another gay man to her collection and ballsing up my work-life balance. I also needed time to process Campbell's backstory mingling with mine. 'What are you doing here, anyway, Daiz?'

'You weren't answering your phone, so I went to the flat, but you were out so I called Harvey.'

'You had Harvey's number?'

'Yeah. Well, Tam had it.'

What felt like a very important valve deep within my chest faltered slightly. Why did Tam have Harvey's number? 'Right?'

'God, Poirot. Harvey said you were here so I said I'd come get you.'

That explained the haunted look. Casually dropping in was not very Daisy – she diarised her bowel movements. Something was happening. As luck would have it, Campbell had stuff to do at home, so it was just the two of us. She drove in silence, eventually pulling up at a cosy pub in Morningside where we used to go underage drinking. She ordered two kombuchas – definitely the first time they'd ever been purchased, the barman rolled his eyes to Skye and back. We sat in the darkest, quietest corner she could find.

'Not drinking?'

'No.'

'Come on, out with it.'

Daisy took a deep breath. Then came a speech I hadn't heard for years, not since I first met Peter. She hardly saw me these days, what was going on with me, why hadn't we chatted lately, how I didn't have to just 'vanish' because I was with a new 'lover'. Lover! I wasn't the kind of wavy-haired hunk who had lovers. But she had a point, even if she was wrong about why I'd gone off-radar. Daisy never did the whole 'now I've got a man, bye forever' thing; she liked the whole gang to stick together. The more swollen the ranks, the better. Maybe she was annoyed I was keeping Harvey to myself.

'So? How is it? Have we done "I wuv you baby" yet? How are you feeling about it? You're glowing!'

My natural instinct was always to downplay, save myself from being gossiped about. 'I'm brand new, cheers. It's going . . . fine.'

She was disappointed not to get any meat. 'Fine! You always say that!'

'Because I always am.'

'Classic Leo deflection. Remember the flat in Finnieston? Sprawling on the sofa for two days, just us? We even slept on it!' She would sleep, spreadeagled, while I perched at one corner, trying my best to fold my legs under me, a flamingo in skinny jeans. 'We had such amazing deep chats. You'd tell me everything.'

This was a slight rejig of history. Daisy would dig deep, unravelling childhood traumas, bad boyfriends and every fear that ever occurred in the darkest cellars of her mind, while I reassured her everything would be all right and kept her glass topped up with 'trampagne' – the cheapest cava from the booze shop on the corner. I stayed shallow, paddled round my psyche. I had nothing to tell. I'd led a perfectly pleasant, if uncharming, life, most of which Daisy had been present for.

Instead of contradicting her and ruining her false memory of mutual outpourings, I repeated everything was fine, and said sorry for not being in touch, before remembering we'd actually spoken over text four days earlier, because I was trying to remember the name of Kim Kardashian's song and Google felt like cheating. ('Jam', if you're interested.)

She sipped her kombucha. 'Nice.' Then the tang hit her and she shuddered. 'Would be nicer with vodka in it, can you get them to put a shot in?'

When I came back, she was sitting up straight. Something was working its way out of her. That same look from our sofa marathons. She tapped out a rhythm on the table.

'I'm pregnant.'

I must've looked . . . well, even more like a gargoyle chewing an oyster than usual, because she laughed and said, 'I knew I could trust you for an honest reaction.'

'Fuck.'

'We certainly did.'

'What are we going to do?'

She mouthed the 'we' back at me, gratefully. Her eyes started to water. 'I'm having an abortion. I'm not crying about that, though. I'm just tired.'

This was definitely the second-most grown-up thing we'd ever had to deal with. My dad dying probably took first place. Now didn't seem the time to draw up a leaderboard. 'Have you thought this through?'

'No, I just checked my horoscope this morning and it said book an abortion whether you need one or not. Sorry. Yes, of course I have. I've done nothing but think. I want a baby. One day. Just not this one, and not . . . '

With Seb? I wanted to say. 'Then you're doing the right thing.'

'You're the only person I'm telling.'

I was ashamed to feel a small tingle of pride, but it didn't make sense, Daisy was queen of the overshare.

'What about the supermodels?' My and Tam's nickname for Daisy's gaggle of girlfriends, all icons to us, statuesque stunners dating men who mostly looked like the 'before' picture on a daytime TV makeover.

'I can't talk to them about this. It's not like our twenties. They wouldn't see it as a disaster. Some of them are trying, too. It wouldn't feel . . . I'd feel so selfish. They might try talk me round or . . . '

'Tell Seb? Why haven't you?'

Daisy shrugged and stared into nowhere. 'He's talked about this kind of thing before. His ex had a pregnancy scare. The one he said was mad, who was trying to ruin his life. Had to ask his dad for money to get . . . to have the abortion. That's how he'd remember me. Another girl who tried to ruin his life. That would be my footnote.'

'Footnote? You're not breaking up, are you?'

There was something on the tip of her tongue. When's the right time to confess that while you like a friend's partner, they're horribly wrong for them? You get people who string others along, and Daisy was at the wrong end of the string. In fact, it was strangling her. If we'd ever slagged off each other's boyfriends it had been way after the front door had hit their departing arses. An unspoken rule: no comment on current flings unless asked. She'd never once slated Peter. During or since. If anyone deserved a slating, it was him. But I'd never offered him up for debate.

'We should go to the seaside this summer. Shall we do Blackpool and get our tarot cards done on one of the piers and puke up on the Big One?'

'Yes. Stop changing the subject. Are you definitely not telling him?'

'No. This is an adult problem. Seb is an adult for about one hour a week.'

'Do you want me to come with you? When is it, the . . . ?'

'Harder to say than you think, isn't it? You'll be in school.'

'I can slip out.' I didn't know how, exactly, but I'd try.

'I don't want you to come in, I don't think that's really a thing, but can you drop me off? And pick me up. They said I'd be in there for, like, half the day. Is this a hassle? Just say.'

'It isn't. I'll borrow Harvey's car.'

'Thanks for not judging me.'

'Why would I judge you? Things happen.'

'I don't know what I'd do without you.' To some, this might seem a gigantic burden, but I wore it like a badge of honour.

'The great thing is you don't have to be without me. Do you?'

Daisy finally relaxed her shoulders, took a slug of the vod-bucha cocktail. Winced. 'God. One day I will have a baby and when I do I promise you, I'll never ask you to babysit.'

'Why? Don't you think I can handle it? My job is basically extreme babysitting.'

'Not that! You'll be the reason I need a babysitter. We'll be out on the town.'

'Even though I can't do tequila shots like Tam?'

'He can't do them either. If he could sing as powerfully as he can boak, he'd be number one on the charts every day of the week.' The colour returned to her face. The relief of a problem shared. The best thing about never being centre of attention was noticing things like this, or even making them happen. 'Tell me about Alex. I didn't realise he was this horrible boss you told me about.'

I was furious to find myself blushing. 'Nothing to tell. He's not horrible, as such, just awkward.'

'I really liked him when I met him at Tam's.'

'I can't believe you remembered his name! You never do that!'

She laughed. It was delightful to see, almost like the previous ten minutes had been expunged from existence. 'It's because he reminded me of you. Ginger Leo, I said to Seb. We all thought so. You, but a bit more, you know, together.'

Like me? Campbell was nothing like me. At all. He had something to prove; I was perfectly comfortable in my own skin. 'More together? Am I not "together"?'

'Well, you weren't, then.' Daisy shrugged. 'He likes musicals too, you know.'

'Groundbreaking.'

She giggled and toddled off to get another round. *A bit more together.* My mind whirred. *He likes musicals too.* Daisy probably found out more about Campbell that night than she had about me in the last five years. *We all thought so.* I'd never before confronted what friends might say about me when I wasn't there. The trick was to treat it as a low hum in the distance – be aware, but never tune into the frequency. But now I had. Daisy returned. Kombucha for me, but she'd graduated to a Coke.

'There's no vodka in it.'

'I don't judge you, remember?'

'I do. Thank you, Lion.'

I got back to Harvey's and he folded me into a hug. I could smell beer and his fragrance and the faint trace of olive oil from whatever he'd been cooking. 'Everything okay?'

'Sorry I'm so late. Daisy needed a friend.'

'But everything's okay?'

I wanted to stay like that for ever but his jumper was making my neck itch so I unravelled myself from him. 'Actually, no. Daisy's not only met Campbell before, but likes him. She said he was like me! "A ginger Leo" were her exact words.'

'Star sign Leo or Leo Leo? Like, my Leo?'

My Leo. Shit, I loved that. I never realised I wanted to be owned so much.

'Your Leo.' Loved saying it back too. Pathetic pathetic pathetic but I didn't care. 'I'm nothing like him! The bloody neck of her! He's . . . he's not me.'

'Certainly isn't,' said Harvey, wrapping an arm round my waist and cupping my balls with the other. 'I love you, you know.'

There it was. The very first one. I felt magical. Saying it back was like finally finding the other half to a locket I never even knew was missing.

Twenty-Two

Highs never last. The next morning, Harvey woke me with an egg-white omelette and: 'I booked your gym induction. Next Sunday. You're free, I checked. I thought we could do spin class together.'

'Sounds very healthy and regimented for a Sunday.'

Harvey chuckled. 'Tell me honestly, other than when you're with me, when was the last time you ate and enjoyed a vegetable?'

'Tempura carrots at my dad's funeral.'

'You need to start looking after yourself. From Sunday, new Leo. Okay?'

Which is how I found myself, just over a week later, standing outside the gym feeling much like I did on my first day of primary school – missing the sofa and desperate for the loo. Harvey stood patiently while I tapped out a reply to Daisy.

'How's she doing?'

'She's okay, still resting. She's told Seb she's got women's problems and obviously he's not bothered enquiring any further.'

'Her biggest woman's problem is Seb,' said Harvey with a concerned smile. 'Give her my love.'

'Obviously she doesn't know that you know, so . . . '

'No problem. I'll keep it buttoned.'

A couple of days earlier, when I was collecting Daisy from what we'd decided to call 'the procedure', she had gripped me so tightly, she brought tears to my eyes.

'Don't, Lion,' she'd said, brightly. 'I'm relieved, honestly. I've never felt more sure. Can we do something really clichéd now like watch a rom-com or eat a massive fucking steak pie? I washed my favourite hoodie specially.'

'All good?' Harvey snapped me back to the here and now. 'You ready?'

'Yeah, she told me to film myself doing a biceps curl to cheer her up. What, er, is, a biceps curl?'

I'd been in a gym a total of three times. I was in alien territory. The grunting, the maleness, the perspiration, the women scurrying to quiet corners to work out so some meathead gym bro wouldn't mansplain their squats. GruntBox was the most select gym in town, on the rooftop of a hotel nobody who actually lived in Edinburgh could afford to stay in. Harvey wandered over to the reception desk while I skulked by some expensive decorative foliage looking like a parcel that had been delivered to the wrong address.

'Bad news,' he said, as he returned. 'The guy doing your induction is ill.'

'Oh, shame, back home we go, then. Another time, maybe.'

He pulled me back. 'Leo. There's also good news. Adam there on the desk said I can show you the ropes. They know me here.'

'How nice of Adam.' I looked over at the buff foetus manning reception who, right on cue, flicked his silken corn-coloured hair out of his eyes. Brilliant.

The torture of spin class was an hour away, so Harvey gave me a tour. He knew his stuff. Well, I assumed he did; I didn't have the faintest idea what I was looking at. A man swung from monkey bars, something I hadn't done since PE lessons, when Claire Dundas had pulled down my shorts to reveal my *Animaniacs* briefs. That's all gyms were – a giant PE class, except everyone was the sadistic teacher.

'What about some strength training?'

What a fantastically horrible idea. He grabbed a huge hunk of metal – a kettle bell, he said – and swung it high into the air while squatting to the ground. The muscles in his arms and legs tensed, their sculpted contours straining against his smooth skin. It would have been a beautiful moment, mildly horny even, had I not known I'd be expected to recreate it in a few seconds. He handed me the weight, and my arm immediately sought earth, hard and fast, the weight thudding onto the mat. Ignoring this, he demonstrated more exercises with fluid precision, staring forward, a light film of perspiration sparkling on his forehead. I liked the sound of his breathing as he lifted, it reminded me of him fucking me, so controlled and determined.

'Think you can manage a few of those while I work on my programme? Try fifteen reps of each, start small, 'kay?'

He had a programme? Would I have a programme? What the hell was a rep? Fifteen?! I had to launch this clump of unwieldy tungsten into the air fifteen times?!? I was a weed trapped in a nerd's body; I could barely lift my griddle pan, let alone this. I smiled. 'Sure, I'll give it a try.'

'I'm really proud of you, tackling your fitness head on,' he said, before wandering off to a scary looking machine that might have originally been used to pull one of William Wallace's supporters in four separate directions. I gingerly swung the kettlebell; the lack of force soon propelling it back, thwacking my shin. I looked round to see if my faux pas had been spotted.

One mat over sat a woman, around early fifties. She didn't look like everyone else here – she had a full face of makeup on for a start, an enormous snakeskin handbag beside her on the mat, and a cashmere scarf round her neck. She grinned at me as she began strapping tiny weighted bands to her wrists and ankles. Once done, she delved into her handbag and pulled out a teaspoon and, excitingly, a small plastic pot with a foil lid. She peeled off the lid and put it to one side – like my mum, she obviously thought lid licking was common – and began to eat whatever was in the pot, slowly.

She looked over at me again. 'Haven't seen you here before.'

'Uh, no. First time. Is that, um, are you eating . . .' I squinted. 'An apple crumble?'

'Aye. Well, it's apple and blackberry. I used to prefer Chambourcy Hippo Pota Mousse, quicker to get through, but they're hard to find now.'

I assumed gyms would be wall-to-wall straining sinew and foaming testosterone; I never realised they could be home to amazing people like this. This woman, this high camp goddess, was speaking my language. 'You come here a lot, then?'

'Contractual obligation.' She licked her spoon tenderly before plunging it into the pot again. 'Three times a week. Insurance. I get my private health care cheap. I don't wanna end up in a corridor up the Infirmary dying of MDMA or whatever.'

'MRSA.'

'Aye, that an' all. He your insurance, is he?' She motioned at Harvey, now strapped into the machine of torture, heaving weights with laser focus, while a sirloin steak in running leggings and an over-gelled quiff counted for him.

'You could say that.'

'I see him here a lot. Lucky boy. Look, I see you're not getting on too well with your, uh, big weight there. Want some advice?'

Fitness advice? From this hedonistic dessert queen? Of course I did.

'The trick is just do enough, you know?'

'Enough?'

'Aye.' She ran her finger round the inside of the pot to get the last of the crumble out, and jammed it in her mouth. 'Go for a weight slightly less huge than the One O'Clock Gun, you know? Don't kill yourself. A little goes a long way.'

'Is that what you do? Just, um, that? Every time you come.'

Her eyebrows met in mock consternation. 'Of course not. Sometimes I eat a banana. Hang on. Big move coming up.' She sat up straight and lifted one weighted ankle around three inches off the ground. 'There. Just enough. See? Ten more of these and I can treat myself to a raspberry mojito in Harvey Nichols.'

I was just about to ask her to marry me when Harvey bounded over with his counting mate in tow. 'This is my pal Akshay.'

Pal. We shook hands. Akshay had lovely teeth; he showed me every single one of them in his unfaltering smile. He'd have made a great ventriloquist. He worked in the beauty industry, he said, doing 'procedures'. I thought of Daisy, and wanted to text her again. Seb hadn't even asked Daisy where she'd been, but she pretended she'd been out having botox; he'd said she looked loads better, the irredeemable hound.

'If you ever need anything doing, I'm your man,' said Akshay, with the cheery nonchalance of someone ordering a milkshake at the drive-thru window. 'I do mates' rates.'

Mates now. Did I want something 'doing'? What about my nose? Harvey had a lamp that threw off an eerie light on my profile; the shadow of Gonzo from *The Muppets* blocking your view in the Odeon.

'Do you think I need anything?' I said it as a joke, but Akshay came closer. His eyes circled my nose like he was trying to focus on a wasp on a gateau.

'I reckon you're all good, mate. Most people are. Doesn't stop them coming to me, though.'

Mate. Again. Was Harvey a good mate? I'd never heard of this man. Harvey talked more about the rude newsagent at the end of his road than he had this absolute stranger. I looked over Akshay's shoulder to see the apple crumble woman now unwrapping an individual quiche. 'What do people tend to have done?'

'Oh, teeth, mainly.' I closed my mouth tight. 'I do a lot of fillers.'

'Couldn't be me,' I said, with the confidence of someone booking multimillion dollar campaigns with *Vogue* rather than someone who had to bite apples sideways. 'I don't want a face like the top of a cappuccino!' Harvey suppressed a laugh, but it occurred to me I was being a little rude to Akshay. 'But I'm sure your fillers are . . . great.'

Harvey seemed to sense my discomfort. 'Spin class now. You coming, Aksh?' *Aksh.* Tiny prickles of jealousy. So this was what it was like to have a hot boyfriend who had secret gym friends with incredible bodies. Were there other Akshays on different days? How many?

As Harvey and I walked into what he was calling the spin studio, he murmured, 'You don't need anything "done", by the way.' But, honestly, never mind Akshay, even the woman eating the crumble had more of a fitness focus than me. Luckily, my insecurities were about to be blown into orbit by half an hour of weapons-grade cardio.

A man who'd never been in the same room as bread, let alone eaten it, stood at the front, next to a weird-looking bike that faced twenty more weird-looking bikes. He said he was Jermaine, and this was a low intensity spin class, suitable for beginners and people on rest days. Rest days from what? Operating very heavy machinery going by the bodies of the others filing in. They weren't beginners – they wore actual gym gear, with swooshes and neon and proper designs, not the free, branded T-shirts from radio giveaways and faded swimming shorts that novices wore. Thankfully, Harvey had kitted me out in tasteful black shorts and T-shirt, so light and airy, and comfortable, they had to have a terrible secret. I looked the part, but now I had to play it. We clambered onto the bikes and Harvey leaned over.

'You got this.'

I wanted to ask what this was, exactly, but it turned out the answer was a major cardiac trauma, or near enough. After promising to 'go easy', Jermaine pressed a button and the room went completely black, save for a few neon beams spiking into the dark and scarring the whites of my eyes. He pressed another button and the room was assaulted by earsplitting landfill dance music, the kind I used to hear piping out of schoolfriends' phones when I was about fourteen. Banging beats and shrill vocals, synths scything through it all with the subtlety of a fat joke in a nineties sitcom. Then, well, I can't think of any other way to describe it: Jermaine hollered at us for twenty-five minutes straight, a sergeant major in a unitard, demanding we stand, sit, pedal faster, scream things back at him. When it was over, I hobbled to the side and took heaving breaths, honking and hooting as my roiling stomach tried to make sense of the world. Harvey rubbed my back, barely even panting, like he'd just climbed down from changing a lightbulb.

'You did brilliantly. Let's hit the showers.'

I slowly soaped my traumatised skeleton, glad to shut the cubicle door behind me so nobody could tell I wasn't a proper gym person and drive me out with pitchforks – or javelins. I dressed slowly, cowering in the corner, not sure which way to face – which was worse, showing my bony arse, or turning round and horrifying them with the front aspect? I watched Harvey bustle from locker to mirror and moisturise his body. Sweeping his hands over his surfaces, like his fingers knew exactly where they were going, and enjoying it. I'd reached an uneasy truce with my body, keeping to safety zones where I didn't stand out. This was contravening our agreement. Harvey turned to me. 'You did great.'

'Did I?'

'Ah huh. Once you get into it, you'll never look back. You'll soar. Shall we sign up on the way out? Maybe Adam can do us a wee deal.'

Another handsome friend only too happy to help out. Did Akshay and Harvey ever get changed at the same time? Did Akshay sit watching Harvey's arse walk off to the shower, lick his lips at the glimpse of what was between Harvey's legs? Which was worse, to sit at home and wonder, or see it for myself?

'Okay, good idea.'

In the foyer, Harvey barely opened his mouth to say Adam's name before I felt my legs give way, and my stomach leaped to my throat, depositing that morning's Coco Pops, banana and two mugs of rooibos into a planter. We decided I should sign up another time.

Twenty-Three

Tam held up two ties and asked, with the gravitas of a funeral director making you choose casket handles, which I liked best. They were identical. Blue. Cornflower blue, maybe? I wasn't sure; I wasn't an interior design gay. Or a fashion one. No matter what I wore, I always looked like I'd got dressed quickly, to the tune of a shrieking fire alarm.

'Tamish. I've no idea.'

'But they're both so different,' he said. 'So hard to choose.'

Hang on. 'Is this a reference?'

'To a film that came out two decades ago, yes, keep up.' Tam flung the ties to one side and a mute shop assistant immediately scurried in to clear them away. 'Your gym-bro boyfriend is turning you straight. When was the last time you watched *The Devil Wears Prada* or *Mean Girls?*'

Tam's handsome brother was 'busy off being heterosexual somewhere' so the suit fitting was only us. Our first time alone since Tam had confided in me about the money issue, and it appeared he'd totally blanked it out – this was not a high street establishment. More shop assistants appeared and hurried Tam into a changing room. He emerged, minutes later, looking somewhere between cologne advert chic and suave mobster. He fussed with his collar, pretending to scowl as he smoothed down the shirt front; this mild discomfort would probably be the biggest problem he'd face all week. He carried on fidgeting. Tam never knew stillness. I told him once: 'I swear on my deathbed, when everything flashes before me, 90 per cent of my greatest hits will be watching you rummage in a cheap tote bag looking for lip balm.'

He'd been indignant, his default setting. 'All my manbags are real leather, thank you.'

As he yanked at his collar, a vision flashed up, of Tam unbuttoning his shirt while Peter watched. Maybe Peter had unfastened it for him. He liked that. The way he'd undress me with glacial meticulousness, order me not to move a muscle, felt sensual and erotic at the time – hindsight afforded me cynicism and the view that Peter might make a great undertaker.

'I think I need something in duck-egg, mix things up a bit.'

'You look stunning. As always.'

Tam stopped mid-pirouette and stared at me via the mirror. 'You always say that like I'm doing it on purpose, to piss you off.'

My cheeks flamed. My mild, occasional resentment that Tam was hot without even trying had been exposed. 'Oh sorry, did you mean to look terrible?'

'No, but . . . oh never mind.'

I remembered what Daisy said about Tam needing reassurance. 'Sorry. I'm in envy mode. Ignore me. It's hard being an ugly duckling surrounded by such beauty.' I tried to giggle to show I was (half) joking, but it came off bitter.

'Surrounded?' Tam looked round the room as if searching for other, hotter men than him.

'Well, Daisy. Seb. Fabrizio has his charms. And my Harvey, of course.'

'Of course.'

'And there's Alex. And you.' Whoops. I said the quiet part out loud. Where was my time machine? Tam's jaw slumped to the floor.

'Like, Alex at work? Fabrizio's Alex? Are you . . . do you fancy him?' He was immediately excited, my sarcasm forgotten. 'Leo! Are you trying to fire into him? That is . . . not like you.'

'Of course not! I just meant . . . ' Why wouldn't it be 'like me'? What kind of things did I do? I wanted to ask how he'd know exactly but it felt spiteful. That feeling again, though, picking up traces of conversations happening when I wasn't in the room.

'A little crush, maybe?'

'No!' But . . . I was warming to Alex, definitely. When he came to workshops, there was a different energy. He was passionate. I knew a thwarted theatre kid when I saw one, the ones who'd been too cool to get involved. Luckily, I'd never been too cool for anything. The more time I spent around him, the more I forgot why I disliked him. He now spoke to me as an equal, rather than a subordinate, and I stopped acting like an adolescent. We'd done one very speedy run-through of the staging for my solo and when it was over, he'd stood up – after a few agonising seconds struggling to get out of the bean bag – and applauded. Fervid, hard, loud clapping, eyes wide, like he was at the opera.

'Admit it,' he'd said, a glint in his eye trying to transmit a message. 'I was right.'

'Alex is good-looking, though, isn't he?' said Tam now, twirling in front of the mirror.

I could appreciate an attractive guy without it meaning anything. I'd been doing it all my life. 'I've never worked with anyone hot before,' I said. 'Except Mica, obviously, and she's a fifty-year-old woman.'

'My ideal life partner, to be honest.'

'And mine.'

'Right, let's pick your suit.' Another assistant – I hadn't seen the same one twice the entire time we'd been there – came trundling a rail of suits and Tam flipped through them as if thumbing through carpet samples. 'Let's find something to make you look extra handsome.'

'They're suits, not wands.' I laughed, but Tam shook his head.

'Try this on.' He thrust a suit at me, the kind of thing I'd never pick in a million years, a tan colour, slim fitting. 'It's not like you're hideous.'

'Easy for you to say. This won't suit me. Can't I wear something blue?'

'How do you know it won't? It isn't easy for me to say, actually. Compliments are disgusting.' He carried on flipping through suits. 'You've got a lovely, warm face, full of character. A great smile when you do.'

'Character!' It landed like the clang of the plague bell. 'My teeth!'

'Get a brace if you're that bothered! Fabrizio's never looked back since he got train tracks, but I wish I'd known him when he still had the gaps. I saw a pic. Cute as.' He held the suit against me, considering me like a painter approaching a canvas.

'Definitely this one. You're not bland. You don't look like everybody else. That's a bonus.'

As often as I'd heard this kind of pep talk, it never failed to amaze me that even my most cherished friends thought five minutes of motivational bilge could magic away years of the mirror's hard truths. I blamed those songs by earnest boy bands in tight T-shirts, convincing plain girls that, no, honestly, they were super beautiful and needed to know it. Or harrowing ballads sung by gorgeous popstars claiming to be outcasts because they had seven freckles in high school. Self-help dosed out in verse-chorus-verse-chorus-fade. But when the song was over, you were still you.

'So what about blue?'

'No! I'm wearing blue. And I'm paying, so I get to decide.'

I glanced at the tag and gasped. 'You can't! What happened to keeping costs down?'

Tam locked eyes with the assistants, who hastened out of sight. 'Can you try not to scream that so loud in front of these snooty fuckers? I want to make sure they finish making my suit. I've factored this in. Call it an early birthday present.' When we were skint students, Tam's birthday presents had included regifted shower gel sets with Christmas branding and a pair of socks he'd worn 'only once for, like, five minutes'; we'd certainly come a long way. 'I want you to look amazing on my photos and I've seen that one suit of yours.'

'Hey! The guy in the charity shop said it had a famous owner.'

'Yes, who drowned in your precious Tay Bridge disaster. Seemingly while wearing it. Come on, let me. Go try. Scoot. Stop being annoying.'

I trooped to the changing room and begrudgingly pulled

on the trousers. A hand appeared through the curtain with a pristine white shirt and a lovely tie almost the same pattern as my bean bags. I emerged, feeling like a competition winner. 'I don't normally wear light colours.'

Tam stood in front of me. He looked proud. 'I know you don't. Forever prepared for a national day of mourning. This is great. How do you feel?'

I felt quite special. Like I was in costume. It fitted me perfectly, but I was slightly uncomfortable. Could I not be trusted to pick my own suit? 'Nice.'

'Nice. High praise indeed. In an alternative universe somewhere, there's a Leo who knows how good he looks in this and we should take a leaf out of his book. We'll take it. And the shirt. Not the tie. It's foul.'

I changed, and the assistants boxed everything up. They offered to send it to me but I wanted to carry it, so people could see. Tam took me to lunch as a supposed thank you for going along, though I'd been the one walking out with a free suit. The restaurant was cosy and buzzy, with that distinct Saturday energy where people are ordering wine an hour or two earlier than they might any other day. The background chatter was hypnotic; I sank back into the plush banquette and breathed out. I appreciated weekends so much more since becoming a teacher – every Saturday was like a mini Christmas Day. Tam flirted a little with the waiter, speaking broken Italian and laughing too loudly at his rehearsed jokes. It worked, though: our portions were huge and the waiter offered us a round of cocktails on the house.

'Am I all right to have a wee glass of fizz? I feel like celebrating. I won't if you'd rather I didn't, though. Unless I can tempt you to join me?'

Christ. I had to laugh. 'For the millionth time, no. But you go for it.'

'Just testing. I'm in awe, as ever, that you can bear to spend time with me sober.'

I looked out for any bite marks on his hand and saw none, feeling a rush of affection as I watched him twist linguine round his fork – he said Fabrizio went mad if he saw him use a spoon. When he finished, Tam made a show of lining up his napkin, glass, and cutlery, like he was building up to telling me something.

Oh.

Not this. Not now.

It was like the restaurant faded to black and Tam was under a spotlight. Was he about to confess? I felt a creeping dread and wanted to scream 'Don't say it!' My head teemed with outcomes; I'd have paid anyone £1,000 to saw it off and give me peace.

'About the costs thing . . . ' The background noise returned, lights came back up, we were back in the room.

'I'll pay for the suit. In, er, instalments.'

It wasn't that. They'd been going through their guest list, he said, realised the numbers seemed swollen.

'Am I out of the wedding? Did you buy me that suit to wear while waving you off at the airport?'

Tam laughed. He had oregano in his teeth; I decided not to tell him yet. 'We're, uh, keeping things intimate, only very close friends and family. We never spoke about your plus one. We assumed you, uh, wouldn't have one.'

'I'm gonna look so great as I watch you go through security, thank you!'

'Dandelion! Stop! You are coming! But Harvey isn't. We don't have the room.'

'Oh.' Oh. Shame, I'd been looking forward to living out that fantasy. On Harvey's arm. Him looking wondrous in his suit and me looking, well, like me, in mine. Harvey would've been the third or fourth most handsome man there after Tam and Tam's brother and their ridiculously hot cousin – the Patel gene pool was a limpid tropical sea. It could've been my ultimate main character moment, as Mica might say, walking tall alongside my ravishing consort, rendered beautiful by osmosis. But no, I'd be alone, saddled with some other singleton's halitosis over the starters.

'Do you mind? Is it bad? I'm so sorry.' He looked guilty, but relieved. 'We really want it to be people we've known and loved a long time. That's definitely you. Intimate, y'know?'

I said I understood. It seemed kinder. 'Totally. More intimate.'

'I know weddings can be shit on your own, but I promise this won't be. It'll be the gang! Better, in a way, no newbie boyfriend to look after or explain our jokes to, right?'

'Sure.'

'Good, that's settled.' He peered at me. I've never been able to paper a smile over the crack in my soul when something doesn't go my way. My face is a billboard advertising exactly how I feel inside. But Tam chose to misinterpret it. 'Lion, about the suit. I wasn't slagging off how you dress. I just wanted to do something nice for you. You deserve it. I'm actually quite into your whole vibe. It's different, it's absolutely you, and you rock it.'

Tam had never complimented my clothes in all the years I'd known him. Quite the reverse. I didn't know what to say.

He carried on: 'And this thing about how you look . . . I know you always joke about it, but . . . that's all it is, right? A joke?'

'I'm self-aware. It doesn't keep me awake at night.'

'But honestly. I mean, if you weren't attractive, you wouldn't be able to get someone as hot as Harvey, would you?'

The alarm bells of Notre Dame started to clang. 'Is Harvey hot?'

'Absolutely!'

A door had opened. Was I willing to walk through it? 'Remember "beast or boring"?' I said, trying to sound breezy. 'What do you reckon Harvey is?'

Tam laughed so hard I felt a spot of pesto hit my face. 'From the smile on your adorable wee face, I'd say beast. You gonna confirm?'

My smile didn't reach my eyes. 'What about Peter?'

Tam began to hum, then paused. Licked his lips. Short breath. I was glued to his every move. 'I mean . . . uh . . . he had something about him, I suppose. So, you see, you're doing better than most. My lovely Lion.'

Anyone else might've been convinced there was nothing to worry about, but Tam had weathered his share of heartbreaks and was a walking masterclass in painting a smile over a thunderstorm. I was about to ask him, I really was, but he leaned in, took my hand. Tam's bombshells never travelled alone.

'You sing, right?'

'Tam, I just spent half an hour in the tailor's moaning about that sodding solo. Why?'

Tam's unexpected credit crunch meant his dreams of floating down the aisle to the dulcet tones of a curvaceous diva would need to be curtailed. 'You'll do it, won't you? You've got a gorgeous voice. I remember from uni.'

Singing in the student bar, pissed. Not quite Broadway. But Tam was hard to refuse. Few men managed it. 'Of course. My present to you.'

He was delighted. 'Related note: do you know any Italian?'

'Quattro stagioni is about my limit.'

'Oh, it'll be fine, I'll message you the song. "That's Amore", dead easy. But in Italian. You can do it phonetically. Or maybe I'll try to convince Fabrizio we should have a Céline number. You've really come through for me, you know.'

Two singing gigs in a matter of weeks; I was going to get ideas way above my station. 'Are you sure about this?'

'I believe in you, Dandelion, always have. But no pressure. One bit of good news . . . Ross and his man are off the guest list too. I'll let you tell him.'

I clinked my Diet Coke against his prosecco. 'It'll be a lovely day.'

I must've looked good in the suit. When I tried it on for Harvey, he was all over me like coleslaw ruining a perfectly good sandwich.

'You'll rumple it.'

'Sorry!'

We'd never discussed it, but he struck me as a 'weddings are boring' type. Turned out he wasn't. He was actively annoyed about the lack of invitation.

'So Seb's going?'

'Yes, but Ross and his partner aren't, so, you see . . . '

He left the bedroom and stalked through to his lounge. I followed, the suit no longer feeling so magical.

'That's not fair on you. Being alone at weddings sucks. Why would Tam do that? I don't understand these people sometimes. What do you actually get out of being friends with them?'

'Get?'

'Yeah. What's in it for you? They're never there for you. You run around after them. So much emotional labour. They sap your energy. All today, helping Tam with his suit. We could've done something.'

It hadn't occurred to me. Tam needed my advice, naturally I was there. It's how things worked. 'There doesn't have to be anything in it for me, although I did get this suit.'

'Not sure about that colour now, actually. Drains you.'

Knew it. 'I don't mind not "getting" anything out of it. It's not a transaction. We've been through a lot. They care about me.'

'I know they do. But you never get to be yourself. It's all wisecracks and deflection. You never confide, in case they judge. And when they say, "oh by the way, no plus ones to the wedding" you roll over. That's not best friend behaviour, it's what you'd do to a distant relative. Or a frenemy like Ross. Know what I mean?'

We hadn't argued yet, not at all. Was I kind of excited to see where it might go? To enter this new phase? It meant you really cared about one another, didn't it, to row? Passionate couples did it all the time.

·'The only friend of yours I've met is Akshay. What are you getting out of that?' That was a low blow, but the pained look on Harvey's face told me I'd hit my target.

'I've lived here two minutes. I don't have many friends yet. And you know what, good friendships are transactional. Being there for each other, sure, but give and take, not give give give.'

It wasn't like that. He didn't get it. We weren't like friends off TV, permanently brunching, calling every day, taking it in turns to be centre of attention if the storyline required it – although Tam and Daisy . . . I shook the thought away. 'Let's not have an argument.'

'I'm not arguing, honestly. But seriously . . . I want to shake you out of this sometimes. I don't mind if they don't like me, but you deserve better.' I could feel the heat of his anger. He'd never raised his voice before and wasn't quite doing it now, but I instinctively knew whatever I said next was key. I didn't want Harvey to unlock too many of my doors; Peter had grown to be disgusted by what he found behind them and I couldn't risk Harvey feeling the same.

'They do like you! A lot! It's logistics.' I found myself saying they weren't so bad really, that Tam would change his mind if I asked. Harvey calmed down, he had a glass of wine, we ordered a takeaway.

Later, Tam messaged to thank me, and said giving up my plus one meant they could keep Alex Campbell in the wedding, and that Fabrizio was delighted.

Shit.

Twenty-Four

I was born on a Tuesday. Wonderfully unremarkable: a day without weather, a digestive biscuit with no chocolate on, eighth place in a beauty contest. The old saying went 'Tuesday's child is full of grace'. My mum would recite it to me while soaping my hair in the bath.

'Mind you,' she'd say, 'you popped out around quarter to midnight. You were nearly a Wednesday.' Wednesday's child is full of woe, apparently. Figures. 'I hadn't smoked a Superkings in seven months,' my mum would say when probed about the miracle of birth. 'I was practically sparking up as they cut the cord.'

I never planned much for my birthday. Making a big show of it, forcing people to celebrate, wouldn't be me. I might, if nagged by Daisy or Tam, send a quick text asking if anybody fancied raising a glass before we got on with our lives. Tam's birthdays lasted weeks and usually involved a trip away and a night out watching him dance on a podium praying this wouldn't be the year he fell off and broke his back. Daisy organised two bashes: a full-on glammed-up bender with her supermodels, with a total photo ban after the third margarita, and then a quieter soirée, with her rainbow crew and any work-mates she'd feel guilty about not inviting. And by 'quieter', I mean she'd hire an entire restaurant, and flit between tables like she was performing immersive dinner-theatre.

This was my first birthday with a boyfriend in four years. Peter liked to pick a ludicrously expensive restaurant with below-par food, and remind me throughout we were 'paying for the experience'. For him, shelling out for an expensive meal was a licence to be demanding of the waiter; he liked lots of bowing and scraping and would send back perfectly good start-ers to show dominance, all with a mile-wide smile, of course. I didn't mention my birthday to Harvey, couldn't find a way to bring it up naturally. Still, my imagination went into overdrive. Would Harvey whisk me off like Fabrizio always did for Tam? We hadn't been a couple long, though, and it wasn't like we lived together, mind you . . . maybe that would be on the cards one day? I wasn't sure whether to bring it up. Then, one morn-ing he announced he'd booked a birthday dinner, somewhere romantic. I liked that word much more with Harvey than I had with Peter, when it always sounded like a threat.

The revelation that this was more than dinner à deux came from Mica. She was whingeing about Emerald crossing bounda-ries in the art department group chat – too many pulsing heart emojis, apparently – when she said, 'At least Harvey don't put no kisses on his texts. You know where you are with him.'

It was true, he didn't. Sometimes Harvey's message carried the detached crispness of an automated bank balance text – no hearts, no pet names, no kisses. He more than made up for it in private. But I'd never told Mica that. After some light interroga-tion about why my boyfriend was texting her, she broke. Harvey had secretly invited all my friends along. I was shocked, especially after the wedding invitation drama. He'd set aside his own hurt, and the considerable rudeness of how the news was broken, and instead focused on how important my friends were to me. So thoughtful, so generous. I felt a lump in my throat. Mica was mortified and swore me to secrecy. It now made total sense why Daisy and Tam had both been noncommittal about meeting for drinks when I'd messaged. Amazing! I couldn't wait.

My birthday was a school day, so my tutor group made the same crude jokes they did every year about birthday blowjobs and sang an explicit version of 'Happy Birthday to You', while I dutifully blew out a candle on a £2 cupcake.

By the evening, I was buzzing as I slipped on one of Harvey's roll necks and put too much wax in my hair. Harvey held my hand in the cab all the way to the Old Town. When we arrived at the restaurant my stomach was halfway through a spin cycle. The anticipation! I practised my surprised face, cleared my throat a thousand times so I wouldn't sound too shrill when I shouted 'Oh my God' or 'You guys!' or whatever people in films shouted in similar situations. Harvey held open the door and I swept in, regally. We were led to a private dining area at the back, where I found . . . Mica, sitting alone, looking embarrassed. Around her were empty seats, like advent calendar windows devoid of chocolate. I composed myself, remembering I wasn't supposed to know about this.

'Mica! Wow! Hey! Why are you sitting by yourself at such a huge table?'

Mica and Harvey exchanged a quick glance, charged with pity, but Mica's grin never slipped. 'Dunno . . . I might be at the wrong one.'

I turned to Harvey, who looked shellshocked. 'Are more people coming? Or is this the wrong table?'

'Bit of both.' He scooted off to speak to the maître d'.

Mica gave me a hug; I stifled a sob. 'What time did you get here?'

'We were supposed to be here at seven.' It was seven-thirty now. 'Are they usually late?'

Sometimes, yes, but not like this. Daisy liked to arrive first to bag the best seat and Tam had a watch that barked his diary at him on the hour. They weren't coming. Harvey returned, looking defeated.

'They've asked . . . they've had a last minute booking. Do we mind moving to . . . maybe a table of six, in case . . . late-comers, maybe?'

'Who did you invite?'

'Well, Mica, obviously, and Daisy and her partner, and Tam and Fabrizio, your mum, and that gay guy you're not massively keen on but . . . more the merrier.'

We moved to the smaller table, everyone else in the restaurant watching us as a jury might awkwardly stare at defendants in a murder trial. The waiter flashed us a kindly smile, and plonked down three glass flutes, and an ice bucket with a bottle of champagne in it.

'Gratis, doll,' he said. 'Happy birthday.' God bless the gay waiters of the world.

I reached out and drew a tiny heart in the condensation on the bottle, picked at the label. 'Let's crack it open.'

Harvey popped the cork, poured a glass each for himself and Mica. 'Let's get you something else, unless . . .'

'Unless what?' said Mica.

'Unless he wants some. It's his birthday.'

'Nah,' Mica shook her head emphatically; I'd seen her do this a dozen times to students asking for assignment extensions. 'He don't wanna do that.'

But maybe I did. It was my birthday. If my friends – and even the enemy-adjacent – couldn't be bothered to turn up for my first ever surprise dinner, I now realised, at the ripe old age of thirty-four, why not? I wasn't drowning my sorrows but I could at least help them get their feet wet.

'Leo?' They both stared. This wasn't a big deal. I could have a small drink; it wasn't like I'd given up because I couldn't handle it. I reached for the third glass.

'It's my birthday.'

I swear Mica gasped. 'Leo, you sure?'

I didn't answer, as Harvey slowly poured, bubbles popping and fizzing in anticipation, the slender layer of foam settling, so creamy and white and inviting. 'Happy birthday to me!' I cheered, and drank the lot in one go.

Harvey held my hand. 'I gave them plenty of notice. Sent reminders. Everything. I'm sorry.'

Funny, but as the evening wore on and the bottle emptied, I cared less and less that Daisy and Tam hadn't turned up. I could properly chat to Mica, and she and Harvey swapped stories about weird fitness regimens – Mica was currently paying a king's ransom for a man with muscles like a bubble waffle cone to shout at her three times a week at boot camp. Her daughter Sasha was going through a well-behaved phase too – 'She ain't slammed a door since last Thursday' – and Mica was meeting a man for a third date next week. Things were looking up. I hugged her harder than I ever had before, bathing in her positive energy.

'Sorry . . . Mica, I, er, thought you, um, liked women, no?'

Harvey fixed me with the stare of an innocent swearing for the first time, concerned he was breaking a confidence. I couldn't remember what I'd told him, really, and it didn't matter at that moment. 'Have I got this wrong?'

'I'm bi, babes.'

'And if you're not good enough for her, it's fucking bye-bye, babes!' Oh, I was feeling that champagne.

Mica managed to pump Harvey for any juicy details I hadn't told her, and in turn laid bare about her last big relationship, with a fellow teacher. 'Not at Bucklemaker, though, that would be disgusting. The kids would never let us live it down.'

This was true: ever since Mel Maths and Dom Design & Engineering got together, older students would make sex noises whenever they passed them in the corridor. 'It's my asthma, miss, honest.'

'So there's nobody hot at your school, then?' I wasn't the only one feeling the champagne; Harvey was the most slouched I'd seen him out of pyjamas. 'No workplace crushes?'

'God, no!' I said, reaching for the bottle – our second – and draining its contents into my glass, now smeared with my fingerprints.

'I dunno, y'know.' Mica's left eyebrow suddenly developed a personality. 'Naomi's a bit of all right, despite the bobbly jumpers and John Lennon specs.'

'Who's Naomi?' asked Harvey. 'Is she the school stunner?'

'It's a he, babes. Mr Campbell. Alex. Our deputy head.' For some reason, I wanted Mica to stop. I had a feeling, I don't know.

'The guy you're doing rehearsals with, right?' Harvey was still smiling, his eyes flicked to me for a second, he winked. 'He's a honey, is he?' A honey! The very idea.

Mica looked like a bird proudly ruffling its plumage. 'Dark horse kind of vibe, you know. Bit like our Leo, actually.'

I couldn't read Harvey's face at all, but thanks to the champagne, I guess I wasn't trying.

'And what, he's taken, is he?' said Harvey, whose curiosity didn't sound entirely casual. 'Married?'

'Well . . . ' Mica lowered her voice, as if Alex was at the next table. 'I heard he got dumped recently.'

Oh. He'd never said. Should he have said? To me, I mean? We didn't talk about anything other than the show; the only glimpse into his non-school life was the revelation he was hoping to catch a couple of musicals in London over Easter, and even then it only signalled that he was more invested in the show than I'd thought.

'That's a shame.' The booze made my head fuzzy and my eyes swivel, but I definitely detected a coolness in Harvey's voice. 'Do you think she'll take him back? His wife, I mean?'

Mica laughed so hard she spilled champagne into her lap. 'No . . . like I said, he's like our little Leo. Loves musicals, you get me?'

Harvey returned her wink and looked at me in a way I couldn't decode. 'What do you think of him, then?'

In that moment, everything I hated about booze came to the front of my mind – the acidic churn of my stomach, my body too elastic and unprepared for danger, my tongue fat and sluggish.

'Not much,' I managed to say, before excusing myself and sliding out from behind the table to plod to the bathroom, whereupon I threw up until the very last bubble was out of me.

Twenty-Five

I used to get terrible hangovers. Proper heart pounding, trembling shame and regret. The whole day on the sofa ploughing through popcorn and movies I'd seen a hundred times while Peter banged saucepans in the kitchen under the guise of tidying. But that morning, after my birthday: nothing. Whither the thundering head, scratchy throat and vague testicular pain that used to haunt me, leave me cancelling any plans other than a quick taxi to a lowkey pub for restorative drinks with Daisy and Tam?

No pain this time, but plenty of shame: my unblemished sobriety record became history in a matter of seconds. I hadn't counted the days since my last drink, that felt like something a person in recovery might do, or someone striking off days spent in incarceration, but it had been a lot. Now I'd slid down the longest snake to day one. I padded to the bathroom, braved the mirror. I found Harvey in the kitchen, making coffee. I'd never met anyone who owned so much navy and burgundy leisurewear, and looked so appetising in all of it.

'Sorry I was so drunk.'

'Don't be. Birthday. Unlock permission to enjoy yourself.'

'I don't drink. I'm mortified.'

'I said don't be. You're not a lapsed alcoholic.'

I felt instantly better and smugly repeated this line to Mica in the staffroom. She shrugged.

'Yeah, but it ain't you, is it?'

'It was me. I used to drink all the time.'

'Right. Used to. Anyway, long as you're happy.'

Something felt off. I was in the doghouse. I had sudden respect for Mica's teenage daughter. 'I won't do it again. Harvey's terrific, isn't he?'

Mica dropped her phone and swore. 'He's very handsome.'

'I know. Can't believe my luck sometimes. But he's nice, isn't he?'

'He obviously sees you as his priority. I've got a one-to-one with Naomi Campbell. See you later. You deserve the emergency fag today. I hope your mates have been kissing your arse on WhatsApp this morning.'

Daisy and Tam were never big on apologising. Tam even had the cheek to call me – a phone call! – and ask whether I had plans for my birthday. 'Shall we do a noodles night? Just me, you, and Daiz?'

'It was yesterday, Tamish.'

On hearing about the missed dinner, Tam feigned ignorance. 'I definitely didn't get an invite. Oh, hang on.' There was a pause, the tip-tap of fingers on a keyboard. 'It went into my other inbox, you know the one . . . from people you don't know. I didn't even see it. Oh God. Lion. Nightmare. Are you pissed off?'

I found myself saying no. I resolved to go easy on Daisy too, after her botox-not-botox. We met for the noodles, at our usual place. Distinctly unglamorous but always busy. Tam had chosen it years ago because its online reviews averaged out at three stars.

'Any more stars than that means white people like it, so it probably isn't as good. No offence, but immigrants know.'

Daisy had reared her head back. 'Your parents are from Paisley.'

Tam had drawn his lips in tight and shot Daisy a pointed look. 'Tell that to the "but where are you really from" crew.'

About my birthday, Daisy was unrepentant. 'Harvey just sent an invitation into the ether? Without following up? Who does that? Has he never organised anything before? It's unhinged.'

It felt rude to point out that my birthday had come and gone without so much as a birthday cake emoji from her.

She peered at her phone suspiciously. 'Found it. Them. From an unknown number. I deleted them straightaway. Looked spammy. Everybody does that. What did he expect?' I'd heard her use this tone on the phone to interns; I didn't love being on the receiving end.

'He did it from his work phone. Can I ask . . . why do you sound pissed off at me, exactly? All I did was dare to have a birthday.'

She sighed a really, really lengthy sigh. I could've nipped away from the table and cruised the Galapagos islands during it. 'Because now I feel like a dick, I suppose. Obviously I would've been there. Harvey should've phoned, physically, with a voice. Words. Details. I'm mad at him, not you.'

Daisy would rather read her teenage diary out loud to her parents than answer a call from an unknown number, but sure.

I was about to say I was mad at her, actually, but was frightened of tipping into new territory. We'd never fallen out before, except over dirty dishes and noise misdemeanours in our student flat. It was always resolved with a cup of tea or a Smirnoff Ice or one of us just agreeing we'd been silly (usually me).

'Nobody turned up, except Mica.'

That got her. 'Oh, Lion. I'm sorry. Proper sorry. I'd have loved to have met your work wife.'

Mica would not have enjoyed that description. She once told me, 'When a man starts calling you his work wife, he expects coffees, bits of admin, clearing up. I'm nobody's wife.' She did call me her husband sometimes but said that was okay. 'Intelligent women don't expect nothing from a husband, which is lucky, because that's exactly what they get.'

I didn't want to drag this out. 'Apology accepted. Harvey tried to do a nice thing, it didn't work. Don't be mad at him. Look . . . how are you? How is everything?'

Another sigh. 'Oh, the same. Daybreak comes, work all day, two glasses of wine in front of the TV, Seb creeps in at midnight stinking of the pub.'

Tam and I looked at each other, as if willing the other to say something that might set her free. Whether he'd had time to reflect, or it was the sight of my miserable face in surroundings we'd usually be laughing in, I don't know, but a wave of remorse suddenly engulfed Tam. 'Lion, I think I'd chuck myself off the Forth Bridge if nobody turned up at my party.'

Daisy covered her hands with her face. 'Please! Don't let me imagine that.'

'Which bit? A party nobody comes to, or me jumping off the bridge?'

'Both. Can we do a toast to our lovely Leo? Charge your kombucha, Dandelion. A happy belated birthday, apologies for being bad friends, and may his otherwise perfect boyfriend Harvey get better at organising parties.'

I almost bit my tongue in half. 'It wasn't his fault.'

'Cheers!' Tam knocked back his wine in one. I'd decided not to tell them about my boozy slip-up, I didn't want them staging an intervention over the yakitori. My internal narrative was that they'd driven me to it, in a way, and I didn't want them to feel guilty.

'D'you think Harvey did it on purpose,' said Tam, 'so he could have you to himself?'

'Mica was there. Who's ever wanted me all to themselves?'

'I do!' screeched Daisy. 'Always! Alone time with my Leo is my fucking dream. Right, I'm off to the loo.'

I looked over at Tam. He gave a thin smile back. Whenever I thought about our group dynamic, I'd always assumed he and Daisy were much closer, being more similar. Maybe he'd been put out by what she'd said, about wanting me to herself.

'She doesn't mean that.'

Tam reached over, touched my wrist. Cold hands. 'She does. It's lovely.'

'No! She loves you more. You're the ideal gay best friend.'

'It's you she calls,' said Tam. 'When she needs someone, I mean. Always you first.'

I didn't know that. 'Only because she knows I'll turn up. You turn your phone off before the last bong on *News at Ten*.' An early riser, Tam insisted on his nine hours.

'I don't think it's that. I was gonna say you indulge her but that sounds catty. You listen. Not everyone does. There's so much noise, we end up talking through it. I know I do. But you actually listen. With your cute wee ears.' My ears are not wee, or cute, and one sticks out at an angle, like a taxi door swinging open. 'You take stuff in. At the suit shop when I was banging on about duck-egg ties, you were really concentrating. Like a wee boy learning to read.'

Did I take stuff in? How perceptive was I, really? I remembered what Mica said about Alex Campbell being dumped, but still turning up to workshops and rehearsals and costume discussions as pushy and passionate as ever, never saying a word. I hadn't clocked even the slightest thing might be wrong. And it should've been obvious, shouldn't it, that his heart was broken? Tam clicked his fingers to bring me back into the room.

'I can't believe you zoned out while I was saying what a good listener you are. Look, don't ever feel you're not appreciated, okay. We're sorry. We love you.'

'I know.' But words were just words, weren't they? Like with Harvey, real 'I love you's were all about the showing, not the telling.

Tam ordered another wine, but Daisy came back wanting to wrap things up. Rowing with Seb on the phone, no doubt. She hugged me tight as I stepped onto the tram. 'Oh, Lion. Don't be mad, will you? I'll see you soon. Ross's birthday, you coming to that?'

Did it sting that she had Ross's birthday committed to memory but not mine? You bet your arse it did. I smiled through my disappointment. 'Wouldn't miss it.'

I've slept wearing ear plugs ever since my mum discovered eating cheese made her snore and wilfully ate more in the hope of accidentally curing it. It didn't work, and my teenage bedroom shook – although it became easier to disguise the noises of my wee midnight chugs to shirtless stills of the boys from *The OC*.

So it took me longer than it should've to hear the banging on my door at 3 a.m., and stumble out of bed.

I squinted blearily through the spyhole. Seb, clammy and fretting under a red baseball cap. His eyes were blood oranges turned inside out. He was in fitness gear, obviously having gone straight from the gym to the pub, followed by a row with Daisy.

I ushered him in quickly, praying my neighbours didn't mention this at the next residents' meeting. 'Been a while, Sebastian.'

'Lion.' It took him three minutes to get every letter out. He flopped onto the sofa. 'She's chucked me out, like a dog. Hope I didn't wake you.'

'No, Einstein, I'm still asleep, this is a hologram.'

'No way.' Seb drawled. 'I was listening to this podcast, this guy was living as a hologram in a virtual world and had, like, a fake job and an animatronic dog.'

'You're talking about *The Sims*. I'll get the spare duvet.'

He was on the verge of passing out as I tucked him in, removing his baseball cap to discover a wrap of cocaine hiding underneath. Daisy had been anti-drugs since reading a pamphlet about trafficking once, which might have explained my unexpected guest. Unless something else had come up – might she have told him about her 'procedure'? Other than tell Harvey, I hadn't breathed a word, but was gripped by paranoia that I'd let it slip somehow by blinking the wrong way or posting on Facebook in my sleep.

'Wanna tell me what happened?'

Seb shut one eye to focus on me. 'Just a wee kiss.' Something about the way he said 'wee' in his cut-glass English accent made me want to invade Berwick-upon-Tweed. 'She saw it on the socials. One kiss. Okay, two, but no tongues.' That meant there'd been many tongues and possibly even fingers and tops. 'Aw, Lion, I don't mean to be naughty, but we're young, y'know?'

'You're thirty-four, Seb, not a horny adolescent.' I'd seen plenty of those in my time. 'You two are getting married one day, aren't you?'

'Yah. Absolutely. I mean. I wanna have fun. I wanna get married but it's hella middle-aged, you know?'

'How long are you planning to live?' I'd never understood men like this, still desperate to be little boys, enjoying adulthood's excesses with none of the responsibility. Seb often said boarding school were the best days of his life and I believed him. 'If you still want "fun" you shouldn't be in a relationship.'

I meant fun as in casual sex, but I suppose I meant it in every sense, from previous experience, before Harvey anyway. Harvey was fun. I had fun. Plenty of it.

'No, I get it, totally. You're always right, Dandelion.'

'My curse.'

'Hey.' Seb looked up through his shiny, dark fringe. I made a note to ask Daisy which shampoo she bought; my fringe stuck to my head like I spent my life pressed against windows. 'Do you fancy me?'

Huh? Seb often talked a lot of shite, but this was unprecedented. I mean, of course, I fancied Seb a bit. Visually, at least. It would be hard not to. He went to the gym four times a week, and ran round the Meadows every morning, come rain, shine or hail. He had his T-shirts taken in by some guy in a kiosk in Dalry so they'd sit perfectly over his pecs, he was very good at taking off said T-shirts at the first hint of summer too. I'd also been reliably informed by Ross, whose boyfriend had been Seb's personal trainer until Ross decided it was causing boundary issues, that Seb had nothing to be ashamed of in the shower. So I won't deny that early in our friendship, I'd toyed with the fantasy that, if I'd been at the same extremely posh school he'd attended, he might have asked me to finish him off after a lacrosse lesson. But every other facet of his personality cancelled out the boner.

He was unreliable. He never charged his phone. He was terrible with money. He made Daisy cry more than is normal in any relationship, and Daisy was not a cryer – she had to pinch herself hard at funerals. He still thought farts were funny at thirty-four and you could always tell when he was about to say something stupid and obnoxious because he'd begin filming you on his phone to catch your reaction. So, no, not in a million years. But I thought it best to humour him and spare his ego.

'Why'd you ask?'

'Just . . . I mean, you're a good guy and if you ever felt kinda . . . bi-curious, I hope you'd come to me first.'

'That isn't what bi-curious means, Seb.' Fuck's sake. An actual pass being made at me, by someone who looked like a statue, but was straight (as far as I knew), my best friend's boyfriend, drunk out of his mind, and a fucking idiot. This was too much drama in one envelope. 'I appreciate the offer. We don't need to mention this to Daisy, but you two really need to chat about your future.'

He seemed unbothered by the mention of Daisy. 'So it's not a "no"?'

I suddenly had a very clear image of Seb ejaculating onto my back while checking emails on his phone. It was the hugest of 'no's. A 'no' that could be seen from the Triangulum Galaxy. 'Sure, it's not a "no". Goodnight.'

Twenty-Six

Harvey found it hugely amusing my friends hadn't turned up to my dinner, but were willing to celebrate the birthday of someone we supposedly didn't even like that much. Breaking convention, Ross had hired a bar for his party – tax reasons, Daisy said, swearing me to secrecy as if anyone I knew would be remotely interested – and to make things extra awkward, it was themed. I was apprehensive – the only thing that suited me less than my own clothes was fancy dress. But when I discovered the theme was the musical *Cabaret*, I was thrilled. I'd have preferred a Sondheim, obviously, but this was my world. I rouged my cheeks, did my best to slick my hair down, and went as a tame version of the emcee, eschewing tights for spray-on trousers, just in case a student saw me.

I wasn't expecting Harvey to dress up beyond a bit of lippy and maybe some eye makeup – which we'd agreed to call 'manscara' and 'guyliner' to retain an air of masculinity – so I was winded when he showed up to mine clad in a fishnet top and a harness he said he'd had 'years'. Whatever he and Matt got up to in London was clearly a tad spicier than drag brunches.

His look was more stage version of *Chicago* than *Cabaret*, to be honest, but no matter. Wow. Flashes of that banging body peeking through the netting. Lips plumped and shiny from Daisy's donated lipstick. Eyes shining through the inky kohl. Everybody would eat it up when we walked in.

Sure enough, eyes dangled on stalks; men who'd only ever sneered from across rooms at Ross's shindigs were careering across the bar to talk to us. Well, to him. I basked in the periphery of his spotlight, delighted when he'd hold my hand and pull me closer and say to Stevie or Neil or Paul or Ian or whoever, that, yes, we were together. That I was his. Super-cool and secure about walking in with one of the hottest men, I let him slip off into the crowd and went to find Tam.

I had to speak to someone about Seb. Tam would know what to do, I was sure of it. If Peter was telling the truth about the two of them, Tam was expert in such moral dilemmas. But, of course, Peter wasn't telling the truth, was he? No. I found Tam swaying by a large flower arrangement, his bowler hat askew; he'd obviously been pre-loading.

'Lion! You look like the guy from *Charlie's Angels*. The one who rips their hair out and sniffs it.'

We hugged. He looked stunning, in a lacy . . . I don't know, blouse? Tie draped at the neck. Cycling shorts cut all the way up to his coccyx. 'You look like Margaret Thatcher got a Nasty Gal gift card for Christmas.'

'Shit. You win.' I was about to launch into my tale of Seb-shaped woe when Tam took my hand and said, with a drunken lilt, that he had a dilemma. 'Do you think I'm doing the right thing?' I looked down. A deep red mark by his knuckle. 'Getting married, I mean?'

'What's brought this on?'

'We were talking about porn. It doesn't matter why. Okay, maybe it does. I wanted to put some on. But Fabrizio says he never watches it. Ever. I mean . . .'

'This is why you're having doubts? I don't watch porn either.'

He laughed like a fire alarm. 'It's not doubts! You do watch it, Lion, you totally do.'

Lucky I'd already smothered my cheeks in blusher. 'I don't.'

'Leo Falconer, I distinctly remember you once telling me your favourite type of porn was Mormons. Or men pretending to be them, anyway. In the full getup. One hundred per cent.'

Wh– I had not. Surely. Never. I . . . 'When did I say that?'

'We were both wasted, somewhere, but that particular detail lives rent-free in my napper, baby.'

Okay, so maybe I did say that. Well, you know, those lovely clean white shirts and immaculate, combed hair, and . . . another addition to the growing pile of reasons it was better to be sober – no drunken revelations could come back to haunt you. Although now I came to think of it, Harvey had quite a Mormon look, all clean lines and order – without the other stuff, obviously. I rubbed Tam's hand, felt the bumps where he'd bitten. 'But you're okay, though, right?' Tam never held back, he'd tell me if something was wrong, I knew it.

'Peachy. I'm being silly. I'll start him off gently. Visiting plumber, or stepbrothers left home alone. He'll be fine. What about you?'

'Actually, I have a dilemma of my own . . . ' I hurried through the story of Seb's unexpected visit, leaving pauses for Tam to react with shock or even hysterical laughter, but instead he scrutinised me throughout with the concentration of a safe-cracker.

'Hmmmm, look,' he said finally. 'Uh, he did that to me too, once. Propositioned me, I mean. Years ago.'

How dare I feel a little less special? Of course he'd come on to Tam first. Who wouldn't? Except me. I gave a theatrical gasp, for effect.

'One difference. I actually, uh, went through with it.'

Oh, not jokes, not now. 'Stop it. This is serious. What am I gonna do?'

Tam leaned in, put his mouth to my ear. He smelled of wine and sandalwood. 'Shush. I'm being serious. I did it. Well, not it. Not all of it. I gave him a blow job.'

My neurotransmitters buckled under the weight of the million visions filling my head. I couldn't picture Seb and Tam, though, which I suppose could be quite horny if you liked that sort of thing; I was imagining Tam and Peter together. I breathed long and deep, like Mariah Carey about to go for the big note on 'All I Want For Christmas is You'.

'You did not. When did this happen?'

'I did.' Tam was unfazed by my reaction. 'Ages ago, couple of months after they first got together. We were both monumentally hammered.'

'You've never said anything.' No, not Tam. Not him being good at keeping secrets. Secrets about sex. Sex with best friends' boyfriends.

'I assumed Seb would, like, fall away, like Daisy's other men did. I didn't realise he was "the one". Daisy knows all the answers on *University Challenge* and Seb can barely get through a wordsearch in the *Beano*. He doesn't exactly have forever energy, does he?'

I couldn't believe my ears. My safe, reliable, wholesome Tam. Everything I thought I knew about him was gurgling down the plughole. 'Why the hell did you do it?'

Finally, the veil of shame descended. 'Because it's the kind of thing I'd never do. Alternative timeline Tam found his way to our dimension. Haven't you ever wanted to be someone else, even for, like ten minutes?'

Had I ever. 'Yeah, but I'd maybe get a haircut or give a fake name in Starbucks. Or switch from my A fragrance to my B fragrance. Not this.'

Tam brushed my arm conspiratorially. 'You know, I knew you had a B fragrance. I noticed. What is it?'

'Tam!'

'Jesus. Fine. Yes, I'm embarrassed. I was feeling low at the time, like I didn't matter.'

I'd always refused to believe someone as hot and adored as Tam could ever feel that low. Uncharitable of me, I know. 'You do matter.'

'I know that now, Dandelion, but right then . . . I didn't. Not my finest hour. I didn't enjoy it, if that helps?'

'Didn't you?' I kind of wanted to ask why. Seb always looked so perfect on the surface. Weird-shaped knob? Hygiene issues? Freaky grunting? I attempted a kinder approach to this unholy mess. 'Do you think we should be helping Seb get to the truth of his sexuality? Maybe he has questions?'

'Seb is getting more than enough help. He doesn't need us swooping in with rainbow badges and flyers about queer bookshops.'

'We have to tell Daisy.' I said it to test him, really, in case it urged him to confess about Peter, right here.

'Oh, we do, do we? Why? We don't live in reality TV.'

'She has a right to know.'

'A right! Honestly, stop. We're stuck with him until she finally decides she's had enough. And she will. You don't wanna be the reason they break up. People get back together all the time, but friendships don't always recover.'

'Was it a one-off?'

Someone walked past with a tray of wines and Tam made a grab for one, but missed. 'Shit. Of course! He's never asked for a sequel and I've never looked for one. I can barely believe it happened.'

'It's wrong.'

'No shit, Lion. But it's done now. I don't know why you're so pissed off. Daisy should be angry, not you.'

'She can't be angry if she doesn't know.'

'Exactly.'

I looked deep into his eyes, scanning for guilt or recognition, any memories of Peter. Nothing. He went off to get a drink.

'Everything all right?' Harvey was at my side.

'Yep. Do you mind if we go? I feel rough.'

'We've barely been here an hour.'

'Please.'

Twenty-Seven

We were quiet in the cab back to his. Harvey put music on, opened a bottle of red, poured me a fizzy water. It was way too early to be home. I chucked my coat on the sofa, and Harvey flopped down on top of it. He looked like a chorus girl on her lunch break. He sighed. There was a weight to it. He swirled his wine round his glass and gazed at me in bemusement.

'So, your friends . . . are they all into musicals, then?'

I joined him on the sofa. 'God, no, Daisy can just about hum "Memory".'

'Memory?'

'From *Cats*. Jesus.' A little sharp. Harvey wasn't to blame, no need for me to snap. I reset, brightened. 'Daisy likes Eurovision. Tam doesn't like musicals as such, he adores old-school divas.'

'Like, uh, Mariah Carey?'

'No! Judy! Babs! Elaine! Patti! Liza! Jane McDonald. Anyway. We don't have to like the same things. You don't like musicals and it works.'

'You gonna tell me what your cosy chat with Tam was about?'

I didn't want to lie and I needed to get this into the open air. I couldn't confide in Daisy, that was for sure. 'I don't want you to think it's a big deal, but . . . Seb crashed at mine the other night. Had a row with Daisy, the usual.'

'Those two. Just break up, already.'

'I know.' I liked that he knew me, knew all of us, well enough to say that. It made our foundations feel unshakeable. He was invested. 'Anyway, he was steaming, and he said . . . God this is so silly, but, well, he said if I ever wanted to . . . actually, I'm not sure where he was going with it. He asked if I fancied him, if I'd ever wanted to get it on with him.'

Harvey sat rigid. 'Get it on?'

'He was drunk. I said it was no big deal.'

'To you.'

'I know. Look, that's not all of it.'

'Did he . . . show you anything? Expose himself?'

'No! Anyway, right, I told Tam and, seemingly . . .' I laughed, I couldn't help it, 'Seb said the same to him too, ages ago, except Tam actually did it.'

'Did what?' I watched sobriety repossess Harvey's soul. A whoosh of clarity.

'He sucked him off.' I laughed again, hoping it might be contagious. He usually laughed when I threw him a cue. This time, my delivery must've been off. He looked disgusted.

'And you think that's funny?'

I straightened my face. 'Tam seemed to. He was drunk, though.'

'When? When he did it?'

'Yes. And when he was telling me.'

I'd misjudged this. Harvey's usually placid expression

shattered. 'This is awful. I am hearing this right? Let me just . . . your friend sucked your, uh, best friend's boyfriend's dick?'

It did sound epically bad, out loud. And convoluted. 'Not just Tam's fault. Seb doesn't exactly come out of it covered in glory.'

'Not glory, no. Poor Daisy. She'll be devastated.'

'Ah. Well, Tam's asked me not to say anything.'

'Asked you? So what are you gonna do?'

'Nothing. I wouldn't know how anyway.'

'Leo, she's your best friend. You've known her a really fucking long time. Don't you think she deserves to know?'

We all deserve to know the truth about the people we surround ourselves with, if it stops us getting hurt. But maybe Tam was right: this was over, history, Tam was sorry, and maybe even if we deserved to know everything about the people we love, it didn't mean it was the best thing for us. Good speech. Instead of saying that, I squeaked out: 'I don't know.'

Harvey reached for the bottle and refilled. 'She's your best friend! Jesus. I'm sorry. You lot are so strange. Don't you see how weird this is?'

Whenever Harvey had observed my friends' foibles before, I'd been able to explain them away, but he was dead right about this, wasn't he? I couldn't admit it, though. I tried to distract him. 'I saw Peter.'

'What?'

'I've been in a bit of a state about it. I've been meaning to tell you.'

The tension in that moment. Pinter would've been proud. But Harvey didn't look mad; there was a serenity about him. I'd always glossed over my life with Peter, but even on such scant information, Harvey knew he had nothing to worry about. But he hadn't heard the full story yet. 'In a state?'

I explained in a nervy staccato. 'I went to a bar, by myself. A gay bar. Like an old haunt or whatever. Few months back. When you were in Frankfurt. I'd had a bad day. Campbell breathing down my neck. I didn't drink or anything. Peter was there. He came striding through the dry ice like Mr Darcy wading to shore.'

'Did you know he was gonna be there?'

'No!' But I knew how it sounded.

'And?'

'He told me something horrible. I don't know what to believe. That's why I was telling you. About Seb, I mean.' I wished I'd sat on the chair, opposite him, so I could see his face front-on, gauge his reactions. 'Peter said he had sex with Tam. When we were together. While I was asleep, in another room. I don't know if it's true.'

Harvey gave a winded, one-second laugh, his eyes straining in astonishment. 'You guys. Seriously. Who's left? When do you get a go on Tam? Or have you already, and that's your next confession?'

'Of course I haven't. I don't know what to do.'

I felt the warmth of his hand on my thigh. 'Leo. You don't have to do anything. You're not with Peter anymore. You're with me.'

I felt that crackling behind the eyes that warns tears are imminent. I wanted to hold it together, show Harvey I was strong. 'What about Tam?'

'God!' he said, heartily. Like he was projecting to the back of the Playhouse. Then, more gently: 'I'll never pretend to understand it. Only you can decide. I don't know . . . maybe wank off Fabrizio so you're even?'

'Harvey!'

He shrugged. 'What do you want me to say? You all have such an unserious approach to life. Never any consequences for anything they do. Any normal person would, oh I don't know, never speak to Tam again, let Daisy know that her boy-friend and best friend are selfish and destructive, then go get some friends who actually enrich their life. But I know you won't do that.'

He was right. I wouldn't do that. I'd shrug and keep it in. Because that's what I always did, absorbed other people's dis-asters to protect myself from the fallout. Harvey filled his glass again. 'Fuck Peter. Forget him. Look, do you want some of this? Have some. It'll relax you.'

'No. I'm sorry for . . . dumping this on you. I should've told you about Peter. He was always good at messing with my head.'

'Don't be sorry.' He stroked my face. 'I understand. In fact, I . . . while we're sharing.' A brief, casual chuckle. 'I should tell you. Remember I stayed on in Frankfurt?'

Oh no. What? No. I nodded really slowly, as if it would delay whatever was coming.

'I didn't. Stay in Frankfurt, I mean. I went to London. To see Matt.'

'Your ex Matt?'

'That's right. Matt.'

I didn't want to ask why but you're supposed to, aren't you, when someone reveals something like this?

'He's selling the flat. Our flat. He wanted to talk about my share, that kind of thing.'

I almost said phew out loud. But did I mean phew? Why tell me now, ages later? What prompted this amnesty? Tam sucking Seb's cock? Had it reminded him of what he'd done? Did he meet Matt, at a train station pub maybe, or a favoured old haunt, had a glass of wine, then another, shared a few 'remember whens' and before long the booze kicked in and they were pressed against each other, pique polo shirts entangled, before Harvey slid to his knees and gave Matt what he wanted. I tried to stay the agreeable, preferable me. The anti-Matt. But I had a million questions. 'Why didn't you say?'

'Honestly? I didn't feel like it had anything to do with you. It was boring admin I had to sort out. But now, I realise, I should've told you. We should tell each other everything.'

I felt sick. I'd seen that photograph in Harvey's glove compartment. I knew what I was up against. Handsome, athletic Matt, trophy perched vaingloriously on the bookshelf. Harvey, bursting with pride in that photo. A love you couldn't just extinguish like a cigarette. It would burn on, the embers of it all round me now. 'Why did you lie?'

'I'm telling you now. You lied about Peter, remember, and that's fine.'

The cogs, why didn't they stop turning, why couldn't I do my usual act of sitting down and being quiet like a good boy and telling myself it would be okay? No. I couldn't put myself there again.

'I didn't lie. I just didn't say. It's not the same thing. You lied about where you were. Said you were in Frankfurt. You weren't.'

Perhaps in recognition of this escalation, we both stood up. 'It didn't seem important.'

'But it's a lie.' I wanted to skip ahead, to everything being sunny again, but felt a familiar sensation – a shift in air pressure I recognised from years ago.

'Fine. I didn't mention it. It's not like I went cruising for cock because I was . . . what was it you said? *Having a bad day? Met my ex in a gay bar.*'

Ouch. That was vicious. 'It's not the same! I didn't know he was going to be there. I wasn't cruising! You planned to see Matt!'

Harvey topped up his glass. The wine looked like blood, so deep and rich, blackening his lips. 'It's a bit much to go on about honesty. You've literally agreed to keep a massive secret from your best friend.'

'This has nothing to with Daisy or Tam.'

'Doesn't it? I think it might. You're arguing with me when you should be shouting at them. They've made a hypocrite out of you, and totally dismissed your feelings. What Seb did is highly inappropriate, and would be seen as traumatic by any normal group of friends. But not yours, Dandelion.'

There's a weird sensation when you touch something very hot. For a millisecond, before the burn takes hold and your skin begins to crackle, it actually feels ice cold, the kiss of a snowball. That was the feeling; certain I'd get hurt, but not sure how badly.

'You know what a dandelion is, don't you?' Harvey shook his head. 'It's a weed. That's why they call you it. They could root you out any time they like.'

I let that uncharacteristic unkindness linger in the air a few seconds. This wasn't the Harvey I knew. I didn't recognise either of us in that exact moment. Our clothes matched the two lovers who'd laughed in the cab to the party, but everything else was different. I couldn't hold off my tears.

'Look, I'm sorry,' he said, his face losing its red glow. 'Here . . . ' He held out his glass, the wine roiling within it, trying to reach out to me. 'Have a drink, go on, chill out. We can sort this.'

'Stop it. I don't want a drink!' I grabbed the glass out of his hand and felt its contents splash my shirt and chin before it slipped out of my hand, empty, and fell to the floor. I was tingling head to foot, heat rising, scorching liquid metal in my veins, every muscle electrically charged. Fight or flight. That feeling, that feeling. I knew it. Too well. I'd been wrenched back to a place I never thought I'd find myself again. I didn't look at Harvey, I didn't want to see this version of his face. I'd ruined everything, again. I wish I looked good wet, I thought, for the millionth time in my life, as I pushed past him, and ran out the front door, and away, into the night.

Twenty-Eight

I don't know why I went to the school. No, I do. I couldn't go anywhere else. I couldn't face going home and sitting staring at the walls. Nor back to the party, to Tam and Daisy's questions. Too much explaining. I jumped in a cab and was getting dropped at the gate when I realised it was 9.30 p.m. on a Friday night, and everything would be locked up. So there I was, coatless, under the first dots of rain, when the gates opened and out drove Campbell. He stopped.

Unfortunately.

Thankfully.

'Bit early for Monday.' Another dad joke from his limited repertoire. He must've noticed the look on my face, not to mention the remnants of blusher and kohl eyebrows. And the super-tight breeks. 'Everything all right?' I almost laughed. I shook my head. 'Get in.'

'I was going in to look over some, errr . . . '

'Forget it, McCluskey's locked the place shut. In.'

As I fiddled with my seatbelt, I heard him sniff up. 'You been out?'

'Uh, a party.'

'I thought you didn't drink.'

'I don't.'

'Rightio.' He put the car into drive. Automatic. I liked to watch Harvey change the gears, so masterful and smooth.

'This isn't the way to my flat.'

He glanced at me. 'We're going to mine. Dry you off, maybe get you a clean shirt. And ummm, some tracksuit bottoms, maybe, as delectable as your pins are in those . . . what are they? Leggings?'

I suddenly understood why he'd asked about the drinking – I stank of wine. 'There was a spilling incident.'

'No offence but you smell like you fell into Lake Chianti Classico.'

His flat was near the Meadows, with a view of Arthur's Seat. It was also where clinical depression came for a city break. It wasn't untidy or anything, just unloved. Transient. One of those new-build crates with a mesh balcony bolted to the front, corridors of heavy fire doors. This place hadn't been chosen as a home; he'd been forced to move here. Unpacked boxes were stacked in one corner of the hall. I remembered what Mica had said – *he got dumped*. He read my mind.

'It's temporary.'

'It's nice.' What was I supposed to say? That plutonium-levels of lonely heartbreak energy radiated off the place?

'If you're fresh out the gulags, yes, it's gorgeous. I've got some cracking tea – camomile and lavender. Fancy it? Unless you'd like another dip in your lake.'

'I really don't drink.'

He set the tea in front of me; our mugs didn't match. Mine

had flowers on – a maternal gift if ever I'd seen one – and his said I SURVIVED THE ULTIMATE AT LIGHTWATER VALLEY. The tea smelled sweet and comforting, but looked like pee.

'So what's happened? Why are you wandering the streets looking like a ventriloquist's dummy who's hit the skids?'

Where was this sympathetic, open smile at school? Something about this new persona disarmed me – it made me confessional too. I gave a précis of the row, downplaying it as much as I could.

'You looked scared when I saw you. Is your partner . . . and you can tell me to mind my own business, but, is he violent?'

'No. Never.'

'So why did you run?'

'Not because of him. I'm not scared of him, just . . . this kind of situation.'

'Flashback to an ex?'

'Good guess.'

'I'm becoming an expert. An ex-expert. What was his name?'

'Peter.'

I'd never told anybody the full extent of The Unpleasantness. I began to babble – my first time saying it out loud to anyone, ever, yet the story had been finessed in my head over years, during sleepless nights, long bus journeys and, some-times, at work.

I thought I'd be glad when Peter left me. After the elation of the last goodbye, I remembered feeling relieved some days, distraught others; there was no unifying emotion. I was glad he couldn't look at me with contempt anymore. But then he was gone. Peter used to take up a lot of space. Coats, scarves and shoes left exactly where he took them off, sitting in chairs he covered as much surface area as possible. I wasn't overly tidy, but at university learned from Daisy: 'don't put it down, put it away' – whenever she came over her eyes would drink in Peter's precarious piles of books, discarded sweatshirts and stained coffee mugs. I explained it away, he was an English teacher, intellectuals were messy. Daisy never said a word. If she had, what might I have confessed? Sometimes all you need is a door to be left slightly ajar, don't you?

When Peter left, the air seemed heavy, like it never moved. No floorboards creaking to let me know he was in another room, no doors slamming, no shower water tinkling down the drain, no phone beeping with messages from his bits on the side. For a while, too long in fact, I'd choke at the thought of calling his name and not having it answered. I'd open and shut empty drawers in the bedroom, day after day, hoping to find I don't know what – out of date condoms and gummed-up tubes of lube, mostly. I felt so stupid missing him, given I loathed him and what he'd done to me. Life is complicated.

Daisy and Tam were sympathetic on a superficial level – not totally their fault, I didn't tell them the full story, which suited me fine at the time. He'd had an affair, yes, good riddance, yes, what a bastard, yes, the comforting clichés. I wanted to leave The Unpleasantness buried. Every now and then, like a terrier, I'd exhume it, inspect it, then plunge it back deep into the soil, clods of earth holding it down.

Alex coughed to let me know he was still here.

'Peter hit me once. God, I'm lying for him even now. More than once. Twice. Two and a half times. That last time was the most scared I've ever been, except when my Madonna tickets went to the wrong house.' Even now, at the peak of my vulnerability, I couldn't stop making jokes to paper over cracks. My curse.

'Printed tickets? Was this concert during the Neolithic period? Do you want to talk about this?'

'Do you want to hear it? I'm not used to talking about it. I never have.'

'I can wait.'

First time was in the car. I'd read the map wrong, I don't really understand satnav, can't bear the voice, so authoritarian and judgey, babbling about yards and miles – who's supposed to know what 750 yards is? Daisy had hired a cottage for the weekend. I was driving, Peter wasn't helping, regally tapping at his phone. We missed a turning. It was getting dark. I told him to wake the fuck up. I meant it as a joke, said it jovially, to hide my annoyance. Maybe it was my fault. He felt attacked, he said later. Yet he did the attacking. He didn't hit me, actually, not properly. A quick thwack to slap the phone out of my hand while I tried to make sense of the gridlines, which were turning into spaghettini before my eyes. Then a shove, hard, with both hands, against the door; I caught my arm on the steering wheel, which gave a mournful honk in sympathy. It hurt. He was shocked by what he'd done, but doubled down quickly. I'd provoked him. I accepted this. I sold the car a month later, thinking if I could remove a weapon it wouldn't happen again.

Second time, he didn't hit me either, technically. Back in the flat after a night at the pub. He wanted to put a song on but couldn't find it. Maybe I pushed him a little, offering too many suggestions, needling him, confusing him. It escalated quickly. He jerked toward me so fast he could've been either about to hug me or hit me, then everything slowed down and he dashed his full glass of wine in my face. I felt every drop hit, could even hear the sound of the splashes that didn't, spraying the floor and the wall. I blinked through the sting of Pinot Grigio, gagged a little at its perfume. My shirt was stuck to my chest, small trickles coursed down my back. I tried to anchor myself with the things around me. There was the geranium we bought together, stopping for a latte on the way home. Syrupy ones, too sweet, we'd laughed about sugar highs. And the rug we finally bought after two months of circling it and various clones in furniture shops across town. The card we'd posted ourselves from Turkey to remind us what a lovely afternoon we'd had. That was us, the real us. Not this, not this wine dripping down my face, this poison seeping into the fabric of my shirt, stinking out the room. I thought if we could get back to being those guys again – geraniums, syrup, laughing, holidays, a bland rug – this would never happen again. I was wrong.

Third time, he definitely hit me. Drunk. In the communal landing outside the flat. I'd made a comment about how many he'd had. Playful, but, if I'm honest, laced with sourness. He hit me with the back of his hand, like they do in movies. The echo knifed through the air, off the stone walls. My ears rang with the sound for days after. When I opened the flat door I felt the force of both his hands on my back and I staggered to the ground, limbs everywhere, so gangly and clumsy and useless. There's a silence after unthinkable things happen that feels like it might last for ever. The longer it goes on, the more likely it will lead to further unthinkable things. I was on the floor. I tried anchoring again, focused on the walls, noticed scuffs from where he propped his bike, mud from my running shoes that I hadn't wiped properly. He stood over me. I could feel his boot next to my face. He was working out his next move. He didn't lift his foot, but he was thinking about it. I could smell mint from the chewing gum stuck to the sole of his boot.

Finally, he spoke. 'I don't like losing control like this. You make me crazy sometimes, Leo. Are we sure we want to spend the best years of our lives like this?'

These were the best years? I'd have hated to see the worst.

'I'm sorry that I make you unhappy, I wouldn't blame you if you left.'

I didn't want him to go, even then; I said it to get him to pity himself almost, in the hope it would make him stay. Instead, he read it as permission for him to have that affair. All I wanted him to do was crouch down on his haunches as I lay beneath him in sacrificial splendour and beg my forgiveness, but he never did. He silently helped me to my feet and went out again. Maybe he even met Ben that very night, who knows? Four months later Peter was gone for good, and I was free, but I still saw the world from inside a cage. Takes a while.

Alex placed another mug beside me. Regular tea this time. 'Can I ask . . . why you never told anyone?'

It would've made it real. Telling Daisy and Tam, or my mum, would've transformed it from something I could box away safe, and into a 'thing'. Police might be called, there'd be shouting matches, drama, perhaps more violence. It would become part of my story, cast up again and again. They'd forever see me only through this filter, another battle scar, like my nose, or my eye, or my vitiligo. I'd take my place in the hall of fame of disastrous relationships, to be pulled apart on the wrong end of a bottle of rosé for all eternity.

'I was embarrassed. Didn't want people to know I'd backed the wrong horse.'

'Is that what you're worried about now? That you've backed the wrong horse again?'

Harvey and Peter couldn't have been more different, but those last moments with Harvey had felt like time travel. The anger between us. 'Maybe I'm the wrong horse.'

'You're not. You're a very cool guy.'

Even in the darkest depths of despair my ego couldn't resist this dusting of sugar. 'Huh?'

'I admire you so much. You're unashamedly yourself.'

'What does that mean?' Although I kind of knew. That was the main thing about never drinking: I was always myself. There was no hiding from me, no anaesthetising the pain or blocking anything out. The highs got rarer and the lows felt tougher.

'Don't take this the wrong way.'

'If you're going to say I'm camp, I am . . . aware.'

He laughed. A different melody from his forced laugh in staff meetings. 'I battled a long time with, uh, masculinity, that stuff. Was ashamed of myself for liking musicals . . . '

I had to know. 'What's your favourite? I'll decide whether you should be ashamed or not.'

'I don't know. One of the Sondheims, I guess.'

'Stop it. You know he sent me a letter once? It's locked away in my pants drawer.' I blushed at the idea of Alex knowing I had a pants drawer, even though everybody had one. 'I wrote to him when I was a teenager.' I paused for the inevitable intake of breath. 'Favourite song?'

'Erm . . . "Another Hundred People". From *Company*. You know it?'

'Of course I fucking do. Good choice. Mine's "Opening Doors". From *Merrily We Roll Along*.'

'Oof. A fan favourite. And a flop. How niche.'

'Shut up. You were saying.'

His life uncoiled like a comic strip. Working in the ice-cream shop in the holidays, peering over the counter at beautiful boys and handsome dads, trying to catch the eye of anyone who blipped his radar. He'd wanted to sing and dance, but his parents thought he was mad, that he should either go into a respectable profession, like being a doctor or teacher or investment banker – 'This is before the recession' – or take control of the soft scoop for good. In his family – Scottish miners and scaffolders on one side, loud and confident Italians on the other – men were men. They only danced, sang and hugged after a few drinks. Any love between them was the type of loyal hero worship that can, at its height, feel lusty. He'd never worked out how to be himself.

'Not like you. I got you straightaway.'

I didn't like the idea of being so easily worked out, but, you know, drama teacher, my voice, my walk, my everything – I'm gay to the core.

'I need to let myself go a bit,' he said. 'For a long time I was frightened of gay stereotypes.'

'You have a *West Side Story* poster in your office. My all-time, overall favourite, by the way.'

'I know!' How did he know?

'What else do you like about me? And do I have to reciprocate? I'll struggle.'

He leaned over and nudged my arm, but backed away quickly, maybe worried it wasn't appropriate to touch someone who's just told you their ex was handy with his fists. I'd have done the same – maybe Daisy was right about us being similar. 'I know that in work mode, I can be hard to like.'

'Yeah. But back to me.'

'Charming. Okay. Your students obviously adore you. That's rarer the higher up the education ladder you get.'

He was popular too, though. I'd heard students yell 'Hi, sir!' to him in the corridor, not even in a funny voice – a rare honour – and the Naomi nickname was definitely affectionate.

'You know Chris is on about retiring next Christmas.'

'Oh?'

'You should apply for head of drama. I'd support it. I'm sure April will, too, when she comes back.'

I felt a twinge of fear. Change. Responsibility. But on the flip side: being rid of Chris.

'I'm not sure.'

He sipped his tea as if he'd been expecting that response. 'I was scared too, becoming a deputy, but once I . . . ' I swear his eyes misted over. What was he thinking of? 'It worked out okay in the end. You're a great teacher.'

A rush of blood to the head, like I'd stood up too fast. 'I wonder what else we have in common.'

We spent the next hour or so flinging random facts back and forth, during which I discovered he peed sitting down, had slept with two women (not at the same time) but had been very bad at it (both times), thought salted caramel was disgusting, was allergic to penicillin and couldn't ride a bike.

'Look, do you want my advice?'

'No. Yes. Maybe.'

'Don't judge yourself, or Harvey, on Peter's mistakes. Go

back, apologise for storming off, but stand up for yourself, set the tone for what comes next. You don't have to be frightened. You don't have to lose him.'

'Maybe you're wiser than I gave you credit for. Whoever dumped you was an idiot. You're actually lovely.' Whoa. Hang on. That was a stupid thing to say. His smile dribbled away.

'Dumped? I wasn't.'

'But this.' I swept my hand out to the room, over empty bookshelves, cushions that were never plumped, the standard issue curtains, and furniture bought for a much bigger flat, elsewhere, one that maybe still contained his ex.

'I left.'

'Oh God, I'm so . . . '

'It's fine. Do you mind if we talk about that another time?'

'I'd like that.' Hang on. My face burned. 'No, I meant . . . '

'I know!'

He drove me home. As we pulled up outside I instinctively reached for my coat. 'Shit, it's at Harvey's. I'll have to get it tomorrow.'

'A chance to clear the air, then.' Alex shook my hand. So businesslike after our earlier confessional. 'Let's keep this between us, okay?'

'Sure.'

He stopped me as I was getting out. 'You're a force for good, Mr Falconer.'

'Oh, back to the misters now, are we?'

'Leo, I mean. *Leo*. Sorry.'

'Don't be.' It had been the heaviest of nights, yet as I walked into my flat I felt lighter than air.

Twenty-Nine

Harvey opened the door slowly, sheepishly.

'Hey.'

The walk along his hallway seemed to take forever. God, I hated this, I couldn't wait to get back to laughing – another reason I hated drama, there was always aftermath to wade through, motives and intentions to dissect and drive yourself mad over.

Harvey took my hand. He had something to tell me. I really hoped he wasn't about to reveal he'd fucked his ex, or got a cab round to Seb's and given him a row. What if he was proposing? Or was ending it? My mind conjured up as many disasters as it could in those short seconds.

'It's about your coat.' Oh.

On the bed, unmade, very unusual for Harvey, was my coat. But it looked weird. I reached out to touch it. The material didn't feel soft and plush, like usual, it was felty, stiff.

'I'm sorry. I tried to salvage it.'

Apparently in my race to strop out of Harvey's flat, I'd knocked the wine bottle out of Harvey's hand onto the sofa, staining my coat with sticky, bloody vino. After a ninety-minute tussle with the washing machine and a frying in the tumble dryer, the coat was, I could plainly see, ruined.

'It's a cashmere mix. Dry clean only.'

'I tried to . . . I can't believe I didn't check the label. I assumed . . . it didn't seem that valuable.'

'It wasn't.' I held up one of the sleeves and looked inside, the lining was brutally ripped from the spin cycle. My dad had still been alive when I'd bought this coat. I was wearing it the day he'd clung to my arm as I guided him into the house from the taxi after his radiotherapy, the day I realised he was going to die. This coat had survived my saddest winters.

Giant tears rolled down Harvey's beautiful face, spoiling it almost, but he made no sound. I didn't want this, it scared me. I wanted to rewind everything, pretend I'd never seen him snarl, or grabbed the glass, or that I'd never gone back to Campbell's and told him who I was. My mum once told me watching a man cry was both the most beautiful and the ugliest thing you'd ever see. Those fat, salty tears. The way his bottom lip curled out. Baby wants milk. I felt drawn to this rare flash of vulnerability. He stroked my face.

'Sorry I didn't tell you about Matt. Seeing him, I mean. It was horrible, he was cold. Like a business meeting.'

I tried to join these dots to the version I'd heard when we first met. Amicable, he'd said. Wanted different things. What changed? Now didn't seem the time to ask. I guessed this was my cue to accept his apology which I did, gladly.

'That must've been tough. I'm sorry I was such a bitch about it.' Of course nothing happened with Matt – Harvey was trying to protect me. He clearly adored me. Why else be so upset by the coat?

'I'll tell you everything from now on.'

I grasped for a laugh. 'Maybe not everything. Toilet habits, how much hotter my friends are than me, that you don't really like "Send in the Clowns". Good to have some mystery.'

He laughed through his tears. 'Sorry about "Send in the Clowns". It's not for me.' We kissed. Man, I don't know. It felt good to be back to normal. He pulled my jumper up over my head, unbuttoned my jeans, shoved his hand down the front of my pants, hard.

As we twisted naked in the sheets, Alex's words from the night before ran through my head and I pulled Harvey's hair back and squeezed him so tight, wringing out every last drop of doubt between us. I was admired, I was a 'very cool guy'. My friends said shit like this all the time, but I barely knew Alex. Why do compliments from strangers always mean so much more?

Harvey lazed in the bath and I dragged my favourite coat to the giant dumpster secreted behind ornate trellising in the grounds of Harvey's block. My phone rang. Daisy. I desperately wanted to talk to her, yet at the same time wasn't in the mood.

'You left so early!' Twenty-four hours ago. What had taken her so long? 'I didn't even see you! Was everything okay?'

'Yes, just tired.'

'You don't sound sure. Look, if this is about your birthday again . . .'

Fucking hell, my goodwill evaporated. 'It isn't! I was tired.'

'Because Harvey should have followed that up. I explained

to you about that, remember?' She was walking somewhere, fast. She'd once raged at me for calling when I was in transit, insisting it was impolite, that the optimum conversation mode was sitting in a lovely chair. I'd laughed hysterically, assuming it was a skit, but she was serious. Predictably, she didn't live by her own lofty standards.

'Yes, I remember you blaming it on Harvey.'

'I'm not blaming anyone, Lion, I'm explaining.'

There comes a point, I think, when you have to stop excusing bad behaviour as eccentricity. Daisy micro-managing every-one's schedule and taking charge with no acknowledgement that people work in different ways. Tam, too, offering no expla-nation for his behaviour other than 'it happened and there's no going back now'. No wonder I'd run to the school the night before, to Alex, and not to either of them.

Maybe I had to accept it: we were growing apart. It was a miracle our friendship had lasted that long. I used to think of us as Frank, Charley and Mary from 'Opening Doors' – us against the world, struggling and winning together. I'd found something comforting about being loyal and accommodating, never burdening them with my worries because I knew, deep down, they were too fragile. Maybe I knew them too well. Daisy's scars from her parents' decade-long finger-pointing, vase-throwing divorce, which on the disaster scale made the sinking of the *Mary Rose* look like a slow puncture in a dinghy. Tam's bizarre inability to be alone for longer than a month or two, staggering into relationships because he'd never known the joy of starfishing in a double bed.

I'd never complained, kept my heartaches to myself, buried my dad and did all my crying in one day, and threw my energy into being indispensable so that when I wasn't there, they might miss me. I think that's all some of us want, sometimes, to know the space we take up is valuable, that someone would care if we weren't in it. Was it so bad if we were drifting away? It happened. You can't stay besties for ever. Things were changing. Seb and Daisy would have kids eventually, Fabrizio and Tam would be doing married shit with other married gays, and I'd have Harvey. I wasn't short of friends – Mica, the running club . . . Alex. I'd be fine. Would I really miss carrying that extra weight of Daisy and Tam's myriad traumas? Would I yearn for Ross's soirees, permanently on edge in case I crushed a canapé underfoot?

And Harvey had a point, actually: that nickname was patronising. Why was I Dandelion? Why did I have to be the lanky, dopey flower bobbing above the blades of grass spoiling the clean line of a manicured lawn, first for the chop when the mower descended? Daisy and Tam were the beautiful flowers, weren't they, who bloomed stronger and more vibrant every year, enjoying every crumb of privilege their allure offered them. Would I have let them get away with so much if I wasn't hoping some of their charm would rub off on me? I didn't like to be cruel, but I felt an urge to push her away, away, away.

'Lion? Are you there?'

'I have to go.'

Most satisfying press of the end-call button ever.

A few days later, I was at home trying to negotiate a peace deal with my central heating thermostat when a delivery came: a huge gift box, the kind that carried apologies, embellished with golden ribbon and a sparkling bow. Inside, a coat that must've cost an arm and a leg, plus the limbs of several bystanders too, an extremely upgraded version of the tatty one claimed by the evil vino. Military style, a collar I could turn up, with exquisite detailing on the cuffs. Buttons with a high mortgage value. Cosy, but light enough to carry over one arm should the sun ever make an appearance in Edinburgh before April. I slipped my arms into it; it was beautiful. It buttoned up fine, but it was slightly too small. I didn't look squeezed in or anything, but I felt the tiniest bit restrained, like I couldn't quite get a deep, satisfying breath. Inside the box was a golden envelope. I stared at in my hand. Willy Wonka luring me to the chocolate factory?

An embossed notelet informed me I now had a year's premium membership to Harvey's gym, GruntBox, and a stark white piece of paper with Harvey's jagged handwriting on it said: 'From now on, the only thing getting ripped is you and me, in spin class.'

One way of getting the coat to fit, I supposed.

Thirty

Once, as we watched a man with a million-dollar jawline eviscerate a waiter at the next table, Tam told us his theory: the cruellest people of all were hot ones who'd once been ugly children. 'It's the old cliché, isn't it? Get hench then forget what it's like to be an outcast.'

Daisy had laughed. 'I don't think I've ever seen a childhood photo of you, Tammy. Did you look like Rocky and Bullwinkle smooshed in a blender?'

'But Tam isn't cruel!' I'd said, believing it. He didn't 'get' hench either – his DNA worked harder than any gym membership.

Nobody asked about my childhood photos – for a start Daisy had seen most of my formative years and knew I'd looked like a rat trapped in a pork pie. But perhaps my luck was changing. Maybe I could disprove that theory. Three times a week, I got up at 6 a.m. and met Harvey in the gym. No, seriously, I did. Daisy and Tam would've been aghast, but I'd been fobbing them off. 'Sorry, too busy with the show' was my favourite, incontrovertible excuse. Eventually their attempts to lure me away tailed off.

Fewer late nights listening to them meant I was now on nodding terms with the delightful himbos on the gym's front desk, had a favoured locker, and even developed the habit of working out in the same corner, carefully arranging my preferred heavy instruments of torture around me – once Harvey had shown me how to use everything. I learned squats, swings, crunches, lifts. Annoyingly, after a few sessions, I started to feel different. Better. Something inside me hated that I'd copped out and was attempting to join the beautiful people. I once overheard Ross saying 'there's no gym for the face' to one of his close friends – about an even closer friend – and it had stayed with me. No matter what I did, I'd still have the same face. This comforted me, actually. I was doing this to recreate Harvey's macrobiotic version of joy, yes, but at least I was still me. The remodelling began slowly – 'always harder for tall guys' Akshay had piped up on bumping into me in the locker room once. As my body's transformation began, it was reassuring to look in the mirror and still see my gormless puss staring back. Leo 2.0. Well, 1.5.

'It feels great having something to aim for, right?' Harvey told me, peeling off my underwear and grazing the white patch on my thigh with his lips. It did. I wasn't aiming for bodily perfection; any change was a bonus. My goal was making Harvey happy, showing him what I was prepared to do. Things had never looked better. Until London.

It was Alex's idea, to prepare the students for their big moment – a quick trip to London to see not one but two contemporary musicals.

'Keep your stars happy,' he trilled as he read the proposed itinerary. One musical's songbook comprised what he called 'modern classics' by Britney, Kelly Clarkson and the Backstreet Boys – the equivalent of scratchy gramophone records to my students. The other was like a pop concert with a historical storyline (I anticipated the students booing) but original, contemporary songs. Between them, they'd show our students what our production could be (if we had money, time, and West End professionals), plus the kids would love us for ever. London! Away from school! Theatre! London (again)!! It was also free – Alex found budget 'down the back of your beanbags, Leo' to make it happen. Best of all, it really pissed off the other department heads. To my surprise, Mica didn't seem keen to drop in on her hometown. I'd been neglecting her a bit. A lot, actually. Things weren't great at home. We stood on the fire escape taking a second or two to be thrilled we didn't need our coats for the first time that year, before she filled me in.

'She's done it. She walked in and I knew.'

'Done what?'

Mica pulled so hard on her emergency cigarette I thought she was going to have an aneurysm. 'It. She's been getting her hole.' It was usually an instant demerit if any student was heard using that colourful Scottish euphemism.

'You can't know!'

'Course I can. I got four sisters, plenty of mirrors. She walked into my kitchen like a woman.'

'Well, she is sixteen.'

Mica flicked the cigarette down into the car park and held out her hand for another. 'I don't give a shit how many candles are on her cake. She's my baby and she's living in my house. If she's doing it, I need to know.'

Mica was wildly popular with her students, but she was no

soft touch. She tolerated no classroom nonsense and insisted on a one-to-one if even one piece of homework was missed. Dedicated.

'You know, with respect, you're not giving off the energy of someone who, like, would take that information calmly. Maybe that's why she's keeping it from you.'

'Parenting expert!'

'No, but I'm an expert on … not always telling people what's going on.'

'Point taken. Either way, I can't go to London.'

'You can't leave me alone with Campbell.' It was out of my mouth before I realised. She made me light a cigarette of my own and demanded I spill. I told a very diluted version of that night two weeks before, leaving out our more personal confidences.

'I respect the pivot to main character, nice, but what's the problem? You're mates now, so what?'

Mates? Not exactly. It was like it had never happened. Unless we were alone, business as usual. Curt nods in the staffroom. 'Mr Falconer' this, 'Mr Falconer' that. 'It's very hard to compute. We might kill each other.'

'Or fuck. Is that what you're afraid of? Thing is, this ain't about you so you're gonna have to be a big brave boy and play nice with the deputy, okay? Go to Soho, get wasted on bad margaritas … uh, well, get him wasted maybe. I've gotta stay here and wallpaper my flat with condoms and leaflets about gonorrhoea.'

Harvey wasn't impressed either. 'Three nights? Permanently on duty? Eating into your downtime when you should be focusing on de-stressing? Sounds like school is taking advantage.'

I prevaricated, yammered on about the students, how it would inspire them, how there was no cost, so everyone could come, and he was placated, until I mentioned Mica wasn't coming, but Alex was.

'Just you and him?'

'No, thank God. Joe Music's coming, and Rekha, the teaching assistant. Beth the French teacher too; her husband's papering the sun-lounge that weekend so she needs an excuse not to help.'

'Why, "thank God"?'

'Errr because he's a bit boring. And bossy.' Neither of those things were particularly true. What was I worried about? 'I'm sick of the sight of him.'

Harvey seemed appeased. 'I'm just sad for you. Sounds like it would be a nice jolly otherwise, a chance to get away from the play.'

'The show.' There's nothing inner about my pedantic streak. 'It's not ideal going on a residential with the boss, no.'

'You two are the only gays?'

'Gays! Who says that? I'm afraid so. I've always wondered about Joe, he's got a lot of sheer scarves, but so far he's not come out and he's never single.'

'Will you be sharing a room?'

'No!'

He wrapped his arms around me. 'I'll miss you. That's all.' Part of me could understand the interrogation; if Harvey went to London, I'd be wondering if he was going to see Matt. Again. But this was different, wasn't it? Alex wasn't an ex, I wasn't remotely interested in him romantically, not at all. Right?

This would be my first time with Alex out of school since

that night. The Campbell Confessional, I was calling it. A memory turned into a joke couldn't hurt you.

I'd anticipated the usual educational-visit hotel, a charmless stack of concrete coffins in illegal cladding miles away from everything, but Alex had booked us into a charming, if rough round the edges, place near Russell Square. Shepherding the students the short journey from King's Cross took ten times as long thanks to stragglers pointing at drug dealers, or swarming the Scottish food market stall outside the station, as if they'd been away from home a century. Most of them had never been to London; I loved watching their faces take in its vastness and noise and joyous stink. There was a room issue – only two staff rooms, one of which had a double bed, the other two bunks. I felt so awkward, I thought my spine was going to work its way right out of my body.

'Obviously Rekha and Beth take the double,' said Joe, pushing his glasses up his nose to show he was taking charge, 'so the lads are bunking in together.'

Lads! Bunking! Joe Music had never been a lad! I wasn't ready to see his nightwear arrangements, either, but at least I wouldn't be alone with Alex. Why did it matter anyway? Was I worried he'd try to talk to me about personal stuff again? Was that bad? It didn't make sense, but sometimes feelings don't announce why they're there, they just appear.

The first night, I volunteered for nighttime patrol, staying up until two, when everyone was comatose. Rekha and I played cards and told embarrassing stories from our childhoods. When I crept to bed, everyone else was asleep. I clambered to the top bunk by the glow of my phone trying not to rouse Joe, who was snoring – in key, though; he really was musical to the core. On the other top bunk, Alex lay on his back, hands crossed over his chest like a vampire.

'How was it?'

I hit my head on the ceiling. 'Shit.'

'Sorry. Didn't mean to startle you. Any problems?'

'It's okay. No, nothing. Well, Rekha could very comfortably have a sideline as a Vegas cardsharp and I owe her £15, but that's it.'

'She was a croupier on a cruise ship, you know. Do you want ear plugs? I brought a job lot. I've already given Joe some, if you're wondering why I'm not whispering. Here.'

I felt a tiny plastic case land on my duvet. Two foam ear plugs inside. 'Very organised.'

'Very light sleeper. Night, Leo.'

'Night.'

Thirty-One

By the second night, the kids were exhausted, and Joe and Rekha volunteered for night duty. I wondered how much cash Joe would lose. Alex suggested the rest of us go to the bar of a hotel he knew round the corner. Great rooftop views, amazing mock-tails, he said, without even putting a sarcastic emphasis on the 'mock'. Beth said she had some reading to do, but I was desperate to be out of earshot of teenagers. The lift to the top was glass and my stomach complained all the way up; I almost staggered out into the main bar. We were shown to a table in a quiet-ish corner of floor-to-ceiling windows. You could see for miles: skyscrapers stacked alongside each other like random books on a shelf, gleaming with opportunity and thrilling menace; cranes in the process of creating more; the dome of St Paul's now dwarfed by glass and steel; the night sky stretching into oblivion. I looked down and saw the street far below, like Lego. I watched a man on a cycle, blissfully unaware of us gawking metres up; I felt like Godzilla, tempted to reach out, pluck him from the street and hold him to my face for a closer look. Alex looked comfortable here, in this lighting, among the decor, which was a rich person's idea of kitschy 1970s squalor – macramé hangings and mushroom-coloured ceramics, dark wood with flecks of gold. I was pretty sure we were the only people in here wearing Marks & Spencer knitwear. We talked shop at first – who'd been behaving, or not, which musical we'd preferred, and what we could steal for *Hidden Talents*, if we binned some of the weaker sections.

'I'm excited to see it all coming together,' he said. 'You've done a fantastic job. Mica and Joe, too, of course. How you feeling about your big moment?'

Honestly? Pretty good. Great, even. I was ready. Nervous, yes, but it helped that I'd be on stage only a few minutes and only from the penultimate number, so the audience's enthusiasm and excitement for the big ending would cancel out my nerves. All those faces, eyes trained right on me. Just for once.

'I'm hoping I can pull it off.'

'You will. You've moved mountains this term. I'm impressed.' He leaned forward now. 'Have you thought more about applying for Chris's job? Deadline is first day back after summer. Just a heads up.'

I had thought about it. I wasn't sure I wanted it, or that Alex's faith in me was enough to take me over the line. 'I'm gonna decide over the holidays.'

'Okay.' He looked at me a while. Only a few seconds probably but, during silence, any glance feels like an intense stare. I could tell where his gaze was trained, and braced myself for him to say my patch of vitiligo was getting bigger. Instead:

'I wanted to apologise.'

He left a gap. Was I supposed to know what he was apologising for? I've never liked a cryptic crossword and I'm not afraid to ask an obvious question.

'What for?'

'That first day. What I said about your . . . paler patch.'

'Vitiligo.'

'That's it.' He'd been tearing himself apart about it since, he said, well, more or less; I may have dramatised. He was embarrassed, hadn't known whether to bring it up again. In fact, he was still nervous, he said, and could he order a wine? Of all my pointless superpowers – knowing the words to 'Losing My Mind' in three languages, being able to tell what make of car was being crushed into a cube at the scrap yard opposite my flat – being the gatekeeper to other people's alcohol intake was probably my least favourite. I nodded like an emperor in the colosseum; his wine arrived.

'It was insensitive. Nobody warned me.'

Warned him! About a few patches of pigment-free skin? It wasn't like I had three heads or arms made of tennis racquets. As reactions went, his was among the least offensive. I told him about my Granny McDougall who'd said at least it gave my face character. And Auntie Sheena, who said my white patch of hair was good practice for going grey – unless my hair fell out beforehand.

'Can I ask how you feel about it?'

'How I feel? I don't feel anything. It's there. I know some people see it as a disfigurement, I don't. There wasn't really anything to ruin in the first place.'

'That's a good attitude. Well, mostly.' I know what people wanted to hear, that it had destroyed my life or been a character-building experience, that I was determined to triumph over this adversity – but it hadn't, and I wasn't. It became as mundane to me as looking down and seeing my bony feet or my strange little belly.

'Everyone used to show me photos of that stunning model with vitiligo, you know the one I mean? And I was like, yeah, great, she's bossing it, but she's beautiful – the patches couldn't take that away from her. I'm already in deficit, you know?'

I sensed that was too much honesty for one evening, and was about to suggest we leave, when I saw Alex's eye track to the bar. He gasped a little, held his breath for what felt like hours, then released. I waited for him to come back to the room. 'Sorry, thought I saw a ghost.'

'Who?'

'My ex.'

'Did you come here knowing he might be here?'

'Very good. You should've been a copper. Not the only reason. We used to come here after work sometimes.'

'You worked together?'

'A fellow teacher. I have a type.' I got a lump in my throat. Alex looked slightly ashamed. 'He was my boss, a mentor. I couldn't find my feet at first, but he took me under his wing.' I could almost see the memory projected onto his eyes. One day after a particularly bad day, the mentor had brought him here. He was impressive, confident, charming. I was envious of a person I'd never met. 'It was a Tuesday. It was fun, I liked him, so he said, why not make it a regular thing, the Tuesday debrief.'

Not the right time to think this, but I did find myself wondering whether Alex wore briefs or boxers.

'One Tuesday I realised after . . . probably too many drinks, that he'd brought me here with an eye to seducing me.'

Illicit drinks ten floors up while the city breathes and boozes and fucks all around you in the dark. It sounded quite hot. But something about it was gross too. Made my skin itch. I tried to take a deep lungful but couldn't reach capacity.

'It worked, obviously.'

'It did. For a while. We got together, and it changed. Don't get me wrong, he helped me a lot, to always be my best, made sure I was flying in my career, but I got sick of being his project. Wanted to find my own way. One day, I came in here by myself, on a Wednesday, and saw him, helping someone else meet their potential.'

'Shit.'

They'd moved from London to Glasgow three years ago in a make-or-break move – it did neither, only kept them in suspended animation. Then, in the summer, another move, to Edinburgh, which finally broke them.

'Sorry it didn't work out. Sounds like the early days were fun. Are you disappointed it wasn't him you saw?'

'No.' He slid his hand across the table, his little finger coming to rest against mine. 'There are rooms below.' He was almost whispering, and although the music was booming I could hear him loud and clear, like we were the only people in the bar.

My heart thumped. Too much sugar in the mockito maybe. 'Oh! So he seduced you ... here? That's literally why he brought you?'

Alex's eyes darkened, he was frozen, lips parted, glass halfway to his mouth. 'That isn't what I meant.'

I could hear blood hurtling round my body, my mouth was dry, I couldn't speak. That moment's hesitation was too long, he came out of his trance and peered into his wine glass, before knocking it back.

'Shit. We should get back. I'll see you there.' He rose from his chair, bundled his coat over his arm and strode to the lift, jamming his finger on the button until the door opened and the light within swallowed him and he disappeared.

I tried to breathe more slowly, blinking away the spots before my eyes. I didn't want to ask myself what the hell had just happened because, to be honest, I didn't know. Although. Well.

There are rooms below.

I knew.

Thirty-Two

Alex pretended to be asleep when I got back, and on the train the next day, he sat as far away as he could without actually driving the sodding thing. When Harvey asked how it went, I glossed over the horror of 'bunking in' with two other men by . . . not mentioning it at all, but I said, quite honestly, that Alex had been weird and uncommunicative.

'That's the thing with hanging out outside of work,' Harvey said. 'You see people for who they really are.'

I wondered what Harvey's colleagues saw? Did he act the same way, so measured, an aphorism or motivational statement for every occasion? Or did he lose his temper, get shirty — like those brief flashes I'd seen? My instincts told me whatever his work persona, they'd adore him. I was about to find out. Harvey flashed his phone at me one night as I walked through the door. I caught a brief glimpse of rudimentary photoshopping, a flyer with too many exclamation marks.

'Wine tasting. With work. In a couple of weeks. Can you come? I wanna show you off.'

Show me off. I hoped they'd manage to conceal their surprise that Harvey wasn't dating a near-identical, brawny gay with a face that could stop traffic for the right reasons. I imagined them as either bespectacled architects in top-to-toe Carhartt or hi-vis wearing, goodnatured himbos – but there was an elephant in the room.

'I can't go wine tasting. I don't drink.'

'Okay, not generally, no, but there are exceptions, right? You had a great time at your birthday.'

I'd tried to blank that out. Easier said than done. Every once in a while, during a quiet ten minutes to myself, I'd succumb to the guilt. No, not guilt, disappointment. Oh, I don't know. Whatever it was. I'd not touched a drop since – unless you count the red sploshed on my shirt on the night of the Campbell Confessional, another reason I wasn't keen to be around a lot of wine.

· 'I thought we could invite Tam and Fabrizio, and Daisy and Seb,' said Harvey, 'so you wouldn't be too outnumbered by my boring work lot. Seems ages since you've seen them. What do you think? You don't actually have to swallow the wine, you know.'

An opportunity for a ceasefire with Daisy and Tam – not that either had noticed we were at war. Something Tam had said about Seb – 'We're stuck with him now' – made me want to properly induct Harvey into the gang. I wanted to buck that trend, have the boyfriend everyone liked. Mind you, they'd liked Peter and look where that had got me. Harvey was making an effort, the least I could do was reward it.

'I'll think about it.'

'Tell you what *I* was thinking about . . . I know there's no space at the wedding but . . . why don't I come to Italy anyway?

We can get a place of our own, have an extended holiday. While you're off at the wedding, I can sunbathe, sip negronis, then we'll have the rest of the time to ourselves.'

It sounded heavenly. When was the last time a good-looking man who owned no fewer than seven pairs of tight swimming shorts had wanted to spend time with me this badly? There was no last time or indeed first time. Yet something clawed at me. Tam talking about it being 'just us', and having fun with no obligations.

'It's quite remote, I think, where the wedding is. Once it's over, there's nothing to do.'

'Ah-ha!' Harvey looked excited. 'I thought it would be the perfect time for you to write!'

'Write?'

'Didn't you tell me once you always wanted to write a play? Now's the time. I've been looking up old typewriters on eBay.'

I felt like checking the label on my jumper to make sure I hadn't come dressed as Tennessee Williams by mistake. Had I ever said this? Then I remembered: on the first date, among the usual flannel you say to impress someone you assume you'll never see again, I may have said I fancied writing a play. But, like, eventually, if there was another lockdown or something, in maybe thirty years, once I'd stopped teaching. Not now, on holiday, when I should be by the pool watching my friends guzzle lethal cocktails and fall off overly large inflatables. And I'd literally spent months writing a pl— a *show* for work. Old typewriters on eBay? I'd never even touched a typewriter. Clobbering a laptop with my bony cigarillo fingers was bad enough. But I didn't say that.

Instead, I took Harvey's face in one hand and put my other between his thighs and said, 'Hmmm sounds like an idea. I'll definitely think about it.' Then I gave us both something else to think about.

If Alex had gone businesslike after our first tête-a-tête, after London it was like communicating through a solicitor. At one rehearsal, he was silent until the end, before coming over and saying, with the condescension of a parking attendant, 'If we really focus, stay professional, the show will be a smash. I'm sure you agree.' I watched him walk away, dazed by his brutal formality, a concrete slab to the head. He'd message me terse notes, signed off with *A. Campbell*. Who signed text messages? Even my parents stopped doing that by the mid-noughties. It appeared I was paying the price for his embarrassment. What better time, then, as we staggered into the final weeks of rehearsals, to do my first full performance of the solo and get feedback? Ugh, I was dreading it. My initial frothy excitement was now dried, burnt milk stuck to the bottom of the pan.

Light relief came in the form of Mica's daughter, who I was so excited to finally meet.

'Hey, Sasha, I've heard so much about you. So lovely of you to come. Assuming you are here by choice.'

'Nice to meet you, Leo.' Sasha, a mini-Mica with eyes even more mischievous than her mother's, smiled sweetly. 'I've come to make sure Mum doesn't sit eating popcorn and put everybody off, like she did at that thing we went to see at the Traverse.'

'She seems a very sweet young lady,' I said to Mica, who

rolled her eyes as her daughter went to find a seat. 'I don't know why you want to pack her off to a convent.'

'You've known her thirty seconds, stick around,' huffed Mica. 'You ready or what?'

'I was wondering actually, for my part, could we do a closed set? You know, just us?'

Mica laughed herself almost sick. 'Look, main character, you'll be doing this in front of everyone you've ever given detention to, and every parent who thinks their kid's shitty attitude is your fault, so let's not go full J-Lo, you know?'

I was nervous. I had limited room in my flat to practise the moves and even though Harvey had a huge lounge, few things make you as unfuckable as your lover witnessing your muscles and joints try to acquaint themselves with rhythm. As we set up the blocks and boxes and laid tape where the set would be so I could practise swerving them as I leaped about, Iqra wished me luck.

There was something in my eye. I told her I'd try to do her proud. She said I was overthinking it, the perfect response. The room went quiet. Just the odd cough here and there. In came the piano, then the drum roll, I could hear the backing singers take that first deep breath. My heart raced. I blinked uncertainly as if an imaginary spotlight had found me and . . . I did it, sang out, fully, in public, almost for the first time since I'd last had a shower in a campsite. Alex stood in a corner, arms folded, one leg crossing the other, his face in shadow. Iqra did a heart sign with her hands before pretending to stick her fingers down her throat. It was over in no time. I stood staring at an imaginary dress circle as my lungs frantically tried to calm themselves, every inch of me sparking with electric shocks.

People stopped applauding, but one person's clapping still rang out, loud and strong, bouncing off the studio's dark walls. Alex. He came out of the shadows, smiled thinly, like he was being held hostage, and left without saying a word.

Mica came behind me. 'Last time a man looked at me like that, I'd just told him I was pregnant with Sasha.'

'Is that a good thing or a bad thing?'

'Well, I ain't heard from him in fifteen years.'

This was silly. I hadn't done anything wrong, and neither had he, really. Why couldn't we talk to each other like normal humans? But that was me all over, burying problems. I didn't go after him.

'How was it, Iqra?'

A wavy hand. 'When you eventually found the key, you smashed it, sir.'

Ouch.

Thirty-Three

I tried to explain to Harvey that rock-climbing might not be the best idea a few weeks before I was due to be grasshoppering about onstage, but he'd been so overjoyed that I'd embraced the gym, he was convinced I was now ready for more competitive activities.

'Be great to see you do something that's not as, you know, aimless.'

For Harvey, participating wasn't enough – there had to be a record to break, or someone to beat. Being challenged was good for the soul, he was always saying; I appreciated the sentiment but wondered if he'd feel the same after standing in for a maths teacher in a roomful of teenagers asking the kind of searching existential questions guaranteed to send their substitute into a spiral.

'How can rock-climbing be competitive? See rock, climb it. No?'

Harvey shook his head and again offered me a sip of his swamp-coloured smoothie. 'I told you, it's bouldering, not rock-climbing. Drink it, it's very energising.' I gave in and his smile stretched to the sun. Helping me discover new things super-charged him. 'You're in competition with yourself, it's about endurance, staying focused.'

'And if I lose focus and fall off this, uh, boulder? Go bouncing to the bottom of Salisbury Crags and land with my head facing the wrong way?'

'You'll be perfectly safe in the climbing centre.'

'Not even outside? Scotland has more rocks than Cartier!'

'Can't properly monitor your progress outside. You need controlled conditions.'

The climbing centre was a church to muscle and spirulina, surrounded by hotties like Harvey but much less charismatic. Jordan, the instructor, for example – he had a proper title and some kind of qualification but my knees were knocking too loudly to hear. He talked me through it with what I imagine he thought was patience. I must've been talking too much to calm my nerves because Jordan said I was 'chirpy'. I used to get called chirpy a lot as a child. In a nice way, I think; adults were generally pleased to see me, because I never sulked. Jordan didn't mean it in a nice way; I saw what he was getting at. Guys like Jordan didn't understand men like me, with awkward personalities and limbs more suited to mincing or lazing than athletics. Jordan's body was harder than a sudoku; he was a granite worktop with hair. He had the kind of face that would have brides ditching grooms at the altar, kings abdicating the throne. He was even better looking than Tam's brother – you would risk it all for a big, beautiful fridge like Jordan.

'So that's all you have to do,' Jordan was saying as I stared up at a plastic Kilimanjaro. All I had to do. I looked ridiculous. Harvey insisted on helmets – 'To put you at ease,' he said – but the only one that fit was purple. Purple was not my colour. I'd been expecting a harness, but apparently if I fell, the thick, padded floor would break my fall. Harvey said I looked great and kissed me – well, he tried to, but our helmets clunked so he settled for a peck on the end of my nose instead. Jordan looked on without cringing, so that answered my one remaining question about him. How hard could this be, anyway? I'd climbed walls before. Back in my boozing days, Daisy and I were always vaulting park railings; I could be nimble when I wanted. Hadn't I danced around that makeshift set like Nureyev just the other day, and brought the house down? I stepped on the lowest fake rock and reached my hand as far up as I could, slowly taking the weight off my other foot. Oh, this isn't so bad, I told myself. Next one.

Thud.

'Don't worry, pal,' said Jordan, with masculine gusto. 'That's your first fall out of the way. It gets easier.'

It didn't.

Thud.

Thwack.

Bump.

'Oooooof,' yelped Jordan as I hit the deck for the seventh or eighth time, I'd lost count. Harvey watched the first few defeats blankly before scrambling up as naturally as a daddy-long-legs might skitter across your kitchen floor. Then he descended, then went back up, and down again, and back up. He was faster than the express lift in the Empire State Building.

I scrambled a quarter of the way up and suddenly froze. I couldn't find an obvious path. My arse felt like it had gone twenty rounds with a meat tenderiser, I couldn't fall again. My forehead dripped with sweat and the inside of my cheek was raw from biting it in frustration. This wasn't fun. My mind flipped quickly through my most embarrassing moments: soiling myself aged three in the sandpit; being caught miming 'Anything Goes' into a cucumber on a caravanning holiday when I thought I was alone, aged thirteen; at uni, retching so hard as I gagged on a dick that halls security rapped on the door because they thought someone was being strangled. This incident, clamped to a pretend wall with anxiety tummy and drenched palms, observed by an audience of pure testosterone, was scaling that leaderboard faster than I was this wall. After what felt like decades but was probably three minutes, I heard someone scamper up alongside me and smelled the unmistakable pong of Joop. Jordan. Oh, so he was straight after all.

'Let's get you down, pal.'

Harvey watched as Jordan guided me down to a lower rock to plummet from. After we'd changed back into our civvies, Harvey unlocked the car and paused, turning to me. His face was red, holding something in, lips pulled tightly.

'I guess that wasn't really for me,' I said, chuckling. 'I'm knackered.'

He shook his head. 'It's like you don't even try.' The way he said it told me this was a recurring thought previously unexpressed but now finally given the breath of life.

'I did try! I have the bruises to prove it.'

'A cat with three legs could've done it.'

The heat of the car mixed with the stress of my failure made me sweat again. 'I wasn't that bad for a beginner, was I?'

He floored it at an amber light, and swung onto Leith Walk, hissing at the traffic. 'You went into that determined not to enjoy it, or be any good at it. That defeatist attitude again.'

What did he mean *again*? I'd tried everything he'd thrown at me. Folded myself into a pretzel in yoga, pretended that being aneurysm-adjacent on a bike that never actually moved was fun and not utterly fucking insane. I'd swung, and enjoyed, kettle-bells and was booked in to taste wine with a bunch of brickies the week after even though I didn't drink – I reckoned I'd passed my Harvey 101 with . . . well, if not flying colours, an honourable mention. Yet somehow I found myself apologising and lying that Jordan had seemed very nice.

'He's married,' snapped Harvey, and swerved so hard to avoid a pigeon that I spilled my ginger and beetroot smoothie in my lap. I wasn't entirely sorry not to get the chance to finish it. I stayed stock still, disoriented, a time traveller yanked through a black hole with no warning. Fear. I was actually frightened. He had finally run out of words of encouragement. He was tired of me. I held my breath, waiting for the bomb to be defused or blow.

'We'll get you another, I'm sorry. I just want you to do more, have fun.' Harvey gave my knee the three squeezes, and it was such a relief that the argument was over, I drank that disgusting replacement smoothie in one go and told Harvey it was absolutely delicious.

'Don't be silly. I swear a flasher on the Meadows actually buttoned up his raincoat as I walked by.'

It's strange seeing someone you've been mad at for the first time since you fell out. There's that surge of affection and familiarity but also tension, knowing things aren't how they should be. Daisy didn't look amazing. She looked good, obviously, she always did, but there was a weariness about her, like she was sleeping an hour or two less than usual, or not getting out on her balcony enough.

'How's everything? How's Harvey?' So polite and formal. Ugh, I hated this.

'Oh fine! I'm brand new, thank you. And you?'

She sighed. 'You always say that. *Fine*. Brand new.'

'It's true, though.' It wasn't. I was having trouble processing the rock-climbing afternoon. Harvey's face. His frustration. What did it mean? And why did it trigger memories of other instances I'd glossed over, suddenly making them seem significant? Daisy was good at decoding men; she'd played them at their own game. Until Seb. He always seemed one step ahead or, more likely, for some reason she reduced her pace, allowed him in front. I could never work out why. Why hadn't I asked?

Should I approach it today? Reunite us through a common problem? Introduce that idea that . . . I don't know, maybe everything wasn't quite fine? Even though I'd defended Harvey so staunchly after the birthday debacle, and not mentioned the whole drama after the party? And my coat . . . something had been bothering me about it all week, like dust in the corner of my eye. Had he actually been holding the bottle of wine? Did I really knock it out of his hand? Or . . . I couldn't remember.

'Okay, good, I'm glad you're, uh, brand new. Look, Lion,

I want to say sorry.' This was a surprise. I mean, Daisy had apologised before, for many things, but only when she'd done something demonstrably wrong: broken a glass; been caught saying something horrible about someone; spilled a drink over someone (that happened a lot). 'I've been a wee bit of a cow about missing your birthday. If that happened to me, I'd be raging. I think I was mad at myself and wanted you to forgive me and you kind of wouldn't . . . ' I tried to interrupt but she held up her hand. 'Not straightaway anyway. I should've been doing something nice for you, and Harvey did it instead and I got it wrong and now I've hardly seen you and you being pissed off with me is awful, so . . . I'm sorry.'

'Okay.'

'Is that it?'

'Yeah. Thank you for saying sorry. I appreciate it. I'm not mad at you anymore.'

'Honestly?'

I clinked my plastic tumbler of wild berry kombucha against her plastic flute of Veuve Clicquot. 'That's it.'

She laughed, a release that sounded a long time coming. 'That's what I love about you, Lion, no messing about, we move on. Fucking phew. Fill her up.'

That rush of relief to be back on track with her. I felt like I could tell her anything. Finally, I had the floor. I could give a quick overview of what had happened at the rock-climbing place. I could leave out everything else. Matt. All that stuff. She could tell me if I was being silly. Deep breath. 'You know, it's funny . . . '

But then her expression changed. Her smile went into a Dali melt, dripping down her face. Her eyes welled with tears and her shoulders slumped toward the ground. Then the sound. Sobs. She squeaked slightly, trying to contain them.

I took her glass and put my hand over hers. Now was not my time. 'What's he done?'

'Where do I start?

Daisy had spent most of her relationship with Seb ignoring the little things. Eventually the little things got bigger and she made a choice, to blank those out too – aside from the odd outburst and chucking him out into the night. He'd arranged a stag do for this, her birthday weekend, and was unrepentant. You can, I guess, ignore the signs for a long time, even with damning evidence of infidelities or at least the intention – blame the other person, alcohol, yourself – but not putting you first on your birthday is a pretty huge sign they don't care about you. Just like that, it had clicked into place for Daisy. The impetus for my apology became immediately clear.

'I know everyone thinks I'm an idiot, for putting up with it so long.'

'We don't.'

'You should. I do. He's never taken us seriously because he knows he doesn't have to. There's always gonna be girls in bars, lining up shots, lapping up his patter. It's how we met. He's living the dream. I'm not The One, I'm this one. And I never wanted to admit it, did I? That I'm a footnote.'

I'd orbited round her for so long, it had never occurred to me that Daisy wasn't the epicentre of every relationship in her life.

She shook her head sadly, as if looking in a mirror for the first time and hating what she saw. 'He'll go off and find some other girl and another and another until, eventually, he'll look round his office and realise all the other pricks he works with have kids, so he'll decide it's time he was a dad too. Because it's always about what he wants. And that's what he'll do. Tick the box. Have kids. With some English girl, probably, to make Christmases and birthdays easier. Bastard. I hope she ruins his life.'

'You don't.'

'I don't. Sometimes I really want to be a much more horrible person. That's the hard part, isn't it, with breakups? You know they'll survive. But you might not.'

So it was over. Strange how abrupt and brutal it felt, even though this day had been looming for years. I couldn't believe I was hearing about this now, in relative calm, and not my usual break-of-dawn phone call. Served me right for freezing her out. I felt awful.

'I'm in Alexia's spare room.' Alexia was one of the super-models. 'Gal-pal flat share. Until I sort my own place. Am I tragic?'

I hugged her and breathed in her familiar shampoo and per-fume smell, mixed with champagne breath. 'No, you're brave. It takes guts to call time on something, even if it's not working.' Said the voice of absolutely no experience.

'At least I'm not having his baby. It was the right thing to do after all.'

'I thought you said you never had a doubt.'

'We say a lot of things, don't we, Lion?' I could've stopped her and asked what she meant. Was my face giving me away? 'I was sure, but . . . so many what-ifs. Maybe I'll always wonder.'

I had a sudden thought – might knowing about Seb and Tam help? Or how about what Seb said to me? But then, was I outing him as bisexual? Did the potential infidelity cancel out his right to privacy? I replaced the lid on that idea. 'You lied to yourself for too long. In relationships, you test yourself, see what you can put up with. But there's always a breaking point.'

Daisy looked at me as if I'd stepped out of the shadows. Ah, I'd said that out loud. If she asked me now, I might . . . might I?

'You're so right. That's why you should enjoy gorgeous Harvey. I've never seen you so happy and . . . frankly, buff. I swear to God, Lion, I think I can see a muscle through your . . . what are we calling that? That's not yours, is it?'

The moment evaporated. 'It's Harvey's. Just a sweater. Are you gonna be okay?'

'You tell me.' We both watched as I filled her glass to the top. 'If I've got you, and Tamish, and you two are happy as Larry, whoever the hell Larry is, and if I can stop Alexia signing me up for every singles' night in Edinburgh, then, yeah, maybe I'm gonna be okay.'

'At least we'll always have the glade.'

'Yes!' exclaimed Daisy with the exhilarated energy of some-one the right side of tipsy. 'The beautiful glade! Our paradise.'

We looked round us. The grass was too long, the dumpster's lid yawned at us, the wasp was back and dive-bombing the champagne bottle. 'Let's get the hell out of here.'

Thirty-Five

Iqra had a problem. She didn't tell me. I just knew. Call it teacher's intuition, or maybe the fact she was sitting in the drama studio at 6 p.m. when I was trying to lock up, working her finger into a hole in one of my precious beanbags. I watched yet another styrofoam ball pop out onto the floor and went over to a) ask what was wrong and b) turf her out before the caretaker shouted at me for not having permission to stay late. It was the song, apparently; she had her doubts.

'Iqra, it's a tremendous song.'

'Aye, I know. But some of the lyrics are kind of hitting different. I don't like them anymore.'

This was the trouble with art you put out into the world. Paintings, plays, books, songs – the 'finished' product is never complete, not to the artist. But you must draw the line and begin carving it into stone. This was a lesson Iqra would learn eventually but it didn't have to be now. We looked at changing the lyrics, workshopped some alternatives. I sang them out. She winced.

'The key not doing it for you again?'

'Sorry I was shady, sir, you're good at singing. It's not that. These lyrics are kind of . . . oh, I don't know.'

Click. There went a cog. 'Ah. Personal. They mean something to you.' I looked at the clock.

'Sorry, sir, we should go.'

We were taught to look for signs children might not be happy at home. Staying late and hanging around school was perhaps one of the most obvious. When you ask the question, your student might immediately pretend everything's okay, they might break down in tears, they might fly into a rage or they might shrug. Iqra sighed for what felt like the entire running time of *A Star is Born* (1954 version). 'It's my mum and dad.'

'Are they not happy about your involvement with the play?'

'Are you racially profiling me, Mr Falconer?'

'No! A lot of parents wish their children concentrated more on the core subjects, you know the . . . '

'Boring ones.'

'Your words. But yes.'

The Habeebs were in the early stages of divorce, it seemed. I remembered Daisy's pain, which she kept mostly hidden and expressed only from the bottom of a bottle of cider on the glade. Iqra found herself in the middle of an identity crisis, not sure how to behave, fearful of favouring one parent over another. 'My dad is into me doing the production side and stuff, but my mum thinks I should perform, she wants me out there being a role model, you know?'

'And what do you want?'

'I don't know!'

'Iqra, can I give you some advice as a very old man?'

She gave me her full attention, like I was some philosopher

and not a lanky idiot who happened to have a teaching qualification. 'People try to push you into things because they think it's what's best for you, and sometimes they're right, but it will never work, and it will never be fun, if it's not what you want. Doing something to please someone else is a nice feeling, but it can make you resent them in the end.'

'Teachers aren't supposed to say "do whatever you want", are they?'

'No, they're not, and that's not what I'm saying. Being yourself is your strongest talent. If you can do it without hurting anyone else, then do what makes you happy.'

'So what are you saying, like?'

'I'm saying, like, do you want to sing the song?'

'I can't, not on my own.'

'We can sing it together. You do your personal bits and I'll join on the chorus and sing the judge's redemption verse. The one with the key I actually know.'

'Sir, that will be cringe.'

'Iqra, I have some news. You're a drama student with insane amounts of talent. Your whole life is going to be cringe. Start early, avoid the post-graduation rush. Be cringe. Plus it will really piss off Lewis.'

'We don't have time!'

'We do. I'll sort out a permission slip and we can workshop it after school this week, present it to Mr Campbell.'

'Will he be okay with it?'

Would he? We hadn't had a single conversation since London. This would certainly break the ice. 'He wants the show to be the best it can be. Course he will.'

Iqra left the room light and unburdened. I tried not to worry about the absolute bollocking I'd get from Mica and Joe Music. Let alone Alex.

'Leo.'

Holy shit, I'd summoned him by thinking about him. Even the Candyman needed to hear his name three times before manifesting.

'You're here late.' I regretted that instantly – it wasn't like he had anyone to get back to.

'I heard you just now with Iqra Habeeb.' Where had he been lurking?! 'Make all the changes you need.'

'Thank you.'

He turned to leave, but stopped.

'Can we start again?' I didn't say anything, hoping a pause might give him the answer he wanted. 'I'm sorry I've been off. I meant what I said about you being a good teacher. I knew this show would be the making of you. Iqra isn't the only one with great potential.'

At that moment, I wanted to run toward him and kiss him. No, scratch that, I wanted to ask him about London, did he mean what I thought he'd meant. Had he really wanted to take me to a room? And if he had, what next?

But I loved Harvey, and Harvey loved me. Yes, Alex adored musicals and shared a passion for cardigans, but what else did we have in common other than a few lasting scars from skirmishes with heartbreak? There had to be more than that, right?

So I didn't run to him. What actually happened was he wished me goodnight, and I went home, leaving the lights off, to lie on my bed, panting, while 'Something's Coming' from *West Side Story* blared out of my headphones, imagining myself in a room in that hotel with Alex, naked, our M&S jumpers folded neatly on a chair while he fucked me against the glass, the London skyline staring back at me in cold and phallic splendour.

Shit.

Thirty-Six

To my surprise, Daisy and Tam were super keen on coming to
the wine tasting, although Daisy couldn't resist 'a little joke',
asking whether Harvey had organised it. 'Should I check my
horoscope to find his invitation?'

She'd had good days and bad days since the split, she said,
but the supermodels were helping. One had been inspired
by Daisy and was ditching her idiot husband too – the wedding, a mere eighteen months earlier, had cost £25,000 – so
Daisy already found herself old news, which was strangely
comforting. There'd been a few desperate late-night texts
from Seb, and in a moment of weakness, Daisy had done a
drive-by of his flat only to see a clone leaving in the early
hours – 'heels in one hand, knickers in the other' – climbing
into a cab while Seb blew a kiss from the doorway. Bastard.
It wasn't exactly an overnight cure, but she felt stronger to
face another day.

Harvey's colleagues were kind and polite, but guarded. We
stayed in the shallow end; I couldn't remember the last time I'd
talked so much about my job, but apparently school dinners (no,

I never ate them) and detentions (I tried to avoid giving them out) were still fascinating conversational currency. My favourite of Harvey's workmates was an amazing woman in her early fifties called Gabrielle who'd spent her twenties overseeing renovations in the south of France for ugly millionaires – 'Money can buy you a new face but ugly rises to the surface, it's in the plasma.' She smoked cocktail cigarettes out of the fire exit and told me Harvey had the biggest, bluest eyes of any man she'd seen. 'Yours are quite black, aren't they?' she said. I didn't talk to her much after that.

Daisy threw herself into it: sniffing, gargling, swishing and listening to the sommelier taking us through the wines, between chatting amiably to Harvey's colleagues. We quickly fell into our ancient double act.

'Leo's like the brother I never had,' she said, squeezing my arm.

'She already has a brother!' Cue polite laughter.

'Well, yes, I do, but he's nothing like you.'

'He's gay! And ... isn't he training to be a teacher?' If we'd left a long enough gap there might have been a ripple of applause.

'Stop splitting hairs!' Daisy sounded quite serious. 'He's not you.'

Tam, dressed in what my mum used to call a builder's tuxedo – denim jacket and jeans – was in naughty schoolboy mode, asking stupid questions and calling £300-a-bottle wine 'vino vomito collapso'. The kind of disruptive dimwittery that's seen as charming if you look like a film star. He was clearly enjoying being off the leash, Fabrizio couldn't come; a couple of his passive-aggressive 'look, babe's were usually enough to make Tam check himself. I went through the motions, smelling bouquets and swirling, but like all good Catholic boys, I didn't swallow. It didn't take that many glasses before Daisy and Tam started bantering, with an argument I'd broken up many times before, over whether Cleopatra was, in fact, beautiful or not, kicked off by Harvey complimenting Daisy's eyeliner.

'Look, Daiz, there's evidence. In old Roman coins or, uh, Egyptian money or whatever, she looks like a horse trying to tongue a kidney bean out of a plughole.'

'Shut up, Tammy, you . . . ' she quickly looked around her to check nobody was listening, 'asshole. She wasn't ugly, as such. But so what? She managed to outsmart two Roman leaders with her charm and wit.'

'But not because she was hot. Got it.'

'Ugh. Shut up. She was very clever. Only sexist creeps, like you, Tamishus Wankerus, were obsessed with her looks. There was more to her than that.'

'Look,' said Tam, 'you should be shouting at Harvey, he's the one who said you look like Cleopatra.'

'Aw, Harvey.' Daisy clasped his arm. 'That's just something men say when they don't know anything about makeup. He meant it kindly. You should know better than any of us about being judged only on your looks, Tammy.'

'Are you saying I don't have anything else going for me?'

People were looking. Felt like a good time to butt in. 'Guys.'

'Actually, Lion can decide,' said Tam, mischief written all over his face. 'Who's better looking, me or Daisy?'

What I wouldn't have given for the confidence of these two vain beauties three or four wines down. 'I want you both to know that if future historians ever find my diaries, they'll discover that Daisy Forbes and Tamish Patel both looked like welders' elbows.'

'Poor Lion,' said Daisy. 'You must be so bored watching us knock back all this booze.'

Harvey shot me a look I couldn't quite interpret. 'I've already said I don't know why he doesn't try some. No big deal.'

I definitely saw Tam and Daisy side-eye each other.

'Leo doesn't do that,' said Tam with a slight slur. Quite defensive too, I thought. I knew exactly what was going to happen next.

'I know, I know,' said Harvey. 'Only special occasions.'

'No, never!' Daisy and Tam looked at each other, then at me. 'Isn't that right, Lion?'

'Actually, I had some champagne on my birthday.' I don't know why I felt so guilty. They glared back, like I was confessing to pouring polonium into their breakfast cereal.

'You're drinking again?!'

'It started that night?!?'

'What is this "again"? It was once. Nothing has started. It was a one-off.'

Tam put his arm round Harvey's shoulder. 'So you've got the old soak back on the sauce, have you? How'd you manage that? The bad old days are back.' His voice rang with sarcasm. Harvey gently disentangled himself.

Soak? What the hell? Daisy wore her disappointing birthday present face. I couldn't understand either reaction. I prided myself on being absolutely no more fun at all when drinking; I'd been consistently, amiably dull for my entire adulthood, booze or no booze.

'Is it my fault, Lion? Did you get pissed because you were mad at me for not turning up?'

'What? To spite you? No! Why would I? Let's not make a big deal of this.'

'But after everything.'

'After what?'

'With Peter.'

I noticed the slightest shift in my breathing as Daisy said his name, my heart picking up the pace a little in response. Was it my imagination, or did my vision go into soft focus? 'Peter?'

Tam put his arm round me now, bringing me into the heavy, suffocating kind of hug that drunks love so much and sober people don't. 'You never talk about Peter. Ever. Are you embarrassed? You shouldn't be.'

What. What? What?!

'Tam.' Daisy's voice was sharp and clear and warning.

'Embarrassed, me? He had the affair.' What??

'Oh, I know, but. Eh. Nothing.' He was having a little conversation with himself. Should he say it, should he not? 'I don't wanna speak out of, eh, turn.'

'Sounds like it's out there now,' said Harvey, quietly.

I'd no idea what he was going to say, yet I didn't want Harvey to hear it. 'Can we talk about this later?'

Tam hadn't heard me. 'The booze and stuff. You were drinking quite a lot.'

I suddenly understood. Keeping everything to myself meant Peter could easily spin a story any way he liked. He'd got to them too. How long before leaving me had he been seeding the idea I had a problem and that's why he was getting out? Did he whisper it in Tam's ear while they had sex?

'There was no drinking! Honestly! Peter was projecting most of the time.'

'Sometimes you could barely stand up, Lion,' said Daisy timidly.

'Usually collapsing under the weight of getting you or Tam over the threshold!'

'We're no angels, I know. But you really could put it away, pal.'

I wasn't having this. 'It was always you two! Legs made of Jenga stacks!'

'Now who's projecting?'

'You, mostly, Daisy! Projectile vomiting. All over my shoes at supermodel Gemma's wedding.'

I couldn't believe this, but it did make sense. When I stopped drinking, they never really asked why, only chucked a few encouraging salutes my way or the odd good-natured dig or pretended to egg me on to have 'just one'. I hadn't had a problem or anything. I mean . . . I got drunk, yeah, but everybody did. I didn't wake up in the morning craving vodka, or shaking, or even drink every day, but . . . okay, when I drank, I drank to get drunk. But that was before.

'I could have a drink now, one sip of wine, and I'd be fine, and never want one again.' I slowly reached for the nearest glass, which had about two fingers of wine still in it.

'No!' yelled Daisy. 'Leo, don't!'

I felt the stem in my fingers. Chardonnay, never a favourite. I could smell it. Sticky. Rancid and abrasive. It would coat my teeth, fur up my tongue, I imagined the sharpness at the back of my throat, that descent toward my belly, which now lurched in anticipation.

'No, Leo, don't do that, come on. Please, pal. I said don't!' Tam slapped the glass out of my hand and I heard that pathetic, auspicious tinkle as it hit the floor. Flashbacks.

'What the hell was that?' I hissed. Harvey's colleagues were starting to stare. The sommelier tried coughing to bring some order, before resorting to tapping out a shrill rhythm on a glass. It didn't work. I looked from Tam's leer and Daisy's tortured face to Harvey, told him I was sorry, but he didn't look mad at all.

'I don't know what just happened, but maybe it's time to call it a night,' I said.

Daisy took Tam's arm. 'Okay, seemingly you're not ready to talk about it yet, Leo, that's fine. Come on, Tam. I think we should go. Let's get a cab.'

'I think that's for the best,' said Harvey, and there was an electrifying look between them.

'Just know we're here for you,' said Daisy. 'Thick and thin. Like always.' She started to hustle Tam out the door, but it was like scooping jelly off the floor with a fork; he'd certainly be vomiting in the back of that taxi.

Harvey grabbed my arm. 'Leave them,' he said, but I shook him off. His colleagues had the good manners to look in the other direction as I raced outside.

The fresh air and inability to immediately hail a cab had only added to Daisy and Tam's irritation; they were snarling at each other sotto voce. I should've left it, said I'd call in the morning, but, honestly, what a display. Why did everything have to escalate into a drama?

Tam dropped to his haunches as if looking for a contact lens or staving off nausea. Daisy tried to hoist him back up. 'We didn't tan that much wine, Tam, sort yourself out.'

I coughed to let them know I was watching. 'Look, to be clear, it's not that I'm "not ready" – there's nothing to talk about. I didn't have a drinking problem.'

'Right. Okay, Lion. I . . . I hear you.' The anguish in Daisy's voice cut through the dark. 'But, you know, there's no judgement from us. We're with you every step of the way.'

'You're not listening to me, as ever. I'm not in denial. I had some champagne on my birthday. The end. Okay?'

'As ever? Not listening?' Daisy's voice trembled; she wasn't confident tackling someone else's catastrophes. 'Look, Lion, come with us now, just us, we can sort this out.'

Tam shakily got to his feet. 'Lion. We know you. Leo's catty comebacks. Leo doesn't drink. Leo doesn't do fancy places. Leo doesn't like dressing up. Leo's brand new, thanks for asking. We can help. We'll stick by you. Just let us in.'

Tam had to be joking. Stick by me? They'd seemed pretty ready to believe Peter, never once asked for my side. When would I find a moment to 'let them in'? There wasn't one sentence they were too afraid to interrupt. They'd break off their own wedding vows if a gossipy text came through.

'You can hear me, but you're not listening. If you really thought I had a problem with the booze, why keep trying to get me to drink it? "Let's get shots!" "Sure I can't tempt you?" What was that bollocks?'

Daisy cringed. 'We thought it might get you talking, tell us what you didn't want to.'

'We were waiting for you to come to us.' Tam wobbled. 'We didn't want to spook you.'

'Like when you were coming out, Lion. You had to be . . . lured out.' Daisy waved desperately at a passing cab, even though its orange light wasn't on. 'You can tell us anything. You never call. You can, you know.'

'I . . . never? Are you . . . are you serious?' I never called? Me? They only got in touch these days if they were making up numbers or their lives needed fixing. The looks on their faces. That belief they were beyond reproach. I really had kept my irritation to myself for too long. This is the trouble with confrontations years in the making – every intelligent thought, the carefully considered points you intend as armour, they get dumbed down, they become missiles, they rip open the ground. Yet even in that moment, I still loved them, and didn't want to shatter their illusions that they were amazing friends. So I assumed my default position. 'Forget it.'

A cab drew up and Daisy heaved open the door as Tam shuffled toward me, arms outstretched. 'Lion, babe, honestly, a problem shared. You know us, we're open books. We don't do secrets.'

Harvey stepped out from the darkness and took my arm. 'Really? No secrets at all? You tell each other everything? All of you?'

I felt like I was falling through time as I watched my best friends' faces instantly change. Once warm and open, they were now cast-iron lids slamming shut on every emotion other than disappointment, as they realised I'd separately betrayed each of them. Where did we stand on involving partners in shared confidences? I supposed it never came up. I was single most of the time, Peter hadn't been remotely interested in their trivia, and I'd always resisted sharing my own scandals – there couldn't have been many times our loyalty would've been tested with Seb or Fabrizio or their predecessors.

Daisy's lip curled. She was, I was certain, about to tell Harvey to fuck off, but Tam was instantly subdued, like his plug had been pulled out. We locked eyes. He knew his time was up; he'd have to tell her about him and Seb.

'Thanks a fucking bunch, Lion.'

Harvey took my hand and squeezed tight. One. Two. Three.

Daisy climbed in the cab. There it was. Her wounded bird face, even though she was hard as nails and we all knew it. 'Get in Tam, you pie. I'll . . . we'll call you tomorrow, Lion.'

'Naw, we won't,' slurred Tam. 'I think we've seen enough of you. And don't be calling us either.'

I almost did it, stepped forward, made things better, but Harvey gripped my hand tighter.

'I won't.'

I covered Harvey's right hand with my left hand. To steady myself, to show unity, to make a barrier, I don't know.

'Goodnight, then,' said Harvey, almost cheerily. We turned away. I heard the door slam before the cab's engine faded into the distance.

Thirty-Seven

I wore a Halloween mask of a smile, twirling awkwardly in my costume. I'd heard nothing from them. I'd sent nothing. *You never call.*

Mica cooed in appreciation. 'I can't believe you sold out and got biceps.'

For reasons best known to wardrobe, my costume for the show was a skintight Breton-striped jersey, tight black trousers and a comedy moustache drawn on my face, hair slicked to one side. I'm not sure why an evil talent show judge would dress like if Marcel Marceau shopped exclusively at John Lewis, but the students had spoken and there was no going back.

'Hardly biceps. My arm looks like a mop handle with a pea balancing on it.'

It was final, full rehearsal. The first show was in two days. The concert hall, as we were now calling it, was usually used at breaktimes by junior students, so smelled vaguely of banana skins and salt and vinegar crisps, but it had never looked better. Where Alex had dug up the money, time and student enthusiasm I had no idea, but the room was festooned with cardboard glitter balls, huge banners and artistic portraits of all the 'contestants'. Before showtime, Iqra shook my hand and asked me not to embarrass her. I saluted in response, which made her cringe all the more. I didn't have much to do until the end, so I was helping Joe Music with the sound, walking around with an earpiece and tuning in and out of different frequencies, feeling very important but looking absolutely ridiculous.

Then it was time. The buildup to the big finish. I awaited my call and stared out into the hall. In a couple of days, these seats would be full of parents, governors, students and Harvey, of course. Daisy and Tam, I had no idea; I'd sent tickets but that was . . . before. All I could see now were a few yawning teachers and the odd student involved in the production. Alex was nowhere to be seen. Didn't he want to witness my first stage performance in about ten years?

'Sir. Sir! *Sir!* You're on.'

'All right!'

Sheer adrenaline kept me going, I think. I was shaking hard, and my body strained against this bollock-squishing costume; I was used to practising in one of my usual shirts two sizes too big. The lights were so bright I couldn't really see into the non-crowd, but just as Iqra was singing her lines – and totally smashing it, by the way – I spied Alex standing to one side, absentmindedly stroking his throat. I don't know what changed, whether seeing a familiar face buoyed me a little, or I got used to having all eyes on me, but I was aware of pulling myself to full height, being able to breathe deeper and smile wider. My nerves evaporated and my costume was now my skin. When it became my turn to sing again, I gave it everything, surprising even myself.

Big crescendo, I reached up my hands to the sky, then pointed over to Iqra as I named her my successor as the head judge. Glittery paper rained from above and the lights dazzled at their brightest, before plunging us into darkness. I felt high. During the ensemble finale, time sped up to a blur; I powered through the motion sickness. Curtain down, house lights up, we assembled for the bow, curtain up. And there was Alex, screaming and cheering and looking right at me. I clambered down from the stage and he ran toward me, arms wide in victory. We hugged, close, right as the lights went out again, and I heard a loud 'Shit, power's down' from Mica. Alex's lips met mine and I felt the lightest brush of his tongue and heard the gentlest, hungriest sigh, before the lights surged back into life and we sprang apart.

What the hell had just happened?

I wished I wasn't wearing such tight trousers.

'You were amazing, incredible! I can't describe it.' Such rapturous, unconcealed joy. He didn't seem fazed, or ashamed. 'I couldn't be prouder, I'll be going out with a bang.'

Then I remembered. Next year, he wouldn't be here. This was it. April would return and everything would be as it was.

Except nothing would be. I wouldn't be.

I don't know what I was about to say – something dramatic gathered in my throat, the letters and syllables arranging themselves into coherent words, trying to convey everything I was too frightened to feel in that moment. Don't go, maybe? Kiss me, perhaps? Just touch me again? I don't know, because I never got to say it.

Harvey was standing there, behind Alex, smiling. But not with his eyes.

'Your chauffeur is here. Bit early.'

'Did you see any of that?' That didn't sound right, so I recalibrated. 'The show, I mean?' How long had he been there? How dark had it been? How quickly had Alex and I jumped apart? I was brimming with nervous energy; I could've powered Leith with electricity for a week.

'Saw a bit of your big moment. You must be Alex?'

They shook hands. I just shook.

'So great to meet you,' said Alex.

Don't say the thing, I thought, please don't say the thing.

'I've heard a lot about you.'

Shit, he said the thing.

Harvey's brow furrowed the tiniest amount but they chatted amiably about nothing for what felt like seven centuries. I considered getting out of my costume but that would mean leaving them alone. Not a great idea. I made overtures about leaving, and Alex did his nice to meet you shtick again, adding 'at last' this time, just to make it sound even more like all I did was talk about my boyfriend to other gay men. Actually, was that such a bad thing? It didn't matter, because what Alex said next obliterated everything that came before it.

'I guess I'll see you at the wedding?'

'Oh . . .' Harvey's face. A gnaw of terror deep in my gut. 'Right, I didn't know you knew Tam.'

'Well, Fabrizio really. Grew up together. Our mums were best friends.'

'That's so sweet.' He looked at me for the first time in ages, trying to read me. He looked down at my crotch, now thankfully deflated, obviously. 'I'm not going, actually. To the wedding, anyway. Tagging along to Italy, but . . . not to the main event. We're getting a place nearby.' None of this had actually been agreed; common sense warned me not to object.

'I see. Oh, that's right, it's a tiny venue, isn't it? Yes.'

If things had ended there, if Harvey and I had said our good-byes and trudged out to the car, if Alex had looked at me and read the signs – do not enter, danger of death – I think my life would've turned out very differently. As it was, we didn't. And he didn't.

'I hope we don't end up sharing rooms again, I think I'm a bit old for that.'

Fuck. Fuck no. God. Why? I needed a pause button, or to unfurl some police tape round this whole conversation. Anything.

Harvey shot me the quickest glance, to let me know he'd be listening very intently to whatever Alex said next. 'Again?'

'Yeah, you know after London? Bunking in together. Not sure things can ever be the same once you've seen a colleague's bare feet.' Alex turned to me like I was in on the joke. 'Fun at the time, of course, nice to have a wee night out.'

Then he laughed, and Harvey joined in after a second or two, then I did, too, a few seconds later, and we stood there laughing, none of us meaning it, the most tuneless of harmonies.

Thirty-Eight

Harvey said nothing as he heated up the deluxe ready meals he'd bought on the way to meet me. It was my favourite, shepherd's pie. I sat tense, waiting, as I heard the tedious sounds of meal prep coming from the kitchen, the creaking hinge on the fridge door, the crack and hiss of a can opening, the cheery, but empty, ping of the microwave. I watched as he calmly spooned it out, stoic as an angel watching the world burn. But I knew it was coming. That's the thing about being in a couple. Your first row is shocking, but you see the signs of the storm more clearly every time. I'd have given anything not to notice his fingers slowly bending and flexing as he rested his cutlery on his plate between mouthfuls – mindful eating, he'd got me into it, too. All that stopping, chewing and savouring the taste; eating a doughnut took several days.

'He's going to the wedding?'

I cleared my throat to make sure my voice didn't sound too squeaky when I replied – always a sign of guilt, according to Daisy, who'd heard Seb croak through a million excuses. 'They're old friends.'

'I didn't realise you'd shared a room. Or went on a *wee night out.*'

I readied myself to explain. Why I'd lied about London. That nothing had happened, even though an adulterer's guilt seemed to colour every thought. If it was innocent, why hadn't I mentioned it? I had no answer. And the 'wee night out' – the way Alex dropped the bomb, as if it were a casual drink between pals, like I'd imagined any undercurrent. Maybe I had, maybe this was all in my head. Who would ever try to seduce me in a hotel bar?

'Did you get pissed together?'

'No! I don't drink.' I was tired of saying that. 'We were on duty, anyway. Kind of.'

'Do you mind if I ask you something?'

Did I mind? If this was heading for an accusation, it was a very polite way to begin. It would be hard to defend myself when I wasn't sure whether I'd done anything wrong. What was happening when Harvey walked in . . . it was just a silly headrush, wasn't it, still high from being onstage (me) and seeing the show run through for the first time (him). I felt his tongue on mine, yes, but I didn't respond. Did I? I couldn't remember. How bad should I be feeling? How would I react if, say, Harvey let Matt's tongue brush his lips? I didn't understand my feelings for Alex; trying to process it was making the room spin. Did I like it? Did I want it to happen again? I wasn't used to my life being so dramatic. But better to rip off the plaster.

'Ask away.'

He took my plate, lined up the cutlery. 'Are you . . . how do you feel? About your performance?'

Oh. Right. Which performance? The one onstage or the near-miss with Alex? 'Um, anxious. Nervous. But excited.'

'I don't mean that. I mean, do you think it's good? Good enough?'

I'd endured the usual negative thought patterns, could I do this, would I do everyone's hard work justice, how I'd feel when the lights were on me, but not whether I was any good or not.

'I think so. What did you think? From what you saw, I mean. Is it not good enough?'

There was such a long sigh. A sigh that preceded bad news, and maybe even the truth. He grimaced.

'Don't take this the wrong way ... ' Pretty much a guarantee I'd take this the right way, and that I wouldn't like it. 'I don't want you to feel like you've made a fool of yourself.'

The warm concern in his voice didn't sound like it went to the bone. 'Why would I feel like that?'

'It's just ... recently, you've been ... I've sensed some emotional fragility in you. All that stuff with Tam and Daisy. You've taken a knock. You need to prioritise yourself, work through things. I wouldn't want you feeling conscious of how you looked up there, in front of all those people. Kids, the parents, your workmates. I'm not sure you'll be happy with how you inhabit the space.'

His voice was so soothing and even, that eerie Californian-esque timbre, like the yoga teacher, but every syllable was a shard of glass burrowing into my skin. I realised I was trembling. 'Conscious? How I look?'

'Oh, you know. Your coordination and stuff. Your dancing isn't as ... it's not polished, and, well, the rest of the cast are kids, so they're kid-sized. You're not.'

I didn't need a dictionary to translate this. I was gangly and awkward and looked like a tit on stage. I was that deluded decaying carcass, thinking I was fabulous, while everyone laughed behind my back. But everyone had said I was good! Iqra, even, my harshest critic. Not to mention . . .

'Alex said I did really well.'

Harvey's face turned to stone. 'What's that supposed to mean?' The air and the heat went out of the room.

'Nothing, just that. Alex said . . . '

'Ah, I get it. I'm some idiot. Don't know what I'm talking about, but Alex knows everything. He's a theatre person, sure, sure. I should shut up.' His voice rose the tiniest amount. 'I should let you go up there and show yourself up, and say nothing, and then try put the pieces back together once you've realised there's yet another thing you can't do. Sure. I understand. I see why Alex would be the authority, why you'd take his word over mine.'

I was frightened. I didn't think Harvey would hurt me, but it was the thought of what came next. Something irreversible. And his face. I'd seen it before, in another life.

'I don't mean that. Any of that. All I'm saying is Alex encouraged me to . . . '

'You know why, don't you? To make himself look good. Set you up. Keep your friends close and your enemies closer. Oldest trick in the book. You've been butting heads all year, all that slog he made you put in, writing the show, you spent our entire Christmas banging on about it, nonstop, and then, when you somehow managed to rise to that challenge, he sets you another impossible task and puts you on stage. You were furious that day! Said he was setting you up to fail. Can't you see? He's laughing at you!'

I'd only seen flashes of this Harvey before; the way he settled into it told me it was his default. Every boring detail I bothered sharing about my work stacked up like evidence in a trial, and he was making it sound plausible, now all the pieces were in place.

'Do you really trust Alex's judgement over mine?'

'No, of course I don't.'

'You understand I'm only trying to protect you? Stop you looking like a prick up there? It's not the showstopper they're telling you it is. Trust me. Alex will be gone in a few days, off to another school, but everyone else will be back in August and they won't have forgotten.'

I had the urge to get out. Was he right? I needed to think. 'Look, I have to get up super early to prepare and . . . y'know, so maybe I'll stay at mine.'

I thought he might try to stop me, say he'd only been teasing, that I'd smash it, that I should stay. Instead, he said, 'No problem, you do whatever you need to do, but you know I'm right. You know you don't have the mental capacity to be dealing with this right now. You're doubting yourself. Sit back and watch the kids perform. Enjoy your success, don't ruin it.'

'I hear you, thanks. I appreciate you looking out for me.' I kissed him on the cheek, robotically, and reached for my jacket. 'Night.'

Outside, I kind of staggered against the wall desperately gasping for a full breath. He hadn't shouted, he'd barely moved, but there was something unsettling, like I'd watched him turn into a werewolf. I was shaking so hard, I struggled to get my phone out of my pocket. I stumbled along the street, eyes stinging as they adjusted to the dazzling phone screen. Daisy. I could call Daisy. I could say, look, let's put what happened on hold, if we can, I need to know whether I'm going crazy.

Suddenly, a bike mounted the pavement and a gloved hand punched me right in the face twice, hard, while another grabbed my phone, giving me a final shove to the ground, calling back, 'Ha, fuck you, you fanny!' as they sped off. Over in a flash.

I sat slumped on the pavement a moment, stunned, tiny traces of comets dancing before my eyes, jagged lines too. There was an insistent buzz in my ears, and my head throbbed. I put my hands to my face slowly, not knowing what to expect. I was bleeding. I felt alone, and scared. There was only one place I could go.

Harvey met me at the street door, his look of indignation switching to panic as he descended the stairs. 'Oh my God, oh my God. What happened?'

We hobbled back up together. Harvey guided me gently to the sofa. There was a faint tang of soap or disinfectant as he dabbed at my face.

'I'm all right,' I lied. I tried to get to my feet but felt woozy, so let him softly push me back onto the sofa. Little spots of my blood landed on the fabric. 'I'm making a mess, I'm sorry.'

'Don't worry.' He knelt before me. 'Take your hands away, let me see.' There was a box in his lap, a first aid kit, I guess.

'My nose feels weird.' I didn't know what a broken nose felt like. I touched it. It was tender, but still jutting proudly in its regular shape. I ran my tongue over my teeth, all still there, I'd expected to spit one out, but I felt a sharpness and knew I'd chipped one. 'What's bleeding?'

'The bridge of your nose is cut.' His voice was tender,

concerned. 'You might get a black eye, I think, it looks . . . angry. This is my fault.' He had tears in his eyes. 'I shouldn't have let you go off, in that vulnerable state.'

'It's Stockbridge, not downtown Baltimore. You weren't to know.'

'But if you'd stayed, we could've talked it out.'

It was a silly argument, he said, he was sorry, he was only trying to protect me. We didn't need to talk about the show again, it was fine. He loved me so much, he said.

I didn't want him to feel bad, and it wasn't exactly like he'd pushed me out into the street. Maybe I shouldn't have stormed off like a stroppy teenager. Like he said, I should've stayed. My fault.

Thirty-Nine

The next couple of days, Harvey didn't leave my side. It was clear as soon as I woke up that I was too sore, and my face too mashed up, to go into work. Mica said they'd do the first two shows with an understudy and she'd rework what little choreography I'd been trusted with so I could potentially do the last show.

'I'm so sorry.' I was so disappointed, I'd wanted to give it my all. But maybe a part of me was relieved, perhaps it was a blessing, saving me from looking like a prick on the stage, like Harvey had warned me.

'It's not over! You get to swan in and steal the show on the final night!' whooped Mica. 'Main character, proper diva shit, baby. I love it.'

I'd hated gazing into mirrors long before the vitiligo appeared or my teeth started to interlace, but surveying this new damage was actually fascinating. Levelling in a way. I could be anyone, a regular person, someone who'd had a bump in the car or tumbled off a bike. My bruised eye was already turning a deep and rich purple. The cut on my nose, with the plaster off, had turned from ketchup red into a darker, duller crimson. My bottom lip and tongue were swollen; I'd bitten into flesh as I fell. And my tooth, of course, had a new jagged edge to make it even more . . . what had my grandma called them? Characterful, that was it. I looked a mess, frankly.

But strangely, perhaps, seeing myself like this gave me a new appreciation for my face in its natural state. I looked like I'd jumped down from a particularly crazed Picasso, yes, but it was individual, real, unblighted by cosmetic intervention other than moisturising and a wet shave. My wee patch of white, and its friends elsewhere on my body, were enhancements, part of me. Now I was spoiled not by how I looked, but how I felt. I sat still in my trap, like a tiny fly in a web, trying to figure out what to do. The mugging was not Harvey's fault, but I couldn't stop raking over the circumstances that had put me there. That smooth evisceration, unravelling the slow progress my confidence had made. What did it really mean when Harvey was trying to protect me?

If I let him go – beautiful, usually kind, Bastille Day Ideal Harvey – what waited out there for me? Back to the boys at Menergize? I was suddenly overcome with guilt for every man I'd wronged or cast aside because I'd not needed them anymore. I could've called Daisy or Tam; they'd know, instinctively, wouldn't they, that something was wrong? Just like I always did with them. Now I felt like I'd lost a layer of protection, force field down. If I didn't have them anymore, if Harvey was out of the picture, who was I? I didn't know how to be on my own.

*

We went for a walk. He drove us through town and parked near Salisbury Crags. I remembered our semi-romantic climb to Arthur's Seat. Aeons ago, another life. We strolled in silence, watching couples brave belting winds in their T-shirts, refusing to acknowledge the weather reports and instead choosing to follow their calendar, which claimed it was June. I wondered what must it feel like to be them, in love, safe.

Within five minutes, we saw Ross coming toward us with a dog on a lead. It couldn't possibly be his; he had antibacterial gel in every room and carried a hand vacuum most of the time, even hoovering guests' shirtfronts at outdoor barbecues.

'Mother-in-law's,' he explained, barely looking at me. 'It likes chasing sticks but the doctor says I've not to throw if I want to be fit enough to limbo in Ibiza in September.'

Harvey loved dogs. He'd had one when we were kids. This one reminded me of it, slightly ratty, excitable, but with a cute, eager face. We watched, mute, as the dog trotted off into the distance, lowered its gaze, and its arse, toward the grass and pushed out a rather pathetic turd.

'I hate this bit.' Ross sighed. 'Carrier bag over my hand. Not very chic. I'd wear gloves but I've none I can spare.'

'Do you have bags, then? I'll do it, I don't mind,' said Harvey. 'Let's find a stick, eh? Good boy.' He wandered off, far enough for me to breathe a little easier, a calm I'd never felt in Ross's presence before. We watched Harvey walking away a while, throwing a stick, calling to the dog with commanding affection. Once his shouts became noise rather than distinct words, Ross looked at me, finally.

'What happened to your face?'

'I got mugged. Some prick on a bike punched me and nicked my phone.'

'But you have your show!' I was as surprised as he was by his concern. 'Have you spoken to Daisy or Tam?'

'I've no phone.'

'They're coming to watch you, you knew that, right?'

My heart leaped for a second or two. I'd assumed they'd be steering clear. 'I was going to try to do the final one.'

'Well, you should, if you can. They can't wait. Honestly! Your poor wee face, though.'

We looked over at Harvey. The dog had tired of running, was looking for somewhere to squat again. I waited for Ross's usual jibe, something about my injuries being a marked improvement.

'Why are you shaking, Leo?'

'I don't know.'

Ross breathed out a sigh. 'A long time ago,' he said, 'I met this fantastic man. He looked like a modern-day Cary Grant, can you imagine? Do you even know who Cary Grant is, actually? Doesn't matter. I thought it was a miracle someone like him could fall in love with me, I still don't see why anyone would but, anyway. He was the perfect gentleman, like, ninety-nine per cent of the time.'

'What about the other one per cent?'

Ross moved away from me a little, threw his head back and laughed as if I'd told him a joke. 'He's watching. The other one per cent of the time he wasn't, and I'd look as miserable and as frightened as you do right now.'

'I'm just cold.'

'Bollocks you are. I see things even if you think I don't. You deserve better, young Leo. I hope you know that. I left my Cary Grant and I've never looked back.'

For the first time in my life, I wanted to hug Ross. 'I . . . '

'Don't say anything. But call me, if you need anything.'

'If you see Tam or Daisy . . . '

'I'll tell them you've had a wee accident, but you're, um, brand new, shall I?' I nodded. Ross lifted his fingers to his mouth and whistled like a sailor on leave. 'Come on, Twiggy! Let's get you home.' Ross turned to me. 'Don't. The last one was called Zsa Zsa. That's too camp even for me. Remember what I said.'

As we walked away, Harvey pulled me in close. 'I've never seen you make Ross laugh before. How did you accomplish the impossible?'

'Oh, he was laughing at his own joke really. The dog's name. You know what he's like. Self self self.'

Forty

Harvey insisted I wasn't up to it, told me I should stay at home, but I couldn't let them down, the show had to go on. Joe Music had come down with food poisoning that morning, so it was all hands on deck for the final show. Harvey reluctantly drove me in. Once there, he headed straight to the makeshift bar at the corner of the hall, staffed by the least uptight school governors serving Guinness out of cans and wine warmer than the sea in St Lucia. Mica had brought Sasha along, in case she decided to have any 'wild parties' or invite boys round. Sasha was carrying a paperback, which Mica said was a front so she looked angelic. 'She's here to assist you, Leo. Whatever you want her to do, she'll do.'

'And you're okay with this, Sasha?'

Sasha handed me a headset so I could keep in contact with everyone backstage. 'Course. My best friend is gay.'

'No, I meant . . . never mind. You haven't even told me how the first two shows went. Who took my place?'

Alex appeared, face rigid with stress and focus, but – and I wasn't imagining this – it softened when he saw me. He mentally processed my injuries for a moment, and for a second I thought he might touch me – his hands came forward involuntarily – until he remembered Sasha and Mica were there, and withdrew.

'What the hell happened?'

I rushed through the story, leaving out some key scenes. 'Did you make Lewis understudy? I knew he'd get his way.'

'I did it, actually,' murmured Alex through a nervous smile.

My mouth did a Pac-Man. No sound came out. My former nemesis turned . . . uh, what were we now? Friends? He'd gone on in my place? Was I proud? Envious? Was it better to have my moment taken over by someone I liked? Did I actually like him? *He's like a ginger Leo,* Daisy had said. A sharp pang of regret took me out of the moment. He could see I was struggling to process.

'I wasn't as good. I didn't wear your costume or anything.'

'Why not?'

'I didn't think it would fit.'

I reared back. 'What you trying to say? What the hell did you wear?'

Mica almost choked holding back a laugh.

'Oh, I mean, I wasn't sure my bod was up to scratch.' A self-deprecating king. Relatable. 'I wore my suit.'

'Your suit?! Al . . . Mr Campbell, it's a show. A performance! Art, not maths! You have to inhibit the . . . Meesh, he could wear the costume, right?'

Mica's smile stretched the length of the M9. 'I'd pay top dollar to see it.'

Sasha piped up. 'You were pretty decent last night. Not exactly Jenifer Lewis, but . . . '

My head snapped round so fast to face Sasha I thought my neck would break. 'Hang on, how do you know Jenifer Lewis?'

'I watch her on YouTube all the time. I'm high-key obsessed with Broadway musicals.'

'I can't believe your mum never told me this. Mica!'

'But now we get the big star!' said Alex, putting his arm round my shoulder. 'You're going to smash this. I'm so excited, can't wait for you to show them what you've got.'

My heart felt like it would burst open. I didn't understand how I was feeling, or why I liked that soft and hypnotic way he spoke to me. So intimate. What did I expect to happen? This wasn't a John Hughes movie; I was a thirty-four-year-old drama teacher who fainted if he stood up too quickly and couldn't go out in the sun without six coats of sunscreen.

I remembered Harvey's warning. Was this sincerity or Alex's plan coming to fruition? My headset crackled with an instruction to get backstage. No time for that now. Showtime! I was so busy covering for Joe Music on the sound team, I couldn't watch properly. At the interval, I was getting Alex ready to go on to make some boring announcements about the school's achievements this year – not exactly the halftime entertainment we'd envisaged, but the governors insisted. I threaded the wire down his back, under his shirt so it wouldn't flap and get caught in his fingers.

'Sorry if this is cold. Can you just . . . '

I kneeled as he reached up his top and helped pull the wire down so I could plug it in. I gulped quite hard at seeing his body for the first time. It wasn't spectacular like Harvey's, it was probably more like mine, a regular body, but that didn't make it any less alluring. That rush of excitement of the first glimpse of flesh you've been desperate to touch. Emotionally, I was in limbo, wanting both something to happen, and everything to stop. He took my hand. 'Are you all right?'

'Yes, of course, it looks worse than it is.'

'I didn't mean that.'

Out of the corner of my eye, through the tiniest gap in the scenery, a spotlight caught Harvey's face. Whether he was even able to see us, I didn't know, but the threat of it knotted my stomach. I stepped back. 'You're on.'

He darted onstage without looking back.

I tuned in to his frequency to make sure we didn't lose him. I could hear every half breath, the faint clicks as his tongue moved round his mouth. It was like he was whispering only to me; my heart quickened in response. Once Alex had made his boring announcements and gone offstage, I heard him tell someone he was going to the loo. I was about to switch off – the last thing I wanted to hear was Alex tinkling out the water he'd been chugging back all night, or worse – when I heard a familiar voice call his name in the corridor.

'Hey,' said Alex, 'it's Harvey, isn't it? We met at the . . . '

'Let's not do this,' said Harvey calmly. 'I don't know exactly what happened between you two in London, and at rehearsals, and in a way it doesn't matter, but I want you to know it will never happen again.'

'I don't know what you mean.'

'Save it, please. Whatever you think this is, sorry, was . . . it isn't. And won't ever be. I'll never give him up.'

What. The. Hell?!

'Look, mate . . . '

'Don't "mate" me. You disappoint me, actually, you really

do. I thought maybe you were a proper threat, that I really had something to worry about. But you're nothing really. Just some nerd trying to fire into him because you both reckon Sondheim was speaking directly to you when he wrote his songs. Two lovable losers.'

I desperately wanted to turn the sound off, pretend I'd never heard this. It was like Harvey had been possessed, slipping into that calculating, brutal tone so easily, traces of which I'd noticed before but tried to ignore. I was shaking. I could hear Alex try to form the words to protest, but Harvey wouldn't let up.

'Me and Leo have something deeper, okay? We've got history. We know each other inside out, pal. A million shared experiences and memories. Our own lingo. You could make pathetic horny fucking geek eyes at Leo across a classroom for a thousand years, but you couldn't replicate a second of what we have, because it belongs to us, and it's more important than whatever's stirring underneath that cheap suit.'

I felt sick. Maybe some men would be excited to hear their boyfriend so menacing, so jealous and protective, but to me it was like he'd wrapped his hands round my throat. Conclusive proof. Wrong horse backed, again. Poor Alex. This was awful. I ran through my options. I could pretend I needed to speak to Alex, and rescue him. Hang on. Alex was speaking. But he sounded different.

'You're kidding, right? Lingo? History? You don't know shit about Leo, but I know plenty about you. I know you're pretty nasty in an argument. I know he can't confide in you. And I know he's not happy.'

'How would you know?' That tone in Harvey's voice again,

transported me back to the other night, stumbling out into the street to get away from him.

'I see his face every day, when you're not there, and it's written all over it. He doesn't love you, he's scared of failure. Just like with his ex. Peter, wasn't it? Ah, that's right, he never told you what really happened.'

'You mouthy cunt.' Harvey's voice sounded closer; I felt like I was there. Their faces must've almost been touching. 'What about Peter?'

'You're more like him than you realise. What happened to Leo's face, exactly?'

'What? What's it to you? He was mugged.'

'Why is he so on edge? Why does his story sound like he's reading it off autocue?' I heard the rustling of fabric, spittle forming in aggression. 'Go on, hit me, you pathetic bully, and lose him for ever. You'll save me a job. And for the record, Harvey, I am gonna take him from you, watch me.'

A light scuffle, some laboured breathing, then the sharp clack of Harvey's shoes on the tiles as he walked away.

Alex muttered something under his breath. 'It's as good as done.'

Mica came to find me, looking flustered. 'Harvey says he ain't feeling well. Wants you to drive him home.' He appeared behind her, smiling weakly, a film of sweat on his forehead that I knew didn't come from any illness.

'That's okay, isn't it?' he said. 'They can find someone else to do the song, right?'

'No,' said Mica, 'we need Leo here. He's doing the song.'

I explained to Harvey that with Joc Music off, I was more

needed than ever, that he should drive himself home and I'd see him later. He'd had too much to drink, he said. Mica took this in, her eyes ricocheting between us, reassessing my injuries, scanning my body language, looking at Harvey, putting two and two together and landing right on five.

'I'll drive you,' she said.

'No, I want Leo.' Just a glint of that tone again. 'Leo, will we go?'

'Tam and Daisy are out there, somewhere. I don't want to disappoint them.'

He smirked. 'I meant to text you. They didn't show. They're not here. So now can we go?'

Mica took Harvey's arm, not firmly but with enough pressure to make him look down at her hand. 'We can't spare him. He's our boy wonder. My Sash can stand in for me, let me take you, I wanna make sure you get home safe, Harv, as soon as possible.'

'Leo.' Laced with menace.

'See you in a bit!' I tried to be cheery; it was like backing away from an explosive. 'I'll come straight to yours after.'

They left, Mica not taking her eyes off mine until she almost bumped into the door.

I peered out into the crowd. I'd almost forgotten: not long until I'd be out there, my big moment.

But.

No.

I couldn't.

Harvey's words rang in my head, and even though makeup would do their best, I looked a mess. You could slather concealer over my bruises but there was no duping the crowd when it came to my stilted dancing, and my swollen mouth trying to navigate Iqra's sharp-shooting lyrics. They might not laugh out loud, but the memory of my failure would have the half life of plutonium.

'Sasha, could you get Mr Campbell?'

Sasha winked and gave a low whistle, and by the time she reappeared with Alex, I'd made up my mind.

'Leo . . . I need a chat, actually.'

'I'm sorry, Alex, not now. I can't go on.' I didn't wait for his questions. 'My tooth . . . it whistles when I try to sing. I can't do it. Can you go on?'

'What? Look, Leo, remember this is about pushing yourself.'

Christ. We were way beyond half-arsed pep talks. 'Could you spare me that for one second and trust me? I cannot go on. I need you to do it. In the proper costume. For me?'

He stammered out a few excuses. Hoping the tears threatening to form in my eyes would show mercy and retreat, I reached for my warpaint: a smile, and a joke. 'The windows of Edinburgh will go unshattered tonight at least. The understudy gets to do the full run. Please.'

'If you're sure?'

'Here.' I gently took Alex's specs off his face and shined them on my T-shirt. 'Let's see you in the costume. You'll be great.'

'Thank you.' He took back his glasses. 'I'll do it for you.' He headed for wardrobe.

Sasha laughed. 'Mum was right, the sexual tension between you two is off the charts. *I'll do it for you.* Like, stop. Drink some water.'

'Sasha, don't make me fall out of love with you even quicker than I fell into it. Go make sure a responsible adult helps him into those ridiculous trousers.'

Once dressed, Alex came to find me. 'Thoughts?'

He really didn't want to know my thoughts.

'Are you sure about this? You must be disappointed, you worked so hard.'

'Don't be silly.' I stood to face him. 'I don't do limelight, anyway. It was fate.'

'At least you'll get to sing at the wedding. Can't wait for that.'

Would I even be at the wedding? Or was Tam not showing up a sign that I was about to be lasered off the guest list like Harvey and Ross? Only now did I realise how much I wanted to be there. Not that I had long to grieve: Alex's face came closer to mine, his arm coiled round my back.

'When it's over, I really need to talk to you.'

'You're on. Break a leg.'

I didn't watch. I stood with my back to the stage. No peeping. I couldn't. I just couldn't. Still on his frequency, I listened to his vocals in isolation. He was good. Strong, confident, only a few bum notes, the same ones I'd flunked. When it was over, I listened to him panting, the exhilaration ringing out loud and clear. Like when you can actually hear someone smiling on the radio. I stayed online, eavesdropping, as he shook the students' hands – no hugging since a scandal back in 2009, apparently – and told Iqra she was amazing. I didn't turn round to see, just imagined it. How it might have felt, to feel that light on my face and see the smiles of the crowd, be bathed in their applause.

But I knew my place. Always had.

Forty-One

I stood at the door as the parents left, painting on a smile as they gushed over Alex and Iqra's duet and pretended not to notice my black eye. Once I'd supervised the tidy-up back-stage and briefed the volunteers coming in the next morning to dismantle the scenery and decorations, I trundled front of house to help clean up the under-chair debris – an audi-ence of baboons would've made less of a mess. Distractions, distractions, because I knew Alex was waiting somewhere. Eventually, he came to find me, right as I was chucking saw-dust over somebody's pre-hangover in the accessible toilet. How romantic.

'I have something to tell you.' He was out of costume now, but stage makeup had settled into the soft creases round his eyes. 'It's about Harvey.'

I felt soiled, somehow. The secret, that Harvey wasn't as perfect as his immaculate side parting might suggest, was uncovered. Mica knew, I could tell. Sasha too. And now Alex. The gig was up.

'Is that right?'

'Aye. I wasn't sure I should mention it. He's . . . we had an altercation.'

I could pretend I hadn't heard, and listen to his version of events, but I didn't see any point prolonging this. 'I heard you. Two stags banging their antlers.'

Something sadistic in me enjoyed his change of expression, his brain going through the pencil and paper routine to work out how I'd heard, and exactly what. 'Okay. So now you know.'

'Now I know what? That you're both two sides of the same coin?'

He almost snarled, raised himself to his full height, as if to show me he and Harvey could never be similar; he had at least three inches on Harvey, it was true. 'He threatened me! We're not remotely alike!'

But they were. Weren't they? Thinking they owned me, could shape me into what they wanted, just sweep me along before I had time to protest. Oh, they had slightly different techniques, but their aims were the same: to solve me like a problem. Harvey's mission, making me his fixer-upper, giving me new hobbies, steering me away from being 'aimless', chang- ing my body, transforming me into his ideal boyfriend which, I now realised, was Matt – that rock-climbing trophy photo was a warning shot.

And now Alex. A nicer guy, on the whole, I could admit, but still pushing, and still out for himself. Telling me I had great potential, so patronising. Yes, I'd loved doing this show, and, yes, I probably could do more with my career, and maybe I should go for Chris's job, but when I looked back, this had been for Alex's benefit, not mine. To give him that buzz of slipping a fiver into the charity tin. A sense of achievement, spotting a potential star and making it happen. A case study to brag about in his next job interview. I'd seen enough teachers whose good intentions tarmacked the dual carriageway to hell to recognise an educator with a god complex.

It was romantic, yes, and exciting, to imagine Alex whisking me away, but it would leave me as dependent on him as I'd become on Harvey. I'd never been enough. I just wanted someone to tell me, you're good, you're done, I like you the way you are. I wasn't a work in progress, the ugly girl at the end of the teen movie who whips off her specs and has jocks swooning. For better or worse, this was me; maybe only Daisy and Tam had ever truly accepted me.

Alex looked astonished I wasn't diving into his arms. That I was immune to the smooth talking that had worked on him, back in that fancy bar overlooking the London skyline, sipping martinis with his boss. I wasn't such a soft touch, not anymore.

'What did you think was going to happen, Alex? Six months of "you can do this, you're amazing" and pressing your dick against me in rehearsals, and it would be game over? I'd come running? Just leave my boyfriend for you? "As good as done," I think you said. I don't come that cheap.'

'It's not like that. You can't stay with him! After the way he spoke to me?'

I washed my hands, glad to feel the chilly spray of the never-hot-enough water on my forearms. It woke me up a bit. 'What happens with me and Harvey is nothing to do with you.'

'We had something. There was a moment. I saw his face when he came to get you after the rehearsal.'

'We're colleagues. You were the one saying we should keep it professional. But you didn't. You told him we shared a room in London on purpose, didn't you? To force my hand, maybe.' It hurt to be so cold. It went against all my instincts, I wasn't even sure it was what I wanted, but it was the right thing to do.

'I didn't know you hadn't told him.' Was that a tear forming in his eye? 'What really happened to your face, Leo? Was it because of me? You feel this. I know you do. This is something.'

'I was mugged, Alex. That's all. Honestly. I'm sorry, but I have to be real here. You might think there's something with, uh, I don't know, with the version of me you think you know. That potential me you're always talking about. I meet a lot of men who fall for that guy. Trouble is, he never shows up.'

'We nearly kissed the other day.'

'End-of-term excitement.' It wasn't, we both knew it, but if I had any hope of picking up the pieces, I had to stand my ground.

He moved towards me, grabbed my cuff. 'I've always regretted that night, when I found you outside the school. Letting you go home, go back to him. Kiss me now. You'll see.'

I removed his hand. Stepped back. 'Stop.'

'Please. Leo.'

'I'll walk you to your car.'

He trudged beside me in silence. His car lock beeped. 'This is . . . I can give you a lift home.'

I knew if I got in that car he'd talk me round. An enclosed space, the tired resignation of a long day. Maybe we'd drive out somewhere, consummate this madness. Maybe I'd like it. Then, he'd drop me off and, no doubt, Harvey would see us and make my life complicated in all sorts of new ways. No. I had to declutter.

'I'm not going home, I have something to do.'

'If you go back to Harvey, you're an idiot,' he spat. That last desperate angry act of the rejected. We've all been there.

'I've definitely been an idiot,' I said. 'But things are going to change.'

'What are you gonna do?'

'I'm going to get over myself.' What he'd said to Harvey was true. I had a history of settling for being unhappy because the alternative was unimaginable. Too afraid of whatever came next. Time to put myself to the test.

'You should let people near. You're a bit of an iceberg. Not much on the surface, but below . . . serrated edges.'

Just as I didn't need someone pointing out my potential, I wasn't interested in being reminded of my faults or my mistakes. I knew them. I woke up to them laid out in front of me like a hotel breakfast. An iceberg – hadn't Harvey said almost exactly the same thing? Proof I was on the right track; I couldn't be with anyone unwilling to take me at face value. 'Then you'll be happy to stay out of my waters, won't you? Goodbye, Alex.'

A man defeated, there's no sight quite like it. I'd seen one often enough, in a mirror, in those dark moments when you're brushing your teeth before bed and marvelling at the indignity of it.

'See you at the wedding,' he said, flatly.

'I wouldn't count on it.'

I watched the rear lights of his car blur into the night, and it felt like little threads of my heart were being pulled away with them.

Mica stood waiting at the main entrance, packet of emergency cigarettes in hand. She held one out to me.

'I thought you'd gone.'

'Not without you.'

'Aren't we breaking protocol? Smoking at the same time?' She shrugged. 'Did Harvey say anything? He took his car keys.'

'I can give you a lift. Nope, not a word.' She took a deep drag. 'You're frightened of him.'

'I was. Not anymore.' I'd never felt stronger; I needed to channel this energy before it left me for ever. 'Where's Sasha? She's great, you know. I don't know why you're so hard on her.'

Mica put her hand up to stop me. 'I put her in a cab. Look, I'm not saying she isn't great, but you've met one version. Paperbacks and *Dreamgirls*, let's say the girl knows her audience. Don't forget I'm with her all the time, and she's the one thing I'd like to get right. When I'm not with you playing sassy best friend, I'm doing leading role duties at home, okay?'

'But . . . hang on. Sassy best friend! I thought I was the sassy best friend?'

'Not tonight. Very much leading man, baby. Stole the show without even setting foot onstage. Whew.'

I hadn't been there for Mica at all; she'd been trying to tell me how hard things were for her with Sasha and I'd dismissed it, too caught up in my own drama. 'I'm sorry. It's none of my business. I back you all the way.'

'I bet. You gonna tell me about it? Like, proper tell me what's going on with this fucking guy? And Naomi Campbell?'

'I am actually. On the way.'

'You want to go home?'

There was somewhere I needed to go first. A dragon I had to slay.

Forty-Two

We all have our own Manderley, don't we? That place we return to in our dreams, over and over, like the second Mrs de Winter in *Rebecca*? I've collected a few over the years. Childhood homes, running my fingers over the woodwork and pressing my nose against frosty windows and staring out at a murky, sleepy version of the outdoors. Chic hotels I've stayed in, surreal versions of Ross's parties where I'm either wise and witty or helpless and tongue-tied. I've travelled far and wide without ever leaving my bed. But the last few years, my dreams took me to the same place night in, night out. The house I was standing outside now, while Mica's car purred expectantly behind me. Even though I'd never been before, and it wasn't quite how my imagination had sketched it, it felt utterly familiar. There was a gate I hadn't expected, the door was green and not the shade I usually dreamed it, but I'd strode up that path countless times, knocked loudly, or tapped gently, sometimes there was a bell to ring, and when the door opened . . . I couldn't remember what happened next. Now it was time to do it for real.

'Leo! What the f— what are you doing here?'

That trace of panic and anger in his voice then the instant correction. Peter was not pleased to see me, but he almost managed a smile. Not so long ago, I'd have been scared witless. Seeing him vulnerable for a change was the fuel I needed. I was ready for take-off.

'Good question. I can either tell you out here, loud enough to make your Neighbourhood Watch newsletter, or you can let me in.'

He showed me through to the living room. My old sofa. A familiar side table. Weird to see my old furniture somewhere else. Did it miss me? Ava's toys scattered about. Peter was still a slob, then.

'What do you want? What happened to your face? Are you drunk?' He even managed to sound concerned. 'Is it your mother? I just saw her. You know it's your dad's anniversary tomorrow.'

Bastard. Like he gave a shit. I was fully aware what day it was. 'My mum is fine. She's part of the reason why I'm here. I think it's time you stopped dropping in on her, don't you?'

Peter tutted. 'With respect, Leo, that's none of your business. I know your relationship with Dawn is . . . strained, but she's always cared for me, you know that.'

I felt unrehearsed. How did this go in the dreams? Did Peter usually talk back, did we argue, or did I spit it all out unchecked? 'Only because she doesn't know what you did. Yet. But I'll tell her.'

'You're being hysterical, as usual. I thought you might have grown up a bit, moved on. But no.' Peter glanced at the door. 'Look, I think you should leave. Ben will be back any minute.'

It started coming back to me, what I used to say in the dream, like a script rolling in my head. Go on, I told myself, you've absolutely nothing to lose.

'I'm not scared of you anymore.'

But of course I was. I was shaking. You can't block out who you were. I was only still here because adrenaline and anger wouldn't let me be anywhere else. But shaking or not, he had no power over me now.

'I know what you've been saying about me, to Mum, to Daisy and Tam. My turn to speak now. It's about time everybody knew who you really are.'

Even then, after years apart, there were vestigial fragments of a couple's intuition, so when he went to grab my wrist, I instinctively moved it away. His usual serene expression melted into a sneer. Here he was, the man I remembered.

'What I did? You're off your head. It was nothing. You were a wreck, and everyone knew it. She won't believe it. Nobody will.'

And then . . .

'What's going on?'

Standing in the door, two pizza boxes in his arms, was Ben.

I realised we'd never met. You wonder, don't you, sometimes, when lovers move on, what traces of you exist in whoever comes next, what you have in common? Maybe you're completely unalike, but usually, there's something familiar, even if it's presented in a different way, a better way. The only time I'd laid eyes on my replacement before was when Daisy and Tam had fired up Instagram and torn through every creative choice Ben and Peter had made at their wedding.

'What did you do? Won't believe what?' Ben turned to me. 'What do you mean you're not scared anymore?'

Looking at Ben, more handsome than me, nose considerably smaller than mine, shorter, yet apparently nervous, I saw a glimmer of a version of myself. Ben had secrets of his own. 'Ben, I'm sorry to disturb you at home. You don't know me, but . . .'

'I know who you are.' Glaswegian, I noticed.

'Honey,' said Peter in that familiar way that melted me that first year we were together. 'It's his dad's anniversary, he's emotional. Drunk. Settling scores. It was nothing. This is what he does. Remember I told you.'

Ben really was like me, a face that said everything his voice could not. A face that had listened to Peter's explanations and excuses before and never been quite sure what to believe, brushing away doubts because it was easier.

'I don't drink, Ben.' I took a chance. 'Does he do this to you? Convince you that you're the problem? Make you second guess yourself?'

Peter pushed me, hard. The mask was off. 'Shut the fuck up.'

As I stumbled against the wall, my knees buckling but finding the last grain of strength I needed to stay upright, I caught the wave of recognition across Ben's face.

'Have you two been fucking? I know there's someone else.' To me, now. 'Is it you? Is that why you're here?'

Bile rocketed to my throat. That was typical of Peter's vanity. It wasn't enough for him to have everything; he had to have two of everything and gamble the lot to feel alive.

'No, definitely not.' I could feel Peter's rage boiling. I had seconds left, might as well go out with a bang. 'Has he hit you yet, Ben? I can get you help.'

Peter put his hand over my mouth. 'Shut up. Don't listen to him, honey. He's fucking mental. Bitter. You're drunk. He's drunk, Ben.'

In a way I was glad to see Ben look so shocked by this sudden violent outburst – it probably meant he'd been spared so far. Peter started to manhandle me out the door. It was a brief, ugly moment of chaos. A lamp went on its side, the pizza boxes dropped to the floor, yet none of us spoke. I managed to wrench my arm away. We stopped, face to face, in the hallway.

'Get out of my house.' His face was red, nostrils flared, mouth snarling; the real him had risen to the surface at last. He wanted to shout, but couldn't. We were right outside a bedroom with a huge painted unicorn on the door. A child was asleep in there.

'Wait.' Ben came between us, touched the door to his daughter's room as if trying to pick up her heartbeat. 'Leo. Why are you here?'

I didn't even know anymore. Because history nearly repeated itself? Because I'd had to watch him lick up to my mum, fool my friends, claim he was the victim? Because I wanted to have it out about Tam, find out whether it was really true? For revenge? To split them up?

'Is this true, Pete? Did you hit him?'

I wished I could enjoy watching Peter squirm, but it was pathetic. 'No. There was a scuffle, once.'

Lying bastard. It didn't matter why I was here anymore; coming had been the hardest part. Maybe things hadn't gone as I'd expected, whatever I expected, but I could hold my head up.

'I came to say my piece. I've said it. I'm not a drunk. And he did hit me. My friend is waiting.'

They stood at the doorway watching me go. Ben's hands over his mouth. Peter's face ghostly, realising his world was falling apart.

'Ben . . . I wish you all the luck in the world. Peter, I meant what I said. Stay the fuck away from my mother. Or you'll be sorry.'

So that was how it felt to have a dream come true.

Forty-Three

I waved goodbye to Mica, promising I'd message her as soon as I got inside, forgetting instantly upon reaching my front door, when Daisy and Tam launched themselves at me, hugging me so hard my ribs almost caved in. They'd been drinking and looked traumatised in the unforgiving glare of the light in the communal landing. I ushered them inside as they winced at my bruises and garbled through the marble run of events that had brought them here. Ross had called Daisy. Alex had called Tam. I felt a tiny flutter of regret. Once fully up to speed, Daisy and Tam had rushed over, they said, and pressed every button on the intercom, screeching 'Delivery!' until someone buzzed them in.

I didn't have to ask how bad Ross and Alex had made things sound; when you've known someone as long as we had, there was no need to speak. That was part of the problem, I supposed; sometimes you really needed to say it out loud or it would fester. They both gawped at me from the sofa. I sat awkwardly in the chair, tried to tuck my legs under me for comfort, but it sent me off balance.

'Why is your phone off? We were sitting out there, up to ninety-nine with worry.'

'It got nicked, remember. I'd hoped you might turn up.'

Tam slapped his forehead. 'We meant to come, we were actually planning to surprise you, but . . . ' They exchanged a glance containing at least three novels' worth of subtext that I was too tired to try to interpret.

Daisy smiled the brave grimace of a widow throwing dirt on her husband's coffin. 'We'll tell you later. First . . . '

Tam got off the sofa and shuffled over to me on his knees. Daisy did the same. They sat before me, as they used to do at university when we were hungover and dissecting the night before, slating anyone who'd crossed us. Younger joints, then, of course; I knew they wouldn't last down there long. I chucked them a couple of cushions.

'Tell us everything. Don't leave anything out.'

Did I really want to do this now? Or at all? Finally unload everything? Shouldn't I be heading to Harvey's, ripping off that plaster? Might he turn up here?

'I was mugged. It's not as bad as it looks.'

'Not that, not yet,' said Daisy. 'Start at the beginning. Peter.'

I'd like to say it was cathartic or liberating, upending everything your friends thought they knew about your life, but I felt I was making fools out of them. Nobody wants to be told they got it wrong, had misjudged somebody. Peter's moods, which they'd interpreted as curmudgeonly charm. His lies about my drinking to discredit me, future-proof himself against any accusations. Harvey's subtle manoeuvres, making me question my own worth. Daisy squirmed at the memory of nights she'd clung onto Peter's arm, doubled up at his jokes, or gushed over Harvey's beautiful face and smooth patter. Tam was more demonstrative. He blamed himself, he said through tears. There was something beautiful about watching Tam cry with such fierce sincerity at my feet, but then he always did look so good wet. He'd met two boyfriends from diving off the lowest board at the Commonwealth Pool.

I didn't want them to feel bad or guilty; at one time I had, definitely. I blamed them for making me feel I could never open up, but misunderstandings are not exclusive to strangers, and we all have secrets we keep from those we love the most. I was frightened of being talked about, but gossip, I realised, is an early warning system. Confessions, confidences, hopes, dreams – sharing them kept you safe, they helped friends understand you better, to notice if you were acting out of character. I'd been mad at Daisy and Tam for not giving me airtime but I'd always convinced myself I had nothing to say.

After about an hour, I'd told the lot. I'd 'let them in'. Careful what you wish for, I guess. Over a decade of lust, heartbreaks and lessons learned, distilled into tablet form, but no easier to swallow. We sat in silence a while. Tam poured out Diet Cokes, Daisy searched my kitchen drawer for the cigarettes she knew I was hiding. We shared one, giggling like teenagers.

'Inside, I think I knew something wasn't right,' said Daisy as she squished the spent cigarette against the top of her can. 'You had a look about you sometimes. Your face always gives you away, Lion. I had a feeling he was . . . sharp, or at least had the ability be cruel. I thought it might be that kind of . . . acerbic thing. Like we put each other down sometimes, don't we, but we know it comes from love, eh?'

'So much love.' Tam stroked my knee. 'Hang on, Daiz, do you mean Peter or Harvey?'

'You know what? Both. Shit. The wine tasting. Harvey, like, puts his hands on you a lot. I thought it was affectionate, but kind of, I don't know. It's like something's been draining away from you. Everything I say makes me feel like I'm overreacting. But kind of possessive.'

'He squeezes your hand all the time,' said Tam, almost dreamily. 'You don't always look like you're enjoying it.'

I was about to explain it was his way of reminding me he was there, until I played it through in my head, and realised how it would sound. We'd all been afraid, in a way, to flag anything because, as Daisy said, it appeared ridiculous, an overreaction, but that's how it always started.

It was a relief, not only to come clean, but be among them again, hear their voices, look into their eyes and feel safe and loved. Us three, always. Common ground is holy ground.

Daisy went to the toilet to fix her makeup even though it was way past our bedtimes. Tam took my hand and kissed it.

'Lion, I never told you something. I wish I had. Maybe none of this would've happened.'

So it was time. The big confession. I was ready. It didn't matter. Peter was ephemera, dusty clothes in the attic, yellowing newspapers in a corner, nothing. 'Go on.'

We'd been out, we were all wasted. I'd sloped off to bed with an Irish goodbye. Peter had made a pass, Tam said. Lunged at him, put his mouth on his. 'I pushed him off. He unbuttoned his fly. It was insane.'

'What did you think of his cock?'

'Lion!' Tam pulled a lemon-sucking face. 'I didn't look! I got the hell out of there. I wanted to tell you but I put it down to booze and I'd been going on and on about being lonely. I blamed myself for giving mixed signals.'

'There's no such thing as mixed signals. There's either red or green. And Peter chose to ignore your red. Nothing else happened?'

'No! I swear. I really wanted to say. I was afraid I'd lose you.'

'You said the same about Daisy.'

He rightly ignored that cheap jibe. 'The thought of you hurting and me not doing anything about it kills me, Dandelion.'

'Ugh, I'm sick of being called that, like a weed.'

'What are you talking about?' Tam was suddenly very serious. 'Dandelions are important. They tell you when spring is here, they have pollen *and* nectar, most flowers only have one or the other, they're good for soil, they can survive just about anywhere. I could go on.' He hugged me tight, but not his usual drunken hug, no pat on the back, or ruffling my hair; he held me like his grip was all that stood between me and crashing to the ground. 'You're no weed, Leo, and I love you.' Another drunken I-love-you to add to the collection. He sniffed up. 'You've got your B fragrance on. S'nice.'

We untangled and Tam's eyes glazed over slightly, his mind going somewhere darker. 'How long? Since you spotted something off about Harvey? How long has this been a secret?'

If I were honest? Subconsciously? The day I got the suit, a happy day, just me and Tam – until I got home and told Harvey he was out of the wedding. His disappointment was understandable, the anger was way over the top.

'I knew it. All my fault. It was Fabrizio's idea not to invite him.'

Weird. 'Why?'

'I don't know. Part of me thinks he was hoping you might drop out. He's kinda jealous of our wee thing.' I knew Fabrizio wasn't a huge fan of, well, anyone but himself really, but I'd put it down to general indifference rather than malice. 'That's why I asked you to sing. To make sure you'd be there.'

'He's jealous? Of me and Daisy?'

'Not Daisy, no.' Tam stared back, eyes bloodshot and brimming with secrets of his own. 'I suppose we can be a bit intimidating, without meaning to be.'

'Should I not come to this wedding?' Maybe it would be easier; I wouldn't have to face Alex, then. And I wasn't exactly looking forward to singing my acoustic 'That's Amore' in Italian – I was no match for Connie Francis.

He took my hand. 'Of course you should be there. I couldn't do it without you. I won't do it without you.'

I remembered Ross on the Meadows, his eyes kind for the first time. 'You should try and squeeze Ross in somehow. He's not so bad.' With my thumb, I rubbed the broken skin on Tam's index finger. 'I hope you weren't biting this because of me.'

'Ah, Lion. May both sides of your pillow be forever cool.'

Daisy returned, face renewed. 'Have you told him?'

'Yes he has,' I said. 'It's fine.'

'Um, no, not that. Something else. Look, Lion . . . ' There was a look between them. 'Reason we missed the show. I kind of preempted this whole confessional energy, and I, uh, told Daisy about, uh, the whole, uh . . . '

Daisy did the blowjob motion with her hand, poking her tongue so hard into her cheek I thought it was going to pop out the other side. 'Ross phoned and I was on my way to get you,

I swear, but . . . Tam picked his moment. We've kind of been, um, killing each other most of the night. We only stopped when Alex called and said Harvey had threatened him.'

These two! 'Killing each other? But you're okay now? Despite the whole . . . ' I tried to do the same blowjob motion but my tongue was too sore so instead I looked like I was eating a hot chip.

'We could do with a third party to talk it through with . . . '

What could I do but laugh? Business as usual. Nothing would ever change, except me. I already had.

'I'm sorry, I'll have to deal with you two idiots another time. I need my bed.'

Tomorrow, I'd have to face Harvey.

Forty-Four

I admit, I haven't been honest. About not wanting to be the centre of attention, I mean. Growing up, it could feel like life was always happening on the other side of a window – something wonderful to observe but never be a part of. All the rituals my classmates went through seemed unavailable or complicated. First kisses and fumbles happened in darkness, behind clubhouses, out of sight. Crushes were risky, my infatuations didn't flatter their objects. People were 'cool with it', with me, they always said so, but that clarification instantly set me apart from the others. I never knew how to respond to this pledge of acceptance, often delivered at emotional gunpoint. There was always that suspicion between us gay kids, an unspoken understanding that if popularity or inclusion came calling, we'd leave each other behind. Liberation was happening all round me on TV or Pride marches but none of it felt like it had anything to do with me. The tragic intersection of my looks, personality and sexuality made me feel I was on my own. The whole world, through glass.

So maybe I did crave the limelight a little. And, yes, watching

Alex go onstage and take my place in my stupid show crushed as hard as if he'd replaced me in a Broadway run. What was my Bastille Day Ideal if not being looked at by strangers and assumed to have it all? The spotlight looked good from my dark corner. But so far, whenever it landed on me, it was out of my control. I never stepped voluntarily into that hot white circle; I was always dragged there. My face. My dad dying. Peter. Now Harvey. What would it be like to orchestrate my own chaos?

He was pleased to see me when he opened the door, hugged me, pretended not to notice my stiffness in response. There was the insouciant chatter of the condemned man, his tone light, loaded questions masquerading as innocent, but I was fluent in Harvey now. I understood what he was really saying when he asked about my performance, why my phone had been off, and who drove me home.

'I didn't go on. Alex made a good stand-in, sang flat in all the same places I would've. My phone, if you remember, is no longer with us. Mica drove me home.'

'Sit down, sit down. I'll get us a drink. Tea? Juice?' His smile was sickening, like he was trying not to reveal he'd hidden a dead body somewhere, treading on eggshells for maybe the first time in my company.

To sit means you're staying, that you're interested in what they have to say, if indeed there's anything left to say. You may as well lie down. Power like this didn't come my way every day. I remained standing.

'I don't want anything. Thanks.'

I imagined I was writing this as a scene. Where should everyone be? What was our motivation? How smoothly could I get offstage? How could I keep this as civil as possible? How did

I make it clear I never wanted to see Harvey again? And if he asked me why, what would I say? I'd missed my performance last night; now was my chance.

He handed me a crisp cream-coloured envelope.

'What's this?'

He gave a watery smile. 'Open it.'

'What is it, Harvey?' So cold and dispassionate. Playing a role to get myself through it.

'It's just a card,' he said, with fake cheeriness. 'It's a year today. Since we met. As adults, I mean. Happy anniversary.'

Sniffing up, I could tell there were flowers in the kitchen. A year. If I could've gone back to that night, what would I say to the version of me smoothing down his hair in the mirror in the loos, and nervously checking his breath? When Harvey had asked if I wanted to do this again, would I be any better, or worse off, if I'd said no, and taken another path? Chipped tooth, aside, that is. It was too late for the man who said yes 365 days ago, but it wasn't too late for me.

'I don't think we're right for each other.'

'Sit, Leo, for goodness' sake. Open your card.'

'Did you hear what I said?' And yet, I sat down. I never could resist doing as I was told.

'Look, we've had a rough few days, you've been stressed about your show . . .'

'No. We're not suited. We don't gel. It's not natural. We're not equals. You're not who I thought you were. You're not the kind of person I can be with.'

I don't know how I was expecting him to react. Fury? Devastation? Instead, it seemed to be denial. 'Wow. This is very big talk, probably coming from a place of anger, and I hear you. I see you. But, Leo, we love each other. Are you sure about this?'

I could've listed every reason, every doubt, but what good would it have done? I didn't want to make him think this was a debate or let myself to be talked out of it. This was my show. 'Last time I loved someone who wasn't right for me, it ended badly.'

'So you admit you love me?'

'Listen. I tried to make that relationship work because I was scared. Scared nobody else would come along. Scared that being alone would be worse.'

'I'm not Peter. I'd never cheat on you.'

'No, you're not Peter. But that's not enough.' The problem wasn't that Peter and Harvey were no different – it was me. They turned me into the same person, trapped, second-guessing myself, trying to smooth things over, be something I wasn't. Next time, if there was one, I had to be with someone who wouldn't push me into that role.

'Tell me what I've done. I'll never do it again.' He pulled himself off the sofa and sat on the floor, folding in on himself, and began to cry. Here came the devastation. Heavy sobs. The tuneless grunting and desperate panting of grief, of knowing it's too late. Once he calmed, he raised himself up on his hands, and kneeled. I'd forgotten he was an ugly crier. Poor Harvey. But I wasn't going to change my mind.

'I bet that cunt Alex is waiting for you. There's always someone lurking,' he said, sadly, looking down at the floor. 'Matt had his little crew, worshipping him, whispering in his ear. The yes men. The hero waiting in the wings. They ran the Berlin marathon together. I can't run well. Osteoarthritis. Only thing

I can't do. Matt was so cold at the end, like he was closing a bank account. He made me so . . . he hated me getting angry, but that's what he did to me. I swore this would never happen again. I tried everything to be more positive. Focused on my sense of self.' He looked up at me and I was reminded of the open, beautiful face that had lured me in before. 'I thought I was safe with you. Someone who didn't need that validation. Someone who knew me before. A little bit of home.'

I remembered the flush of excitement when he'd said that to me up Arthur's Seat, but now it made me feel sick. That's all I was, a homely substitute who'd never run off with a rock climber, who Harvey could gradually mould into Matt's image, rescue me like an underprivileged teenager.

But I was no better. I loved Harvey with blinkers on, chasing my Bastille Day Ideal he could never live up to, when all we had in common was our history. I followed my dick, too. My heart and my head barely got a look in.

My mind returned to my number one obsession: my face. Months ago, Tam claimed I'd never have got someone like Harvey if I weren't attractive. Tam was wrong. Harvey liked my compliance, my gratitude, my plasticity in the palm of his hand. Maybe he even targeted me directly; maybe my mother had told him how lost I was, or perhaps the damage from Peter hung around me, like that cloud of bacterial junk he talked about on our first date, a year ago today. A microbiome of every mistake I'd ever made.

I knew where this path ended, time to leave it. I stood, and Harvey shuffled over to kneel at my feet. When I was a teenager, lying in bed thinking nobody would ever love me or touch me, I never dreamed one day a man would beg on his knees for me not to leave. Maybe this happened to hot people all the time. This didn't feel like a victory, though.

'I'm sorry, Leo. I love you. I'll never hurt you.' He shouted into his hands, then hugged my knees, trying to get the words out. 'I can change. Stay.' I watched snot bubble in one of his nostrils and then ping to nothing. 'Why doesn't he love me anymore? Why doesn't he want me?'

Ah. He wasn't crying for me. Typical, I couldn't even be the main character during my own breakup. This was about a man I'd never met. Matt's love, then his rejection, and now his ghost. He'd left scars on Harvey, who tried to inflict new ones on me. Harvey reached for my hand and lightly squeezed my fingers. One, two, three. I sighed, looked round the room. Life is complicated and love is not electricity; you can't just switch it off and sit in the dark.

But I'd come this far. Time to bring the curtain down.

I gently peeled Harvey's fingers from mine, let his hand fall to the floor with a pitiful thud and stepped away from him. He didn't look up. Maybe he'd been right, maybe my life was aimless until I met him, but I was focused now. I left the room without another word, closing the door behind me, crossing that threshold to the outside world, elated, as if it were a finish line.

Forty-Five

The sun feels different in other countries. I dangled my long arms out of my window, daring the Italian rays to burn them a little. It was too warm to get dressed for real until seconds before I needed to. My suit was laid out, waiting. I was going to look good. A new me. As I slipped on my shirt, there was a gentle knock at my door. A little flutter inside. But it was only Tam, looking movie star knockout in that breathtaking suit, now complete with famed duck-egg tie.

'You look like you've seen a ghost.'

'I thought it was one.'

I hadn't seen Alex arrive the night before, only heard his laugh pealing through the courtyard below, wheeling his suit-case over the cobbles.

Tam checked my suit for imperfections. 'Not too late for you two, you know.'

'Alex is a great guy. But not what I want.'

My bruises had faded, my lip was healed and my dentist had fixed that chip in my tooth; the year with Harvey was starting to feel like a dream. One I didn't want to relive. With anyone.

Today wasn't about me, anyway. I quickly scanned Tam's hand for bite marks. Clear.

'How you feeling? In an hour you'll be Mrs Fabrizio . . . I don't even know his surname. How's that possible?'

'Difiori. I'm feeling . . . can I be honest?'

'Under the terms of our new agreement, yes.' Since that night – the Night of the Shock Reveals, we'd taken to calling it for sheer melodrama – we'd been trying out an 'honesty first' policy.

'I really want to say this. Like, so badly. But I'm not sure I should.'

Second thoughts! Knew it. Made sense, really. Fabrizio had a fortnightly scale and polish and owned ISAs; Tam brushed his teeth in the shower and his savings plan was an empty brown envelope stuffed under his cutlery drawer. Fabrizio was a nag, too. Only the night before, Daisy had watched him pout and pick through dinner and whispered to me, 'Fabrizio is so uptight, I bet he nuts talc.'

As if summoned by the telepathy she was convinced we shared, Daisy's voice came hollering from the courtyard below.

'Lion!'

Tam shrank into the farthest corner of the room and put his finger to his lips. I poked my head out the window. 'It's not very dainty and bridal to shout on the day of the wedding.'

Daisy was holding a folder crammed with god knows what in one hand and her phone in the other. 'Shut up. I'm not the bride. And I'm certainly not dainty. Have you seen Tam?'

'What are you doing? You on a treasure hunt?'

I was skating close to the edge; Daisy was in work mode and always left her sense of humour in her car during office hours.

'Tam dropped this list of final snags on me this morning. Some of it's ridiculous.'

A twinge of jealousy. Why hadn't he asked me? I risked a quick peek back at Tam, his hands locked in fervent prayer I wouldn't give him away. I knew how to send Daisy on her way. 'Need a hand?'

'Of course I don't! But if you see Tam, tell him I need him, or give him a swift kick in the balls, see how you feel.'

I watched her troop off, tiny notelets fluttering to the ground behind her, and turned to Tam, who peeled himself off the back wall.

'Most of that list is already done. I wanted a bit of time with you.'

'Without Daisy?'

'Without Daisy.'

Maybe this could be my wedding present to Tam, listening to him spill one more of his petty, but kind of adorable, insecurities before they became Fabrizio's problem. 'Go on then, pal.'

He chuckled, but it rang hollow. 'I keep trying to picture what my future looks like. With Fabrizio. And I can't.'

'Let me get Daisy.'

'I don't need Daisy.' Even in anguish, his face lost none of its beauty. 'Tell me, Lion, honestly. Are you serious about Alex? Not being interested?'

'Yes! Anyway, you can't compare my stupid . . . whatever, emotional affair that went nowhere to what you and Fabrizio have.' What did they have, though? A shared love of city breaks, maybe. Emotionally, they were on different planets. Fabrizio was robotic; Tam would cry at an egg boiling.

Tam nodded and swallowed hard. 'I'm glad. Selfish bitch alert, but I don't think I could stand seeing you two together.'

'Huh?' By which I meant whaaaaaaaaat the hell? So that was it! Tam and Alex! At it! My head filled with sordid penny dreadfuls.

'My Leo. You've always been right there.' His voice lacked its usual brio. 'I could kick myself. If I'd said something before, Peter might never have got to you, there'd have been no Harvey. Two of Earth's leading shits, in a strongly contested field. I'm sorry. Maybe I didn't know, then.'

My train was running out of track, no idea what was coming next. 'Uh, right.'

'But I know now. It's you, Leo.'

The air felt different. 'What's me?'

'It. You. The one I want.'

Boom. Er, what? Me, the . . . the one he what? Derailed. I couldn't take this in. He was being silly, doing one of his bits. I laid my hand on his shoulder, suddenly very aware I had no trousers on.

'Tammy, what are you talking about?' I was trembling. This was way beyond 'honesty first', this was madness.

Wasn't it?

'I don't know.' He grabbed my hand. 'I want to look after you. Make you safe. I want to be with you. Like, all the time. Properly.'

'Tam, what the fuck? You're getting married in actual minutes and I am still in my pants and I have to sing. In Italian!'

'I mean it.' If this was a joke, someone needed to tell Tam's anxious face.

'Why are you doing this now? Boys who look like you do couldn't possibly find . . . '

He sighed. 'Stop that. It's not flattering. I look how I look. Lion, you've no idea.' His eyes burned into me. I saw the start of tears and felt my own eyes sting in sympathy. 'Most of the things you don't like about yourself are exactly what I love about you. You're beautiful, in a way that suits you. You've got edges and corners. Your soul . . . it radiates. You're a delight of a boy.' He ran his hands through his shiny hair, as I tried to process this surreal confession. 'I can do hearts and flowers, I'll write a terrible poem, I'll drink Diet fucking Coke for the rest of my life if I have to, but believe me, if you asked me to go down there and blow this whole thing up, it would be an honour.'

What went through my head right then? I wish I could re-create it sometimes, the thrill and fear of the unknown, staring into the dazzling spotlight of possibility, tasting the heart of the sun. Who did I love more than Tam? Who understood him more than I did? Who would I rather see gazing back at me than anyone else right now and possibly for ever?

Last chance to parachute out of here. 'Is that you want, Tam? Do you want me to ask you to blow this up?'

'Lion. Leo.' Both his hands on my shoulders. Catastrophe imminent.

'Shall I get you a box to stand on?'

'Cheek. Tiptoes is fine.'

'I want you to know I'm giving up the gym. I'll lose those edges and corners.'

He laughed. 'No you won't. I don't care.'

'And please promise me, you'll never call me "babes".'

'Understood.'

So this was how it felt to be in control. I decided what

happened next. This was new. Exciting. Wrong, yes, because people would get hurt. But right, because it felt like it was correcting other, deeper wrongs from our past. So when he brought me closer, I didn't shrink back. When he stroked my face, I didn't pull away, I smiled. When he put his mouth to my ear and said he loved me, it was like hearing my favourite song, and saying it back was as natural as breathing.

'If you're going to kiss me,' I said, as if reciting lines, barely recognising the sound of my own voice, 'you'd better do it now.'

For the first time in his life, Tam did exactly as he was told.

Even when the door opened, and I heard a gasp, then stunned silence, I didn't turn to see who it was, because whoever was standing there, whatever happened next, this moment belonged to Tam and me. I wanted to savour it. The future, the fallout, could wait.

Acknowledgements

It might seem strange to say the acknowledgements are the hardest part of a book to write, but they are. They mean so much, but there's so little space. A book doesn't write itself and there are many people involved in turning it from an idea in my head into the glorious product you see before you – or are listening to – today.

My talented editor, Cal Kenny, who quickly grasped what is, really, a complicated story as I gabbled a synopsis at him in May 2022, pootling around West Yorkshire in his mum's Mini (the car, not the skirt). He has a knack for immediately understanding who my characters are, and helping me to make them shine, and laughing at all my jokes. I couldn't have done it without him. Huge thanks too, as ever, to my previous editors Dom Wakeford and Anna Boatman.

My agent, Becky Thomas, powerhouse of Lewinsohn Literary, for always being my champion and reminding me I'm probably at least a tiny bit better at writing than I think I am. Shoutout to Saliann St-Clair too!

The whole team at Sphere and Little, Brown who've taught

me so much and have worked so hard to make my books look hot and get them, and me, in front of as many people as possible. Including, but not limited to: Gaby Drinkald, Clara Diaz, Henry Lord in publicity; Lucie Sharpe in marketing; Hannah Wood for my amazing cover; Jon Appleton in operations. Also Mallory Heyer for the wonderful illustration on the cover and Angus Yellowlees and Joe Jameson for their incredible, impressive vocal talents on my audiobooks.

All my friends and family who, four books in, remain excited and enthusiastic about my weird job, especially my partner Paul, for listening to me drone on. Special mentions: Kim Falconer for the name and the dancing; Adam Kay for general wisdom and afternoon tea; Dom Ibbotson for the shutterbug expertise; Mel Jarron for the world's best welcome, every time; Ian Nicholson for unofficial Edinburgh fact-checking; and every fantastic friend I made in Scotland.

Booksellers, reviewers, Instagrammers, book bloggers, people who've come to events, festival organisers, social media followers – this machine can't run without you. My wonderful community around my newsletter *The Truth About Everything**, my *Impeccable Table Manners* readers and fans of The Guyliner – I have the most incredible, generous online supporters who keep me going.

I'm so fortunate to be a tiny goldfish in a huge pond of friendly writers and authors who I may not know very well, but they're all very generous with their time, whether it's supporting my work, inviting me to their launches, or reading my proofs, or generally saying great things. Among them: Amy Jones; Daisy Buchanan; Emma Hughes; Harriet Tyce; John Marrs; Henry Fry; Laura Kay; Laura Price; Lauren Bravo;

Lily Lindon; Lindsey Kelk; Louise Hare; Lucy Vine; Phoebe Luckhurst, Matt Cain; and Mhairi McFarlane. Terrific cheerleaders all.

Everyone who reads my books! You have great taste, and it's a huge honour to be read by you. Let's do this again sometime.

Finally, Edinburgh. Home from home. Thank you for teaching me how to be myself. Basically, this is all your fault.